'I was enthralled
 Stella Gibbons

'Mr Guthrie sees no reason why we cannot
settle a small allowance on you,' continued
Millicent, speaking as if the lawyer held the
purse-strings, 'something to allow you to live
modestly but in the style my son would wish.
You may decide on London, but I should have
thought the North, Derbyshire or
Northumberland, might be preferable. It is
healthy there.'

'Oh, thank you,' burst out Stella, blushing a
deep, happy crimson, her dark eyes brilliant
with relief, even joy. 'It would be wonderful to
have my own home, and of course it will be
small and . . . and . . . I'll bring Kit to see you
any time you wish.'

Millicent looked her full in the face.

'You seem to misunderstand. The Marquess and
I are willing to make this allowance, to give you
what we consider is a generous opportunity to
have a life of your own. We certainly would not
consider doing so if Rupert's son left Aston.
The allowance, naturally, is dependent upon
that. Kit will remain here.'

Floodtide
SUZANNE GOODWIN

SPHERE BOOKS LIMITED

SPHERE BOOKS LTD

Published by the Penguin Group
27 Wrights Lane, London W8 5TZ, England
Viking Penguin Inc., 40 West 23rd Street, New York, New York 10010, USA
Penguin Books Australia Ltd, Ringwood, Victoria, Australia
Penguin Books Canada Ltd, 2801 John Street, Markham, Ontario, Canada L3R 1B4
Penguin Books (NZ) Ltd, 182–190 Wairau Road, Auckland 10, New Zealand

Penguin Books Ltd, Registered Offices: Harmondsworth, Middlesex, England

First published in Great Britain by Sphere Books Ltd 1983
Reprinted 1988

Copyright © 1983 by Suzanne Goodwin
All rights reserved

Printed and bound in Great Britain by
Cox & Wyman Ltd, Reading
Set in Linotron Plantin

L'amour et la guerre
Sont deux marées montantes

M.M. de C. 1912

PART ONE
Meidoorn 1902

Chapter One

A wind sprang up after sunset, and although summer was far advanced the air was cold. Stella shivered as she led the ponies out of the yard. She made sure the strongbox of sovereigns was safely hidden under a pile of sacks, then climbed into the driving seat and drove away from the smouldering ruins of her home.

She was physically strong, with the ripening figure of a girl still not seventeen who had spent her life in the open. Her breasts were large and firm, her waist small, her rounded hips concealed in a voluminous old chintz dress. She had swathed a black shawl round her shoulders, folding it to cover her hair. Stella Vredenberg was too handsome for severe Boer tastes. When the commandos rode into the farm for food and shelter, the older men regarded her dourly: she did not look right. She might busy herself helping her aunt to wash and mend their tattered clothes, she was willing and quiet enough. But her hair screwed into the unbecoming Dutch knot at the nape of her neck was a startling silvery blonde. Her face sparkled and her eyes were not the Afrikaner blue but a dark brown. She did not look right.

Driving along a grassy track covered after the recent rains by sheets of tiny flowers, Stella halted the ponies and turned to stare back at the farm. How hideous it looked in the moonlight: the ruin of what had been a handsome house standing in the veldt for over sixty years. A plain white house with large airy rooms, a stoep where her aunt liked to sit and sew, a jumble of stables and barns, and the stretching land planted with oats and maize and sheltered by tall protective lines of eucalyptus trees. Meidoorn had been part of the landscape since the Voortrekkers had come

3

across the grassy plains with their trundling ox wagons, families, cattle. Here the Vredenbergs had halted, built the house and made the farm. Meidoorn had become part of the veldt itself. Until yesterday.

Stella and her old aunt, the black house servants and farmworkers had lived so long knowing they were in danger that they forgot it. The war had dragged on for three years. Other farms were burned, but not theirs. Across the veldt the roll of distant gunfire sounded – but was it thunder? Once Stella saw camp fires twinkling in the dark along the line of the hills; they looked like the lights of a city. But the next night they were gone. When the Boer commandos rode into the farm, they always said, 'God be thanked. Meidoorn still stands.'

'Yes. We thank Him. We are too isolated for the enemy to come this way,' said Aunt Maria.

'They may hold the railways and the cities and the minefields, but they cannot conquer the whole veldt,' said the Commandant. 'To win they must subdue all our country. They will not.'

'The flame of independence burns as strong now as it did in the breasts of our Voortrekker parents,' said the old lady grimly.

But the English soldiers finally brought another flame to Meidoorn, turning it into one more burning farm to light the war for a few lurid hours.

Stella used to think how long the war had gone on for. When it began she was scarcely thirteen years old. Her uncle and his three sons had welcomed the news. 'It will not last long and we shall return in triumph,' said Uncle Hendrik. 'Every Boer man, woman and child is part of our great struggle.'

'So *you* are part of the war too, Stella,' teased her favourite cousin, Karel, the youngest Vredenberg boy. He was flushed with excitement at the idea of going on commando with his father and brothers. 'Don't you wish you could come too? But you're only a Boer child. I am sixteen!'

Yes, Stella had said crossly, she did wish she could fight.

4

Some women went to war, and so did young girls. Arguing with Karel, she forgot she was not a Boer child at all. She had come to Meidoorn from America as a miserable scrap of five years old. Her parents, distant cousins of the Vredenbergs, had lived near New York. Both had died in an epidemic and the only relatives of the orphan child were in South Africa. Hendrik Vredenberg, his wife and sons lived a remote life in the High Veldt in the farm his father had built. When news of the child came from America, Hendrik offered her a home. She had been reared as the only daughter of the family and often forgot she was once an American.

The war had been stirring at the beginning. Uncle Hendrik was a field cornet, and the commandos had assembled at Meidoorn. For days beforehand there were busy preparations at the farm, baking, packing; riders arrived and left all day long, everything was bustle and excitement. At last the great morning came and the horsemen began to gather on the veldt near the farm. What a crowd! Farmers the Vredenbergs had known for years, big bearded men in the prime of life, elderly weather-worn men, sunburnt and thin, young boys like Karel with shining eyes. The commandos all wore broad-brimmed hats, bandoliers slung across their shoulders and carried their rifles at the slant. They rode with the easy slouch of men who live their lives in the saddle; they looked rough, good-natured and stubborn.

Uncle Hendrik, usually reserved and dour, made a speech alight with fervour. A hymn was sung and prayers followed. The men's voices were loud and deep, and to the excited little girl the sound was magnificent as everybody sang the national anthem, the *Volkslied*.

She and Aunt Maria watched the troop ride away, disappearing into the dust across the plains. The elderly woman was dry-eyed.

'They have gone to drive the English into the sea.'

It was a phrase which Stella heard over and over again as the years dragged on. In the girl's mind she had a picture

5

of her uncle and cousins driving red-coated men into the ocean, just as they drove cattle across the veldt.

Letters, weeks old and collected at the end of a fifty-mile ride by Adam, the old black servant, brought news of victories. And defeats. News came, too, from the Bantu tribes travelling across the veldt: they knew everything about the war. Adam and his wife Ruth took any man arriving at the farm into the kitchen, fed and questioned him, and the tribesman would tell his story dramatically, with gestures of battle and retreat, triumph and death. Aunt Maria and Stella always came into the kitchen to listen, and Adam translated the story from the dialect. Afterwards Aunt Maria went back to her seat on the stoep and sat, her sewing forgotten. Stella never noticed how old and pale her aunt was growing.

'Our men cannot be defeated. They are in their own land. They know every *kopje*, every *laagte*.'

'Yes, Aunt.'

'They have led the lives of hunters and now they hunt our enemies.'

Stella muttered her usual agreement. The war bored her now. She was growing up and it was dull at Meidoorn with her cousins gone. She missed the cheerful past, the journeys to other farms. News from the Bantu was sombre, the war was going badly. Stella worked in the house, sewed, helped to make the soap and candles, often now without her aunt, who unwillingly took to her bed. Once Adam heard a story that it was not only the English who looted and fired the farms, but the commandos as well. Aunt Maria refused to believe anything so horrible.

'Our men would never touch their own folk.'

'Maybe they're hungry, Aunt,' said Stella, who half believed the story, which frightened her.

'If they are hungry, we are their women and will feed them,' said the old lady, shutting her eyes.

'And Meidoorn is so isolated,' added Stella comfortingly.

But she had tempted fate. She drove the cart faster as if to escape from the memory of yesterday. First a frightened tribesman had come and then, before they could do more than begin to barricade the house, there was the sound of many horses, and mounted troops poured into the yard. There were shouts and screams and running people and the sudden terrifying roar of flames.

Stella had rushed to her aunt's bedroom, falling up the stairs in her haste, dragging herself to her feet and throwing herself into the room. Aunt Maria was out of bed, in her nightgown and trying to pick up the huge copper-bound family bible. She was supporting herself against the table.

'Aunt!' Stella sobbed, clasping the old woman in her arms as they tottered towards the door. But even while the panic and thickening smoke filled the house, there were shouts of command in English, troops clattered from house and barns, a final torch was thrown and the enemy galloped away at full tilt towards the sound of gunfire.

Hours later, Stella and Adam, Ruth and bands of terrified workers had doused the fire. One corner of the house and the kitchens were saved. The servants' quarters at a distance from the farm were still untouched. But most of Meidoorn was a roofless smoking ruin.

Her aunt never knew her home was destroyed. Even as the English soldiers galloped away, she fainted and fell into a coma which Stella and the servants mistook for a deep sleep.

During the night she died.

Driving now across the great moonlit veldt, hearing the far-off hungry yelp of a jackal, the shriek of a hyena, Stella thought of her aunt with a stab of pain. The old lady had come to herself just before the end.

'God be with you. You are a good child. Go to the Maritz farm. Neeltge Maritz will do her duty by you. Take the bible and your uncle's strongbox . . . tell what happened . . . our people need help and you . . . must have a home. Do you promise?'

'I promise, dearest Aunt.'

'You will miss me . . . when I am dead.'

'Don't die! Don't die!' sobbed the girl.

7

But her aunt muttered the beginning of a prayer. And was gone.

Stella set out to obey the dying words. She did not dare take Adam or Ruth, who must stay with what remained of Meidoorn. The other servants were too frightened, she could not possibly take any of them. The journey was hateful. She had always disliked Mrs Maritz who grimly disapproved of the fair-haired child so popular with her sons. Aunt Maria had been strict, but Mrs Maritz was a hundred times worse. How can I bear to live there, with the boys gone, thought Stella. There will only be Mrs Maritz and that stupid Petronella. Must I go? Can one disobey the dead?

Her practical head told her one could do that very easily, save for the risk of being haunted by Aunt Maria's poor accusing ghost. But where else could she go? The Maritz farm might, only might, be still standing. Stella could not remain alone in the ruins of Meidoorn. Other women had joined the fighting and gone on commando. Aunt Maria's friend Hendrina Joubert had gone to war with her Commandant-General husband. She had actually had her children in camp during a campaign. Stella tried to imagine herself riding out with the men, but she could not.

What waited for her at the end of this midnight journey? Mrs Maritz, thin-lipped and cold. How could Aunt Maria have liked her? But Stella had never understood her adopted aunt and now it was too late and she never would.

Stella, Adam and Ruth and everybody left at the farm had gathered for Aunt Maria's funeral that morning. Ruth had found some black linen for a pall, and a great hole had been dug under the eucalyptus trees. It was seven feet deep and when the coffin was lowered by four of the farmworkers and covered with earth, large flat pieces of rock had been laid on top of it, it was the custom to protect the dead against wild animals. Then more earth and afterwards more large stones placed over the grave. Aunt Maria lay near Uncle Hendrik's parents, who had both been buried in that way. All the servants dressed in their best clothes, although

8

many were still shaken and trembling from the fire of the previous day. Adam read the burial service and almost everybody wept. There was a wooden cross fixed at the head of the grave, with her aunt's name painted on it and the date – February 1902.

My whole Meidoorn life was buried this morning, the girl thought as she stared across the huge plains silvered by moonlight. Accustomed to the distances, her sight was sharp and she would see enemy or friend at once. The weight of the old revolver on her lap was comforting. Uncle Hendrik had given it to his wife, and it had remained by the bible in her aunt's bedroom until tonight. Stella felt a certain satisfaction at possessing it. She was sad and dreaded arriving at the Maritz farm, but it was exciting to have a gun.

Ahead of her, far far away, was the great amphitheatre of the mountains. Nearer, a dark line showed where the river wound through rocks and outcrops of stone. The treeless veldt gave place to bush, with thick clumps of thorn trees, and there were woods closer to the river. Stella approached the first rocks cautiously, her eyes enormous. It was exactly where the enemy might hide, or where animals – there were lions occasionally – came to the river to drink. But the only way to the Maritz farm was across the river. She turned the cart in the direction of the *drift*, the place where waggons and oxen could cross. She reached the shadows of the rocks, climbed down and led the ponies, holding her breath and as alert for danger as a veldt animal . . .

The undergrowth rustled. Then it was quiet. She could hear the waterfall further upriver. Suddenly, she almost screamed as a hideous noise broke the silence. Not the click of a trigger, the whine of a bullet, nor the heavy ominous sound of an approaching animal, but a long gurgling groan. The ponies, sensing something, tugged away from her and she had to wrench them back. There it was again, a horrible choking sound uncannily like her poor aunt's gasping breaths on her deathbed.

Tying the ponies to a thorn tree with shaking hands,

Stella advanced towards the sound: it was the bravest moment of her short life.

She stumbled over something lying across the path. Looking down she saw with horror that it was the twisted figure of a man clutching a rifle. He was in the foreign uniform she recognised from the enemy troops yesterday, and she did not need to touch him to see that he was dead. Averting her eyes, she held her skirts up to keep them from brushing against him. There it came again – the gasping groan. She crept round the rocks.

Another soldier lay among the bushes, feebly moving his head and making that dreadful suffering noise. She threw herself down beside him and burst into broken English.

'Poor man, poor man! Where are you hurt?'

He stared up with the vacant gaze she had seen on her aunt's dying face. One of his legs was dark with blood, in the moonlight it looked black. His face was ghastly, his lips cracked.

'I'll get water.'

She scrambled through the undergrowth down to the river bank, reached the ford, cupped her hands, and came back with scarcely a drop of water remaining to moisten his lips. But she laid her wet hands against his face. Then she sat down, awkwardly pillowing his head in her lap. Her heart hammered, she was filled with pity. Poor thing, was he dying even now? His delicate face, with a skin like a girl's, was greenish, he had a silky moustache and fair hair. The commandos had not robbed him of his clothes, which they did to the fallen enemy now they themselves were in rags. Perhaps they had been forced to retreat hurriedly. Accustomed to her countrymen's scarecrow figures, the wounded man's fine khaki, puttees and leather boots were very strange. The uniform did not belong in this wild place, and nor did the man who wore it dying in the bush.

What can I do with you? she thought. I must find the commando and give you up. Or should I leave you here? You will bleed to death if I do. She looked intently at the face in her lap, thinking – poor creature, if only I could save you.

Suddenly she had a thought. Why shouldn't she save him? He was young, almost as young as she was. She had been grieving for her old aunt who had died yesterday, wouldn't it be a levelling-up to save this man's life? Isn't it the will of God? thought Stella, who often ascribed to heaven the things she strongly wanted. And she found she passionately wanted him to live. Nervously she touched his head, chest, stomach. Perhaps he was already dying of worse wounds than that in the leg. But there was no sign of blood on her hands when she looked at them in the moonlight: no sign of wounds except that in his blood-soaked leg.

As she pressed her hand for a second time to his head, he slowly opened his eyes.

'Who – are – you?'

'I found you. You're wounded.'

'My s-sergeant?'

'The other man is dead.'

He sighed and shut his eyes.

'Do you want water? I'll get some more.'

'Don't leave me!'

The cry reached her heart.

'I won't leave you. But we can't stay here, it's dangerous. I must move you. Can you stand? I'm strong. I'll help.'

She laid his head on the ground, stood up, then stooped to fasten her arms round his waist. A groan of agony came from him but somehow she managed to get him to his feet. He began to sway.

'Don't fall! Don't fall down! If you stay here you'll die, I must get you to the cart, oh for God's sake *don't faint!*'

The strong voice reached the swooning man and somehow she half-dragged, half-supported him to the cart where he collapsed. Gasping, she covered him with the sacks which hid the strongbox.

'Don't move. Don't make a sound,' she said to the shape under the sacks. She led the ponies back down the path to the veldt and climbed into the seat. And took the track back to Meidoorn.

She drove carefully and slowly, grimacing every time the

11

cart shuddered over a stone. Once she stopped to peer under the sacks. He had lost consciousness. It was beginning to grow light, the sky changing to a dim gleaming blue, the jagged outline of the mountains dark against the far horizon. The grass was wet with dew and as the sky began to turn golden, she saw a long line of silhouettes, gazelles grazing under far-off trees. She relaxed for a while, concentrating on driving as gently as she could. Then glancing up she saw the gazelles suddenly scatter – and saw what had disturbed them. A procession of horsemen was riding across the plain towards her and by the very way they rode she knew they were commandos.

Mounted on Basuto ponies, the men approaching her looked all alike, saddlebags bulging, blankets fastened to the pommels of their horses. Had they come from Meidoorn, and what had they asked for, or stolen? As they neared her, the leader reined in his horse.

'What are you doing, *m'vrow*?' he said in Afrikaans, speaking kindly. The girl, scarcely more than a child, was white as a sheet.

She stared at him.

'Minding my own business,' she said with Boer abruptness.

He gave a slight smile. He was a big emaciated man as ragged as a beggar. He pushed his old torn hat back, and where the hat covered his forehead was a white stripe above the darkly tanned face. His eyes had great shadows under them.

'You're too young to be out on the open veldt alone. Been foraging?'

'Maybe.'

He and his companions looked at her for a moment.

'How have you escaped being captured like the rest of our women? Caged up in an enemy camp like chickens and dying of fever?'

'Don't frighten the girl, Gideon,' said an older man beside him.

'I don't frighten her. I warn her.'

'Maybe I go on commando to join my husband,' ventured

12

Stella. The remark slightly amused the men, who grinned. Facing her countrymen she felt a wave of shame. They were such a tattered, weary, worn-out crew. The days were gone when the Boer women could wash and mend their uniforms; now the men's clothes were made from grain bags or pieces of stolen enemy uniform, a sleeveless ragged jacket, torn trousers tied with rope. One commando wore a coat of monkey skin, another a Bantu blanket. Their faces were thin with hunger and sleeplessness. They were exhausted. These were *her* people, still fighting with stubborn heroism against the most powerful country in the world. They fought the men who had set Meidoorn ablaze and hastened her aunt's death. How dared she hide an enemy from them?

The man called Gideon yawned.

'We're tired, *m'vrow*. We've been stalking the English for two nights like we stalk rock rabbits. We picked off a few. A scouting party was out last night, we're off to see if we bagged any game by the river. What's in that cart of yours? Hiding something?'

Stella was so frightened that for a moment she was speechless. Risking everything in a split second, she managed to fix her eyes on her questioner.

'I don't do any harm,' she muttered. 'It's true I'm a woman but they haven't caught me yet.' And she quoted the hymn the commandos sang before going out to fight. '*Slechts vertrouwen, dat is al*'. (Simply trusting, that is all.)

'You sing the same hymn we do, poor child,' Gideon said slowly. 'Keep whatever you're hiding. And God be with you.'

He gave her a kind of wave, and they rode away.

It was broad daylight when Stella turned into the gates leading to the farm. The sun was up and the air diamond clear. In its brightness, the farm looked the picture of desolation. The ground trampled by men and horses, the door of the biggest barn split, the house blackened and charred, the main part of the roof fallen in. The smell was horrible. There was something disgusting about the

13

reeking blackened thing that had been Meidoorn. She felt sick as she climbed down from the cart. Peering nervously under the sacks, she saw her prisoner, as still as death. But when she took his wrist she felt a flutter, like the feeble pulse of a tiny bird. He was still alive, but barely.

She ran into the ruined house, climbing fallen timbers. Blue sky shone where the roof had been, but the stairs leading to two end bedrooms had not been destroyed. She went up, slithering on the wet ash, to her aunt's bedroom. Adam's old wife Ruth was there. Ruth was a Basuto who had been her nurse and friend since she was five years old. As Stella came into the bedroom, the old woman was sadly folding her aunt's clothes. She started when she saw Stella and looked frightened.

'Why are you back, Mis' Stella? Is the Maritz farm gone too?'

'I never got there. There was fighting by the river.'

'Holy God! You're not hurt!'

'I am perfectly safe, Ruth,' said the girl calmly. 'But I have a wounded soldier in the cart outside. I found him near the *drift*. We must get Adam to help us carry him in.'

'A wounded commando, oh, the poor man, the poor man!' cried Ruth. 'I must get Adam and Charley. Is he bad? How brave you are, Mis' Stella, a wounded commando . . .'

She hurried down the stair with Stella behind her. They found Adam at the back of the house, helping two farmworkers to stack burned spars of wood. All three men had ash smeared over their clothes and dark faces, they looked tired and dispirited. Ruth ran up to exclaim – a wounded commando, Mis' Stella had rescued him! All talking at once, the servants and the farmworkers went into the yard where a boy was unharnessing the ponies. The shape under the sacks had not moved. Stella pulled off the covers.

Recoiling at the sight of the deathlike figure, old Adam turned to her.

'He's one of them!'

'So he is!' she burst out, 'and what harm can he do when he's bleeding like a pig? We must save him.'

'Save him?' repeated Adam, stupefied. 'Why?'

The dark faces round her stared accusingly.

'He may be dying,' shouted Stella, guilty and furious.

'But he's one of them. If he dies, it's just after what he did. The Lord says I will make thine enemies thy footstool,' said Adam. No black people fought in this white man's war, both Briton and Boer had agreed on that. But Adam's loyalty was to the farm, the Vredenbergs, the Transvaal, everything the bloodstained figure in the cart had come to destroy.

'The Bible says do good to those who harm you,' answered Stella, glaring. There was a second when Adam hesitated. Then he sighed and shook his head and ordered the rest of the watching men to help. Ruth said nothing. A procession of dark-faced people carried the unconscious man indoors.

'Take him up to my aunt's room.'

It was done.

'The rest can go. Ruth, boil some water and I want some sharp scissors. Adam, get antiseptic from the medicine cupboard.'

'It's locked.'

'*Then break the lock*,' she said, stamping her foot.

They obeyed but deeply resented what she was making them do. They did not want to save the man's life and knew their old mistress would have sent him to the nearest commando *laager*. If he died, jolting and bleeding on the way, that was the will of the Almighty and none of their business. They thought the girl wicked to go against her own people. The human wreck lying in the sacred bed of their dead mistress was one of the devils who had fired the farm. Maybe his friends had already killed their absent master, who could say? Certainly their mistress would not be dead if it had not been for the fire. Obeying Stella from custom, they were shocked to the depth of their souls.

Stella knew next to nothing about nursing. She tried desperately to remember her aunt's instructions, that time

15

when one of the Basuto boys had accidentally been shot when hunting. She knew that the bullet must be removed, but how? When Ruth came back with the boiling water, she brought half a dozen or so bandages, saying, 'That's all we've got.' Adam brought a little antiseptic, that, too, was all. 'Missus used to say brandy does,' said the old man, and produced the dusty bottle of brandy which had been kept for emergencies.

Ruth set the steaming jugs on the washstand.

'I need more bandages.'

'There aren't any.'

'Then cut up some sheets and towels. Have we two pairs of scissors? I want the sharp ones.'

Ruth gave them to her and gloomily began to cut a sheet into strips. Stella bit her lips and began to cut gingerly through the bloodsoaked puttees round the man's leg. When she shudderingly pulled off the final stiffened covering the leg was a horrible sight, crimson, blackened and welling. Ruth groaned. But Adam was unwillingly interested and joined Stella beside the bed.

'You got to clean it, Mis' Stella, that's what the mistress did.'

She dipped a cloth into a bowl of hot antiseptic and began to dab, starting at the outside of the wound. Adam watched.

'Bullet's still in there. See? You got to get it out.'

'Adam!'

Bent-backed, he reflectively stared at the wound.

'I'd do it, but look at these.' He held out his veined hands; as they had done for years, they shook.

'You'll need a knife, small and sharp. I'll get one.'

He left the room and Stella tied back the curtains. Strong sunlight flooded down on to the bed. She rolled up her sleeves and tied a sheet round her waist. She was very pale. Ruth, faint at the sight of blood, had retreated into a corner.

'I brought the sugar tongs, Mis' Stella,' said Adam with satisfaction, coming back. 'We'll dip 'em in the brandy.'

The next five minutes were gruesome and bloody and

16

only Stella's will, a vein of iron in her sixteen-year-old breast, carried her through. She did not know when she began with screwed-up face to cut into the wound that the bullet was lodged in a muscle, and that muscles automatically tighten when probed. The bleeding had almost stopped but the bullet was stubbornly difficult to move as she prodded, until at last, with a grunt, she had her blade half under it.

'Adam, the tongs!'

He took them dripping from a saucer of brandy. Holding her breath, she managed to get a grip on the bullet which was nearly half an inch long. Slowly she pulled it out.

There was a great gush of blood. She and Ruth frantically padded the wound with torn-up sheets, then bound the leg tightly. When it was done, Stella was violently sick.

The Englishman did not regain consciousness for two days. Hour upon hour, Stella sat by his bed, moistening his dry lips and listening to his delirious muttering. Adam and Ruth wanted him to die. She wanted him to live. Fiercely. Why do I care? she wondered. He's only an enemy I found on the veldt. But he had become a cause, something other than wailing over the death of her aunt and the burned house or riding like a coward for help.

'Eat something, Mis' Stella,' Ruth said, on the second night, bringing in coffee, porridge made from mealies, and honeycomb. 'No good you gettin' sick too.'

'Ruth, will he die, do you think? How his head burns.'

'He has a fever,' said the old woman, looking critically down at the restless figure in the bed. 'You goin' to try boiled willow, then?'

It was an African remedy and so bitter that Ruth's own people dreaded it.

'I can't even get him to drink water.'

'Then you can't do nothing. What happens will be the Lord's will.' Foretelling death matter-of-factly, the old nurse looked pleased. But when she was back in the kitchen, Ruth grumbled to her husband. They both felt angry and helpless. Their old mistress had told Stella to go

17

to the Maritz farm. That was the right thing to do. By now everybody should have left Meidoorn and been safe. What were they doing, stuck here? Some of the workers had run away to join the nearest kraal. If *they* weren't going to Mrs Maritz like their old mistress wanted, Adam and Ruth could go to their cousins upriver. They loathed staying in this ruined place, but the girl kept them. They could not leave her so they simply hoped the Englishman would die.

It was after midnight, and Stella was sitting by the bed. It had rained heavily all day and the farmyard lay in pools of water full of stars: the air was warm. She had turned down the lamp which threw a soft light on her silvery-fair plaits and her eyes heavy with sleeplessness. She looked at the man on the bed with mournful curiosity.

'Poor creature,' she said aloud. 'Where do you come from? I only know the name on that paper in your pocket. Rupert Flood Coryot. That's an outlandish name. If you die, do we bury you as well under the eucalyptus trees? And who will know in your country that you died at Meidoorn?'

She wrung out a cloth to lay it on his forehead, but as she bent over him, she gave a gasp. His eyes were open.

'Where am I?' he asked in a slow dazed way.

'In a farm. Near where you were shot.'

He gazed at her with pale uncomprehending eyes.

'We beat them off, did we?'

'This is a Boer farm.'

He shut his eyes, sighed and began to breathe evenly. He had fallen asleep. She put her hand on his forehead – it was cool for the first time. A feeling of triumph so fierce that it took her breath away went through Stella. *She* had fought a battle too, here in her aunt's room and her enemy had been more deadly than any khaki soldiers. And she had won.

When she woke the sun was coming through the gaps in the curtain in long bright bars, and as she stretched after sleeping in a chair she saw that her patient was awake, staring at her.

'So I didn't dream it,' she said.

'Who are you?' His voice was weak and he looked lost.

'A Boer girl. I found you. We will talk later, but now I will wash and change and then *you* must eat. Sleep a little.'

He shut his eyes. Stella washed and put on a clean dress, screwed up her hair and ran to the kitchen. The walls were smoke-blackened but the roof was undamaged, and when she came in she smelled cooking bread. There were pans in the sink and a big bowl of fresh milk; but no Ruth.

She went into the yard, shading her eyes from the sun, and a little boy with curling hair and black eyes, the son of one of the farmhands, stood looking at her and laughing.

'Kinto, where is Auntie Ruth?'

'Dunno, dunno,' said the child, laughing and running away. Then Stella saw Ruth coming slowly into the yard. She went across to her in haste.

'Is he dead, then?'

The words were a slap in the face.

'No, he isn't,' said Stella sharply, 'he's going to live. Bring me some gruel for him and say your prayers. Should a Christian wish a fellow creature dead?'

The man was watching the door, his face fixed and helpless; a childlike relief came over it when Stella came back. She put a hand on his forehead.

'You are getting better, Mr Coryot, if that's your name. Many times I thought you were dead.'

'I owe you my life.'

She noticed the curious English drawl.

She sat down, and looked at him for a moment.

'Were you one of the men who burnt our farm?'

He did not understand her.

'Is it burned?'

'The English came. I thought maybe you were there.'

'No. My regiment . . . we fought in fits and starts. The Boers were on the hills . . . I went on a scouting p-party.'

'You had a man with you. He was killed.'

He looked at her fixedly. He remembered crawling through the undergrowth, the insects biting, the crack of a rifle – pain – and darkness. And now the bright sunlight which hurt his eyes and a child with a Dutch voice sitting by him.

'I am Stella Vredenberg. And you are Rupert Flood Coryot, that's what your papers say. English officer?'

'And your prisoner.'

'So you are,' she said, and laughed.

Ruth came to the door but would not enter the room. She brought coffee and bread and gruel. Stella fed her patient with a teaspoon. Now he was no longer a wax corpse-like figure on her aunt's bed, the man began to interest her. Everything about him was odd and unfamiliar. His fine skin, his white hands, his delicate face, his English voice. He was weak as a kitten, yet had a most extraordinary politeness. Nobody was as polite as that and Stella thought it ridiculous.

'Stop thanking me and eat your gruel, Mr Coryot. No, I shan't call you Mister when I feed you like a *lammetje*, a sucking lamb. Rupert is a queer kind of name.'

'You are accustomed to Dutch names, Miss Vr—'

'Stella. Nobody but servants say Miss.'

He refused more gruel. He was sorry, it was delicious, but he could eat no more.

'When I am recovered, your family will hand me over to the commando,' he said after a pause. He wondered where the woman of the farm might be. He had met a few Boer women; they were formidable.

'I have no family, no mother, nobody. You are in my charge. Yes, I daresay I shall give you up, *lammetje*!'

Stella, who could not remember as much as a day of illness since she had come to Meidoorn, was surprised at her prisoner's slow recovery. The wound was healthy but it was large and had to be dressed three times a day. The pile of sheets in her aunt's cupboard, previously firmly locked, was dwindling. But she did not grudge her patient a minute of her time; what else was there for her to do? She was constantly in the sickroom. The girl with her vitality, the Englishman weak from loss of blood and fever, were

20

dependent upon each other. She was his nurse and protector, he was her reason for staying at the farm.

The feared English did not come back to finish the job of destroying Meidoorn and killing or stealing the cattle.

'If they come,' Rupert said calmly, 'I will stop them.'

But there was no reverberating thunder of far-off guns, no clatter of horses and shouts in English or Afrikaans. While Rupert grew very slowly better, the place settled into a half life. There was food enough: corn and mealies from two of the undamaged barns, milk from the cows, and game now and then. Ruth did her best in the kitchen, and Adam, with the farmworkers who had not run away, repaired the least-damaged parts of the house. Adam sadly missed Aunt Maria, and came to Stella with every problem. If she answered impatiently, he went away despondent.

During the long days together, Stella and Rupert learned something of each other's lives. She asked what 'The Viscount' meant on his papers; was it an army rank? He laughed and said it was a title, his father was a Marquess. She put such oddities down to his being a foreigner, what did they know of titles at Meidoorn? Did it mean they were rich and important? He laughed again and said yes. His father's name was different from his own, that was how it was in these matters. His father was Marquess of Tyrrell. He talked about the ancient family seat in Oxfordshire where they lived, it was called Aston and had belonged to the Flood family for generations: 'Yes, that is another name, our real name, the others are just the titles.' She listened in silence. She could not make much sense of his stories. In turn he heard of her life at the farm, her three cousins and her uncle and aunt. He was curious when she told him she had come from America, and asked what she could remember of that other life when she was very young.

Stella pondered.

'It is stupid how I forget. There was a river and pretty boats went by. And I do remember snow and going in a sledge thing, and my mother had fair hair and she could sing, she was always singing. My parents laughed together.

21

Uncle and Aunt almost never. Then I was in a ship for a long time with a woman and her horrid children and I cried. Then ever so long in a wagon, with the driver shouting the names of the animals and cracking his whip. Then it was Meidoorn.'

'Your adopted home.'

'Yes. It is home. I was never allowed to say I was American. Uncle said it showed ingratitude. So I am a Boer. You English think us only half civilised, don't you?'

'Of course not,' said Rupert. But it was true.

'If I am American or Boer, I wish we could drive you out of our country,' said Stella brightly. She was mending his khaki jacket.

Rupert lay in bed, dressed in one of her uncle's thick cotton nightshirts. His hair, washed and shiny, was soft, his delicate face slightly coloured with the return of health. He pushed a pillow under his head and lay watching her. Her back was bent, he could see the curling lashes which edged her brilliant eyes. She always wore chintz dresses that were too small for her, and this one, sprigged with small blue flowers, was drawn tight across her full breasts. He felt a stirring of desire. Life during the tedious weeks of convalescence had been dreamlike; the big ruined house of which he knew only this whitewashed room was Spartan as a monk's cell ... the reek of burning which came to him each time the bedroom door opened ... the old black servants gloomily waiting on them. He felt languid and content, the leg wound ached less, he slept well. And wrapping him round was the soft company of this girl, hour upon hour: this sixteen-year-old warrior who had saved him from death.

For the first time, tracing the contours of her face, caressingly looking at her silvery blonde hair, he wanted to kiss her. To kiss her cheeks and eyelids, cradle her in his arms. She was so close that he could smell the scent of her skin.

Looking up, she caught his expression, and blushed scarlet.

22

Chapter Two

It was already May, there had been a great deal of rain and when the sun did come out the air was cool. Rupert thought how curious it was to realise that it would soon be the winter. After the rains the veldt was smothered with sheets and sheets of flowers. They grew in such profusion that even from a short distance one part of the plain was shining red, another pure white, another glowing yellow.

Rupert could walk now, but painfully and with a stick, and he spent the days at the far end of the stoep, by the only part of the house which was undamaged. Lying in a chair with his legs stretched out, he watched distant herds of wildebeests or gazelles. And waited for Stella.

He was bored. There was nothing to read at Meidoorn and never had been. 'Uncle Hendrik permitted only the Bible. It is always so with us.' Until recently he had been weak, and thus content to do nothing. But now he was only happy when Stella was with him. The tingle of desire came often, making his blood throb. He was stirred by her rounded figure, the tones of her voice, her shining eyes, and by the way she thoughtlessly touched him when she talked. He wondered if it would be very wrong to seduce this girl. He supposed so.

He was a man who had always preferred women to men, their company soothed and flattered him and since he was a child they had spoiled him. But English girls were not like Stella Vredenberg, they were well-behaved and well-bred, and their Mamas were on the lookout for a suitable husband for them. Sitting on the stoep, he thought often about those girls at home. How delicate their complexions were, how they wore white dresses. They moved in his thoughts, pale figures in dark shining rooms. He had a sudden sick longing for England. Staring blindly at the enormous landscape round him, he saw the ancient house, half manor, half castle, where he had been born, heard his mother's voice as she said goodbye to him. She had been standing at the top of the terrace steps.

'I shan't come to London to freeze to death on a foggy platform, dearest boy.' Before he went, she had loaded him with gifts: a dressing-case with silver fittings, a gun made for him at Purdy's, leather luggage with the Flood crest, and a beautiful saddle.

'I like my son to have the best.'

Rupert's thoughts lingered with his mother. She was small, fine-boned, with a thin face which curiously resembled the Tudor portraits of Queen Elizabeth; she had the same still, hawklike profile and steady eyes, the same carriage of the head. He cared more for her than anybody in the world. 'Mother's pet,' his brothers used to tease when they were all in the nursery and he had fought both of them over that. He understood his mother, he thought, as the other two did not. There was something strong and hard in her, quite different from his father's aristocratic indifference to rank and wealth. His mother's devotion to Rupert was part of her family pride; he was the eldest.

Leaning back against a cushion, Rupert's face wore a look of self-satisfaction. Primogeniture, settling title and possessions on the eldest, was right. Where would the Floods be if things had been divided and sub-divided as they were in Italy or France? The Floods had lived at Aston, the family's great Oxfordshire house, for over three hundred years, steadily acquiring land and renown. And they married heiresses and bred sons.

'What a blessing you were the first,' his mother had once said. 'Desmond is a dear creature and I know your father dotes on him, but even I admit he is dull.'

'Des will do very well,' said Rupert with the generosity that needed to give away nothing.

Desmond, two years his junior, resembled his father, was big, heavily-built, but without his father's wordly nature. He was a steady fellow. Harry, the youngest – nobody counted Catherine the sister – was another matter. Thinking of Harry, Rupert frowned. There was something irritating about his younger brother. He took nothing seriously and if ever Rupert spoke of being heir, Harry would salaam. It was ridiculous and Rupert disliked it.

'Harry will settle down,' Lady Tyrrell soothed. 'He needs a strong hand. Some suitable girl. We'll see whom we can invite for the summer ball.'

The summer ball! The words sounded ludicrous as Rupert came back with a jolt to the long stoep, the ruined wall and charred rafters, to the blinding sunlight, the endless flower-starred veldt, and the sound of Stella talking to Adam in Afrikaans.

She came out to join him, jumping across the gaps between the new roughly-nailed boards of the veranda.

'Adam annoys me,' she said, sitting down on a stool. 'He keeps saying I ought to go to see Mrs Maritz and tell her my aunt has died. I said you were not well enough to leave yet.'

He said nothing for a moment. Then, 'Stella, why don't we go out sometime? Just for a short drive. We could go in that cart of yours. I know I can't ride, but you could drive and we'd be safe enough. I've been staring at the veldt for weeks. We might as well be on a desert island. What do you say?'

It was thought of England that made him speak.

Stella frowned. It was the first time he had shown he was not content simply to do as he was told. He put out his hand and touched hers.

'Oh, very well,' she said cheerfully, 'we'll go. Meidoorn is no safer than the veldt, so I'll take you driving.'

They set off the next morning in cool sunshine. Rupert had a feeling of relief as they drove away from the farm. He looked up at the great bowl of the sky, down at the flowers, across towards the far violet-coloured mountains. He sniffed the sweet air. Stella pointed with her whip towards some feathery acacias. Under the trees half a dozen circular huts were grouped, while some Bantu men were putting together the frame of a new hut. Their women were busy with the cattle.

'The kraal wasn't there yesterday,' she said. 'They take their homes to pieces and pack them on the back of the oxen and just move on. I expect some of our Meidoorn folk are there.'

'Don't you want them back?' he asked, surprised at the matter-of-fact way she spoke of the workers deserting her.

'Oh, they wouldn't come. They ran away after the fire. I daresay,' she added mischievously, 'the Bantu will prefer the English now, since you tell me you are winning. When Uncle Hendrik comes back, they will all appear at the farm like magic. The Bantu have relatives and family in every place in the Transvaal. They know everything that happens. Just now they don't want nothing to do with Meidoorn.'

He laughed at the mistake and caught an answering gleam from her anything-but-prim brown eyes. As the cart bounced along the flowery track, her arm brushed against him.

Since the day before, he had thought repeatedly of his home, walking in his imagination across lawns by yew hedges clipped into the shape of peacocks, hearing bells across water meadows. Everything in England seemed small, enclosed and secret, but here the world was at its dawn. After the rains the atmosphere was so clear that the huge distances were reduced, the very air glittered, and mountains thirty miles away seemed scarcely three miles distant. The mists of Oxfordshire were a world away.

Stella was silent for the rest of the drive. She had spoken unthinkingly of 'when Uncle Hendrik comes back' but the words reverberated in her mind. He would come back. No young man with a girlish face could kill Hendrik. 'Africa for the Dutch, the English into the sea.' When she and cousin Karel used to play 'Boers and Brits', the Boers always won, but she had begun to see that this time the game would end differently. During these weeks with

26

Rupert he had talked of the war and she had listened, at first incredulously and then with dismay.

'But we thought Russia would stop the war for us!' she once said.

He laughed, not unkindly.

'Yes, the world is on your side. Everybody is full of sympathy for your cause, even many in England. But who has helped you?'

Now she was sure that defeat was coming, although the commando fought on. Soon it would be over and Uncle Hendrik would ride back to Meidoorn. I shall have to forget I ever was with an Englishman.

'I keep expecting to see commandos,' Rupert said suddenly. 'Perhaps we should not have come.

He felt unexpectedly nervous out here away from the protection of a house and realised just how helpless it meant to be so lame. Stella shrugged carelessly.

'We'd see people from miles away. You wanted to come, so now we will enjoy it.'

At last she reined in the ponies by a mass of scrubby bushes. Nearby a lofty tree was filled with storks which as they approached flapped away heavily. After the fear of the empty plains, Rupert found the shade of shrubs and trees a relief as he limped after her. She made her way through the thick undergrowth until they reached the head of a small ravine, walled on either side with sandstone rocks. The river had formed a rocky basin filled with clear green water into which a little waterfall tumbled. Two young black girls were playing in the water with their babies, but when they saw the white people they snatched up the children and vanished into the trees. Stella gave a grimace.

'They run from us now. How I hate that.'

She sat down beside Rupert on the flat rocks by the water. The air was filled with the waterfall's small roar, the willows bent over the water, trailing their branches. It was a beautiful place.

'I'm so glad I came here with you,' he said slowly.

'Yes. It's good. And if soldiers come, yours or mine, we swim for it!' She gave him an innocent laughing look.

'You're brave, Stella.'

'Well, I had one brave moment anyhow—' but before she finished speaking he had kissed her. She answered the kiss awkwardly, she had dreamed of this. But his tongue forced open her mouth and when she tried to close her lips he would not let her. She began to be frightened. He unbuttoned the bodice of her dress, pulled out her breasts and buried his face between them. They were full and white, two peaches tipped with pale pink nipples, and with eyes shut he moved from one nipple to the other, covering it with his mouth. Stella trembled like a terrified horse. The virginal instinct to scream, to wrench away, to flee from the marauding male was strong in her. She looked almost with horror at the man with his mouth over one of her breasts like a suckling child. His hand moved down her skirts, he pulled them up to reveal her white stockinged legs.

'No – no—'

In that moment she knew, she was certain, that she could still escape what was waiting for her. He opened eyes drowned with desire – but they were still Rupert's eyes.

'If you don't want me to love you, Beautiful, I'll stop.'

But he spoke while beginning to caress, very slowly, the inside of her thighs. Stella, though taut with fear, was strangely and suddenly excited. She lifted her mouth to be kissed again.

The sun was sinking as they returned to Meidoorn. It shone straight in their faces and Stella had to drive while shading her eyes with one hand. Rupert had the physical sense of well-being, the after-pleasure of sex following months of abstinence. But although his body was satisfied, he was horrified at what he had done. He looked at the girl whose strong profile was lit by the dark golden light. Her head was lifted in the determined way he had noticed many times, as if she faced an invisible destiny. Her hair was untidy and he saw with a stab of something like love the kiss bruises on her neck. What had he done? A crime. His relaxed body denied it, telling him he had taken a luscious

28

female and enjoyed her. But his conscience shuddered. He had violated a virgin. A parentless sixteen-year-old girl alone in the wilderness who had saved his life.

Rupert was a self-loving man who could not bear to believe he had done wrong. In defence against conscience he found excuses. This was no gently-reared English maiden, she was the child of pioneering stock, hardy and hard-headed. She had proved that by the very way she had rescued him, braving her own folk to hide an enemy, extracting the bullet from his wound as courageously as a man.

Yet he felt guilty. How innocent she still looked, shading her eyes like a child. He had taken her twice and the fact that she still looked untouched made what he had done seem more sinful.

Out of the bright sky came a deafening clap of thunder like the firing of twenty cannon. Rupert started violently as the sky darkened in a moment, and in the next the rain came pouring in sheets, followed by a wind so fierce that it nearly overturned the cart. The poor horses bent in the tempest; Stella, hair glued to her head, face pouring with water, seemed about to be swept from the cart and Rupert had to hang on to her. A quarter of an hour later the storm stopped as suddenly as it had begun, followed by a ringing calm. A sky without a cloud. When they drew up at Meidoorn and climbed out of the cart, they were dripping.

'Stella, where are you going?'

'To my room.'

'Won't you come to mine?'

'No.'

She ran to her bedroom and locked the door. She had behaved calmly now from pride, but part of her wanted to scream, not at Rupert but at herself. She had never meant to submit to him and had known for days what was in his mind, reading it in his face time and again. Young as she was, she had seen that look in men's faces before. At first it had disgusted, then fascinated her. Yes, thought the girl, sitting on the bed in the small white room, I knew he

29

wanted to seduce me. But I did not make up my mind. Why did I let him do it? What will happen to me now? Aware of sex in a world of nature, birth and death, she had been totally ignorant of any detail of the human act of sex and when he first possessed her she had loathed it. It was an invasion of her body, an outrage. Yet she had not stopped him. And that second time she had not been afraid and in a shameful way had enjoyed it.

She hugged her thin shoulders, wondering at herself. She no more blamed the man who had taken her virginity than she blamed the African sky for suddenly drenching her with rain.

A second hurricane followed during the night and while it roared in fury through the roofless house, Stella went to her aunt's bedroom, carrying a lamp. She set it on the table and looked across at Rupert. He was awake, and had been thinking of her, wanting her. He held out his arms and she climbed into bed beside him; a moment later she was beneath him in the now familiar embrace, her heart thudding as he made love more fiercely than before.

Flowers covered the veldt: extraordinary, sudden flowers. Shrubs full of showy yellow blooms and sharp spines, poppies four feet high, crimson and orange nemesia and winding creepers sweet as honeysuckle. Stella and Rupert sat under the eucalyptus trees or drove to the river, which was rising steadily after the rains.

His feeling of guilt was gone, he was utterly under the girl's spell and the passion he roused in her in return almost frightened him. She was ready for love any time he wanted her and often when he did not. She had changed. Her modesty, that Dutch reserve which had touched him and which he had thought pathetic, vanished. She flowered as the veldt did, suddenly and completely. They slept together every night, Stella joining him when she knew Adam and Ruth had gone to their own quarters. It was amusing to slip barefoot down the passage, past the gaping ruined old room below, and know Rupert was waiting. In the dawn she left him, returned to her own room and slept the love of the night away like a healthy young animal.

One late May morning when she went to the kitchen hungrily looking for breakfast, she found Adam with a young Hottentot, talking earnestly. The man was small, with a delicate face and figure and brilliant eyes, and when he saw her he bowed deeply before continuing his conversation in the language Stella had never mastered. She stood uneasily, watching Adam's face.

'Mis' Stella, this is Abram,' said Adam at last, speaking in the slow deliberate way she found so irritating. 'He is my sister's cousin's husband. You remember my sister, Mis' Stella?'

'Adam, what has happened!'

He slowly cut a hunk of bread.

'Abram's come from the south, and the commandos, they're just falling back and falling back. Day of wrath to come. Maybe the war is over, maybe now while we're speaking.'

'*Rubbish*!'

'It isn't that, it is the truth,' said the old man. 'Abram said there was five hundred English last night, they made a *laager* round the Maritz farm and Mrs Maritz and the girls, they was taken away to a camp, the Almighty knows where.'

Stella's face drained of colour.

'So it comes to my mind,' said Adam, 'that the Englishman will want to join his own people right now.'

Stella was silent. The Hottentot man was looking at her with satisfaction – the effect of his news was great indeed.

She took some coffee and bread and went down the stoep to join Rupert. The sight of his familiar figure, relaxed and graceful, stretched out in a chair, gave her a most intense feeling of pain.

'There's a man come, a Hottentot from the mountains. He says the war may be over and the English are quite close,' she said flatly. 'The Maritz family have been captured.'

There was a silence.

31

'I suppose we've been expecting it,' Rupert said at last.

She shrugged gloomily and he misunderstood her.

'Don't worry, Stella. I'm here to protect you.'

'I'm not bothered about *them*.'

She walked away.

A pall hung over her all day. It was very hot and they sat under the trees in the shade. They scarcely said a word, yet each knew what the other was thinking. It was almost over, their time together, their idyll. Every hour going by through the breathless, hushed afternoon was bringing it closer – the moment they must be separated. Stella looked dour. Rupert felt restless, almost feverish.

At last night fell, with a full moon and a sky of enormous stars. The servants were gone. Now, she thought, we can make love. She came barefoot into his room, peeled off her nightgown and stood naked for a moment, then ran to him. It was too warm to be covered by a sheet and they made love in the flood of brilliant moonlight. She was frenzied, and when it was over was gasping for breath. Twining their arms closely round each other, they settled down to sleep.

Rupert stirred.

'What was that?'

'Nothing.'

'I heard a noise.'

'Stupid ... it will be the dogs. You know how they root about.'

She pressed her face into his neck. But still he lay listening.

'Let's sleep . . .' she murmured drowsily, moving so that her long hair brushed across his face.

But just as he relaxed he heard a noise. A noise that filled him with horror. Footsteps.

The bedroom door smashed open. A voice shouted in Afrikaans.

Standing in the doorway were two men with rifles.

Chapter Three

She never remembered what happened next. Stark naked, legs and arms entwined, they somehow rolled apart and found the sheet.

A big tattered man in the doorway shouted to his companion,

'Go away, Karel, away, away! Leave me.'

Stella heard her cousin running down the stair.

'Uncle Hendrik—'

He did not look at her, turned his back, unslung his rifle and slammed it on the table. Still with his back turned he said:

'Put on your clothes. Was it burned, your room?'

'Uncle—'

'*Answer me!*'

'No, it was not burned, but Uncle – Aunt Maria is—'

'*Do you think I don't know she is dead*! Do not speak of her, I forbid it. Go to your room. Lock the door. I will speak to you tomorrow. Go!'

She crawled from the bed, dragged on her nightgown, gave Rupert a beseeching look – and fled.

Rupert groped for the old cotton nightshirt and pulled it over his head. Hendrik Vredenberg lit the lamp and stood at the end of the bed. He was tall and strong, perhaps sixty years old, with a lined ugly face, dark from exposure and wasted with exhaustion and hunger. His narrow eyes stared unblinkingly. In a Dutch accent more marked than Stella's he said,

'You are English.'

'Yes, sir, and will you allow me to say—'

'I allow nothing. You are a sinner and a seducer and to look on you disgusts me. Did you rape the girl? Do not

33

answer, I will not listen. You burned my farm. Holy God! This is the enemy who has stolen my country.'

Shuddering, he picked up his rifle and went out, slamming the door.

Rupert dressed slowly in his uniform. On the floor below, in the ruined roofless sitting-room, he could hear the two men talking in Afrikaans. When he looked from the window, he saw horses tethered in the moonlight. How *could* he and Stella not have heard? But they had been making love and people were deaf when they did that.

Dressed in khaki shirt and jacket, sweating from nerves, he made his way downstairs.

A lamp and candles were lit, and in the far end of the shattered room were Adam and Ruth, both fully dressed. Hendrik Vredenberg was talking to them. He was seated, but the two Africans were in a semi-kneeling position, one knee on the ground. The sight of the two kneeling figures gave Rupert a shock. He gaped. Hendrik ignored him, finished his conversation with the servants and dismissed them.

A man not much older than Rupert, round-faced, fair-haired, was sitting beside Stella's uncle. He, too, was thin and worn and dressed in rags; Rupert recognised him from Stella's description, it was her youngest cousin Karel. He glanced at Rupert, and then looked away.

The servants had gone but the Boers did not ask Rupert to sit down. He felt as if he were in the dock. Refusing to accept the humiliation, he pulled up a chair and sat.

'Mr Vredenberg,' he said, using chill formality as a cover, 'I take it that I am your prisoner.'

Hendrik Vredenberg looked at him stonily.

'Don't they tell you the war is over? You aren't my prisoner, whoever you are?'

'I didn't know.'

'At Vereeniging, Botha and De la Rey accepted. Even de Wet agreed. It is over,' Karel Vredenberg said.

'The grave of our Republics,' muttered the old man in a voice of indescribable bitterness. He paused a moment, then looked at Rupert and said, 'Get off my farm.'

'I will go at once, sir, if you wish. If I may borrow a horse.'

Vredenberg looked at him with contempt.

'You go, do you? With the woman? You take her also? You marry her now you have ruined her.'

Rupert had been tensed for that – and could not answer it. How could he marry Stella Vredenberg? It was unthinkable.

His silence spoke and Vredenberg turned to his son.

'You see what they are like. So what do I do with her, mm? Mm?'

He was so savage that Karel laid a hand on his arm, speaking in low hurried Afrikaans.

'My son tells me to be merciful. He is afraid I will whip her. This is what we did to harlots in past days. I tell him, yes, she is a whore but I will not lay a finger on her. She can stay. But *you*. A seducer and a sinner. Get off my farm.'

The violence, the hatred – it was nothing less – in the grim old man was like a physical force, a demon in the room. Faced with such passion, Rupert could say nothing. The old Dutchman spoke with the voice of his own smothered conscience.

'I will go, Sir. But I have been wounded and cannot walk across the veldt, I can scarcely walk ten yards. If I might have a horse . . .?'

'You shall have nothing of mine.'

Karel interrupted again and his father grunted.

'My son says if I do not give you one, you shall have his. He is young and soft. Leave this house you burned – sleep in the barn. Get out of my sight.'

Rupert went out into the yard and across to the barn where he lay down in the straw; he felt like a sentenced criminal. It was not making love to that passionate girl which shamed him, it was that he refused to marry her. But the thought of making an ignorant Dutch girl his wife had never once come into his head. Bring *her* back to Aston as his bride? It was impossible. When he married it would be into his own class. He would choose a young girl not only

35

for her high birth, beauty and innocence, but – yes – for her inheritance. He supposed he loved Stella in a way. But his feeling for his family was more than love, it was a religion.

'I must go,' he thought, and unconsciously spoke the words aloud. But first he knew he must ask Stella to forgive him. She would get over it, she was young and strong . . . convinced that he would never sleep, he was woken by somebody roughly shaking his shoulders. It was cold dawn and Karel Vredenberg stood by him.

'Best you go now,' the young man said in halting English. 'With my father, it is not good. I give you the Basuto pony, he will take you to the hills.'

Rupert scrambled to his feet, brushing the fragments of straw from his clothes.

'How may I thank you?' Even to his own ears the words sounded insulting. Karel said nothing and they went to the stables. Still in silence, Karel led out a horse and saddled it. As they walked away from the farm, he stopped and looked back at the roofless building in the cold dawn light.

'It is over. All finished.'

'But I am sure the farm can be rebuilt,' Rupert said.

'I mean the fighting. We commandos, we wished to fight on until we die. My two brothers are dead, you know. We fought so long . . . so long. All no use. No ammunition, no clothing, scarcely any horses. Our women made prisoners, our homes burned, our cattle killed. Now we must hand over our rifles and sign surrender. Father said he will not. Those who don't sign must leave our country.'

They stared at each other, the emaciated scarecrow Boer and the fair delicate Englishman.

'I am sorry,' was all Rupert could think to say.

'Here is a blanket. And biltong.'

Karel pointed across the veldt growing golden in the dawn to the hills where Rupert would 'find the English'. Rupert hesitated. How could he ride away without seeing Stella? He did not admit he wanted to see her for his own rather than her sake. But almost as if forced to do so, he mounted the pony, grimacing from the pain as he put his wounded foot into the stirrup.

In silence Karel led the pony towards the farm gates.

'Mr Vredenberg, I would like to see Stella to say—'

'It is not possible.'

'But surely before I go I must say goodbye.'

'No, no, you cannot,' said Karel, shocked. He continued to lead the pony away from the farm.

'Then could you tell her—'

'I tell her nothing. The family is not your concern.'

Rupert was ashamed of his own relief. As Karel dropped the reins Rupert turned to him.

'All our people have said the Boers are magnificent fighters. We have fought a noble enemy.'

Karel gave a strange smile.

Cape Town was crammed to bursting. It clattered with carriages, horses and riders, loitering troops filled it, and now and again there was the loud inspiriting sound of military music. The atmosphere of rejoicing at the war's end, of triumph at victory, was like champagne. Rupert had been in the city for a week. His regiment was waiting to sail home and it had been great good luck that he arrived in time to join them. When he appeared at the Regiment's temporary headquarters, his Colonel and fellow officers were astounded. A telegram had announced his arrival in advance. 'Otherwise, Sir,' said Rupert to Colonel Talbot, 'you would think you were seeing a ghost.'

'My dear boy, I am seeing a ghost,' said the Colonel, shaking him warmly by the hand. 'Wallace swore some damned Boer sniper got you.'

'In the leg, Sir, fortunately for me.'

'And for us, and for us,' was the reply. Colonel Talbot liked the Flood family and was a friend of the Marquess, but privately he thought the young man too lame to continue an army career.

Rupert's journey to the Cape had been long and exhausting. He had ridden the Basuto pony for three days before he found the English troops, had had some narrow escapes and had a distant view of a lioness. He had travelled by ox wagon and by train. Although his leg pained him and he felt weak and depressed, he found Cape Town delightful. The city was clean, busy, rich and the surrounding mountains were magnificent. Table Mountain towered high, seeming in the diamond air far closer than it was. The city, usually staid, was temporarily lit with a hectic gaiety and cheer from the presence of all the assembling and departing troops. The mood suited Rupert. Since the day three months ago when he had left Meidoorn he had thought too much about Stella. He remembered their sexual pleasure occasionally but far more often with remorse. Now the guilt had begun to fade. He could think of Stella more easily for he had told himself, convinced himself, that the Boers were a religious people who would never treat a young girl badly. They would blame *him* and they would be right. She was safe with her family which was where she should be.

It was evening and he was dressed for dinner at Government House. He looked at himself, thinking that the tight-fitting scarlet jacket suited him. As he bent to the looking-glass to brush his hair his servant knocked and came in.

'A visitor, Sir. Sergeant showed the lady into the library.'

A lady? Heavens, it must be Cousin Hester, thought Rupert with an inward sigh. She had come over to the Cape months ago to nurse the wounded – an elderly, worthy, dull lady. Rupert clattered down the stairs to the entrance hall which was filled with officers arriving, others leaving, and a continuous bustle.

Dusk was falling, and as he opened the door to the library he saw that a large fire had been lit. Standing in the doorway he stopped dead. A figure in a chintz dress, a rusty black hat and a shawl was by the fire. She turned and gave him a tentative smile.

'Stella! By all that's wonderful!'

For a moment she thought he was going to kiss her and she lifted her face, but he merely took her hands and gave an embarrassed laugh. Stella, too, was uncomfortable. Rupert looked utterly different from the man who had been in her thoughts night and day since her uncle had told her savagely, 'I sent the English enemy away.' His unfamiliar uniform, his – to her – stupidly formal manner, even his smile was not the same. He looked a rich foreigner.

He also found her altered. She was scrawnier, the bloom had gone from her pretty cheeks, her nose seemed more prominent. The hideous clothes made her look as dingy as a scullery maid. But she lifted her chin in the old way.

'You are surprised to see me. It is also a surprise for me to be here. What a dusty place,' she said, wrinkling her nose. 'I do not like towns. Are you well? You look wonderful,' she said and added indifferently, 'I look dreadful but that is nothing.'

'You must have a glass of madeira,' he said, ringing for the steward. 'Sit down, my dear. Why are you in Cape Town? How did you find me? It is indeed a delightful surprise.'

She waited in silence while the wine was brought. When the steward had left them she did not touch the drink. Laughter rang out in the hall outside, there was a rattle of carriage wheels in the street and the fire crackled busily. Sitting near her, Rupert sipped his madeira and began to talk vivaciously, describing his adventurous journey, how he had finally joined his regiment and how soon they were sailing home.

'I daresay you noticed that I'm still a little lame,' he said, 'but the surgeon is encouraging about the wound. And very complimentary about your skill. At first he could scarcely believe my story!'

He laughed, showing his white teeth. 'You haven't told me where you are staying.' He had not given her a chance to say a word. 'Have you relatives in Cape Town? May I call on them?'

'I have no family here. Karel told me the address of Mrs Zeederburg where I stay just now. A little house in a suburb. She is quite kind, but I have left Meidoorn.'

'I don't understand.'

Something in her voice made him oddly uneasy. Yet the girl sitting by the fire was very composed.

Stella shrugged.

'Cousin Karel gave me money and arranged the journey for me. It was he who found where your regiment was. I could not tell Uncle Hendrik I was going, he would think it his duty to stop me. I come to you for a reason,' she added. 'I am to have your child.'

He blanched. He was no longer the elegant self-possessed man: she could have been facing a horror-stricken boy.

She slightly smiled.

'*Ge skok*. You are shocked. It is very dreadful, then, an Afrikaans girl for a wife.'

A silence fell.

Never for a second, looking at the man she had dragged from death and whose child she now carried, did Stella consider a refusal. In her journey across the huge unhappy country mourning its defeat, down endless roads where soldiers, women and children, white and black, stared at the wagon going by, through storms and sun and bitter cold day upon day, it had not once come into her mind that Rupert would not marry her. Her certainty filled the air between them. He could feel it, smell it.

He swallowed.

Stella was driven back to the suburban house on the outskirts of Cape Town. Rupert, due at Government House, could not accompany her but he ordered the cab and paid the driver. The city sparkled with lights and jostled with crowds; the cab crossed a square where a building as elaborate as a palace towered into the dark sky. She saw nothing. It was the first time in her short life that she had discovered a person could change. Her uncle and aunt, Karel, old Adam and Ruth, the people who had reared her had been changeless. She could depend on them for their good traits and bad, for severity and piety, humourlessness and unspeaking affection, disapprobation – honour. But Rupert was not the man she had known. With clear eyes she had seen, the moment he walked into

40

the library, that he no longer loved her. It had been a chilling shock. I was a shock to him too, she thought. There it is. We must put up with it.

She never thought she was wrong to expect the Englishman to marry her. It was his duty, just as it had been her uncle's duty to give her his protection, although he had found her in bed with an enemy and thought her a harlot. Her uncle had wanted to turn her out of the house, she knew that very well. He kept her at Meidoorn from duty and when she told him bluntly that she was pregnant, his resolve did not change. Yes, he would have kept me with him because he thought it was right. And would make us both suffer for it.

It was Karel who had told her that her uncle was determined to refuse to sign the oath of allegiance. Meidoorn was ruined, Maria was dead and he hated the English. It seemed that some of the Western states of America were offering free land to any Boers who were deported. Hendrik would go there.

'He will take you with him, Stella,' said Karel. 'You will make a new life, as an honourable widow and a mother. Some good American will wed you, maybe. You are quite pretty still. And after all, you will be back in the country of your birth. Perhaps that is the will of God.'

'No,' said Stella flatly, 'I shall marry the Englishman. *That* is what's right.'

Karel was deeply disturbed. She was still almost a child, he said, and his father would care for her.

'You belong with him. He is family. Please think again. You know nothing about the Englishman.'

But Stella could be as stubborn as any of the Vredenbergs, and who did she know better than the man who had been her lover for all those weeks?

So now he will marry me, she thought, unsurprised. She climbed from the hackney outside a small house with white railings, flowering shrubs and chickens scratching in the back garden. Mrs Zeederburg was sewing in the front room. She was a plain-faced woman of the kind Stella had known since she was five years old.

'I will not be needing the room after Thursday, Mrs Zeederburg. I am to stay with friends,' said Stella at the door. She had a sudden childish impulse to startle the impassive woman by saying casually, 'I'm going to be married.'

But what was the point? Mrs Zeederburg was a stranger who cared nothing for her and in any case Stella was tired. Being pregnant was tiring. She went to her room, lay down and fell into a peaceful sleep.

When they met for luncheon at a smart hotel the following day, Rupert said he had obtained his Colonel's permission to marry. A special licence would be granted – the ceremony could take place in two days. He did not speak about the interview which he preferred to forget, but mentioned the name of the church. It was small and out-of-the-way, not far from the house where Stella was staying.

'I chose it because it is convenient for you.'

Stella enquired its denomination and was surprised when he snapped, 'Church of England, of course. What a ridiculous question.'

She was silent. The Vredenbergs were strict members of the Dutch Reformed Church. Their church, their *predikants* – ministers – and their Calvinist principles were as much part of their lives as the air they breathed. But Stella could see Rupert was nervous, he scarcely ate a thing and when she talked he answered in monosyllables. She thought, it's the ceremony that matters, not which minister he got us. And suddenly it came to her how very far she was from Meidoorn.

Rupert was kind enough during the next two days, but made no move to be alone with her and when they parted, merely kissed her cheek. Like Uncle Hendrik, he was doing his duty. He gave her what seemed a great deal of money 'to buy a hat for the wedding'.

Stella thought about that. A hat? She only possessed one which she had worn once every three months when she and the family travelled to church, a fifty mile drive. It was a

42

stiffbrimmed old black straw which had belonged to her aunt, and was slightly too small for Stella's head.

Up in the cramped bedroom of Mrs Zeederburg's house, Stella decided it was time to give up wearing the black shawl. She must not mourn any longer for Aunt Maria; it would not do to depress Rupert. For the wedding she would wear her favourite chintz, white, sprigged with little purple flowers. She went off in the afternoon to a Cape Town emporium to choose the hat.

Visiting a large shop was a strange experience for the country-bred girl, just as the large city was. She disliked the noise and hurry and although the city did not frighten her, she wished herself out of it. The shop was overheated and smelled of scent. She looked at the padded velvet gowns, the appliqués of thick lace, the sweeping trains, with derision. What guys the women made of themselves. And the assistants did not look at her politely. She knew they guessed that she had no money.

An assistant in black silk rustled up.

'I want a hat,' said Stella dourly.

The woman, who had dyed hair and a powdered face, arranged a gilt chair in front of a looking-glass. She began carefully to place hats, one by one, on Stella's blonde head. Stella gazed at her own haggard face, topped by a series of broad-brimmed confections: some were heaped with stiffened ribbon, some with veiling, some had great curled feathers or flowers or the wings of birds. She finally chose a white hat wreathed in lilies of the valley, paid for it and left the emporium carrying a very large hat box.

She had ironed her best dress the night before her wedding day, which proved to be a mercy as she was violently sick the next morning after breakfast. Hoping that Mrs Zeederburg did not hear the retching, Stella washed her face for the second time, screwed up her hair, carefully pulled on the clean print dress and put on the hat. She skewered it with the long pearl-topped pins which had been provided, and looked at herself with interest.

I wish I didn't look so washed out. How plain I've got;

but anyway the hat is jolly. She pinched her cheeks but the pink faded at once.

Pretending not to hear the landlady calling from the kitchen, she slipped out of the house. The cab sent by Rupert was punctual and waiting at the gate.

'St Mary's Church, Miss?' The hackney set off at a brisk trot on a day warmer than usual for the cold Cape Town June. It was rather airless and the sun came through a white haze. Stella's spirits rose for the first time since she and Rupert had been together at the farm; they were going to be happy, they were fond of each other and she would do her best. Her passion had strangely left her, but Stella put this down, as with everything new, to pregnancy. She accepted her lonely state, her altering body, the unwillingness of her future husband, the chill dusty city, even the hat bobbing on a head accustomed to a sunbonnet or freedom, with philosophy.

There was the church, small, black and white with a little spire and a porch with thin pillars. As she alighted from the cab she saw two officers in the porch waiting for her. Rupert was in uniform, and there was a strange young man in another kind of uniform of dark blue. For a moment neither of them saw her, they were talking, or rather arguing. With her sharp sight she saw that Rupert looked angry and she knew they were talking about her.

Turning, they watched the white-clad figure coming through the churchyard towards them. She walked easily, chin lifted, innocently presenting so ludicrous an appearance that they were both appalled. The old-fashioned Boer gown made her look like an under-housemaid, yet her head was topped with an elaborate hat which only a beautiful woman of over thirty would dare to wear, a woman of their own class, soignée, poised . . .

'Good God,' muttered Harry Flood, 'what have you done?'

'What choice had I?' muttered his brother in reply.

With a forced smile, Rupert greeted her.

'Stella, this is my brother Harry. His ship only docked

44

last night, I was not sure he would be able to be with us; I kept his arrival as a surprise.'

Stella primly held out her hand. But as she looked at Harry Flood, her ideas of Englishmen scattered. The man was as tough as an Afrikaner. He had a round face, a strong jaw, thick dark hair. His skin was slightly olive, very different from his brother's, and his eyes were bright and grey and very sharp. Beside him, Rupert was like a lanky girl. Harry touched her hand and the trio went into the church.

The vicar, an elderly long-nosed man in a lace-trimmed surplice which Stella thought a garment of nasty popery, was waiting by the altar steps with his curate. He greeted Rupert with respect, whispering as if they were by the bedside of somebody gravely ill. 'And this is the bride, Miss—'

'Vredenberg,' said Stella.

'Yes, yes, exactly. The Viscount did not tell me if your parents will be here, Miss Vredenberg. Should we wait for them? Who is giving the bride away?'

Stella's poise faltered for the first time.

'My family—'

'Miss Vredenberg's family are deceased, Vicar, sad to say,' said Harry Flood. 'Shall we begin, please. I am giving the bride away.'

PART TWO
Aston 1902–1908

Chapter Four

Rupert stared out of the train window at the cornfields beginning to turn grey in the autumn sunshine. Oxfordshire. Every turn of the wheels, every meadow with its isolated luxuriant oaks, meant he was nearing home. The sun had shone when he and Stella had left London, but it was now a richer gold in the late afternoon. He felt a moment of joy at the thought of seeing Aston: then the familiar dropping of the heart. How could he help resenting the girl he had been forced to marry? The thought hurt and never left him, it was like a gorse spine caught in his clothes. Whichever way he moved, it pricked his skin.

He had never learned to look on the bright side. His face, petulant and spoiled, showed how little he had of philosophy. He could not get used to what had happened through his own fault. When he remembered the moment when he had, so to speak, accepted Stella's offer of marriage, he could not recall how on earth he had agreed. His brother had tried to dissuade him – literally in the church porch. Rupert did not think of Harry with any more affection because of that.

Taking his eyes away from the ripening country, he looked across the carriage at his wife. She was asleep. A small hat decorated with purplish grey feathers was pinned on top of her head. He had spent more than he could afford on clothes for her during their brief stay in London. The town was deserted, but one or two of the better stores were open. But whatever he chose for his wife, she looked ill-dressed. She had no more idea of how to wear clothes than a scarecrow. Wrapped in a pale cape to hide her growing bulk, she slept deeply, the hat he had chosen with finicky care looking absurd.

49

When she finally awoke, she looked at him and smiled.

'Have I been long asleep? I dreamed of Meidoorn. How much longer is the journey?'

'We arrive at Aston Magna in twenty minutes.'

'Day of wrath to come!'

'I have asked you not to use that expression, Stella.'

'I forget I am to talk like an Englishwoman.' Her voice had become as sharp as his. She had been listening to such criticism since their wedding night when he had sat on the bed in the Cape Town hotel and talked to the yawning girl about her 'duty to have good nerves and a calm temper'. She must take her place in the world beside him, he had said, and learn the right standards. Stella had fallen asleep twice during what had resembled a sermon and a long sermon at that. He had not made love to her that night. There had in fact been singularly little love since then, but Stella found that she did not very much mind. Now that she was pregnant her desire, as well as his, seemed to have gone. But her husband's irritability hurt her and although she was sorry for him – he was very nervous – she had decided he must stop nagging. He must make the best of things as she was doing.

And there was a good deal, thought Stella as she looked out of the train window, for her to make the best of. My God, how small this country is. Nobody said it would look like this. No distances, no mountains and no sky. Little fields where a few cattle grazed. Dolls' house cottages. Nothing savage or wild and everything the wrong colour and the wrong size and the wrong season. September was the start of spring, not autumn.

'Rupert.'

'Yes?' He was trying to read.

'I think it good we try to behave.'

He slammed down his book.

'What on earth do you mean?'

'I mean we can't arrive at your parents' house like squabbling children. I know you are worried.'

He laughed sarcastically but she went on, 'Yes, you are. Don't pretend it is not so. You think your family will not

50

be pleased. They will get used to me, you'll see. It will come right.'

She grinned almost cheerfully. A trick of the light banished the drawn, pregnant look and for a moment she looked like the same girl who had teased him, sitting on the stoep with the beautiful background of the veldt's flat rainbows.

He had the grace to lean over and take her hand.

The train drew up with a sigh of steam at a toy-sized station. 'Aston Magna' was planted in red flowers on a bank. The compartment door opened and a stout porter appeared.

'Welcome home, your Lordship and Ladyship.'

Rupert and Stella were respectfully ushered out of the station. A carriage was waiting, the footmen in livery, the grey horses perfectly matched. As they set off Stella almost said, 'A bit different from our Meidoorn cart.' But inwardly sighing, she knew she must not. She had discovered that such comparisons deeply offended him. Faced with the great scattered jigsaw of her husband's nature, Stella had pored over the pieces and now had the firm edge of the portrait. Each day she put another fragment into place. He was English and rich, to start with, and she was foreign and poor. But that was too neat. Uncle Hendrik had not been poor at all, but frugal as a Boer farmer must be to make his land prosper. Rupert's way with money was to preface it with an unspoken 'Of course'. Of course they must stay in a luxurious hotel in London, of course the carriage would be drawn by superb horses, of course the stationmaster would bow and scrape. And of course his wife must not make jokes about farm carts.

Rupert was piqued that she said nothing on the journey. They trotted through beautiful woods and Cotswold lanes tall with feathery late summer weeds. The air smelled of pollen and drying hay. Then the carriage slowed down and turned in between pillars decorated with stone stags awkwardly clasping shields between their spindle legs. The gates were already open, and the carriage bowled into the drive.

51

It was two miles long and crossed a huge stretch of parkland dozing in the afternoon sun. The vast domes of oaks stood in circles of their own shade. In ferny distances a herd of deer slowly moved. The carriage topped a rise and the house floated into view like a vision in the golden light. A jumbled mass of buildings, a confusion of stone and brick, with Tudor pinnacles and a Dutch orangery, eighteenth century façades, broad terraces, pavilions. Aston had been a monastery dedicated to Saint Astonwold and the life of fervour. Henry VIII had given it to the first Rupert Flood. It had been raped by Cromwell's soldiers, caught fire when Dutch William was on the throne. Built and rebuilt by the Floods and their rich wives, it was not a house, it was a dominion.

In the courtyard, a cluster of servants in starched white, sober black, maroon and green, stood waiting to bow and bob. Rupert was gracious, but Stella scarcely took them in. Had she thought England was small? The size of this place stunned her.

'The Marchioness is in the conservatory, my lord,' said the butler, who reminded Stella of a Dutch preacher.

Rupert took her through what she later learned was the Great Hall, a stone-floored chamber lit by stained glass windows. Rows of antlers along the walls clustered like dead branches and round the hall ran a gallery, leading to scores of bedrooms. But what Stella looked at was the line of flags. Suspended from poles under the timbered roof, they hung motionless, and so thickly laid with untouched dust that all the once brilliant reds and blues were changed to a strange, ghostly grey. The silks were old and rotten, and on many flags there was little more than a network of threads supporting rags.

'Those are the flags of the regiments we have served in,' Rupert said, following her eyes. 'They go back as far as Plantagenet. That little brownish one in the corner.'

'Your family fought in many wars.'

'One or two,' he said.

She did not reply. They fought in many wars, these people, and I have been in only one, she thought. My cousins died in it, and I cannot bear to think of their laughing faces when they rode away to drive the English into the sea.

He took her down a corridor with doors on the left, one of which stood open and led into a library, its windows overlooking the sunny gardens. He was in a hurry, leading her up little flights of stairs, through doors, down passages, until she quite lost her sense of direction. At last he said, 'Here we are.'

The conservatory smelled of damp earth and the scent of flowers; a tree pressing against the domed glass roof was covered with white waxy blossoms. A woman of about fifty was sitting at a tea table. She put down a silver teapot and held out her hand. Rupert rushed forward, kissed the hand and then her cheek.

'Mother.'

'Rupert.'

He still held her hand.

'Mother, may I present Stella. I cannot tell you how much she has been longing to meet you.'

The two women began their life together with a barefaced lie.

The Marchioness glanced at Stella, slightly inclined her head and turned back to her son. She was handsome in a bony, patrician way. She had the aquiline nose and well-set eyes of the most famous portraits of Queen Elizabeth, when the face, pale and still, seemed a kind of mask of majesty. She wore remarkable pearls and her mouth had Rupert's curve, but she looked hard and strong and Stella's spirits sank to her shoes.

Gesturing to the footman to draw a chair for Stella, Lady Tyrrell briefly enquired how Rupert was, and how was the voyage home. She made no mention of Stella and paid no attention to her. Rupert talked eagerly and obsequiously, once or twice including his wife in the conversation. His mother disregarded this, her manner to her son was cold, she might have been speaking to an acquaintance. Stella was chilled and miserable, but she had expected it. She had heard, like thunder rolling among the hills of her homeland, the sound of Rupert's fear of his mother. The lady sitting bolt upright under the flowering tree in this hot damp place epitomised everything Stella had heard about the English.

'That will be all, John,' said the Marchioness without turning her head. The footman silently left.

Lady Tyrrell waited until they were alone, then said, 'Well, Rupert? Your explanation.'

He looked alarmed.

'I wrote to you and Father and explained, Mama.'

'You explained nothing. Your father and I are shocked.'

'Mama, please!'

It was a kind of groan, and Stella was suddenly so angry that she blushed to the roots of her hair.

'Rupert is twenty-five, he has a perfect right to choose his wife,' she burst out, her Dutch accent thickened by temper.

Lady Tyrrell appeared to see her for the first time.

'I don't question his right to "choose his wife" as you call it. I merely wonder whether he has either reflected or indeed informed you that he is totally dependent upon his family. Doubtless you would have behaved differently had you known he has not a farthing of his own.'

'What do you mean? You are very rude!' shouted Stella, jumping to her feet.

'*Stella, be quiet*! How dare you speak to my mother like that in her own house?' cut in Rupert.

Stella turned on him.

'Why is it different if I speak in her house or Meidoorn or a pigsty if she insults me? Why don't you tell her that's what she does. She insults your wife.'

'Oh, we know all about that,' said Lady Tyrrell, with a tinkling laugh.

It was much, much worse than Stella had imagined. Here she was in a great threatening palace, facing a woman who detested her, and her own husband, the man supposed to protect her and whose child she carried, standing there like a sick girl. The Marchioness stood up, shaking out the folds of her pale silks. She glanced briefly at Stella.

'We will have no more scenes, if you please. Rupert. Has your wife brought her maid?'

'I didn't have no maid at Meidoorn except my Basuto nurse and *she'd* not come here if you dragged her,' said Stella rudely.

Lady Tyrrell ignored her.

'Wilkins can maid your wife. She is well trained and Mrs Briggs tells me she is perfectly suitable.'

'Of course, Mama. Thank you,' said Rupert, ashen.

When she stood up, Lady Tyrrell was smaller than Stella had imagined, quite a little thing who appeared larger because of her elaborate clothes and presence. She walked to the door, managing her skirts with perfect skill, kicking her slight train behind her.

'I will see you at dinner,' she said to Rupert. And was gone.

In gloomy silence Rupert took Stella along the gallery which overlooked the Great Hall, and after many passages, finally into what was called the Lauderdale room, where a peculiarly wicked Earl had slept when he visited Aston in the seventeenth century. The Earl's four-poster was hung with curtains embroidered with his cypher. Bay windows overlooked formal gardens, a distant lake and a vista of low hills. Stella threw herself down on the window seat, looking at the exquisite man-made landscape and not seeing it.

Rupert pulled at his silk stock as if it choked him. 'You must apologise.'

'I will *not*. She is to blame!'

'My God, how old are you, twelve?'

'Seventeen a month ago,' she said, like a child.

He walked up and down, angry and pale.

'How could you speak to her like that? How dared you? *Nobody* speaks to my mother—' words failed him. 'Can't you understand that my marriage was a great shock? Have you no imagination?'

He was angry with his mother for showing him the side of her nature that he was afraid of and with himself for even imagining that she would accept this raw foreigner. But most of all he was furious with Stella, and waited for her to burst into repentant sobs. She unpinned her hat.

'She said there will be a maid, who will unpack, I suppose? It offends the English when I do things for myself.'

'Don't say "the English". You are English now,' he said bitingly.

Thinking in Dutch that she was no such thing, Stella did not reply.

The arrival of the Viscount's girl bride had been received with horror by his family and with scandalised disapproval laced with curiosity in the Servants' Hall. Only the scullery maids thought it romantic. Stella had no idea that her appearance at Aston resembled a great lump of rock hurled into a tranquil lake. She never wondered what these people thought of *her*, she saw things from no point of view but her own. Her feelings were hectically-coloured fragments in a kaleidoscope: one shake and the pattern utterly changed.

A gaunt maid arrived to dress her for dinner. There was scarcely a year in age between the two girls but Wilkins was already middle-aged. She unpacked, hung up each gown with care, ran Stella's bath and sprinkled in rose geranium bath salts. She set out her underclothes and when Stella had bathed, laced her stays gently and knelt on the floor to pull on her stockings. Somehow she managed to avert her eyes from Stella's bulging stomach. She brushed Stella's thick blonde hair and skilfully dressed it. Stella felt she was being waited upon by a ghost.

Rupert had retired to his dressing-room and Stella was glad. She did not like Wilkins but at least the maid was silent and Stella could think in peace. She already detested this huge kingdom Rupert called his home, and it was only too clear that the Marchioness detested *her*. Reared among strong women, Stella knew a considerable enemy when she saw one. As for her husband, where was his loyalty, let alone his love? She wondered why his lack of affection did not hurt her more. Pregnancy had blunted her feelings. She felt as if she were wrapped in a thick protective cloak which even a righteous indignation could not penetrate.

When Rupert led her into the drawing-room the sun had begun to set behind a group of distant trees. The sky, turning from orange to crimson, filled the high windows with colour. An elderly man and a child stood looking at the sunset together.

'Oh, it's Rupert!'

The little girl spun round and darted forward to throw herself into his arms. She was pretty and dark, her face alight with joy as she exclaimed, 'Dearest, dearest Rupert, did you absolutely forget me?'

Watching Rupert hugging and petting his sister, Stella smiled for the first time since she had entered the house. The elderly man was also watching the scene in silence and Rupert, detaching himself from the child's embrace, said 'My dear Father!' and went to him. Stella had seen many fathers and sons reunited after painful separations during the war. They always embraced and said a prayer together, and she always felt her heart would burst. The Marquess and his son merely gripped hands and laughed slightly.

'Father, may I present my wife? Stella, my father. And Catherine, my little sister.'

Catherine bobbed a curtsey and Rupert's father gave her his hand, murmuring something: 'Pleasure ... feeling fatigued?' The tone was kind enough. He was a heavily-built man with strong shoulders and a head of thick crinkled hair turning to silver. He was cleanshaven, with a big jaw and a sensual face. The manner was negligent, the voice more drawling than his son's. Both had blue English eyes.

When they sat down, Catherine leaned against her brother like a dog with a newly-returned master. The Marquess, incapable of being ungallant to a woman, asked Stella one or two questions and smiled at her slightly. When courtesy allowed he turned to Rupert who positively glowed during the conversation which followed – that of war. Sitting in the lofty and elaborate room hung with pictures, set about with great vases of roses, among velvets and garlands and trophies, Stella heard familiar names; Spion Kop and Majuba and Talana. They echoed like bells for the death of friends.

'Desmond is home on leave soon,' said the Marquess, turning to her again. 'You'll meet a new brother, don't you know.'

'I already met Harry in Cape Town.'

'Indeed? Rupert did not say.'

Stella almost replied that he had come to the wedding but Rupert cut in, saying Harry's ship had docked in Cape Town and wasn't it a stroke of luck. Lady Tyrrell rustled into the room just then. The atmosphere changed.

William Flood, Marquess of Tyrrell, had been forced to listen to many long and exhausting harangues from his wife about Rupert's marriage. The news, a telegram followed by a letter, had prostrated her. William knew his wife only too well. She was not going to accept the girl and he groaned inwardly at how much all this was going to inconvenience his comfortable life. The Flood tradition was to marry heiresses, and William had married Millicent Dacre when she was eighteen years old. The Floods needed to marry money, they squandered it with such skill; they gambled and were passionate about horses, they pulled down and rebuilt Aston, they lived like Royalty, continuing in their extravagance when their wealth inevitably dwindled. But heiresses came along to save the day. Rupert had broken the tradition with a vengeance. It was, thought William retiring to bed, a surprise. His eldest son rather bored him, it was Desmond who was his favourite and most like himself. He considered Rupert's submission to Millicent ridiculous: it was not manly. True, the boy was handsome and healthy and had done the family credit until now. William was secretly amused by the mésalliance: what had possessed the boy?

As he retired to bed – he rarely visited Millicent in the state bedroom – he decided upon a trip to Paris. He would take his poodle Gustav to be clipped, to avoid the inevitable unpleasantness that would follow.

When he had been a child, William's nurse had said, 'His young lordship does like to give hisself a treat'. He had not changed. As a young man he accumulated fearsome debts, and Millicent arrived in the nick of time. He was in love with her for a while: she was spirited and pretty, well-born and wonderfully rich. Coal mines. As a bride, she took to Aston with a passion which surprised him because he had never felt thus. Power did not stay long in William's well-shaped hands, he gave it to Millicent. When he needed a change from her, he and Gustav went to Paris.

Certainly Millicent was superb. In the last thirty years she had become one of the great ladies, magnificent, autocratic, never swerving from her exalted standards and often refusing to know brilliant wealthy people close to the King. Millicent stood for what she had venerated since her Victorian childhood: majestic position and irreproachable conduct.

The arrival of a penniless Colonial – her son assured them she was American but Millicent ignored that – was a savage blow. She had raged. Oh, thought William, it had been tedious. He might have sympathised had she not repeated herself so often. Useless to suggest she came to terms with the marriage, Millicent never made the best of things: she changed them. But she could not un-marry Rupert. No wonder she looked as if made of stone.

On the day following Rupert's return, the Marquess went riding. Returning in the perfect evening, the sunshine beginning to fade, there was a hint of autumn in the air. As he rode through the trees near the lodge, he saw a figure sitting forlornly by the sundial. He dismounted and walked over to his son.

'And where is the young lady?'

'Resting, Sir. The journey tired her.'

His father raised a bushy eyebrow, which gave his face a touch of caricature.

'Gals of that age don't tire. Is she with child?'

He smiled dryly at his son's start.

'I thought so. There's a look about the face. Pleased?'

'Of course, Sir.'

'Quick off the mark, though. How old is she?'

'Seventeen last month.'

'Good God!'

'But I wrote and said—'

'You did not tell us you had raided the nursery.'

'She's older than a girl of her age in England,' said Rupert defensively. 'Women out there age more quickly.'

'You ain't going to like that, are you?'

His father took pity on him and looped the reins over a branch. The horse began to crop the short turf.

'We're in the soup, my boy.'

'But surely all this does not affect you, Sir!'

'Makes a difference to everybody. Quite a bolt from the blue . . . sudden wedding at the other end of nowhere. Your mother don't understand you.'

'Stella saved my life.'

'Very remarkable.' A pause. 'So that's why you married her, eh?'

'I fell in love with her,' said Rupert and believed it just then.

His father thoughtfully smacked his riding boot with his crop. Talk of love was not his style.

'Don't try to smooth your mother down, my boy. Best thing is to lie low.'

'Keep Stella out of her way?'

'That's the ticket,' said his father, with a hearty smile which promised nothing. He remounted and rode off.

Rupert walked back under the beech trees. He looked towards Aston, seeing its familiar jumble of roofs, arches, turrets. Somewhere inside its walls was one mute girl of seventeen. He wished his father would take his side. It isn't a game or a war, he thought irritably, why do I think of sides? But of course it was a war. His handsome face, pale, with silky moustache and skin like silk, was strained as he tusselled with the problem of how to regain his mother's affection. He loved her. And *her* love and admiration were necessary to him; if she did not look at him with softened eyes, he felt less than himself. There had never been a time in the past when she had not treated him tenderly. He was

60

Chapter Five

It took Stella many weeks and much of the dour self-control she had been taught at Meidoorn to become accustomed to life at Aston. She did not feel well, her pregnancy was not as effortless as anyone so healthy, strong and young might expect. She sometimes felt very sick and always languid. Her malaise worked in two ways. She had none of her hardy energy to face an extraordinary new life and she accepted things she felt too tired and unwell to fight.

The world into which she had ignorantly forced herself was incredible. The Floods lived in an oriental splendour: fifty servants in the house, footmen in velvet with powdered hair, lodgekeepers, gamekeepers, carpenters and dairy-maids. At Meidoorn the whole reason for workers was to make the land and the farm prosper. These flocks of skilful servants were for nothing but glory. There were green-houses filled with orchids, dinners stretching to twelve courses. When Rupert had tried to describe Aston to her when they first met, Stella had thought it sounded unreal, absurd and shocking. No wonder, she had thought, we fight these folk. Now she was supposed to be one of them.

As the days passed, Millicent adroitly allowed visitors to come to Aston, a few intimate friends at first, then a larger circle, until finally the house at weekends was crammed with guests. They treated Stella as her parents-in-law did. The gentlemen were kindly but casual, the ladies looked at her with a glassy stare and addressed her as little as possible. At her first large dinner party, faced with forty strangers, Stella was breathless with nerves.

She began to see her husband in perspective, the jigsaw made a picture. Beyond his shoulder, like the miniature

63

detailed landscapes behind figures in Mediaeval paintings, was a way of life which had not much changed since the Civil War, merely growing more elaborate. The Floods, whose ancestors had died for Charles I, spoke of it as if it were yesterday. The family's sense of itself, its rank and history, seemed to the girl to be summed up in the flags rotting away in the Great Hall. Nothing was discarded or thrown away: it hung above them coated with dust, for pride.

Aston was enormous and seemed to the wondering girl to spread for acres. The high windows overlooked the gardens, lake, parkland, meadows. In the picture gallery were portraits of the Floods in lace and satin, ermine and mail, some of whom slightly resembled her husband, staring down at her with Rupert's girlish face. The armies of servants puzzled her. She was used to house servants obedient to the extent of falling on one knee when Uncle Hendrik gave them an order, but her uncle and aunt had treated them as children. The upper servants at Aston had authority, they were like sergeant majors keeping the army in order. You never complained to a footman or a groom, but to the butler or housekeeper. There was precedence wherever you looked.

The strangest sensation was the idleness; since she had come from America as a little child, Stella had been schooled in the Dutch belief in work. It was God's will. At evening prayers her uncle constantly referred to the deep-felt belief. 'The sleep of the labouring man is sweet' he quoted. 'Whatsoever thy hand findeth to do, do it with thy might; for there is no work, nor device, nor knowledge, nor wisdom, in the grave, whither thou goest.' She and Cousin Karel had talked about that. Stella had said daringly, '*I* thought we were supposed to enjoy ourselves sometimes.'

'It is never possible to be idle and happy, Cousin,' Karel had said.

She had been trained to duty, sighing over the washing and ironing, the making of soap and candles, the ache of her young back and the state of her bleached hands. Now there was nothing to do at all, except to be changed from one dress to another, to sit, to listen (since people did not talk much to her), to drift round the park and to play the piano.

One evening, sitting beside a somewhat livelier young man than usual at dinner, Edwin Saltash, she spoke of work at Meidoorn. He was short and curly-haired and laughed a good deal; he was very amused. When they were in their bedroom that night Rupert said, 'Stella, you say you love me.'

'Say it? Of course I do. And you love me.'

'Then you must promise here and now, solemnly swear, that you will never speak of Meidoorn even if you are asked. Learn to avoid answering. Edwin, this evening, simply did not understand. You do see, don't you?'

As a matter of fact, she did. Touching on the subject of darning commando uniforms, she had seen a smiling but pitying look on Edwin's face. It had annoyed her.

She promised.

In the quiet hours that she and Rupert spent in the Lauderdale room, Stella was not unhappy. One morning after breakfasting in bed, she brought up the subject of work.

'It is so difficult, doing nothing. And you and all the others do nothing too.'

'My dear child! Of course we work. It is simply that the kind of work we do is not what you can understand. We have great responsibilities. We built the village hospital here, and my grandfather built the church. The new one, that is, not the little old one by the bridge. My mother endowed the free school, and all the cottages in the village are ours as well as those on the estate. And what about our other properties? Flood Place, Llantrip, the London house and so on. A great number of people are entirely dependent upon us for their welfare.'

He spoke ponderously. Stella was unimpressed.

Certainly the Aston servants worked invisibly and skilfully; but all Stella saw of the family at work was Lady Tyrrell occasionally talking to the butler or condescending to have a word on Sunday with the vicar. *He* bowed low as a Basuto, thought Stella scornfully; a minister should not bend to a woman just because she paid for the church roof.

But despite inward censures, she began to accept her life. The luxury, the service, the flowers, the ebb and flow of visitors, the music at night which was for pleasure and not for hymns. Her greatest cross was listening to Society talk, which consisted of references to people she did not know and parties she had not attended. Oddly, stocks and shares were much discussed. Apparently it was not ill-bred for ladies to talk over their investments. And there were, of course, long tales of the hunt.

The high veldt, the fierce heat and violent rains, the clear air across which one could see so magically far, the thorn bushes and sneeze wood trees, the whining of jackals and roar of waterfalls, the great lost panorama of her young life had begun to fade. This enamelled enclosed world about her grew familiar. Rupert was kind – sometimes tender.

Stella's dislike of Aston eased – when her mother-in-law was not about. But Lady Tyrrell's manner did not alter by the quiver of an eyelash. She was either freezingly cold or managed to behave as if Stella were not there at all. Being in the same room with her mother-in-law often made Stella feel rather sick with nerves. She had met such treatment before – Lady Tyrrell was not unlike the hated Mrs Maritz.

Knowing herself detested, Stella returned the feeling, although its edge was blunted as everything was, by pregnancy. She said little about her mother-in-law to Rupert. And he was too afraid of losing his mother's love to wonder at his wife's endurance. Naturally Millicent did not show her feelings in public – when Aston filled with visitors she managed a kind of imitation politeness to her daughter-in-law. Rupert's expression of eager gratitude when this happened also made Stella feel a little sick.

But to her surprise she found that Rupert's ten-year-old sister appeared to like her. Catherine was still in the schoolroom, and her governess was kind to Stella in a respectful way. Catherine was friendly. She and the increasingly-pregnant Stella went for walks in the park, talking of horses about which Catherine found her new sister-in-law even more knowledgeable than herself. They returned to the house to share a hearty schoolroom tea.

The two members of the Flood family still missing to make the circle complete were due home on leave in early October. Desmond arrived first; his Regiment had returned from Africa far later than Rupert's. One soft autumn afternoon walking across the park with Stella and two of the Aston dogs, Rupert caught sight of a figure on the terrace.

'Why, there's Des!'

He limped as quickly as he could up the terrace steps.

'My dear old fellow!'

The brothers greeted each other heartily. When Rupert introduced Stella, she was given the usual veiled Aston look of curiosity. She was curious too. Here was the brother whom Rupert preferred, and the favourite of his father. The missing card in the pack. Desmond was everything Rupert was not. He was thick-set and solid, much resembling the Marquess, with the same aquiline nose, heavy jaw and strong figure. He had none of Rupert's overbred racehorse looks, he reminded Stella of a Dutch farmer. He also had a curiously conceited manner. Perhaps he had assumed it years ago when made to feel the difference between the heir and himself. Destiny had robbed Desmond by eighteen short months, of everything he prized. To be head of the family one day. To carry the huge weight of Aston on his powerful shoulders. Physically like his father, he was as tough-minded as Millicent, and had always thought his elder brother's nature a most inexplicable weakness.

Desmond had been aghast at the South African marriage. Now, looking at the girl, he thought her plain as well as being a nobody. He was perfectly polite to her but Stella felt patronised. With a rare feeling for taking her husband's part she decided Desmond was doing exactly the same thing to Rupert. Later, when she saw him with other people, she noticed that Desmond was the same with everybody except his father. To the Marquess he was warm. But nobody else, not even Millicent, penetrated his self-regard.

Rupert was delighted at his brother's arrival. He was shy with his father, and Stella now saw that he had sorely missed masculine family company. The two young men talked eagerly. Desmond's regiment had fought under Lord Roberts when Bloemfontein was occupied. Fighting the commandos, Desmond had won an MC and promotion; he was now a lieutenant.

The brothers soon fell into the habit of going riding together early every morning. Stella stood at her bedroom window to watch them as they rode down the drive. Desmond was confidently mounted on his favourite chestnut hunter, he rode well, but Rupert's seat on a horse was appalling. It shocked her, and she had already told him more than once that he should either give up riding completely or learn to ride well. She had grown up among men who spent their lives on horseback and knew what she was talking about. Why, it was incredible, he actually fell off sometimes! Who but children fell off their horses? Rupert had been extremely offended by her bluntness and ignored it.

Desmond was very friendly to Rupert on their long rides together. For the first time in their mutual lives he felt more fortunate than his elder brother, for Rupert was not only saddled with this pregnant foreign wife but was sadly lame. He asked kindly about Rupert's wound.

'Oh, the bullet damaged a muscle. The medico says it will mend in time. I was lame for an age at school after I put out my cartilage, remember? The leg is already better,' said Rupert cheerfully.

Desmond knew otherwise. His father had told him that there was doubt about Rupert returning to the army. Desmond was sorry for his brother, and quite fond of him. They got on excellently, talking of the war and its peace, of Aston and its estates, of cousins and friends. Everything but his wife. In his private conversations with his father, Desmond agreed that the marriage was a disaster. His father said that Millicent was adamant. 'Nothing to be done, my boy, when your mother sets her face against somebody.'

Desmond wore his heavy look. Could not something be made of the girl, since Rupert and she would inherit? His father looked lazily amused.

'Your mother will live to be a hundred.'

Stella was lonely now that Rupert was so much with his brother. She knew it was foolish but she was hurt at how eagerly he escaped. She went out, one blowy autumn day, and sat on the East Terrace. Lady Tyrrell had left in the carriage an hour ago, and Stella felt free to sit and sew without being sent messages telling her it was unsuitable in her condition to be in full view of the gardeners. Dressed in brown velvet, with tartan ribbons, and a small bonnet she sighingly wore, wondering when one could be bareheaded out of doors, Stella sat embroidering a small fragment of white lawn destined to be a handkerchief for herself. Her head was bent, her thoughts on Rupert. After the baby was born, would his feelings alter? Would hers? What happened to our love? she wondered. We were in love, weren't we? I don't seem to be able to feel any more. I drift about getting heavier and behaving like a sheep. Now I come to think of it, they're all like sheep here. They do the same things at the same time. They even talk in the same way: 'Dashed funny', 'Very plucky', 'Blessed if I know', 'For mercy's sake', 'What was the evening like?', 'Oh, the usual crush, don't-you-know...'

'Good morning, your Ladyship,' said a voice suddenly.

She literally jumped. She had heard nobody approaching. Looking down at her with an impudent smile was Harry Flood.

'How I startled you,' he said, sitting beside her. 'Didn't your husband tell you I was arriving? And where is everybody? No sign of the parents, and not a soul about but one little sister-in-law looking at me as if I'm the old duke's ghost.'

'The Marchioness is paying calls, I don't know if your father is in London, the Staffords have left and Rupert and

Desmond are shooting in Shelley Woods. Then they're going to climb Bassett Hill. Desmond said one can see six counties when it's clear like today.'

'Don't six counties appeal, Sister-in-law?'

'Rupert said the climb is too steep for me.'

'And you didn't want to go anyway. Yes, John, tea please. For two. And all the trimmings. Tell Cook I have not eaten for a week.'

The footman went away looking pleased.

Harry turned to Stella, looking her over with more frankness than the usual brief Aston glance. Out of uniform, he was even more handsome, she thought, olive-skinned, round-faced, unlike any of the others. She was not sure he made her feel very comfortable.

'So why is it you don't like the idea of six English counties lying at your feet?'

She shrugged, looking Dutch, and he burst out laughing. It was the first loud laugh at anything to do with *her* that Stella had heard since she came to England. She laughed too.

'I got used to looking at the veldt. Things here seem small.'

'Well,' he said imperturbably, 'they are.'

'But I can't tell nobody that, can I?'

'It is "can't tell *anybody*", Sister-in-law. I heard you make that mistake on your wedding day, hasn't Rupert cured it yet? I don't see why you can't remark that England is small. Who would care? It's our smallness which made us spread the Empire and paint many other countries red on the map. We'll talk of that interesting subject another time. Here is tea.'

An unusually elaborate repast was brought by John and another footman and laid on the terrace table. Stella poured out and Harry told her stories of his life in Aden, where his ship had been based for some months. The place had surprised him, friends in the Navy having described it as arid, unbearably hot, and nothing but a lump of volcanic rock at the end of the Red Sea.

'For me,' he said with zest, 'it was the most romantic

place in the world.' He had liked the dry heat, the spicy, Eastern smell. There was a tower towards which the people turned at dawn and sunset to pray, he had gone to the races on the Salt Flats which looked like stretches of silver sand, and to a concert in a place called Crater 'and that's what it is, the crater of a volcano'. He had swum 'with friends', which Stella knew in the Flood vernacular meant with a pretty woman, in a bay of deep water surrounded by wire netting. 'They kept assuring us it would keep the sharks away.' One day ashore, he had lingered for hours on the hotel terrace, enjoying the scents and sounds and multicoloured crowds. 'But what do you think? That night I came out, not in bites, but great hideous lumps over every inch of the back of my legs. From the bugs in the wicker chair!'

She listened and laughed, thinking him everything his family was not. She had thought that when they met in the Cape Town suburb but then he had not been at all pleasant to her. Now for some reason he had changed and she felt quite easy with him.

'So,' he said, offering her more cake, 'how do you find Aston? Judging by your expression just now, I should imagine you are not enjoying the old place.'

'It isn't bad.'

He raised his eyebrows drolly.

'Could this lack of enthusiasm be something to do with my mother not being the soul of hospitality?'

'Maybe.'

'And does that not upset you?' he enquired. She amused him. She was changed from the housemaid in the unsuitable hat whom his brother had taken for better or for worse on that ill-fated morning. For a start, she was well dressed. Being pregnant had taken away what looks she had, but she was very self-possessed.

'You can't go on being upset by the rainy season,' she said. 'You get used to it.'

'Ah, but the rainy season ends and flowers come out. Besides, you need the rain after the drought. It is not the same, Stella.'

She shrugged, saying indifferently that she still thought that a person disliking you resembled the bad weather. There was nothing to be done about it.

'Rupert is very devoted to my mother,' Harry said, quite kindly. 'I'm sure he is trying to smooth things over.' He himself had thought about the marriage and had arrived home determined to see what might be done for the best.

'Maybe Rupert has made it up with her,' said Stella vaguely.

'What do you mean! That he and my mother are friends again and you remain out of favour?'

'Do you think that impossible?' she asked, still with her odd lack of emphasis.

He finished his cake, flicked the crumbs from his fingers and leaned back. It seemed appalling, supposing it were true, that his mother and brother had healed the breach and left this young creature to shift for herself.

'I don't know what I think, because I've seen nobody in the family yet,' he said. 'What do *you* think has happened?'

'Rupert is friendlier with his mother, I'm not and she isn't and never will be. It don't – doesn't – matter because after the baby is born we leave this place.'

'Leave Aston? Of course you cannot.'

She looked at him blankly.

'Why not, then?'

It was on the tip of his tongue to tell her the truth. Because Rupert hadn't a penny piece, his mother paid the piper, called the tune, held the whip and used it. Because she would never allow Rupert to go out of her power with *her* money, and make a life with this original girl. Harry had not the heart to say any of this. Stella's face was haggard and horribly, undeniably young. He found himself liking that face which looked at times quite boyish, as much as his elder brother looked girlish. He liked her big expressive brown eyes, and the way she lifted her chin. She was a silvery blonde and he was bored with dark-haired women.

'Perhaps you can escape later, which may be a good

72

thing,' he said comfortably. 'Shall we go for a walk? Is there anywhere which you won't compare unfavourably with the veldt?'

'I like the kitchen garden.'

'I asked for that. Let us go and admire the cabbages.'

Harry's arrival after his long absence in the Mediterranean was welcomed in various ways. Catherine hung on his arm. His father declared he must hunt, adding 'but you'll not outshine your brother Des, you should have seen him yesterday'. Desmond and Rupert were affable and Millicent very warm, actually calling him 'Dearest boy'.

'Your mother behaves as if she flirts with admirers instead of talking to her children,' remarked Stella one night when she and Rupert were going to bed. He looked put out.

'I wish you would not say things like that. They're unwomanly. You shock me.'

'No, I don't. Your mother does flirt. With Harry. With you when she's in a good mood. Even with Des.'

'I see it is taking you a long time to understand us.'

She pushed a lace-frilled pillow into the small of her aching back.

'I don't want no arguments with you, Rupert, I don't feel well enough. We won't talk of your mother because we only argue . . . Your father said Des rides so well but I don't agree, he is stiff-backed and straight, he isn't easy, like the commandos. Yes, I know I mustn't talk of Africa but we are alone and we need not tell ourselves lies, so don't let's try, mm?'

She put up her arms and laced them round his neck and kissed him. Drawing back, looking up with her melting eyes, she said, 'You *are* handsome. Much better than the other two. I am the lucky one.'

He kissed her tenderly.

As it happened, Rupert was pleased his unconventional brother was home. Harry was kind to Stella, and more important still, Harry knew his secret. It comforted Rupert that at least one member of the family knew why he had married. Of course Harry would never reveal it to a living soul. But there was a certain extra warmth between them. And yet . . . it dimly occurred to Rupert that had it been Desmond with him in Cape Town, things would have turned out differently. Des would have been firm: even brutal. Des, in plain language, would have got rid of Stella. Harry had left him room to move, but Rupert had not managed to get himself free.

He continued to leave Stella on her own, went shooting or played billiards, drove out to call on friends. Stella stayed in the house a good deal reading or sewing. She went to the schoolroom to have tea with Catherine and they played Brag and Beggar my Neighbour. And there was Harry. He turned up in the library or the drawing-room to amuse both Stella and himself. Rupert noticed and was grateful, but another eye, a narrowed blue eye, also saw Harry's attentions to Stella.

Safe out of earshot of elderly aunts or visiting London grandees, Harry led Stella on, questioning her about the past.

'Tell about your uncle, Stella. I thought the Boers were all surly and uncouth?'

'What horrible words,' she said, unmoved. 'The Boer farmers are not like all of *you* with false manners and no hearts. Uncle Hendrik had great strength of will. Very stern, he was. But, oh dear, when he talked it was a sermon. Slices of the Bible.'

'What did he look like?'

'Big and strong and ugly. And so ragged, poor man, when he came home from commando.'

'You must have missed him very much when he was away fighting all those years,' he said carelessly. For a second he forgot what Rupert had told him, that the uncle had burst in when the couple were naked in bed.

Stella was silent for a while. They were alone in the library and it was getting dark.

'My aunt missed him to her death. And he came home to nothing. No wife. No Meidoorn. No country, for he won't sign your English oath. Cousin Karel wrote that Uncle is gone to America. See how it changed. The great

74

farm and a happy life burned away, and poor uncle with nothing, living with foreigners. And I—'

'And you?'

'I am a foreigner too.'

'Of course you are not. Particularly when you lose that accent and stop thinking nothing here is as good as your beloved Transvaal.'

'Maybe I want to stay a foreigner. Somebody else wants it too.'

'Oh, I can guess who she is!'

'You get it wrong. It is you.'

He laughed and changed the subject. But when he was alone, and remembering the talk, he knew she was right. He made her feel a foreigner by encouraging her to remember the past whereas Rupert wished her to forget it. She must grow into being Viscountess Coryot, into little statelinesses, into blandness, smoothing out (at any rate on the surface) the passionate and courageous girl she must surely be. He wondered if she were happy. His mother treated her badly. What of Rupert? It was impossible to guess.

Millicent sent for Harry one evening to come to her room before dinner. When he entered, she was lying on a *chaise longue*, wearing a good deal of cream-coloured lace. Jasmine scent hung about.

'Sit down, my dear boy.' She looked him up and down. 'I have never liked that shirt.'

He laughed, showing beautiful teeth.

'Change it before you come down, my dear.'

He grinned again and did not reply; it was unlike her not to notice the lack of obedience. She was looking critically down at her ringed hands.

'You know why I wish to see you.'

'I haven't a notion, Mother.'

'Indeed? I have decided you are, how shall I put it? too friendly to Rupert's wife. You mean well but it is unsuitable.'

'Her child is due in three or four months, you can't mean I am flirting with the lady,' he said teasingly.

'I dislike frivolity. You understand quite well what I am saying. I know since the Queen died it has become fashionable for men and women to be free and easy, I do not subscribe to that and never shall. In a word, I don't like your manner with Rupert's wife and nor does he.'

'Has he told you so?'

'Do not argue with me.'

He scratched his nose. The unconscious gesture was one his father used when he and Millicent disagreed. Her hawklike face hardened.

'I will put it plainly. It displeases me to see you with that girl. You positively approve of her. She will end by imagining she is one of us, and her Colonial colours will come out then. You will be responsible, and you will regret it.'

'You mean to keep Stella under hatches?'

'Yes.'

He considered. His mother never shocked him, he had grown up in her shadow and admired her. She was as hard as nails, which was better than being like his father and Rupert. He leaned over to take her small hand, she tried to pull it away but he held it more firmly.

'Mother. I sympathise with your feelings, and don't imagine I do not understand them. I *know* there could not be a worse match. It's a damned bore – sorry to swear, but it is. However, I shan't promise to change with regard to Stella. You must behave as you wish, that is your privilege. Rupert must make up his mind what *he* is going to do—'

'He will do as I tell him.'

'I daresay he will. But, I repeat, I shan't promise. I like her. She is going to be the mother of an heir as like as not, so perhaps it's better if she has one friend among us. Don't glare like that! You're much handsomer when you smile.' He kissed her soundly and left the room before she could recover her breath and her temper.

Chapter Six

A plant uprooted and thrust into a foreign soil often gives up and dies, but some hardy shrubs manage with little nourishment to hang on until their very leaves adapt and change. For the second time in her young life Stella's roots had been dragged out of the ground. She could dimly remember how frightening Meidoorn had seemed after she lost her nearly-forgotten parents and their indulgent love in the land of her birth. But children cry and accept, and soon the huge country and the dour faces were her only reality.

At Aston she had oddly returned to the position of the five-year-old waif in an alien land. But this time her eyes were dry. She could scarcely wail over a destiny she had chosen herself.

It was less than a month to the child's birth and she was tired and subdued. Her parents-in-law were going to London 'to see a play or two'. 'And I need to see my dressmakers, there is a gala on the 15th,' said Millicent. 'What a pity you cannot be with us, Rupert.'

The family were lingering over dinner. It was bitterly cold, the fields white with frost and frost-flowers on the windowpanes. Great logs burned in the downstairs rooms, tended every hour by the servants, but the fires in the bedrooms were minute, the rooms freezing.

'Mama thinks it good for the health,' Rupert said, laughing when Stella grumbled.

The large gatherings at Aston had lessened as winter advanced; tonight there were no visitors at all, except an ailing Great Aunt, a wispy creature who looked alarmed if Stella uttered a word to her.

When the cloth was removed, Millicent glanced at Stella,

77

indicating that the ladies must leave. Rupert and Desmond remained with their father. Harry had returned to Portsmouth some days ago.

It was the first time Stella and her mother-in-law had actually been thrown together by themselves; there were usually at least two, often a dozen, other ladies. Stella wondered if she would address a word to her. When they were in the drawing-room and the silver tray was placed in front of her, Lady Tyrrell said:

'Do you wish coffee?'

'Thank you, no, it makes for me to be sick.'

Stella spoke involuntarily. Day of wrath to come, she thought, why do I blurt out things like that which prove I'm so vulgar?

Lady Tyrrell poured her own coffee in silence. Above her, over the chimney piece, was a full length portrait painted by Sergeant when she was in her mid-twenties. She was fond of saying that it was his first successful portrait at the Royal Academy, he had been only twenty-eight. The girl in the painting wore white satin to which he had given a pearly, greyish sheen, her waist was tiny, a swirl of tulle and satin formed a magnificent late Victorian bustle. Her white neck was set off by a black velvet ribbon. With soft hair and swimming eyes, the young Millicent gazed dreamily into the distance. How could she possibly have looked like that? thought Stella. I don't believe it. She was full of wonder that anyone as old as the woman opposite her had ever been truly young.

'Lady Tyrrell.'

The older woman bridled at being directly addressed.

'You said it was a pity Rupert can't go to London. Why can't he?'

'It is scarcely necessary for you to ask.'

'Because of the baby, you mean? I don't mind being here without him.' A meaningless laugh was the reply, but Stella persevered. She was feeling fond of Rupert. He had been kind when she could not sleep, and had crept down to the kitchens to fetch her some jam sandwiches. They had had a fit of the giggles, sitting in the four-poster in the middle of the night like children having a midnight feast.

'Rupert would like to go to London with you after being stuck with me for so long. In the Transvaal wives didn't keep their husbands by them just because they were pregnant. I don't want to burden him.'

Millicent, ignoring the allusion to the girl's deplorable past, reflected; she was sure that her clever son was responsible for this.

'Certainly he ought to accompany us,' she said. 'The Queen will be at the Gala, and she has been most gracious to Rupert on three occasions. Yes,' continued Millicent to herself, 'the monthly nurse is not due until the end of February, Rupert can come to London to the Gala very easily.'

It was only when Stella heard the ominous word 'February' that a thrill of alarm went through her. She turned dreadfully white. Lady Tyrrell, glancing up, said in exasperation, 'Gentle heaven, are you going to faint?'

Stella did not.

It had been insane of them both, but she and Rupert had avoided the painful subject of when the child was due. During one embarrassed conversation on board ship, he had looked so agonised that she had not the heart to go on. She had said stolidly, 'Then we shall tell them it is a seven-month child.' He had escaped from the state room, 'for a breath of air.'

This evening, when she and Rupert left the drawing-room and walked down the gallery overlooking the Great Hall and its ghostly banners, she wondered whether to speak to him. Glancing up, she saw his profile. Oh Rupert, I wish you didn't look such a boy. I wish you didn't frighten easily, she thought. Other faces which were stubborn and strong haunted her. Feeling her eyes on him, he turned and grinned. The look settled it.

The morning was frosty when the family were due to leave for London. Rupert, looking as fresh as the gleam of winter sunshine, came into the bedroom to say goodbye.

'Are you certain you don't mind my leaving you, Stella?'

He sounded like a schoolboy given an unexpected holiday.

'Oh, I'd much rather be here than at that stuffy old Gala. And what do you think I found in the library? One of the visitors must have left it behind. Your mother would be shocked. I shall go to bed early tonight and *read it right through!*'

Holding up a book, she burst out laughing. It was the scandalous *Three Weeks* by Elinor Glyn.

'I must go, they're waiting,' he said hurriedly, kissed her and went out. Stella was filled with wonder – she had actually embarrassed him.

Forgetting her pregnancy, she jumped too energetically out of bed, her stomach dropped and she grimaced. Then she went to the window to watch as the carriage drove away. She sighed with pleasure as it disappeared. She was free, free from her mother-in-law's enmity which flowed into every room like a poisoned river. And free from suspecting that Rupert was only tied to her by duty. His alacrity at leaving just now had annoyed her.

During the sharp winter days that followed, Stella enjoyed herself more than she had ever done since first arriving at Aston. She did not miss her husband in her bed or during the day either. She liked her own company. She walked through the enormous house, frankly gaping. She examined paintings and vases, clocks and silver, dinner sets on which each plate had a detailed and different view of a castle or a mountain, a manor or a river. There were curious old treasures of every kind and nobody to stop her staring, or to stare at *her*. Aston's vastness still had the power to astonish: she was coming to grips with what she had actually married. Not the nervous young man she had saved from death, and with whom she shared giggles or moments of tenderness, but this huge strange honeycomb, with its chains of rooms and its unexpected staircases, its ante-chambers and galleries and tapestries, its passages lined with glass-fronted cupboards filled with jade and with majolica, its state rooms crammed with every kind of object, precious, odd, unexplained, ugly, over hundreds of years.

One sunny afternoon in the picture gallery she discovered a portrait painted on wood, the head and shoulders of a young man. One pearl drop hung from his ear, his hair was black and thick, his eyes bold. He was uncannily like Harry Flood. Leaning back in her late-pregnant attitude, she stared at the man in the picture, wondering why he had been hidden away in a dark corner.

Walking back to the drawing-room she felt slightly lightheaded. Perhaps I am getting a fever, she thought. In Africa people described most minor complaints as 'fevers' just as in England they called them influenza. She crossed the Great Hall, averting her eyes from the flags. A footman opened the drawing-room door for her.

'Sister-in-law?' Harry was standing by the fire. 'I'm told the family has waltzed off to the Londonderry Gala and nobody's at Aston except my Great Aunt, Des due for the weekend, and your little self. Why did your wretched husband desert you?'

'He wanted to go to the Royal Gala and I don't need a nursemaid.'

He laughed and said he never doubted it. They chatted for a while. He asked if Stella had met Elinor Martindale, the young girl Des apparently wished to marry.

Stella, who had met her and had not liked her, said, 'She's what my cousin would call a typical Brit.'

'Don't let the family hear you say that.'

'I am not a fool, Harry.'

'You certainly aren't.'

She blushed crimson. For a moment she actually looked as if she were going to cry. He was horrorstruck.

'My dear girl!'

'Don't say nothing, I'm all right,' she said crossly, and walked over to the window where the winter day was dying. She turned her back to him. He looked at the ungainly figure and the wisps of hair at the base of her neck.

'Stop being stupid and come and sit down.'

81

He ordered tea with heartless good humour, and she consented to return to the fire but said nothing. He sighed loudly.

'Are you going to punish me by sulking? Why are you offended just because I said you are not a fool?'

'What you meant was that I got Rupert to marry me. That's what you meant.'

Did she expect a gallant apology?

'You didn't want me to be his wife,' added Stella, with a kind of gloomy satisfaction.

'Of course I didn't,' he said annoyingly. 'You were scarcely a catch, were you? If it hadn't been for a certain matter, the wedding wouldn't have come about. That doesn't mean I am not glad you are here. The Floods have been running after money for hundreds of years and you're a nice change. They've run after it, caught it, wasted it, and chased the next big prize. Even Des's Elinor Martindale is padded with the stuff, not that one would guess it from looking at her.'

'I don't agree. It's obvious she's rich.'

He stretched his long legs.

'Rupert told you, I suppose.'

'Nobody did. I saw it by the way she walks.' Harry guffawed loudly. Stella, still annoyed, scowled and that made him laugh the more. He finally persuaded her to tell him what she meant. She said that since she had come to England she had noticed that people with money walked in a certain way. And people without it did not. Enchanted, Harry ran through a list of relations and friends who regularly came to Aston, all of whom she unerringly labelled.

'Stella, you are a comedian and a witch.'

Tea was served, and for once she was hungry, eating hot muffins from under their silver cover. She stopped being annoyed with Harry, since it had no effect.

'I was in the picture gallery this afternoon. I found a picture stuck away in a corner. A man looking just like you. He had a frill round his neck.'

'A *ruff*, Stella. How like you to ferret him out. That's

Gervase Flood. He was a pirate. When they were caught, men were hanged for piracy.'

'Was he caught?'

'What do you think?'

'He looks like you, so I bet he wasn't.'

'Correct. But the family prefers to forget him. He was a friend of Raleigh's, who was beheaded, poor fellow, and as we were busy sucking up to James I, Gervase wasn't exactly the most popular member of the family.'

'All those dead people. You'd think they were still alive.'

'So they are, Stella. In us.'

The evening grew dark, and a footman came in to draw the crimson curtains and make up the fire. Harry looked at the young woman opposite him. It was curious that she should be part of the Aston tapestry now. Of course she was changed from the ugly Cape Town girl. Her clothes were elaborate and graceful and her hands – he remembered those roughened hands – were silky and covered with rings. But her eyes were the same.

'Do you know, Stella, there's something you've never told me. How you saved my brother's life.'

'He said I mustn't say nothing about that.'

'Anything, Stella, anything.'

'I mustn't say *anything* about Meidoorn or finding him in the *drift*.'

'Yet if you'd been a brother officer, they would have given you the Military Cross, like Des.'

'Oh, it wasn't so brave, I wanted to save him so I did.'

'Do you always do what you want?'

'When I was a child, I couldn't,' was the curious reply.

'You dug the bullet out of his leg. Even a man would have jibbed at that.'

'Maybe I did it bad. Badly. He limps so,' she said with terrifying truthfulness. 'To do it wasn't so hard. It only made me sick.'

After dinner they went back to the drawing-room to talk, but as the evening passed he thought she looked very white.

'Are you all right, Stella? You aren't going to faint or anything ladylike of the kind, are you?'

'I never fainted in my life.'

'You never expected a child in your life either. Are you quite sure you are well?'

'Don't fuss, Harry. And stop looking at me like a sick cow.'

But when they said goodnight and Stella was alone in her room, she could no longer pretend she did not feel strange. Her back had ached all the evening but the pain was worse now. There it came again, so sharply that she gasped. Then as she clutched at the bedpost, it was gone. Suddenly Stella saw a vivid image of Meidoorn. Aunt Maria and she were by the servants' quarters in the moonlight and she heard her aunt say to a young girl, 'How many minutes between the pains, Hannah? Ten? Good, there's a while to go, then. Stella, run to the house and fetch Ruth and my medicine box.'

Oh God, thought Stella, the baby is coming. She went over to pull the bell, she had begun to sweat. She thought passionately – *why isn't Aunt Maria here!*

Stella's labour pains were the start of the most dramatic birth at Aston since a daughter had been born to the then Countess Flood during a Royal visit of King George II. After that historic night, nothing of the kind had been done without careful preparation. The event now shook Aston from attic to cellar. A terrified Wilkins fetched the housekeeper, who summoned the butler, who went in search of Harry. He found him with Desmond newly arrived from the last London train. The doctor was sent for, and the housekeeper despatched to cope in the meantime with Stella who was groaning so loudly that she turned the elderly woman's blood to ice.

Aston, quietly settling down to sleep through the winter night, suddenly shone with lights and echoed to the sound of maids hurrying to and fro. The doctor and his sister arrived, there were whispered orders and running foot-steps, and every now and then through the shut doors of the Lauderdale room came the dreadful sound which resembled an animal in pain.

Harry and Desmond returned to the study and a brandy apiece.

Desmond's heavy face was frowning, he was more offended than alarmed by what was happening. He had his father's attitude to women, and particularly to women in childbirth. The further he could keep away at such times the better.

'No monthly nurse. Mother and Rupert in London,' he said, underlining the fact that this drama was nothing to do with him or Harry either. 'The child is not due for weeks. It will probably die.'

Harry could not bring himself to reply. He finished off his brandy and poured himself another. The groans had upset him deeply. A few hours ago he and that young girl upstairs had laughed together – that noise made him afraid. How long did the agony continue? He faintly remembered his mother once saying that her first-born, Rupert, had taken two days of labour. Great God, if that happened! thought Harry, savagely blaming himself for the situation. He and Rupert had known the child was due far sooner than the official story. He should have thought about it and – God's teeth! – why hadn't that dolt Rupert done so? They could have prepared against tonight's panic.

Desmond yawned, drank too much brandy and fell asleep in his chair. He began to snore. He had successfully removed himself from trouble. Ignoring him, Harry rang for tea. He looked at the clock. It was nearly dawn, but pale servants were still up and dressed. Suddenly he noticed that the dreadful sound which had caught him in the guts had ceased. What had happened? Was Stella dead? He rushed from the room and up the stair, brushing past a footman dozing at the corner of the corridor. Hurrying down the passage towards the bedroom, Harry arrived just as the doctor came out of the room. An extraordinary silence reigned.

Doctor Croft, grey in the face, managed a smile.

'All's well that ends well,' he said, with an attempt at his

85

usual manner. 'A boy. Healthy, fat and no trouble at all. My sister is tidying up Lady Coryot, then you can see her and your nephew.'

'She's all right – she really is—'

'Right as a trivet. A strong young lady. Courage of a lion.'

'How may we thank you—'

'All in a day's, I mean a night's, work,' said the doctor, swallowing a yawn. 'Congratulations, my lord, and I'll be off to my bed.'

The doctor's sister, a virginal spinster who looked nunlike despite a midwifery training, beckoned Harry into the room. Stella lay on a heap of pillows, her hair damp with sweat now smoothed away from her face. He was awed at how beautiful she looked. All the haggard lines were gone. She was languorous, swimming, like a woman who has been making love. She gave him a dreamy smile and stretched out her hand weakly.

'Dreadful of me, taking you by surprise.'

He kissed the hand.

'A son,' she said, blurring her words. 'Rupert will be pleased. Want to look at him?'

'I'd rather look at you.'

'See him tomorrow, then,' she said, smiling this time as if she had made a wonderful joke. She fell asleep.

Millicent could not believe her ears when Desmond telephoned the news. The arrival of the child without a female member of the family in the house or the monthly nurse either was indecent. A seven-month child, too, it was a miracle he had survived. Doubtless Rupert's wife had run up a staircase or done something equally dangerous which had brought on the early and perilous birth.

'We must return at once,' pronounced Millicent.

'I think I will stay on in town for a day or two,' said William, looking at her through the eye-glass he wore sometimes.

She turned over in her mind whether to insist but decided

it did not matter. She agreed. As for Rupert, he irritated her by smiling all the time.

Waited upon by Miss Croft who suited her, Stella was not particularly pleased to know the family had arrived back from London. She heard the carriage draw up, the sound of voices, and felt guilty that she was not more excited at seeing her husband. She had enjoyed today. Harry had called now and then and Desmond had signalled approvingly from the doorway, giving her the kindliest look he ever had since they had met. Stella had slept. The baby interested her up to a point, a little fat thing with a bald head and when he opened myopic eyes, a winking dark gaze like her own. Rupert's nose? Who could say? Stella most enjoyed the flatness of her own stomach. She turned on her face, she stretched, her body was her own again. She had a feeling of seeing everything for the first time. The winter light. The distant top of a tree. The fire brightening Miss Croft's greyish-red hair. Even Harry's face, when he called to talk to her. Had she noticed before the deep dimple in the centre of his chin? She vaguely remembered the pirate with the pearl earring.

The bedroom door burst open, and Rupert, blushing with emotion, hurried into the room.

'Stella!'

He embraced her closely, then said at once, 'Where is he?'

'Miss Croft has taken him to the nursery. I have to rest just now.'

'May I see him?'

Without waiting for a reply, he darted out. Stella drifted into sleep thinking – Harry was more pleased to see *me*.

It was clear from the first that Rupert was a doting father. He spent far more time in the nursery than Millicent thought necessary or even natural. She found him most tiresome, with his fond smiles and tedious talk. She had never seen him so taken up with anybody as he now was with the child. Stella listened to his praise of the baby, and gave lazy smiles. Rupert had become rather boring, but he was touching too.

The monthly nurse arrived, and proved to be a fat competent woman who creaked with starch and had a loud voice. Stella disliked her and was pleased to notice that Nurse Digby, destined to be in charge of the new baby as she had been in charge of Rupert, Desmond, Harry and Catherine, also disliked her. There was a mute alliance between Nurse Digby and Stella, both waiting for the monthly nurse to leave.

Stella had first been introduced to Nurse Digby on the day she had arrived at Aston. Rupert took her up to Nurse Digby's kingdom, in the oldest part of the house, a little Tudor wing which still survived. Stella already knew about the nurse from her husband, just as she knew about the Aston tower, the ghosts, the visit of George II and his hardfaced Queen. Nurse Digby belonged. She was a heavy woman of formidable aspect, with an impassive large face and small observant eyes. She had the quiet strength of a sea captain who knows how to resist storms and hidden rocks and mermaids. Stella was given a keen look when they were introduced.

Nurse Digby welcomed the arrival of young Lord Thomas Christopher Lauderdale de Tournai Flood – whom Stella nicknamed Kit – without emotion. The nursery suite was the only part of Aston which had not been taken by surprise at the birth: it had been ready for weeks. Nurse Digby had not joined in the drama of the arrival but had been, so to speak, hovering in the wings. In creaseless white apron and high starched collar, attended by two nursery maids, she removed the leading actor and took him to his own quarters.

The christening was set for the end of February. Aston was festively busy with guests, and Stella was strong enough to dance at a celebration ball. Rupert, flushed with all the congratulations at the birth of an heir, was very affectionate to her, danced with her much of the evening, and encouraged her to sing.

Stella had not sung once since the day she came to England. At Meidoorn she had sung the day through in a sweet, oddly thrilling voice and a repertoire entirely

88

consisting of hymns. During the evening, Stella's first official appearance after her lying-in, Rupert noticed that his friends looked at her with slightly altered interest, even with smiles. Certainly she was looking very pretty. After a waltz he suddenly said, 'Can you read music, sweetheart?'

'Yes, why?'

'I think you should sing for us. Elinor can accompany you.'

Elinor, whose engagement to Desmond was soon to be announced, was small and thin and dark and cool. And rich, as Stella had rightly perceived when they were first introduced. A poised little heiress in virgin white who looked as if nothing in the world could ruffle one strand of her high-coiled hair. Desmond's manner seemed to have been caught by Elinor, like a cold.

'Shall we try this?' said Elinor, passing her some music.

It was a new setting of Leigh Hunt's poem 'Jenny kiss'd me'. She played a little run of chords, saying, 'Is the key right?'

'It's a little low,' said Stella, looking at the music, and Elinor transposed it.

There was a quietening of conversation. The walls of the ballroom, in smaller imitation of Versailles, were lined with mirrors joined by branched golden joints like elaborate, thin stems of trees; the effect was to show an endless succession of ladies in pale gowns, their heads nodding with plumes or crowned with flowers and diamonds. The gentlemen in black and white set off the female display. Fans furled. The eyes of every person standing in the ballroom were not on Elinor but on Rupert's wife. Stella was nervous, but found that she intensely wanted to sing. She lifted her head.

> Jenny kiss'd me when we met,
> Jumping from the chair she sat in;
> Time, you thief, who love to get
> Sweets into your list, put that in!

The voice rang out. It had such grace that the audience was still. She tightened her grip on them.

> Say I'm weary, say I'm sad,
> Say that health and wealth have miss'd me,

A long pause, she held them close, then with the last lines, she pushed them away.

> Say I'm growing old, but add,
> Jenny kiss'd me.

There was a burst of applause.

'What a success you were tonight, sweetheart,' said Rupert. They were lying in bed. The fire had burned down to a glow, the room was all shadows. He leaned on his elbow, looking down at his wife. She seemed a seductive stranger. He had not made love to her since Kit was born and before that for months he had not been attracted to the stout companion she had become. Now she stirred him. Stella knew it, and remembered from the past how she had responded and what bliss she had enjoyed. She had believed that desire, the tiger which had clawed at her until she gasped, would come back. It eluded her still.

'You're so beautiful,' he said, burying his face in her long silvery fair hair. He pulled up her nightdress, rolled on top of her and began to make love strongly and hurriedly. It was over very soon and he lay back, saying 'Was that good, sweetheart?' and fell asleep.

She put her arms behind her head and lay for a long time with open eyes, thinking about the future. She saw that this man breathing deeply beside her, this brief lover, was to be her particular helping of life. She had lifted an empty plate to destiny and had been given Rupert. Certainly the plate was gilded. But – but she remembered with a stab of the heart how passionately she had loved him at Meidoorn. Where had it gone, the trembling excitement, the rush of desire, the tenderness? She simply did not know. Nobody had talked of love at Meidoorn except the love of God which had sounded, when Uncle Hendrik spoke of it, more like fear and self-abasement. She had never imagined she could fall out of love with Rupert. Perhaps too much had happened to her too soon. Was that why she no longer wanted the man asleep at her side? Lying quietly, she put his lovemaking out of her mind and began to think instead of another blissful embrace tonight, given her by her audience.

As the slow spring began, Stella was reasonably content. Lady Tyrrell managed an imitation politeness to her in company, and Nurse Digby and Catherine were positively friendly. Catherine persuaded her to come riding. As with singing, pregnancy had robbed Stella of the pleasure of riding and she now found just how magnificent the Aston horses were. Riding out in the leafless woods, she forgot to criticise England for its smallness.

An unexpected piece of bad news shattered the pleasant days. The Army authorities wrote to Rupert after he had visited them in London, to say his leg injury prevented him from continuing his career. He was shocked. He had taken it for granted that he would stay in the regiment his family had served for generations. Millicent was as upset as he was. She had bred three large handsome men, and she hated to accept that her first-born was no longer physically perfect.

Stella was very sorry for her husband but his gloom over the news was something she thoroughly disapproved of; she had grown up with men who accepted such things as the will of God. Rupert did nothing but complain. She tried to raise his spirits by pointing out that since he was going to be out of the Army, he would see his son every day.

She saw, in her matter of fact way, that she had little influence over her husband nowadays. When they had fallen in love at Meidoorn her sway over him had been complete. If she coaxed, he submitted. He loved her, desired her, indulged her and she was queen of their burned-out sun-baked kingdom, and of him. It was not like that any more. Her sway over him only returned when he wanted to make love to her: a short reign indeed. She had recently come to an important decision about their future and knew it was going to be difficult to get her own way. She must choose the moment carefully.

There was an evening of music, she sang three times to much applause, and Rupert was pleased and flattered. Earlier that day when he had visited the nursery, the baby had looked at him short-sightedly and made a noise like the coo of a pigeon. His father had been overwhelmed. Now, as Stella brushed her hair, Rupert kissed her bare shoulder. She smiled at his reflection in the glass.

'Rupert. I want to say something to you.'

'Mm? You smell delicious . . .' He nibbled the lobe of her ear. Stella waited until he had taken his face away and was again looking at her own mirrored reflection. She said lightly:

'We must make up our minds, you know. About when and where we go.'

'Go? For a visit somewhere? It's too cold for Kit, sweetheart, and the Season begins in a few weeks.'

'Rupert, I'm not talking about a visit. I mean leaving Aston. We don't need to stay now Kit is born. We can't do nothing – anything – we want in your mother's house. So we go.'

He was thunderstruck. They had been at Aston all these months and he had seen with growing relief how his wife had settled down and even, to a degree, that his family had become accustomed to her. They were really quite kind, especially when one remembered exactly who Stella was. Of course his mother had not altered towards Stella, but he felt that she had taken *him* back. Staring at his wife, whose odd pale face and great brown eyes looked back at him from the depth of the glass, he saw that he had forgotten the real Stella Vredenberg. When they married she had been merely the homeless victim of his seduction; and at Aston the pregnant wife had behaved differently from the girl on the veldt. She had been meek. He had not realised that the alteration had been physical and that she had now returned to herself. He walked irritably away from her.

'You don't seem to have learned much since you came here.'

'I've learned two women like your mother and me can't live under one roof, even if it's built over a hundred bedrooms. It isn't large enough. Not nearly large enough.'

'Don't use that tone of voice!' he exclaimed.

She said nothing, biting her lip.

He stood hesitating, and then came back and put his hands on her shoulders.

'Listen to me quietly, Stella. You will have to put these mad ideas out of your head. It is quite, quite out of the question for us to leave Aston and have a separate establishment. We must live here.'

She made her eyes enormous.

'You can't mean that.'

He was beginning to be angry. 'You know very well how things are. You know that there is nowhere we can go.'

'Don't be so *stupid*! How many houses have the Floods got? Your father told me seven! Great big places empty all the year and if they're too big, and they sound horrible, we'd best have a smaller one. A little house quite nice and gentlemanlike to suit, where you and I and Kit—'

'Stop!' Not daring to raise his voice, he hissed, and actually put his hand across her mouth. Above his hand her eyes glared. When he saw she meant to be silent, he took his hand away, exclaiming.

'Don't you understand *anything*? Don't you realise we have no money?'

'Oh, for God's sake!'

'*Will you listen*? We haven't a penny. All the money in this family belongs to my mother. My father's fortune was practically lost. I told you, he gambled it away. Yes, my mother is exceedingly rich. She gives us all allowances and mine is generous. Even when we first married and she was so angry, she never cut my allowance by a farthing. She won't allow her son and his wife to lack anything. Aston is my father's and will be mine when he dies, but the money is Mother's and that's that. Do you think she'd let us go? Take away her grandson and go off to live somewhere on her money? Aston is what she cares about. It matters more than my father, her children, anything. I told you to get on the right side of her. You're so pigheaded. I realise she has not been particularly pleasant to you—'

Stella gave a violent laugh.

'You must accept it. We can't leave and that's that.'

'You don't want to go!'

'Perhaps I don't. Why should I?'

With an effort of will that cost her a good deal, Stella did not continue. In any case she knew she had lost. They went to bed.

But both of them lay awake in the dark: silent, separated, in the huge old curtained bed.

To Rupert's surprised relief, accustomed to the long campaign waged by his mother, Stella was quite pleasant the following morning. When he left her after breakfast, she turned her cheek to be kissed. He left the room cheerfully. His mother's anger had been bad enough, thank heavens it was almost gone, but to quarrel with his wife as well was more than flesh could bear. He began to understand why his father took that ridiculous poodle to Paris so frequently.

When she was alone, Stella thought over what had happened and knew she had been naive. During the months of pregnancy she had accepted this life of rules and riches as a sort of Pilgrim's Progress. Doubting Castle, Mount Error, the Slough of Despond, a series of trials and punishments for sinfully giving up her virginity. But although she was now lawfully married and the mother of a son, it seemed there was to be no end to the punishment. Did Rupert truly mean he had no fortune at all? Money had never come into Stella's life until the night of her aunt's death when, obeying instructions, she had taken the sack of sovereigns. Later, she had poured them carelessly back into her uncle's strong box. Never having had money, she was ignorant of its power. Were all young men in Society chained to their parents? She wondered to whom she could talk now that her one friend, Harry Flood, was away in

Malta. I must be patient, she thought uncharacteristically. Rupert will want to leave Aston in the end. She almost believed that . . .

It did not suit Millicent to be at odds with her favourite son, and they had made it up in a way, but she still felt that the bruise was never going to heal. Nobody in the Flood family behaved as she did; she knew her husband was pleasant to the Colonial girl behind her back. Even Desmond and Elinor were polite, and as for Harry, when he had been at Aston he had behaved disgracefully and made a positive friend of the girl. Millicent could not help being interested in the child who one day would be the heir, but she would not accept the mother. While appearing to ignore her, Millicent had observed her closely and saw that her daughter-in-law cared nothing for Aston and was too low-born and ignorant to understand what it represented. Millicent disliked everything about the girl, the pale blonde hair, the tones of her voice, her singing – heaven knew why people praised it – her figure. Worst of all, she could not abide the emerging signs of confidence in such a nobody. They boded ill for Rupert. If I am cruel to her, thought Millicent, *she* was cruel to us. She had no right to accept my son's insane offer of marriage. Millicent never thought of Stella as a very young girl but as a hardy adversary, self-centred and an alien.

One morning towards the end of March, Millicent alighted from the dog-cart at the doctor's house near the church. When she rang the bell, the housemaid who opened the door blushed and bobbed a curtsey.

'Good morning, Rogers. Tell your Master I am here.'

'Doctor's out, your Ladyship.'

'Who is that, Rogers?' said a voice, and Miss Croft stepped into the hall. Seeing her visitor she smiled effusively.

'Lady Tyrrell, how very delightful. What may we do for you? Please do come in, the wind is so cold. Come to the fire.'

Millicent was respectfully ushered into the drawing-room. She was gracious as she accepted the best chair and

95

a string of commonplaces. She had called, she informed Miss Croft, to enquire about the croup in the village. Had there been any new cases? Hearing that the epidemic was now on the wane, Millicent picked up her gloves. Miss Croft's girlishly freckled face had become rather pink. She said eagerly:

'May one enquire how the young heir is progressing? It was such a pride and pleasure to me, Lady Tyrrell, to be allowed to help him into the world. I know he arrived unexpectedly and our stalwart Miss Bouverie missed the delivery. But her loss was my gain, as I've said to my brother. What a magnificent child! I remember as he came into the world I said to Lady Coryot, "A lovely boy, and just like his father".'

Millicent smiled condescendingly, agreeing that the child was handsome. Miss Croft dreamily returned to her moment of triumph.

'It's odd what mistakes young ladies can make about the most important day of their baby's life, is it not, Lady Tyrrell? It was a great surprise to me that Miss Bouverie was ordered to arrive so late. She called to see us and told me she had not been required at Aston for weeks.'

Millicent bridled at what sounded like impertinence.

'When a child is premature,' she began coldly, but Miss Croft gave a merry little laugh.

'Goodness gracious, one cannot truly call a baby premature when he is a day or two early, can one? That beautiful boy arrived on cue, as my brother amusingly said. A full-term child and weighing eight and a half pounds. Lady Coryot must be one of those many young ladies who miscalculate. My brother often chuckles over them. Imagine, the Viscountess was quite two months wrong!' And Miss Croft gave another, perfectly innocent laugh.

Rupert was in the nursery when a message came that his mother wished to see him. It was before luncheon, a time when she was busy with her secretary, and he supposed she wanted to discuss the guests expected on Friday. She was in her study, a small panelled room which had once been a private chapel. She was alone at her desk, hands folded.

'Close the door, if you please.'

There was no mistaking the tone of voice. Elegant and tall, exquisitely dressed in grey with a camellia in his buttonhole, he began to look as nervous as a girl.

'I wish to talk to you. About your wife.'

His heart thudded.

'Please, Mama!'

'Don't wail in that ridiculous manner. I have just had a great shock. I had always imagined that you and I were close.' She stated it without affection. 'I had certainly imagined that you would not lie.'

'I don't understand.'

'Indeed? I called on Doctor Croft this morning, he was out but his sister received me. In all ignorance she told me an interesting fact. That your son was not premature but full-term. Croft, it seems, confirms that.'

There was disgust on her face as she added, 'So that was why you married her.'

He was silent. His mother wanted confession, subjection, entreaty – he felt her desire for them like an outstretched claw.

When he spoke, his voice shook.

'I kept it from you because I knew it would set you more against her. She saved my life and *I* seduced her. I can't talk to you about this – I refuse!'

For the first time in his life he walked out of her room and slammed the door.

She stared after him, her mouth so thin that no coral of the lips showed. She had willed him to break down. He owed that to her. Did he imagine rushing away like a hysterical girl would make things any different? They were as bad as they could be. The momentary triumph she had felt knowing herself proved monstrously right was gone and she felt icy cold. That foreigner who had trapped him into marriage was an immoral woman, an object of repugnance in society. How to defend Aston against such an enemy? There must be a way and I shall find it, she thought. I need time.

Chapter Seven

On a clouded March day in 1907, Stella watched her son
trotting ahead, wearing a little cap with ribbons. He was
making for a spot near the lake where there was usually a
string of muddy pools. After heavy rain, the pools were
larger than usual and the child turned to give her a
triumphant grin. Then he bent double and began to play.
Nurse Digby never allowed water games, which made them
all the more fascinating.

The wind from the east had a bite in it, and Stella
wrapped her furs closely round her and sat down on a seat
to watch him, her hands in her fur muff. Her face was
slightly flushed by the chill, the hood of her long dark coat
framed it, pulling her hair slightly out of its golden coils.
She was changed from the raw girl who had come to Aston,
she was less of a fledgeling although still only twenty-one
years old. She had learned to wear clothes with grace and
had utterly lost her Dutch accent.

But Rupert was not satisfied with his wife's progress, and
at times irritably accused her of not 'joining in'. Stella did
not bother to answer that you can join nothing if the people
making up the circle, game or dance do not invite you.
Society resembled those noisy gallops popular at the end of
a ball, when the dancers, redfaced and laughing, race and
slither round the floor to the rising music. If Stella put out
a hand as the dancers skimmed by, they dodged. For
whatever reason, Society did not exactly accept her,
perhaps because *she* did not accept them. Rupert's accusa-
tion was true, she had not joined in. There were times when
she was happy, she could scarcely escape from being so as
a young, pretty woman. Young men admired her, particularly when she sang, and she knew she could make them

laugh. For the most part, the life chafed her. Every spring the Floods, with the rest of Society, moved to London, opened up their great houses and began the glittering season. There were balls and levées, receptions and every kind of stately entertainment. Money showered down in a rain of gold. In the summer 'everybody' went to Cowes, where the sea was covered with beautiful yachts, and to Scotland afterwards, arriving as the heather began to bloom, to kill birds and wear tweeds. Then back to Aston for the long months of winter. A year-in year-out parade of pleasure. Stella wondered sometimes if those sermons she had yawned through as a child had taken root in her after all. Where was this sense of duty and responsibility about which Rupert bragged? She saw none. Everything to do with work was left to people who served them, to tough-minded bailiffs and stewards, to experienced upper servants, to strong women like Nurse Digby. Stella watched the Floods waited upon with reverence. Their own preoccupation was to entertain themselves and their friends, to dress in elaborate style, spend money like Indian rajahs, and eat those endless, endless meals . . .

She still longed for a home of her own and envied other young women in the Flood circles who married and stepped into their carriages, moving through the open gates of their parents' houses to freedom. Desmond and Elinor lived in this happy state. But whenever she had spoken of leaving Aston, Rupert became so angry and reproachful that she had not the heart to upset him. He would not leave Aston. She must settle to that.

Sitting in the cold wind idly watching the little boy, Stella looked up to see a girl coming through the trees, carrying a bunch of wild daffodils. She walked with a light, bouncing step.

'Alone and palely loitering?' said Catherine, smiling. 'What do you think I just saw? A tawny owl.' She sat down beside Stella and examined a splash of mud on the hem of her furred coat.

Catherine Flood had changed as much as Stella in the last four years and would soon be an attractive young woman.

She was rounded, slightly taller than Stella, her face heart-shaped with a chin like a kitten's, her hair dark and curly. However carefully it was dressed, stray locks escaped as springily as the tendrils of a vine. She was the only female companion apart from Nurse Digby with whom Stella had any rapport in a world filled with women. Women as a whole did not like Stella. Was it the singing voice, rather too good for her position in society? Or that her mother-in-law, symbol of high morality, mutely ignored her? Catherine herself never took sides but looked blank and relied upon jokes.

She glanced at her nephew.

'Have you seen your son's gloves? Caked with mud.'

'I don't see why he shouldn't have some fun.'

'Nursie can't see that mud is ever fun,' said Catherine vaguely. She put her nose to the flowers. 'I picked these in the Dower House gardens. I popped in to see Great Aunt and she was all of a doo-dah. You will never guess. She is leaving us!'

She did not see the effect of her words which for an instant made Stella's whole face change. But Stella said casually enough, 'I thought your Great Aunt was settled there forever.'

Catherine laughed and agreed. It seemed that the aunt's old friend Lady Drake ('you know how devoted they are to each other!') had begged her to come and live in Cornwall. Lady Drake's husband had died some months ago and she longed for her friend's company. After many heart-searchings, very flustered and nervous and driving the servants out of their wits by her indecision, Great-Aunt Margaret had agreed.

'Mama is rather amused, I hear, at getting the Dower House back. She had quite given it up, except to take tea there every Thursday.'

The girls walked back to the house followed by a small and muddy boy.

Aston was over-full at present. Guests arrived in droves, bringing their own servants to swell the forty-five who lived and worked for the Floods. There were visitors invited because Millicent enjoyed their company – most of the young men being in that category – or because they amused William, or because as cousins, uncles, all kinds of relations, they always came to Aston in March. There were friends of Rupert's and of Catherine's. Millicent spent a good deal of time on her list, and the mixture was successful.

Rupert had been hunting that morning, which Stella disliked; his seat upon a horse was still appalling and he had had one or two bad falls. One had been the occasion of a quarrel between them. Why must he ride like a sack of potatoes, Stella demanded. 'If you can't learn to do it well, give it up.'

'I ride perfectly well. The damned mare slipped.'

'Every horse you ride can't be at fault.'

He was offended and sulked for so long that Stella finally apologised simply to keep the peace.

She found him this evening in his dressing-room, changing for dinner. The hunt had been long and he looked strained. Standing like a doll while his valet brushed his shoulders, he glanced at Stella with an expression which silently said, 'And what do you want, pray?'

The valet gave a final flick to the impeccable shoulders and left the room. Stella, wearing turquoise and white silk and a good many jewels, looked beautiful and vivacious.

'I've come with some very interesting news!'

'Well?' He scarcely bothered to reply; he had not enjoyed the day.

'You are not very nice sometimes. You might try to look pleased when I tell you something which could make us both happy. What do you think? Your Great Aunt is leaving the Dower House. She's off to Cornwall to live with Lady Drake.'

'I know. Why should that please me? She's devoted to Kit.'

'Oh Rupert, how slow you are! Why, there's going to be a pretty house standing empty at the other end of the park and we could move in there in a month! In less! We can have our own home at last.' She clasped her hands and added merrily, 'When will you speak to your parents? I know you'll want to arrange everything without me seeming to interfere.'

She smiled radiantly.

'What nonsense you talk. Such a move is out of the question.'

She gaped at him.

'*Why* can't we live at the Dower House? It's a lovely place and it's going to be ours. Our first home after five years of marriage, just imagine that!'

Sighing, he said in a tone of exaggerated patience, 'We cannot live there because it is too small. And one does not live in a Dower House unless one is a pensioned-off relative. I've told you time and again, and I wish you would have the good taste to remember, that our home is here. At Aston. And this is where we are going to stay.'

There was a profound silence. Then she walked out.

That night when her maid had left her, she sat brushing her hair and thinking of the little Jacobean house at the other end of the park. Soon it would be deserted, empty and dead. She could have made it live again. It would have been full of music and songs and Kit's little marching step . . .

There was a tap at the door and Rupert came into the room. He wore a dark red brocaded robe and that Rupertish look of being freshly washed and smelling of cologne. He took off the robe and climbed into the curtained bed. She knew by his expression what was supposed to happen next. She plaited her hair and walked across the room, her long lace-edged nightgown trailing. She lay down beside him. He made the familiar movement towards her, putting his hand between her thighs. She pulled down her nightgown and moved away.

'Stella.'

'What?'

'You're not going to be childish, are you? Taking your revenge because you can't have what you want.'

'If I can't, nor can you.'

★   ★   ★

On the following morning his manner was as cold as hers, and although Stella felt no compunction at what she had done, she was thoughtful. She felt the need to talk to somebody in this world of no friends – the only possible person was Catherine. Of course Catherine never took sides, but she was more aware than most girls of sixteen. At least she showed through her reserve that she liked Stella. She tried to be friendly despite loyalty to her mother being absolute.

When Stella asked her to go for a walk, Catherine looked pleased. The morning was chilly and both the girls wore furs as they walked at a brisk pace towards the lake, enjoying the challenge of the biting wind. Catherine talked for a while about the latest visitors, making pointed little jokes. Finally, after a pause, Stella suddenly said, 'I need your advice, Cathy.'

The request was flattering and Catherine's expression was interested.

'You said yesterday that your Great Aunt is leaving the Dower House.'

'We shall all miss her,' said Catherine inevitably.

Stella was not listening. 'I told Rupert that he should ask if we can make our home there.'

Catherine looked extremely surprised. She raised her delicate eyebrows.

'You don't mean that. You can't.'

'But I do!' exclaimed Stella, 'I mean it with all my heart. The house is large enough, isn't it? It seems large to me. Cathy, you're sensible and clever, although you're only sixteen; surely you can *see* that I want my own home! Desmond and Elinor have Fallowfield. You'll have a home when you marry. Everybody does.'

'But you're at Aston,' said Catherine as if this answered any argument.

'Aston belongs to your parents.'

There was a pause.

'You and Rupert are in the South wing, miles from everybody.'

'Oh Cathy!'

The girl looked flummoxed. She nervously pulled her high fur collar closer. Stella continued.

'I can't even get Rupert to ask for the Dower House.'

'Of course you can't. How could *Rupert* of all people live there, or Kit either? You have to remember who they are, Stella. It simply wouldn't be suitable.'

The girl's tone was flat and unemphatic, but it was like listening to Rupert all over again. Stella had never felt so complete a stranger. She said without bothering to hide her resentment, 'You can't deny we need our own home.'

'It's a pity you feel like that. You've been at Aston so long that I thought you were quite settled,' said Catherine kindly. 'But since it is *you* who want to go, Stella, what happens depends entirely on your fortune.'

Stella burst into a laugh of exasperation.

'Didn't you know I came to England without a *randt*?'

'Your uncle was a person of property, was he not?' Catherine sounded very English and elderly.

'Certainly. Meidoorn had thousands of acres.'

'And land is money, Stella,' quoted the girl.

'The farm was burned down.'

'But the Government gave compensation. Des told me that when he was talking about the war.'

Stella sighed. 'Catherine, my uncle refused to sign the oath of allegiance to the English. He had to leave his country. He is in America now and quite poor.'

'Oh.' Catherine looked straight at her. 'Well, I'm sure you know Rupert has only what dear Mama gives him, as we all do. I'm afraid you'll have to give up your idea of leaving Aston after all.'

Stella might have made it up with her husband and buried the whole miserable subject, but that afternoon she went to look at the Dower House, taking the Marquess's retriever for company. The housekeeper told her that her mistress was out, and Stella said she would leave a note. Alone, she stared round. How *could* Rupert refuse this house? It seemed to her the very size of happiness. It was friendly and comfortable and well proportioned. No huge

104

portraits glared down from the walls. No flags hung rotting in stone-floored halls. Even the fire was small.

She wrote her note and left the house. As she and the big dog came through the gate there was a sound of horses and two riders approached, reining in their mounts when they saw her. One was Rupert, seated in his usual awkward manner, the other was Mary Flood French, a statuesque young cousin who wrote poetry.

'Stella has been lookin' over the Dower House after all, Rupert,' said Mary with a mischievous smile. It said clearly that she knew what had been going on.

Rupert looked vexed.

'I hope you have not spoken to my Great Aunt,' he said to Stella in a hectoring voice which told on her nerves.

'She was out or I would have done,' Stella said rudely, called the dog and walked off into the park.

Her feeling against Rupert hardened as she returned to the house. She went to her room, telling Wilkins that she had a headache. But it was her thoughts which were aching. Rupert had told that girl about her wanting the Dower House as a home; she had seen the condescending look on the girl's stupid face. She hated him for discussing her with his stuck-up cousin, for sneering at her simple longing to have a home. Stella had an idea that Mary Flood French was slightly in love with Rupert. They are the same kind, she thought, closer than he and I could ever be. I don't blame him for that. But he treats me badly. He bows and scrapes to his mother who hates me, and he makes up to that girl who looked at me as if I were a servant. Why should I let him into my bed?

Rupert was too occupied to be upset by Stella's coldness. He was with Mary Flood French. She was nineteen, only three years younger than his wife, but she seemed as fresh as the dawn. She was that magical being, an innocent and high-bred girl with whom, had things been different, he would have fallen in love. Millicent took care that the two young people were never actually alone. Young girls in society must be looked after with tender care, not the slightest whisper must be made against anyone young, pure

105

and unmarried. Yet Millicent felt a pang of regret. Everything about Mary was right: pedigree, fortune, even the way she walked and smiled. If only . . .

The two words also rang in Rupert's head while Mary remained at Aston. Stella was confined to her room with a feverish cold and apart from calling every morning to ask how she was, and receiving a reply as brief as his question, he was with Mary. They rode together – with a groom. Played billiards – with Mary's brother. They sang duets – in a roomful of people. Yet they still flirted. It was only when she had said a lingering goodbye and the motor taking her and her family away had set off up the drive that Rupert gloomily decided he must make it up with his wife.

Between Stella and himself now stood the ridiculous matter of the Dower House. How could she have imagined he would consent to live in that poky place? She still shows her breeding, he thought. Perhaps she always will. He was in the library, postponing the moment when he must see her, when a message came saying that his mother wanted him.

Rupert was relieved at not having to face Stella's hard resentment yet awhile. He would talk to his mother about Mary, he would enjoy that. He was smiling as he entered her study. She did not return the smile but gestured for him to sit down.

'Catherine has told me,' she said, 'of your wife's unbelievable suggestion.'

Oh God, he thought, there's no escaping it.

'You mean about the Dower House? Yes, it was foolish of Stella and of course it is out of the question.'

For a full minute his mother said nothing. Then,

'Something will have to be done.'

'About where we shall live, you mean?'

'Where *you* shall live?' she repeated. 'At Aston, of course. You don't question that this is your home, I suppose.'

'Mama, what is this? You know how I love Aston.'

'I had thought you did. I will be blunt, Rupert. I must tell you that I do not intend to keep your wife at Aston any longer. How many years is it since she came here? Five? To me it seems a humiliating eternity. Do you suppose that this Dower House affair will be the end of her ill-bred notions? She will think of some other vulgar idea which will show just how much you married beneath you. Are you aware that people laugh at her behind our backs? When one compares that creature with Mary! No, Rupert, your wife does not belong here and proves it by wishing to live elsewhere. Are you prepared to let her ruin all our lives? She must go.'

'Of course she cannot go, she is my wife!'

He had begun to tremble.

'We are in no position to forget *that*,' she said.

He had a surge of hatred for the implacable woman facing him. And for the sulky girl who tugged him from *her* side, who refused his marital rights and humiliated him in his own thoughts. He detested them both.

'Mother, what are you saying? That Stella and Kit must leave Aston?'

'Kit? Naturally he will remain.'

'But what you suggest is impossible! How can Stella and I separate – why *should* we!'

'You are so devoted to her, are you? We saw no sign of it this week while you were dancing attendance on Mary.'

He blushed. Looking at him, his mother read his face. She read it as accurately as a lover might do. She had lovingly studied that sensitive countenance when he was a little child, she recognised every nuance. She saw he was not going to spring to his wife's defence, and that he was frightened.

Changing her tone, she said quietly:

'Of course I suggest no such thing as a separation. Good heavens, should we go to lawyers with our private affairs? We will do this. Your father and I will make Quenington House over to you. It's large and comfortable and has a good deal of land. Derbyshire in summer is pleasant enough. You will move there with your family, and later return to Aston on a visit. A long visit. You can travel up to Derbyshire now and then. For form's sake. As for Kit,

Aston is far healthier than Quenington and with Nurse Digby here, it is best if he remains.'

Rupert saw the full reach of her words. Saw Stella's joyous acceptance, his own craven role, saw himself returning to Aston, and the look of triumph in his mother's face. He trembled more, and it took all his courage to say in a choking voice:

'I can't do it. No, I can't. What has she done to deserve such a thing?'

'*Done*? Trapped you. Seduced you. Don't tell me what happened in the past was your fault, I will not believe it. If it had not been with you, she would have done what she did with some other man – some Boer. She had no respect for her purity, she is an immoral woman. I no longer intend to have her under my roof.'

'She saved my life.'

'Not that old history again. Listen, Rupert. Do you pretend to have an undying affection for this woman? She gets on your nerves. Of course she does, she is not one of us. You, of all my sons, know what Aston means, what I have done for it and still will do. The only possible, indeed honourable thing, is for you to separate from her. Do you suppose a name like ours has remained great without sacrifice?'

He stood up, shamefacedly brushing away the tears. With a faltering, 'I'm sorry – I can't talk now —' he went out.

Knowing Mary Flood French was gone, Stella was anxious to see Rupert, and left messages asking him to come to her. She felt tense after the week of separation from him, but still had no intention of giving in. The more she thought about it when alone and miserable, the more she became determined to make him see that they must get away from this great rich prison. She knew when they did that she could make him happy. And was certain that she *would* somehow succeed in getting him to leave Aston. She felt as she had long ago, when she had been sure of making him marry her. You only had to stay strong.

It was cold and rainy, the rain blew in gusts against the

108

panes as she stood in her bedroom looking out into the dull afternoon. She could see the curve of the drive down which earlier in the day she had watched the car taking away Mary Flood French. Now she heard the sound of hooves, and to her surprise saw it was Rupert, urging his big black hunter into a gallop. Her first thought was, why didn't I catch him in his dressing-room? But Rupert disliked her doing that. He did not answer my messages, he is going to look for the hunt, she thought. She felt quite angry, watching him ride away so fast. He's riding off his low spirits because that stupid girl has gone – he never even came to see me this morning. My God, how badly he sits on a horse . . .

Yet something in his figure touched her, even his back looked miserable. Her anger melted as she stood watching him disappear into the winter distance. She felt a pang of impatient affection, and wished – she did wish – they had not quarrelled.

Hours went by. Luncheon was over long ago, and finally the Marquess and a group of friends returned, tired, muddy and satisfied from a good day's hunting. The Marquess, bathed and changed for dinner, was in his study reflecting over the day's sport when the Master was announced. William was amused.

'Hello, Beresford, I thought we'd seen enough of you for today—'

The words froze. Beresford's face was ghastly.

'Good God, man, what has happened?'

'It's Rupert. They discovered him just now by Fawley Brook.'

'Discovered him? You mean the boy's hurt?'

'He must have taken that hedge. That damned high hedge. His neck is broken, William. He is dead.'

Chapter Eight

On a day in early April just over a year after Rupert's death, Stella received an invitation to sing at Ransome Manor, the house nearest to Aston, where the family's cousins, the Fairfaxes, lived. At the bottom of the letter, in Maud Fairfax's neat hand, was a P.S. 'It would be a great pleasure to us all if you would consent to sing.'

The fact that Stella sang well, and that people loved to listen, had been remarked upon when Rupert was alive. It seemed to have come into prominence lately, and Stella often received such requests. The family was out of deep mourning, and when visitors came to Aston, or invited the family to visit them, it was almost expected. No longer in the black silks which forbade any kind of gaiety, Stella enjoyed it.

The first shock of her husband's death had made her very ill. The Marquess had been seriously concerned and had sent for a specialist from London; he had said the young widow was suffering a nervous collapse. She must have complete rest and freedom from anxiety.

The girl was in a bad way. She vomited, grew painfully thin, could scarcely reply to a kind question without weeping. Rupert's parents were shattered by the tragedy, yet even Millicent did not take Rupert's death as badly as Stella. Desmond, Harry and young Catherine grieved deeply. But during the elaborate funeral, in the church hung with black and filled with dark-clad relatives, the young widow was so weak and ill that the Marquess had to support her up the aisle.

Society was impressed with such an excess of sorrow and thought her depth of feeling remarkable.

Nobody but Stella herself knew it was not grief which

prostrated her but conscience. Her strength in the past had enabled her to bear both the hard narrow life at Meidoorn and the galling life at Aston. But when she knew she would never put her arms round Rupert's neck again, never answer his quick desire with at least some warmth, she could not forgive herself. She was convinced that his death was her fault. They had not made love. She had been cold. He had always ridden badly, and she could have forced him to give it up for Kit's sake. She had saved his life at Meidoorn and killed him at Aston and the thought made her retch.

But even such an extreme of grief began eventually to heal. She was twenty-three years old, and a day came when she woke from a natural, not drug-induced sleep and remembered with a smile that Harry was due home on leave.

It was months since she had seen him, and she looked forward to it. One day she would tell him that she blamed herself for Rupert's death; it would be a weight off her heart.

The day was changeable. In the distance across the park she saw her son's sturdy little figure, followed by the even sturdier one of Nurse Digby. Stella sat on her favourite seat near the lake, watching the wind-ruffled water. It's strange, she thought, that I'm still here. If it weren't for Kit, I would have left Aston five minutes after Rupert's funeral. Packed my trunks, gone to London and earned my living somehow. The thought of such liberty was unimaginable.

'Greetings, Sister-in-law!' said a laughing voice. Turning round, she saw Harry Flood. He wore uniform, and had arrived scarcely five minutes ago, having seen her across the park.

'Harry, you aren't due until the end of the week!'

'Their lordships changed their minds. I saw you from the drive. Are you glad to see me?'

'Very.'

He looked her up and down critically.

'You're better, and about time too. It wasn't like you to be so pulled down. You're quite pretty again. Too pale,

111

though. You must go riding and get some roses in those cheeks.'

'Oh, I never ride now.'

'You used to ride like a huntress.'

'Did I?'

She changed the subject, and asked him about Gibraltar. He answered breezily and made her smile. Looking at him, she thought how unfamiliar it was to see anybody so darkly sunburned; he reminded her of Cousin Karel at the end of the Transvaal summer. There were pale laughter lines etched on the brown skin at the corners of his eyes.

'I must go up to the house and change before I pay my respects to Mother,' he said, 'but first I want you to promise me something. That you'll let me take you riding.'

'Harry, no. I told you that I don't ride now.'

He studied her somewhat blank face for a moment.

'Did you lose your nerve because Rupert was killed?'

'Lose my nerve? Of course not. It is just that – well, it reminds me. You understand.'

'No, I don't. Poor old Rupert breaking his neck is no reason for you to give up something you are good at. Very silly. We will ride this afternoon. See you at luncheon.'

He sketched a salute and walked away.

Millicent was busy with her dressmaker from London when she heard that Harry had arrived. She did not send for him, but dismissed the woman and sat in her boudoir, waiting. She looked older since Rupert's death. She had accepted the terrible blow in a grim silence; she was like the Spartan mothers, grey-faced and stony. Stella's extremity of grief had offended her as deeply as everything else about her impossible daughter-in-law. Millicent never blamed herself for the accident. Certainly Rupert had been upset after their argument on that fatal afternoon, but he had been upset scores of times before that. He had been in a permanently nervous state since his disastrous marriage. The boy had been dogged by ill-fortune – and had died.

She had not altered towards Rupert's wife, never spoke to her unless it was unavoidable, and when she wished her to do or not do something, she used Catherine as a go-between. Catherine was biddable, and it was useful that she got on reasonably well with her sister-in-law while still doing exactly what Millicent told her.

There was a tap at the door and Harry strode in.

'Mother.'

Millicent gave him a true, not a social smile. Putting his arms round her, he kissed her, pressing her close. She broke away with a laugh.

'Don't hug so, you'll make my hair come down and Moffatt spent an hour doing it. How do you like the new way?'

'Glorious, and so are you.'

'Oh, good.' It was her answer to all compliments. 'Did you have an amusing time in Gibraltar? Did you fall in love? What fascinating news have you? Are you going to tell me that you are marrying the Governor's daughter?'

Harry said that the Governor's daughter weighed twelve stone but was irresistible. He adored fat women. Mother and son talked, and while she smiled and questioned him, she also consulted her green morocco-bound diary to tell him that Desmond was home from Dublin this week. And would Harry be here for the Londonderry House ball? Sprawling in a chair, Harry thought how unchanged his mother was. Her life was lived by that damned great diary, she knew the exact dates of everybody coming and going. And as usual seemed to think he and Des thirsted for each other's company, like those two warriors Harry had seen on the outside of a church wall in Venice, their arms round each other's necks.

'How do you find Aston?' she asked. 'We've had some repairs done in the Great Hall. And electric light under the most important paintings in the gallery. De Lisle's idea. Incidentally, he has been painting me.'

'Who has painted Stella?'

A little pause. She raised her head.

'Nobody. Sergeant has done a very pretty little drawing of Kit.'

'Stella ought to be painted, my dear mother. To hang

113

beside the Orpen of Rupert done before he went to South Africa.'

'I don't know why you bother yourself with that, Harry. *She* would not wish it.'

He was listening to her thoughts, not her words.

'You're an unforgiving creature,' he remarked. 'Stella has done you no harm. No, she has not, so don't put on that grim face. How like Queen Elizabeth you are, you should wear a great lace collar and have your hair dyed red! Stella is getting quite pretty and stylish. She might do Aston credit one of these days.'

Millicent folded her lips thinly and stared at him without blinking, more a bird of prey than a Tudor queen.

'I cannot discuss Rupert's widow with you, Harry. I am quite aware of your ideas on the matter. It has always been a source of astonishment to me that you should be so lax. I shall never change. And I wish to heaven,' she added in a voice more chilling because it lacked expression, 'I could rid Aston of her for ever.'

Harry's easy smile was gone.

During luncheon, Lady Tyrrell kept up a pleasant talk with her newly-returned son, and his father said little but looked benevolently at them both. Stella openly listened to the conversation and when Harry made a joke, she giggled. She seemed not to notice the occasional icy look thrown in her direction by Millicent. At the end of the meal Harry said:

'Father, have you a horse in the stables for Stella?'

'Bertha's a lady's horse. A nice little mare.'

'I had no idea you had decided to ride again,' said Millicent to Stella in her most unpleasant voice. 'I understood you could not do so.' *You were supposed to be too grief-stricken* hung in the air, unspoken.

'My dear mother, you underrate my persuasions. I told Stella a ride would do her good,' Harry said, smiling.

When she came out to the stables, wearing her tight-fitting black habit with its trailing skirts, Stella was nervous. She had a real revulsion against riding, which was inextricably tangled in her mind with Rupert galloping to his death. Avoiding horses had been a way of stopping that vision. She did not know that memory which rises like a spectre at a scent or a tune can disappear as water sinks into the sand. The groom held the stirrup, she jumped lightly on to the mare's back and she and Harry rode under the stable arch. She rode with the old Boer droop of the shoulders and he bit back a smile.

The afternoon was sunny, Stella quickened her mare's pace, Harry urged on his horse and they rode across the meadows, dismounting to walk down a long hill towards a little fast-flowing stream.

'You ride like a boy, Stella. We must ride often together.'

She did not answer but walked beside him leading her horse. He said after a while, 'How do you get on with my mother nowadays?'

It had occurred to him that it was high time things were patched up between his mother and this enigmatic young woman.

'There's no need to join in, Harry, whichever side you favour.'

'Must there be sides?'

'Until I came to Aston, I never thought so.'

'We are not talking of the past but of the present. You know Society now and this emnity between you both is talked about among our friends, who all disapprove.'

'They don't speak about it to me,' she said indifferently. 'In any case they know your mother hates me and they'd never disagree with *her* since she's the one with the cash.'

'Stella, don't be vulgar.'

She laughed, showing her teeth, and said impudently, 'I don't see why not.'

But he remained serious.

'Family feuds are a grave mistake. They're wearing and bitter and as people get older the feuds grow worse. I must find a way of mending this one.'

'You'll be clever,' she said, mounting her horse with a spring, 'if you do that.'

Harry was a general favourite at Aston, there was

something about him which Nurse Digby called 'sailor-like'. His father, planning a trip to Paris, decided to stay at home and take Harry shooting. Millicent was all gracious smiles and treated Harry as if he were a visiting Cabinet Minister, with flattering attention. Catherine captured him whenever she could. It was annoying of Harry, thought Stella, to have a talisman into everyone's affections.

Charming and clever he might be, but she knew he would not succeed in improving things between Lady Tyrrell and herself. And she was not going to help him do so. She detested her mother-in-law who had treated her so badly for so long. In one thing Lady Tyrrell was right – Stella was an outsider. Stella never had settled for Aston and still disliked it. The round of pleasure, the red faces of the nobility drinking too much champagne, the iron faces of mothers hunting husbands for their daughters ... most of all Stella was repelled by the knowledge that money was in everybody's mind. It flowed at Aston and in every other great house, a subterranean river under the floor-boards and the stone flags. How ungrateful I am, she thought, was I happier at Meidoorn? I don't believe so. Neither the Boer farmers nor English Society accepted her. But at least now many people liked to hear her sing ...

Invitations poured into Aston, everybody knew that Harry was on leave. A few days later Desmond was home from Dublin and a letter from Elinor was delivered by hand, saying how much they looked forward to seeing Harry.

'Elinor says you've agreed to sing,' Harry remarked, as Stella came into the drawing room before dinner, looking poised and cool in satin. A swan.

'I'm not looking forward to it. Elinor has ordered an orchestra from London. I shall feel so stupid, piping away accompanied by all those professional musicians carefully not showing what they think of my voice.'

'You sing like a nightingale.'

She laughed, but wondered why his presence made the idea of singing tonight alarming. She had never felt like this before, she had sung as a bird does, for the joy of it. And

116

had known she put a spell on her audiences. But when Harry was there the spell might fail. He would wait for her to fly and she would fall like a stone.

The evening at Fallowfield proved a success after all. The concert and her songs went well. Little self-possessed Elinor was gracious and Desmond, whom Stella had never learned to like, actually paid her a compliment. She knew that this was not due to admiration but to her success. Desmond's manner to her never lacked its flavour of patronage, but his friends' approval of her impressed him.

When Stella and Harry went home in the cumbersome old Flood carriage, she was – for the first time in what seemed a hundred years – rather happy. Harry took her hand. He undid the pearl buttons of her glove and kissed her palm. They drove in silence and April moonlight back to Aston.

She found Harry's company during the weeks of his leave a wonderful relief. He was never cold or critical, never drunk and given to paying her unwanted compliments. His voice was not loud. When he went to the nursery to play with Kit, he never cheated to please him but played to win.

One evening when Stella was dressing for dinner, Catherine gave her light rat-tat-tat on the door. She came in wearing pale green chiffon with a white overdress embroidered in pearls.

'I'm here to chat,' she said, sitting down.

Wilkins, as deeply respectful to Catherine as she was subtly not to her own mistress, fastened Stella's bracelets and left the room.

'You look sweet, Cathy,' remarked Stella. 'What a lovely colour. But why the glory?'

'Dick Manders, I'm sorry to say.'

'Sorry? But he's so fascinating,' said Stella, laughing. Dick Manders had a romantically haggard face and women fell in love with him.

'So people keep telling me,' said Catherine with a shrug. 'Why does he make eyes at all the ladies and think it acceptable to turn them on me as well? Mama told me to wear this dress. I think she wants Dick as a son-in-law. *Quelle horreur!*'

Catherine never much liked any man specially invited to Aston for her by Millicent. She was bright and charming but swerved away.

'I'm a great disappointment so far. I'm being sent to Paris to be finished, Mama tells me. That will get me off her hands for a bit.' She gave Stella a glance from under her thick eyelashes. 'You and Harry seem very thick.'

'Just because we ride together.'

'Isn't that the point? He got you on to a horse again.'

'Harry is persuasive,' said Stella, who did not want to talk about him. But his sister did.

'Harry is the clever one,' she said pensively. 'He should have been the eldest, not poor darling Rupert who took everything so seriously. Harry copes with Mama. He manages her much, much better than Papa ever does. Or me. Or Des.' She fiddled with a bracelet, looking down, her dark eyelashes in two crescents. She was very pretty.

'But all Harry does is blow into Aston and out again like a sea breeze,' said Stella, amused.

'That sounds as if he comes and goes without thinking. Harry would never do that.'

'Don't you approve of him?'

'He has always been my favourite.'

'But now you are grown-up, you have found him out.'

'One doesn't find Harry out, Stella. He invites you to understand him. He simply says, "This is what I'm like".'

'You're too clever tonight. I pity poor Dick Manders,' said Stella, as she and Catherine walked down the corridor.

Catherine criticised any man who came to Aston on her account, but she frankly admired Harry. Is she slightly jealous, wondered Stella, and has she reason to be? After dinner that night, with Millicent down at the other end of the long drawing room, Harry asked Stella to sing.

'Cath knows the music. It will suit your voice,' he said. He had given the music to his sister.

Seeing Catherine at the piano, and Stella standing beside her, there was a lull. Catherine played the opening bars. It was a poem by William Blake, set to a melody which had a kind of magical sadness.

> Never seek to tell thy love,
> Love that never told can be . . .

When it ended there was applause and Dick Manders begged her to sing again. She smilingly refused. She scarcely heard the compliments. During the song she had looked across the room at Harry, and he had returned the look. His eyes were narrowed, his body seemed relaxed but it was not. His face spoke and what it said she did not resist but only sang more thrillingly.

They did not speak to each other during the evening, and when she looked in his direction sometimes he was always energetically talking to somebody. At last the evening ended and she trailed upstairs along the gallery to her room. Wilkins was waiting, her face very pale. It was after one o'clock.

'Go to bed, Wilkins. I don't need you.'

The maid obediently vanished. Stella took off her pearls, her thick satin dress and petticoats. She undid her corset and peeled off her white stockings, pulled on her nightgown and modestly beneath it, as she had been taught as a child, took off her bloomers. Her hair was incongruously still shining with jewels. She took out the diamonds and unpinned its coils. Then she put out all the lamps except one. Her heart beat so fast that she felt she would suffocate. She sat looking at the door, not directly but in her looking glass. Five minutes went by. Ten. She did not stir.

Very slowly the handle began to turn and Harry came softly into the room. He closed the door and locked it. In the dull golden light he seemed ominously tall and dark. Saying nothing he came towards her, lifted her to her feet and gave her a long exploring kiss. He put his hands flat on her buttocks and pressed her so close that she could scarcely breathe. He was extraordinarily strong, his body

119

seemed of solid muscle and Stella, who had known no other male body but her husband's, was half frightened as her senses began to swim.

At last he stopped the kiss, picked her up and carried her to the bed. He looked down at her.

'You've had nobody but Rupert, have you?'

Dumbly she shook her head.

'Good. Now I'm going to show you what it's really like.'

Sex knocked Stella spinning after her first night in Harry Flood's arms. He was passionate and skilful, tender and violent, and she responded like a land waking from a dream to find itself vanquished. Looking at him when they met in the house or garden made her heart stop, she felt she would faint. When he touched her hand on occasions when he found her alone, she went white. But it was not only the violent physical attraction which took her by the throat. It was being in the power of a man so strong and mocking whose nature was harder and surer than her own. She could not bear it if he did not approve of everything she was. He loved her and said so. He came into her bedroom every night, stayed until dawn, taught her about love as Rupert never had and talked about it as Rupert never would. He had no shame and nor had she. She counted the days of his leave like a miser, grudging every minute they were not together. He never let her have her own way.

'We will *not* ride together, I'm going to the hunter sales with my father. I will see you at tea.'

'I shall die if I don't see you until tea.'

'What a pity. Then I shall have to find another bedfellow. Come here, you shameless hussy, I know that look.'

He organised their brief span of days at Aston so that there was little opportunity for her face to betray her. She did as he bid her, busying herself with the little boy and it was easy in Kit's company to find reasons to laugh. But when she was with Catherine she noticed that the girl's manner was not as warm as usual, it was offhand and quite brusque. Perhaps it is my imagination, thought Stella.

Catherine is so reserved, one can never really guess what goes on in her head. She's probably worried about something to do with her mother. Always a new young man is being trotted into Aston for her. And anyway, Catherine can't *know* anything about us. That's impossible. Yet Catherine was odd with her. Once when Stella looked at her, she thought she saw in her young sister-in-law's eyes something cold and changed and aware.

But she forgot it. She was happy. Ridiculously and carelessly and meltingly happy. Harry's love gave her a golden armour, she could no longer be hurt by anyone for she was his. She felt in the mood to love everybody and everything that belonged to him. Except, she thought, inwardly smiling to herself, Lady Tyrrell.

From the first night when he had taken her she knew that everything was going to change. She and Harry would be married. With her new happiness and this iron-willed partner, every difficulty would be solved. Rupert's pale shade evaporated when she looked at the man who possessed her now. She compared him to her uncle and cousins, male creatures whose strength had never been doubted. Harry was as strong as they. She was too rapt to think of anything but love until the final night before he was due to leave, rejoining his ship at Portsmouth.

He came to her as usual, very quietly locking the door. The very turning of the lock affected her. They scarcely slept, made love over and over again until she, not he, was exhausted. Once or twice she fell asleep but he woke her again, smiling in the lamplight, he never made love in the dark. 'It's no good, lovebird, I want you again.'

At last he allowed her to sleep. She woke suddenly, to see the grey edges of daylight between the curtains. He was tying on the belt of his dressing-gown, carelessly flicking away his dark hair from his forehead.

'Harry. Dearest. Must you go?'

'Alas, I must. It is the lark and not the nightingale.'

'Romeo and Juliet is a horrid play.'

'You like happy endings,' he said, in the half-whisper

they used. Suddenly her love and longing swept over her like a wave, knocking her down. She held out her arms.

'Sit by me for a moment.'

'My dear one.'

He never refused to do any small thing she asked, and sat on the bed taking her hands and looking at her with smiling fondness. She gazed at him, remembering everything about his face, the olive skin, the blue eyes and heavy eyelids, the mouth with its betraying lower lip, the glossy hair, the cleft chin.

'Do you love me, Harry?'

'And do you love *me*, Beauty?'

Her soul was in her face just then.

'We are going to get married, aren't we?'

Harry's expression did not change. He did not look surprised or cease to smile. He touched her nose.

'My darling girl, of course we are not.'

She pulled herself away.

'*You don't mean it!*'

'Of course I do. Why in heaven's name should we wish to marry?' he asked and pressed her breasts. 'We have this, don't we? What could be more delicious?'

He looked at her and shook his head.

'What a romantic creature you are. I've no intention of getting married, Stella. On a lieutenant's pay? And can you imagine how much my mother would settle on me, if I decided to trot up the aisle? In any case . . .'

He paused and smiled.

'In any case your brother had me first.'

'Stella, you really *are* a child.'

She stared at him fixedly. 'I speak the truth. In England men like you marry well-born girls who are still innocent. That's it, so why not say so?'

He threw his eyes up. 'What society rubbish. I've never had a taste for virgins; I shouldn't have been enjoying myself so blissfully in your bed if you had been one. No, we will not marry, we will have a glorious and unending love affair. Now *you* should get to sleep, Beauty, because you look a wee bit exhausted, and after last night I am not surprised. I won't see you to say goodbye. My train goes in two hours. Don't forget me.'

He sketched a teasing salute and quietly left her room.

If the loss of Rupert, taken by destiny and death, had prostrated her, her break with Harry must be borne. The emotion flooding her was not grief but bitter resentment. He simply did not want her – no, since that was absurd, he wanted her only as a secret mistress he could enjoy without a single responsibility. It was not that she wished to lean upon him: she leaned on no one. What she had believed was that because they were in love, they must be united. They would be each other's next of kin. They would be one. It came to her, during the later weeks of April before the annual migration to London, that no couple could be less 'one' than she and Harry Flood, except in each other's arms.

She spent more time than usual with Kit, and Nurse Digby welcomed her in her customary reserved way. The older woman rarely said more than a word or two to anybody who was not a child, although she stretched the point to gossip to Catherine sometimes. Kit thought his mother beautiful and kind.

Along the corridor beyond the Nursery Wing was the old schoolroom where the three Flood boys had learned their lessons before being packed off to preparatory school. Stella took to the room, which was shabby and, in the Aston way of keeping everything, retained the battered desks and blackboard and cottage piano. Here, with high windows showing nothing but the sky, she played and sang alone, the music for a while subduing her bruised and longing heart. Nurse Digby, sewing in the nursery, stopped to listen to the voice floating towards her.

Stella was practising a new piece one sunny morning when a footman came to tell her the Marchioness wished to see her. Stella closed the piano, and took as long as possible to walk to Millicent's study.

Her mother-in-law glanced up as Stella came into the room. Both women were in half mourning, Stella in lilac, with a broad collar slightly resembling a sailor collar, the ends tied with silk tassels. Her dress was fringed at the hem and sleeves. Millicent was in severe grey with black braiding.

'Please sit down,' she said, indicating a chair she had ordered to be placed at a certain distance before Stella arrived.

Millicent's desk was so crowded with silver-framed photographs that there was little room for the flowers and heavy silver inkwell engraved with the Flood coat of arms. There was a new photograph Stella had not seen before – of a young cloudy-haired Millicent with the baby Rupert on her lap.

Her mother-in-law looked at her and said abruptly, 'You are not happy at Aston, are you?'

Stella was astounded. When had she been asked such a question in all their mutual life?

Not waiting for a reply, Millicent went on, 'It is rather boring for you, I do see. You are not in a very advantageous position, since Rupert was unable to leave you anything. Besides, there is always the possibility that you might wish to remarry.'

For one gasping minute Stella thought that Harry's mother knew what had happened. But the idea was impossible. Harry had rejected her, and Millicent's manner was calm.

'Don't think I have not realised during the years that life has not been easy,' continued Millicent in this new reasonable voice. 'You were, so to speak, catapulted here.' She gave a mirthless little laugh. 'And then – poor Rupert's loss. It has not been easy. Particularly for you.'

The last three words contained the usual threadbare insult about lack of breeding. Much Stella cared. She sniffed freedom.

'I drove to Oxford yesterday to see Mr Guthrie,' said Millicent, leaning her chin on her hand. 'We had a good talk.'

The name Guthrie was weighted for the listening girl. He was the head of one branch of the Flood's lawyers, and often

124

travelled to Oxford when the family wished to consult him. Rupert had sometimes spoken of doing so, but his courage had failed him.

'Mr Guthrie sees no reason why we cannot settle a small allowance on you,' continued Millicent, speaking as if the lawyer held the purse-strings, 'something to allow you to live modestly but in the style my son would wish. You may decide on London, but I should have thought the North, Derbyshire or Northumberland, might be preferable. It is healthy there. I should like you to think this over seriously. My daughter could accompany you, if you wish to look at some suitable small properties.'

'*Oh, thank you!*' burst out Stella, blushing a deep, happy crimson, her dark eyes brilliant with relief, even joy, the first since Harry had gone. 'It would be wonderful to have my own home, and of course it will be small and . . . and . . . I'll bring Kit to see you any time you wish.'

Millicent looked her full in the face.

'You seem to misunderstand. The Marquess and I are willing to make this allowance, to give you what we consider is a generous opportunity to have a life of your own. We certainly could not consider doing so if Rupert's son left Aston. The allowance, naturally, is dependent upon that. Kit will remain here.'

On the following morning, after a sleepless night of helpless fury, Stella rang for her maid early, rose, dressed in her most elaborate morning dress, and went downstairs to the Marquess study. He was alone.

William looked uncomfortable for a moment as she walked towards him. She was pale and very handsome. He kindly asked her to be seated, while he stood with his arm along the chimney piece, looking at her thoughtfully. She blurted out her story with no idea of how pretty anger made her look.

He, of course, knew the tale already. He nodded, not without sympathy, and lit a cheroot. Various thoughts drifted through his mind as the smoke drifted in bars across the sunlight. The girl was very inviting. That young rip

Harry had been having a devil of a time with her. He'd seen his son leaving her room on two occasions. And his own little mistress, a dancer in London, was becoming tiresome. Here was a luscious piece of female flesh. She was in difficulties, too.

'My dear child, I realise you are a little upset,' he said, with his pleasant drawl, and came across the room, putting down the cigar. Seating himself beside her, he put a manicured, slightly hairy hand on her knee. Through the silk of her dress and two petticoats, Stella could feel that hot hand. Lowering his eyes, he gave her knee a squeeze. Then his hand dropped towards the calf of her leg. She started as violently as if she had been scalded.

He laughed, and took away his hand.

'Come, come, child, I am not going to eat you. Although you would make an appetising meal. You wish to leave Aston, mm? And who's to blame you?'

A footman came in just then, to make up the fire, and Stella stood up, said something polite and made her escape. She wished she had slapped the Marquess' ageing face.

Aston continued its leisured harmonies. Millicent, Catherine and Stella wore their billowing greys and mauves. Visitors came and went, music was heard, Stella's voice sang out. A barrier of courtesy kept the Floods and Stella separated. They were polite because they were polite to everybody. But Catherine had taken away her friendship, just as if she had come into a room and removed the only flowers which had graced it. Stella missed her. She saw now that she was never going to be able to rely on Catherine's affection, which came and went according to her mother's attitudes. When Millicent merely ignored Stella and no more than that, Catherine acted as a convenient go-between, and actually seemed quite fond of Stella. She could be an enchanting companion. Stella had been glad and even grateful for Catherine's smiles and jokes and friendship. But now they were gone.

Stella began to feel literally desperate as the days went by. She had never realised before to its full extent the position of a woman with not a farthing of her own – a woman with a child who could not run to freedom, even a poverty-stricken one. She was chained to Aston as surely as if the bracelets she wore were iron rings.

One morning when Harry had been away at sea for over a month, and the Aston preparations for the London exodus were almost complete, a letter was brought to Stella with her breakfast tray. Picking it up idly, she felt a pain as sharp as a stab wound. It bore a Transvaal postmark.

My dear Cousin,

I hope you receive this. I write in English for I daresay you forget Afrikaans. And *I* forget your right name, I think it is Lady Flood but maybe I get that wrong too.

I do sincerely trust, dear Cousin, that you are a little recovered from the great cross you had to bear. I pray for that to God. And thank Him that there may be for me the joy of seeing you soon.

If all is well I sail from the Cape and will be in London by April 20, that is if we do not run into bad storms. There is business I must do for my father. He is in Washington State where he has been offered some land. He never did sign the Oath and he writes wishing me to join him now he has a farm. But I am not sure. I have begun to rebuild Meidoorn.

A good friend, Theodore Jensen, has visited me. He is American and was the good man who knew your dear parents and helped for you to come here as a little child. He also will be in London and is glad to meet you. And I also am glad. And shall always be

your very affectionate cousin,
Karel Hendrik Vredenberg

Chapter Nine

Karel Vredenberg, sitting in the lounge of the Warburton House Hotel in Piccadilly, tried to read the newspaper and failed. He kept looking at the swing doors. The porter had assured him that the young lady would be brought straight to him but Karel was convinced she would never arrive. London was a dreadful place. He disliked the jostling horse traffic, the noise, the new motor cars; he detested the raucous shouts of newspaper vendors: 'Orrible Murder!' The people had grey faces, the buildings were caked with soot, even the air floated with smuts. The hotel might be seven storeys high and very magnificent but he was sure his cousin would never find her way to it. He continued to stare at the doors.

His travelling companion from Cape Town, Theodore Jensen, had been very amused last night when Karel confided to him that he was anxious. Theodore had said that Stella would find the hotel easily. But Theo was rich and worldly and thought other people resembled himself. He had talked to Karel of a house-party to which he had been invited on his last English visit. The King had been a guest, with a lady who was his latest bedfellow. Karel was deeply shocked.

'My dear man,' remonstrated Theo, 'you must try to see things from a different point of view, mm? The English Court is no longer stuffy, it is entertaining and filled with amusing women. Times are changing, you know. And since your cousin is in society, I daresay she will be changed too.'

But Karel had smiled and shaken his head.

The doors swung open and a lady came into the lounge. For a moment, merely thinking he looked at a stranger, he saw a beautiful young woman approaching. She walked with grace and was dressed in a dark tight-waisted coat elaborately trimmed, her fair head topped with a hat swathed in soft veiling which also covered her face. But the veil was fragile, and dark bright eyes shone through it.

Involuntarily he opened his arms and she ran into them.

'Cousin!'

'Oh, Karel, you are just the same!'

'Oh *lammetje*, you are not!'

They sat down, talking eagerly first in English and then slipping into Afrikaans. She had not used the language of her childhood for six years yet it came as easily as yesterday. Talking to this big bearded man, she felt frank and free.

She said he had not altered but that was not true. The years had thickened and broadened Karel, his hair was bleached almost white by the suns of the veldt while here in England a long dark winter had only just ended. There were lines round his blue eyes. But if she saw what time had done to him, Karel was bewildered at the changes in her. He had recently begun a slow courtship of Elly Maritz, youngest daughter of the family living fifty miles from Meidoorn. He could not help comparing his shy Elly with this foreigner looking at him with Stella's eyes. Yet what she spoke about, affectionately and eagerly, was the past. Of her uncle and aunt, Adam and Ruth, even of the childhood games Karel and she had played, the 'Boers and Brits'. Looking at him, Stella thought it a kind of miracle that he owned the same past as she, saw it as she did. Because of that, the girl she had been still lived – in a way. She asked about Uncle Hendrik. Karel's face changed.

'I told you, yes? He wishes me to go to Washington State and join him on his farm, Stella. I have prayed about it, and now I know it is right I stay at Meidoorn. I am sad for Father, and wish he would return to our country. But his choice is to be an exile. I cannot give up the Transvaal even for my own flesh and blood.'

She put her gloved hand on his.

'He'll understand, Karel.'

He gave her a solemn, curious look.

'Do you forget his nature? He will not forgive me or the English either. We are both the enemy now. But Theo has travelled to see him and other Afrikaaners who are his friends and says Father is not unhappy and the farm not too small. Theo is your parents' old friend,' he added kindly.

'How odd, a man who knew my parents. Uncle Hendrik and Aunt Maria were my real mother and father.'

He paused, then said as he used to do, 'You are a good girl'.

Stella had written to him when Rupert died, and now she saw that Karel believed as he questioned her about her own life that her husband's death had broken her heart. His sympathy made her uncomfortable. When she tried to describe Aston, it was clear that he could not grasp its suffocating grandeur. He frowned, saying yes, it was a heavy responsibility to be rich and powerful and Stella must pray about it. And pray too to do her duty by her little son. Kit was a fact Karel could grasp. The frown left his face, he gave her a charming smile.

'I brought a miniature to show you,' she said.

He studied it carefully.

'He has just your eyes.'

Elly Maritz's name came into the conversation more than once, and Stella suddenly exclaimed, 'I do believe you are going to marry her!'

The young man quite blushed, embarrassed and pleased. Elly was a good girl too, it seemed, and they had many plans for Meidoorn.

Stella listened, smiling with her brilliant eyes, but her heart had sunk. Hopefully and foolishly, she had imagined Karel would help her in some way, yet how was that possible? She could not tell him about Millicent, it would shock him to his soul. And supposing he did manage to grasp that she was unhappy and penniless, what could he suggest? That she returned with him to the Transvaal? She could just imagine poor Elly's face at that idea. Besides, there was Kit, who would inherit the title and Aston too when the Marquis eventually died. That might not be for years, but Kit could not be at the other side of the world when the day came. What could this kindly man, his hands on his knees like a farm labourer, do for her? Give her a serious affection. She felt guilty because that was no help at all.

Before they parted, he told her Theodore Jensen had invited them to dinner. He lived, said Karel, in Park Lane. Did Stella know which street that was? She laughed, saying it was round the corner from the Floods' London house.

Theodore Jensen, working in his business room, looked amused when his servant told him Mr Vredenberg had arrived. He had been shown into the upstairs drawing-room.

Theo found Karel adrift, looking very out of place among the Frenchified furniture.

'My dear fellow, are you always early? Do your friends at home have the uncivilised habit of arriving half an hour before time?'

Karel smiled, looking younger than when he had been with Stella.

Theodore regarded him benevolently and rang for sherry.

Karel's host was a powerful-looking man in his late thirties, with heavy shoulders and deep-set dark eyes. He could have been Italian but was of pure Dutch blood. His family had settled in New York a hundred years ago, acquired land and grown rich. Theodore was wealthy enough to do nothing, but money interested him: he liked, he said, to make it breed. He was on the way to being a millionaire, and doors opened for him with that golden key. He knew the King and Queen of England, English dukes and French countesses, statesmen, jockeys and actors. On the voyage from Cape Town he was the most sought-after traveller on the ship, but chose to spend his time with one young Boer farmer.

Years ago when Theodore had been still almost a boy he had been an unexpected friend for Hendrik Vredenberg to make: the two men were poles apart and in the ordinary way of their disparate lives would never have met. They did so because of Stella. Theodore and his family had known the young Vredenbergs in New York and had been deeply shocked by the tragedy of their twin deaths. The Jensens had managed to trace the orphan child's relatives in the Transvaal. The youthful Theo had travelled to South Africa to see Hendrik. The two men talked farming, for Theodore's father had thousands of acres of good Pennsylvanian land. They had liked each other. Theo admired the Boer's hard, upright nature and his patriotism. Hendrik could not deny that this young American's quest for a home for a bereaved child was a Christian act. And few people could resist Theo Jensen when he wished to please. Travelling with Hendrik's son had interested Theo, as had the story of what had happened to his little protégé of long ago. Now, he sat down and looked expectant.

'How was your cousin? Changed, I'll be bound.'

'She is not the same.'

'And you are not very happy about that.'

'I can't tell. She is a widow. It is a sad life.'

'She's young, my dear boy, she will marry again,' was the casual reply. Theo had played destiny to Karel's cousin once but as Karel now spoke, the idea of the young woman she had become began to bore him. Widowed and clad in ugly black. He had invited her to dine because Karel made him feel he ought to do so: the young man had a way of nudging one's conscience. Sipping his sherry, Theo briefly remembered the pretty New York house and the two enchanting friends of his boyhood. They had been dead a long time. That winter had been full of death through an influenza as fatal as cholera. Karel, too, was silent; he was thinking about Stella. She troubled him. She was too easy, too promising, too fluid ... if he had not deeply believed that she had reformed after the sinful way her womanhood had begun, he might have thought her loose. But that was impossible. It could not happen twice to a woman raised by his parents.

'The Viscountess Coryot,' announced the footman.

The two men stood up. Stella, in fullskirted lilac silks

132

with a wide sash the colour of an orchid, came into the room. Karel took her hand and made the introductions.

Theodore Jensen and she looked at each other, Stella with interest and he with surprise. Where was the bereaved figure in rusty black? The boy had not warned him that she was a beauty. And Stella, smiling coolly, had remembered why this man's name had sounded familiar when Karel mentioned him. Jensen. She had read it in *The Times* social columns. He was a friend of Royalty and someone at Aston had spoken of him as 'wildly rich'.

Dinner was served in a sombre heavily-furnished dining-room, all crystal, red hangings and portraits, of the kind Stella was accustomed to and Karel had never seen in his life. The food and wines were excellent, but Stella scarcely touched hers. When the cloth was removed Jensen said:

'We can't say we will join the ladies when we have only one present. Would you consent to stay with us and break the rules?'

'I would like to and the rules are very stupid,' she said gaily.

The trio talked in a relaxed and friendly way and Stella asked her host about her parents. 'They seem,' she confessed, 'quite unreal to me.'

He looked at her somewhat dryly. 'They were charming and happy and when I was a boy I was devoted to them. Is that enough?'

She was not abashed, saying that it was a good beginning.

Observing Theodore Jensen during the meal, Stella had made up her mind to speak out. She waited until they had returned to the drawing-room and were sitting round the fire. Then, drawing a breath, she said frankly, 'I would like to ask you both a favour. I need advice.'

Karel looked surprised. Theo Jensen rubbed his chin.

She had realised this morning when she met Karel that it would be impossible to describe her difficulties to him. He would never begin to understand either her life or the people who surrounded her. But Mr Jensen, she thought, would understand very well.

'I want to get away from my husband's family,' she said, adding bluntly, 'And I have no money.'

Erect and graceful, her hands in her lap, she briefly described her first arrival at Aston, her life during her marriage and since her widowhood. She did not mince words: money and authority belonged to Millicent who detested her.

'But how can she feel so?' Karel was confounded.

'I am of no birth. And a Colonial.'

'In actual fact you are an American,' remarked Jensen.

'Oh yes, Americans are accepted, Mr Jensen. When they are rich.'

'True.'

'As I'm sure you know, one must be a rich somebody. I am a poor nobody.'

Karel looked very distressed and muttered that it was terrible and wrong and what kind of people were they?

'The same that one finds everywhere,' said Jensen. 'I gather that you wish to work for a living?' He turned to Stella, his courtly manner apparently gone since they were to discuss business. 'Have you any assets apart from a pretty face?'

'People tell me I can sing.'

'Why the grimace if what you say is true?'

'It seems a small thing. Yet a lot of people have said they like my voice and I am always being asked to sing.'

'In society, Lady Coryot, in society. To be paid for performing is a different kettle of fish. Let's hear you, then.'

'But Mr Jensen!' broke out Karel, recovering from the shock of his cousin's revelation only to grasp at another deplorable fact. 'You cannot suggest my cousin should earn her living as a *singer*.'

'I don't suggest anything, my dear fellow. Sing, young lady, if you please and we will listen.'

Karel fixed her with gloomy blue eyes. Jensen leaned comfortably back in his chair. Stella sat down at the piano and hesitated for a moment; then she played the opening bars of the William Blake song which she had sung on the first night Harry had made love to her, *Never seek to tell thy love*.

Her voice floated out through the windows which were slightly open on to the spring night. At the sound of her singing, memory swept back to Karel. He saw a time that was long ago and the little girl who had been his beloved playmate, who had sung the hymns more sweetly than any other child. But the past had cruelly gone and taken the child with it. Jensen sat with his dark eyes on the girl at the piano. He did not budge.

Stella was staying at the Floods' London house in Upper Grosvenor Street for a few days, having invented dressmakers' appointments. She had been joined by Elinor also in London for pre-Season fittings. On the morning following her dinner in Park Lane Stella came into the breakfast room to find Elinor already seated, sipping coffee and going through her letters. Small and neat, Elinor was set to be a Millicent when she reached fifty. She gave Stella a probing look.

'I was rather surprised that you did not dine, Stella. And left no messages.'

'A cousin of mine is in town.'

'A cousin?' repeated Elinor, rounding her eyes. She did not much like Rupert's widow and she did not approve of her. Besides, the Marchioness could not bear her.

'One does not produce relations like a conjuror out of a top hat,' she remarked.

'You mean, who is he? His name is Karel Vredenberg and we grew up together,' said Stella shortly. Elinor got on her nerves and she had a good deal to think about just now.

There was a knock at the door and a footman came in. He carried a very large and ostentatious bouquet of white orchids. Elinor's pale eyes grew even rounder. The footman said, 'We was particularly instructed, my lady, to give these to you immediately.'

Stella looked in silence at the showy and rather ridiculous bouquet. She took the envelope attached to it.

'Come at four if you are serious about changing your future.

T.J.'

Putting the card in her pocket she glanced across the table at Elinor.

'My cousin knows how much I enjoy a flower or two,' she said, and gave an urchin's grin.

When she arrived at the Park Lane house she was not taken up to the drawing-room but down a corridor on the ground floor. She was left to wait in Theodore Jensen's business room. It was full of ugly Victorian furniture, and dominated by a large desk covered with red embossed leather and heaped with papers. Too excited to sit down, she roamed about looking through the French windows at the sooty garden, and at the bookshelves filled with volumes of American history. The door opened.

'Good afternoon, Lady Coryot. Do please sit down and make yourself comfortable. Will this chair do?'

She sat down sedately. She was dressed in black but it was not a widow's mourning, it shimmered. The effect, thought Jensen, was of a black pearl in a silk-lined box.

He sat down at his desk.

'Well, young woman,' he said matter-of-factly, 'surprising as it seems, you can sing.'

'And you thought I couldn't.'

'Society women all chirp like sparrows. But yours is a good thick throat which gives room for the voice. Yes, you can sing. But are you quite sure you want me to help you?'

'I am certain.'

'Wait a bit. If you sing for your supper it means you'll leave Aston. The Marchioness may be a Tartar but you can't say you are not secure. Venture out from behind those thick walls into the market place and who knows what may happen.'

She said simply, 'I must leave Aston.'

'You know nothing about earning your living,' he said almost roughly.

But she was ready for that.

'I know what life is like in the Transvaal, Mr Jensen. I had to work hard. All the women did. I suppose you think that Aston has softened me.'

He looked her up and down with heavy-lidded eyes.

'I should have said you were soft as butter.'

A lady would have been offended. She burst out laughing.

'Very well,' he said, as if the laugh itself answered him. He scribbled a letter and handed it to her. It was addressed to Patrick Bird Esquire, Kean Theatre, Strand.

'Go and see him tomorrow. There might be an opportunity of some kind. But I promise nothing.'

When Stella returned to the Floods' house she went straight up to her room and lay down. She had taken her first step towards escape. And she knew it was not only from Millicent and Aston that she wanted to run and run until she dropped. She was *glad* to go from them, and still furiously angry at the attempt to take Kit away from her. But her wild desire was to separate herself – soon! now! – from Harry. She saw him in her mind, heard the lilt of his voice, put her hand against his olive-skinned face, remembered the bliss of his violent lovemaking. And their parting.

She thought of another man who had looked at her, this afternoon, with desire. Jensen. Strange to remember he had actually known her parents. How selfish she had been not to have spoken of them again. She was wrapped in her own trouble and those two poor dead people who had created her were forgotten. She was sure Jensen had noticed her omissions and counted them against her . . . or perhaps they had simply amused him. He looked hard as nails and was apparently as rich as Croesus and a friend of the King's. And of mine? she wondered. Does he only mean to help me if I go to bed with him? She decided that was not so. A man so wealthy must be able to buy a beautiful woman at any time . . .

Standing up, she went over to the looking-glass and stared critically at her reflection. Her eyes were large and overbright, her figure was rounded and promising. I am

137

behaving like a whore, she thought, and thinking like one too. But it came to her that she had never in her life had a moment of real freedom. Not at Meidoorn. Not at Aston. Perhaps that sardonic American was offering it to her.

Stella had seen musical comedies at the Kean Theatre on a number of occasions. The most popular shows were still with catchy music, pretty girls, a sentimental story and dances which were a whirl of frills. Stella had enjoyed the entertainments so much that one young man sitting beside her at the Kean during *The Chocolate Box Girl* had remarked disparagingly, 'You *do* enjoy things, don't you, Lady Coryot?'

She took a hansom to the Kean and alighted at the Stage Door. The Kean, built in the 1830s, was a stylish little theatre with a pillared entrance up four shallow steps, a small gem of a place polished and treasured and made to sparkle by its owner-manager. The Stage Door was not polished at all, it was a dark cramped entrance in a side alley, and an old man popped out of his sentry box, took her letter, and asked her to wait.

'Name of?' he added, before setting off into the shadowed interior of the building.

'Bredon,' replied Stella.

It rhymed with the beginning of her maiden surname. And she had liked Bredon Hill, where she had once driven with Rupert. After a short time, a disapproving woman of middle age with gold pince-nez and a frilled blouse came to fetch her, informing her that Mr Bird could see her now. Stella was taken up a stone staircase and along a passage as cold as a prison. Finally a door was opened and she was shown into a warm, red-carpeted book-filled room. A bright fire shone. Bow windows overlooked the street.

'Miss Bredon, Sir,' said the woman, and vanished.

A slender smallish man was sitting at a desk tidily heaped with papers, holding Theodore Jensen's letter. He glanced at her in a manner which slightly resembled the look Jensen had given her earlier.

138

'Sit down, please, Miss Bredon. Is Mr Jensen a friend of yours?'

'Of my cousin's. He knew my family when I was a child.'

He nodded absently, and continued to hold the letter as if he were weighing it. Patrick Bird was odd-looking. His face was perfectly round like a turnip, but unbecomingly ruddy instead of thick and pale. There were broken veins on the cheekbones. His nose was shapeless and his chin seemed to have been stuck on as an afterthought. He looked waspish and womanish, yet intimidating. His clothes were of exaggerated elegance, with a good deal of gold tie pin and jewelled links and satin stock.

'Mr Jensen tells me you can sing,' he remarked, adding, 'I wonder if I believe him.'

'Shall I sing now?' she enquired. It was, after all, why she had come.

'Of course. In a while. Stand up.'

Surprised amusement went through her. Where had 'the polite world' as it was called, disappeared to and what man in the whole of Society would say to a lady 'Stand up'. Jensen was right when he called it a market place.

She obeyed and Patrick Bird frankly looked her over.

'Turn a little. Now walk up and down.'

She recalled a visit to Tattersall's with her father-in-law. 'Walk the mare about a bit.'

Patrick Bird studied her sideways and frontways. He narrowed his protuberant blue eyes and told her to pirouette. She did so, her grey skirts flew in a circle revealing an embroidered petticoat and bronze shoes. Moving the mounds of paper carefully, Bird passed her a thumbed piece of manuscript music.

'Try this. Alter the key if necessary.'

She sat down at the upright piano in the corner by the window, and played the introduction. A nice little tune. The song was called 'No one loves me' and the refrain asked plaintively, 'No one loves me, no one hates me,

Tell me, do, what fate awaits me?'

Stella sang and Patrick Bird listened. When the song

ended he said, 'From the beginning, please.' He made her sing it four times; by the end she knew the words by heart.

'Thank you, Miss Bredon.'

She left the piano and returned to her seat. She had no idea what was going to happen next. Might it be a vague promise? To sing at a charity matinée, perhaps, for which she might actually get paid? Or to be accepted for some kind of training. Her knowledge of the theatre was limited to sitting in a box and watching the stage. Even entering by the Stage Door just now had seemed very strange.

'The voice is pretty,' remarked Patrick Bird after a pause. 'I can offer you a small engagement. Our new show, *The Holiday Girl*, starts next month. You will be in the chorus. There are twenty-five young ladies, all of whom can sing and dance, and you will need to work at your dancing, I don't doubt. You will receive your contract tonight. Give my secretary your address.'

She said nothing, and he was struck by the oddity of her expression.

'I take it you are pleased.'

'Overwhelmed.'

He permitted himself, for the first time, a faint smile.

'Yes. Not every girl gets her first engagement at my theatre. I have owned it for six years and I flatter myself it's in a class on its own. Well, Miss Bredon, that's a passable little voice but we will have to work on it. You are going to do a great deal of work. Good hard work.'

He sounded like Uncle Hendrik.

Karel was leaving for Tilbury the following day, having settled his father's business affairs. Stella sent a note to his hotel saying she would call to say goodbye. She would come mid-morning, an hour before his departure.

The day was very dark, the rain heavy. The London pavements shone with greasy mud and bobbed with umbrellas.

He was waiting in the foyer, but did not throw open his arms. He led her to a quiet corner of the lounge.

'Mr Jensen told me the news about you,' he said, his

voice scarcely above a whisper. 'I could not sleep for thinking of it.'

'Karel—'

'Hear me out, Stella,' he went on in English, his accent sadly distorting the words. 'It grieved me more than I can say to know you so unhappy. You are very young, and your good man already in his grave. But to be an actress! It is not right. You do not know the world you wish to enter – a sinful world where my cousin should never go. We must think of another way for you to earn an honourable living.'

Stella did not know whether to laugh or cry. She, too, had not slept for the excitement of her thoughts. At last she was going to escape. From Aston and everything it stood for. From being an interloper and never allowed to forget it. And most of all from Harry. She would never see him again and *that* was what she wanted.

'Dear Karel, don't be angry with me.'

'I am not angry,' he said looking at her with his truthful eyes.

'But you are shocked. Don't be. Everything in this country is different. They do not understand the way *you* are and the way I used to be. They respect nothing but birth or money and I have neither. And now no husband. You can't want me to go on living among people who despise me.'

'No,' he said in a desolate voice. 'I don't want you to do that. I ask you to come home with me.'

He was not thinking of himself – only of her. He was willing to do anything to help her. He would sacrifice his hopes, give her money needed for his farm, there was no limit to what he offered her. It was beautiful and impossible and the tears stood in her eyes.

He went on talking, questioning, making suggestions with all his kind seriousness. For a while he believed she must change her mind. But Stella was affectionate, warm, and adamant.

When he kissed her goodbye, he knew he had lost her.

* * *

141

Stella drove later that day to the Park Lane house and enquired if Mr Jensen were at home. The butler told her that the Master would see her in his business room. It seemed she was expected. Theo Jensen might never have stirred since she had seen him the previous day. The same fire, the same desk, the same cheroot and the same papers. He rose.

'I came to thank you,' said Stella. 'Mr Bird has engaged me.'

'So I hear, Lady Coryot. I broke the news to your cousin.'

'Oh, of course, how stupid of me. I said goodbye to him this morning.'

She gave him a look in which distress and determination were mixed. He remarked that they had both realised Karel would be upset. There was a pause.

'I feel rather dreadful,' said Stella with an unconscious Aston intonation, 'after all you have done for me . . .'

He laughed at that. 'But you need more help, is that it?'

The laugh was amused but not encouraging. Stella carefully explained the difficulty. She must come to live in London and find a house or a flat; she must bring her little son with her.

'So you would like me to lend you some money.'

'Good gracious, of course not!'

He continued to look amused.

'Then forgive my impertinence but how shall you make out? You say you have no money of your own. Patrick Bird might advance you a week or two's wages, but they'll be small enough.'

She pushed down one of her long kid gloves and showed him her wrist. Round it was clasped the only valuable gift apart from her pearls that Rupert had given her. It had not been bought with his mother's money but bequeathed to him 'to give your dear wife when you marry' by his godmother. Emeralds and diamonds.

'Do you think my son and I might live on this for a

while?' She handed him the glittering band, and Jensen looked at it with an expert eye.

'Very comfortably. For a year. Probably two. Do you wish me to have it sold for you?'

Her pale face was slightly flushed.

'You are very kind. I thought I must do it for myself, and came to ask you how.'

'I tremble to think of the price some country pawnbroker would give you. Always provided he was willing to risk offending the ruling family, Lady Coryot. My bank has a branch in the City. We will open a small account for you there.'

She smiled and positively glowed as if sunlight, or perhaps footlights, shone on her.

'How shall I ever thank you?'

'By succeeding.'

Aston did look beautiful now that she knew she was leaving it. It stood at the end of its tree-edged drive in all its pride that dull spring evening, beginning to shine out here and there with lights. Such a vast and elaborate monument, its honeycombs filled with the booty of hundreds of years, swarming with servants, hung with tapestries. She detested its tyranny. But it did look beautiful.

It was an hour before dinner, and she changed rather earlier than usual and walked from her wing of the house to the nurseries. She found Nurse Digby accompanied by one of the nursery maids. Kit was being bathed. Both women stood up as Stella came into the room, tall and pale in a white gauze dress striped with satin and a deeply fringed silk scarf.

'I would like to speak to you alone, Nurse.'

Nurse Digby dismissed the nursery maid, and Stella sat down at the table.

'Yes, my lady?'

'Nurse. I am leaving Aston. And taking Kit with me.'

There was a silence as the older woman looked at her.

143

Then, 'I beg your pardon, my lady. But I had gathered Kit was staying here.'

Stella had forgotten the way the most confidential family news always travelled through the house in some mysterious way.

'Yes, it's true,' she said, 'Lady Tyrrell asked me to go, providing that I left Kit behind. What she does not know is that I mean to leave and take him with me. I'm going to work in London.'

It was a bombshell indeed but Nurse Digby's face did not show it.

'Nurse,' Stella went on earnestly, 'I know you belong to the family and can't approve of what I'm going to do. But my mind is made up. You're the only person I shall tell because of course you are with Kit and he is leaving. I've been very unhappy here. I'm sure you know that. I suppose everybody does. Well, I can bear it no longer. You've been so good to Kit. I want to thank you for everything. I don't know how I shall manage without you.'

Nurse Digby picked up her knitting in silence. The needles clicked.

Stella looked round the nursery. Her eyes took in the things she had never exactly noticed and certainly never prized. The silvery glitter of the high brass fireguard. The nursery pictures and the flaring nostrilled old rocking horse Rupert had ridden as a child. The comfortable furniture, worn and solid. Nurse Digby's kingdom was safe and created for a child. To what kind of life was poor little Kit going to next?

Without realising it, she sighed.

Nurse Digby looked up from her knitting.

'You won't have to manage without me, my lady,' she said.

Stella blushed crimson.

'You never thought I'd let him out of my sight, did you?' went on Nurse Digby. 'If we must go, then we must. We'll be packed by morning. Do we take the 10.15?'

'*Oh Nurse!*'

'The 9.15 would be better, come to think of it. The

144

Marchioness always has her late breakfast of a Thursday. We'll be gone before she knows it.'

The trio left on a morning of low grey cloud and not a breath of wind. As the carriage went down the drive away from the great house, the little boy chattered merrily. Neither his mother nor his nurse replied.

With the unquestioning service of the upper servants, nobody had thought the departure out of the ordinary. Where Nurse Digby went was always organised to the last gold safety-pin.

Stella left a letter in her bedroom for her mother-in-law. With no address.

PART THREE

London and France 1914–1918

Chapter Ten

On a Sunday afternoon in July 1914 the bell of a pleasant house in Victoria Grove, Kensington was pealed impatiently by a tall young man standing in the porch.

The door was opened by an elderly woman; she looked at him with some disapproval.

'Mr Collingwood, she is not expecting you.'

'Nursie, when am I not welcome?'

Nurse Digby showed him into the house, thinking to herself that actors had more wheedling ways than children. Teddy Collingwood threw down his straw hat and strode confidently down the passage towards the garden door. It was open, and framed a brilliant picture of sunny lawns and flowerbeds. A woman in a trailing white dress lay reclined under a cherry tree.

When she saw him Stella stretched out her hand.

'Teddy, how nice. But I thought you were on the river, elegantly punting and making eyes at Pansy Lonnen.'

'Perhaps I'd prefer to make eyes at you.'

She gave a lazy smile. At twenty-eight Stella had lost the constraints of being 'the Colonial girl' and had flowered. Her creamy face had charming lines and angles, her cheeks were slightly hollowed which gave her at times the look of an impudent boy. Her great dark eyes swam, and her alluring voice now and then had a faint echo of a foreign tongue. Life in the theatre suited her and it showed. Engaged by Patrick Bird at the Kean as one of twenty-five frilled and simpering girls in the chorus, she had soon learned to twirl a parasol, to dance, and to sing the catchy tunes of the absurd musical comedy songs. The first of these began 'Little Heart, beat-beat-beating,' and described Stella's own state of mind at the start of her career.

By one of those chances which later seem inevitable, Patrick Bird gave her a duet with Teddy Collingwood. The two had things in common. Both were young and ambitious, both were beginners and curiously enough, both were fugitives. Stella had run from towers and terraces, Teddy from the suburbs. He had been ill as a boy with a patch on his lung, and much coddled by his parents. When he grew up and his health improved, he announced that he wanted to go on the stage; his family were horrified. They behaved as if he had chosen a life of crime.

Teddy Collingwood had the face of a monkey, with a big mouth and long upper lip; his figure was thin and lounging with a gawky grace, his singing voice was not strong and slightly hoarse, but there was something engaging and boyish about him. Stella had beauty, Teddy had charm. From their first duet onstage, they matched. Teddy's health, it was true, was uncertain and once he was away in a sanatorium in the country. Stella missed him dreadfully as a companion as well as a partner. Then back he had come, and together they steadily rose in the public's affection. They were now the twin stars of the Kean's latest success, *Sweet Violets*.

Sprawling in the sunshine, Teddy remarked that it was a relief to be with somebody who was not talking about the crisis.

'Everybody says we're on the brink of catastrophe,' he said. 'At the Garrick last night, though, most of the fellows agreed that if there *is* a war, it's nothing to do with England.'

'I hate talking about it,' Stella said.

He looked at her.

'I always forget you were once in a war, darling. It wasn't a very big one, was it? I remember how excited we children were at the relief of Mafeking. We waved flags.'

'I was on the other side,' she said dryly. Adding, for she preferred to talk of work, 'Didn't the "Don't Really Know

You" number go badly last night. Shall we run through it?'

'*Must* we? It's Sunday.'

Looking sulky, he followed her through the French windows into the drawing-room. Stella's house was spacious and fashionably decorated; there was a good deal of satinwood, much white paint and quantities of flowers. Sentimental water colours hung on the walls, and gold-framed programmes printed on satin. There was a romantic pastel of Kit looking uncannily like his dead father.

Sighing, Teddy sat down at the grand piano and played the opening bars of the number Stella had mentioned.

'I don't really know you, do I?

You don't really love me, do you?'

They sang with feeling.

'Mm,' said Stella as it ended, raising her eyebrows.

Looking cross, he played the chorus again. When he began to sing he looked into her eyes, smiling like a lover: but only during the song.

'Not bad,' Stella allowed.

'Slave driver.'

But he stayed on and she invited him to supper.

'Oh good, champagne. Now, Stella, I shall tell you some news,' he said, brightening. 'I saw somebody you know at the Garrick last night. Have a guess. Mop of silver hair. Big heavy figure. What one would call a presence.'

Stella shrugged.

'No idea. Any actor who specialises in dukes and fathers.'

'Warmer than you think! I'll surprise you – it was your Pa-in-law!'

He burst into a roar of laughter. Stella did not join him. Teddy, Patrick Bird, and other people who were friends knew something of her history. Society people coming to the Kean occasionally recalled that the actress Stella Bredon had been married to poor Rupert Flood, years ago, hadn't she? But the story was too old to be interesting. Stella's fame had been gradual and her previous life had never made a stir. When journalists found that she closed up like a clam

151

if questioned about it, they stopped doing so. Her silence proved surprisingly effective. She did not even talk of the past with her friends.

Now she was snappish, saying to Teddy that she could not think how he had recognised the Marquess.

'But I didn't. He was pointed out to me. It will annoy you, Stella, when I say I thought he looked a jolly old buffer. He was dining with Herbert Tree and being very happy and gracious.'

'He used to be quite kind to me.'

'Stop scowling. Your secret is safe with me and half London. But it would be fun if you told me something about your life as a Viscountess. It would help me from brooding over the newspapers.'

'There's nothing to tell.'

He ignored that. 'When Minnie married Lord Whatshisname, she met the Floods,' he said reminiscently. 'She told me they were a lot of Victorian diehards. You chose the toughest bit of the upper crust.'

'I didn't know one crust from another. How would I? A little girl from the Transvaal.'

'You can't wipe out your one-time life as if it had never happened, Stella. For instance, Kit will have to know sometime. He's a Viscount, isn't he? You haven't let on but I bet he's found out. Children are so sly.'

'Kit is eleven. The old buffer you admired at the Garrick will probably live to be a hundred. One of his aunts lived to be ninety-eight and drank a pint of stout for breakfast every morning.'

'Now darling, that *is* what I call a romantic past.'

It was impossible to stay annoyed with Teddy, and she consented to tell him a little about Aston. He asked numerous questions, laughed, and disagreed that she had been badly treated.

'They had a point of view too,' he declared, annoying her again.

When he said good night, he kissed her tenderly.

'I enjoyed hearing about you in Society, darling. But

your present's quite interesting too. Whom do you love now?'

'Perhaps nobody.'

'I can't believe that. You look much too pretty.'

When he had gone, she smiled to herself as she went up to her room. She sat down and unpinned her long hair. Most of the girls at the Kean had lovers and were afraid Patrick Bird would find this out. He had worked with George Edwardes and knew the value of keeping beautiful girls at the arm's length of their throngs of admirers. Some girls ended their butterfly careers in brilliant marriages, flying from the stage door through the lodge gates into Society. Despite Stella's fleeting vexation at other girls succeeding where she had humiliatingly failed, she would not have exchanged the highest Aston success for her life now. Her career moved from one success to another. Young men begged to be allowed to take her out. Flowers did not come in bunches but in cascades: lilies and Malmaison roses, big bunches of Parma violets in which, sometimes, a diamond brooch was hidden. It was the fashion to send back the diamonds.

Being a musical comedy star was not all bouquets. Three times a week Stella went to the rehearsal rooms to practise her dancing, working for hours to the sound of a tinny piano in a building jangling with other tinny pianos. She worked daily on her voice and had singing lessons. On Sunday mornings she answered scores of letters, posting her admirers photographs of herself, signed with a flourish. She enjoyed it all, the discipline, the work, the applause, the popularity.

During the first year in London she and Kit and his nurse had lived in a small shabby house at the end of Fulham. They had been supported only by Stella's small wage and the emerald bracelet. With Stella at work morning, noon and night, it was Nurse Digby who found a way of making the poky rooms comfortable, who kept Kit healthy and happy, and who faced without comment the loneliness and lack of any luxury in this unfamiliar new life.

But things improved as Stella's wages rose. If she

flowered in the warm theatre air, the other Aston deserter, facing the cold wind of the park and the uncongenial London atmosphere, did not. Hazel Digby remained the same self-contained and formidable person who had accompanied Stella into the wilderness. She had lived for years wearing the glory of 'her' family's high position, and had been called Nurse Flood. Society nurses took the name of the family they served. She had driven away from Aston without a backward look, her eyes fixed on the child in her lap.

The early years during which Stella had little money had not appeared to worry Hazel Digby. Stella was too busy and self-absorbed to appreciate that Kit had well-made clothes, nourishing food and a warm nursery. When Stella began to earn more and they moved away from the Fulham back-street, Nurse Digby did go as far as mentioning a few extras needed for her boy. Later it was she who reminded Stella to put Kit's name down for a suitable school (she suggested one of good reputation, little used by the aristocracy). Suddenly, it seemed to both women, Kit was eight years old and leaving for his new school, Pearson House in Sussex. Dressed in brand new uniform, his large eyes brimmed.

'There, there, my lamb, you look a treat and mind you write to your Mama every Sunday, and to old Nursie too if you have time,' said Hazel Digby, hugging him.

'I shall write to you every day,' sobbed the child.

When the little boy, delivered to the school, was accompanied into a crowd of other small boys, disappearing like a fish into a shoal, Stella wailed.

'Oh, *why* must we send our children to these awful places?'

'They are not awful. Rupert, Des and Harry thoroughly enjoyed school. Rupert won two cups at Eton, and Des was a wonder at the paper-chase. Harry was the boxer of the family. Come to think of it, we should have taken those cups of Rupert's with us. Kit will appreciate them when he grows up.'

'Nurse, *please!*'

It was Stella's usual sigh if Aston was mentioned between them.

Hazel Digby took a train to the new school when Kit had been there for a week. She found her charge perfectly recovered, and demanding a parcel of home-made cakes.

Kit loved the two women in his life. His mother was beautiful and famous, and postcards of her were in the tobacconist's window in the village near school. He was envied for having a remarkable parent. One small boy said, 'Every time my father opens a packet of cigarettes, your mother falls out!' Kit confided in his friends that his father had been killed while hunting.

'He jumped this huge high fence and was thrown. I was too young so I don't remember him.'

The story gave Kit a further cachet.

'I s'pose they didn't take you to the funeral?'

'No. I wish they had.'

But although his dead father was a romantic legend and his mother a fascinating fact, Nursie was Kit's reality. She looked after him when he had splitting headaches followed by vomiting: he had unknowingly inherited the 'Flood migraine'. When he woke as a little child and walked into Nursie's dark bedroom, he had only to stand like a silent ghost by her bed for her to wake at once.

'I feel sick.'

'Do you, Lamb? Let's see how we can make it better.'

It was in his letters to Nursie that he boasted of triumphs or confessed disasters. Now that he was at public school (also selected by Hazel Digby as neither too large nor too small) the elderly woman realised that her charge would soon be gone from her. She knew that the season of childhood was brief and beautiful and could not last. But he still kissed her goodnight with a throttling hug, and saved only for her his most appalling jokes.

While they were living in the narrow Fulham house Theo Jensen visited, his glittering motor looking very out of place in the back street. He always visited them when banking affairs brought him to London. He made a fuss of the little boy and brought Hazel Digby a silk umbrella from New

155

York. He made a point of seeing all Stella's shows at least twice each, and commented acutely on her performances. He took her out to dine, but did not pay court to her.

From the first they liked and understood each other. They had something in common for both had grown up in a strict atmosphere of duty and piety. New England and the Transvaal might be separated by oceans and national flags but were originally and essentially Dutch. When Theo talked of his father Stella saw an image of Uncle Hendrik; one of his aunts had the same grim character as Neeltge Maritz. There were even hymns which they discovered they had both sung as children.

Theo Jensen enjoyed work and she had an idea that in the world of finance he was something of a pirate. He was also a man of the senses who appreciated beautiful women, fine food and good wines. He had an eye for the way things looked and Stella always wore her prettiest clothes when she was with him. During the first years of their friendship he taught her a good deal. She had lived among the rich without a penny of her own, and Theo said she must learn both how to earn and how to spend. Although she still had little money, he knew she would borrow nothing from him, he had to be content with giving her expensive presents. He also talked to her about her parents, having remarked with amusement that he had noticed how she was 'wonderfully disinterested in the authors of her being', and had asked him nothing about them. Stella was rather annoyed since it was true. The fact was they had never seemed real to her, but figures she felt she had invented.

Theo had known them well. They were much older than he and he had admired them, often visiting them in their pretty riverside house outside New York. George Vredenberg was the son of a Dutchman who had grown up in New York. He had had little education but was clever, ambitious and interested, like his forebears, in land. He began to buy and sell property and in his short life (he was thirty when he died) had almost begun to be rich. His wife was a tall shy New York girl with the same thick silvery-blonde hair as her daughter, warmhearted, domesticated and with a singing voice like a nightingale. They had been devoted to each other and to their spoiled little daughter. They had died of a virulent influenza in the winter of 1886, and when the lawyers had paid George's business debts, many of which in future would have made money, there was scarcely enough left for the child's fare to South Africa.

'So you see,' Theo finished, 'from whom you sprang.' When she was alone, Stella thought about all he had told her, imagining those two lost parents. She had inherited two things: her father's determination and her mother's voice. They had left her nothing and everything.

During Stella's second London winter the Kean was dark for some weeks, following the failure of a lavish musical comedy. It had cost a mint of money, had been set in early eighteenth century France with châteaux and gardens and real fountains and a scene at the Court of Versailles. Apparently the public did not want historical romance and the show closed. Patrick was desperately looking for something modern.

Stella was unemployed and fretting when Theo arrived from America. Over tea at Fulham he suggested a visit to Paris.

'You're too thin. We'll fatten you up at the Ritz.'

Stella, paler and more nervous than usual, managed a laugh.

'It's kind of you, Theo, but how can I leave Kit and Nurse?'

'I never suggested that you should. Bring 'em with you. They can chaperone us. Nurse can walk the little chap round the Luxembourg Gardens and disapprove of all those statues of the French Queens. Meanwhile I shall take you about.'

Stella accepted.

The Channel crossing was rough and Nurse and Kit, with most of the other passengers, stayed below. But Theo and Stella went on deck to watch the huge waves showing yellowish teeth and to listen to their roar. She was excited by the fierce weather and the knife-sharp air. The ship heaved, she slipped and he put out a strong arm to support

157

her. As she leaned against him, he gave her a violent kiss. Stella responded passionately, and Theo, drawing away, looked at her with heavy eyes.

'We will be together in Paris,' he said, tracing the shape of her mouth with his finger. 'Good.'

It had been good. It was a long time since she had been in Harry's arms, and although thoughts of him still had the power to hurt, it was impossible to yearn any longer. Theo and she had a satisfying week in Paris. He was a sensual man and a practised lover who knew how to give pleasure. He enjoyed life and Stella too. If he did not love her, and Stella thought he did not for all their mutual physical delight, why, what did that matter? Her own feelings seemed to match his and there was never a time when he appeared to ask for more than she gave. Since then, whenever he was in London they made love. Their feelings were steady . . .

Remembering Teddy's teasing remarks about her looks, Stella smiled, thinking that if it were true then Theo must be responsible. She liked the idea. She wondered why tonight she had actually been willing to talk to Teddy about the past. And then she thought of Harry and of Aston. Wasn't tomorrow the day in August when Millicent always gave her yearly garden party? I suppose she still does, thought Stella, for nothing in Aston changes. The tents and marquees will be up by now, and the roundabout will have arrived. I always wanted to ride it.

The next day dawned in London and in Oxfordshire with a clear blue sky. It was a wonderful summer, a time for picnics, boating and swimming in the river, for playing croquet or lying in a hammock under the trees. It was a pastoral. When Catherine left her books on the lawn one night, she had found them bone-dry the next morning.

The flag on the Aston tower drooped in the windless air; pigeons cooed. The tents were all in place and the children's roundabout and the trestle tables, covered with starched white, were placed in symmetrical rows. There were two bran tubs, stalls of home-made jams, honey, and cross-

158

stitched tablecloths. There were bucketfuls of flowers, the blue spires of lupins, cabbage roses, roundfaced daisies and huge vivid poppies.

For two hours Millicent moved about, up and down the rows of stalls, in and out of the tents, pointing with her furled parasol, examining and commenting to her attendants, the bailiff and the head gardener. Her garden party was organised down to the last detail. By midafternoon the crowds had arrived. Ladies in cartwheel hats wreathed with artificial flowers and fruit, moved about under fringed parasols. The villagers wore Sunday best – suits and sprigged prints – and looked hot and jolly, their hands tugged by excited children. The roundabout wheezed its music and shots cracked out from the shooting booth.

Harry Flood, on his last day of leave, had been flirting with the pretty cousin whom Rupert had half loved once upon a time. Mary was now married with three children, but still gave swimming looks which she did not mean. Desmond and Elinor were graciously talking to the villagers; since his brother's death Desmond had assumed a slight manner of being heir. His father was enjoying himself with his own friends, having no sense of duty. Catherine, whose sense of duty was over-developed, was busy all the time. She was at her mother's beck and call, ready to help in the smallest tasks, and most of all ready to agree with anything Millicent suggested: a perfectly trained lady-in-waiting.

Strolling through the crowd after Mary had left him, Harry saw a certain straw hat piled with pink silk roses. He came up behind his sister and pinched her arm. She grimaced at him and offered him her tray of real roses.

'You're supposed to buy one and pay me a sovereign.'

He gave her the coin and sniffed the flower's petals.

'Sergeant should paint you in that hat, Cath.'

'He already has.'

He burst out laughing.

'Nobody told me. Where is the picture?'

'Back in Mr Sergeant's studio. Mama asked him to redo it a little. She said he made my nose too big.'

'But he's right. It is a beak,' he teased her.

'He could have lied, couldn't he?'

Threading their way past a row of stalls, they finally came to the railing which separated garden from park. The hay had been cut weeks ago, the sloping fields looked dry. The sky's intense colour was reflected in the lake which shone like blue steel. Brother and sister leaned on the railing.

'I wish you weren't going. You said your leave would be longer.'

'I know, Cath. But I've been recalled.'

She hesitated, then said, 'Is there really a reason to worry?'

'People think so.'

'But Papa said everyone in London believes we should stay out.'

'They do. But can we stand by and watch one little country being gobbled by a larger one? And you know how the Germans are determined to rival us at sea.'

She sighed. 'I don't know anything,' she said discontentedly. 'I can't talk about things like this to Mama, she thinks it "unsuitable". As for Papa, I listen when he's talking to other people, but women even being interested in politics, unless they're married to Cabinet Ministers, are *not* his cup of tea. And one's friends, Harry! A lot of silly young men playing that silly game with tin soldiers invented by the Churchill set.'

She described a visit the previous week to a local manor house where their friends the Fairfaxes lived. Basil Fairfax 'has boringly asked to marry me'. He and half a dozen other young men had spent the evening lying on the floor in the conservatory, playing with battalions of toy soldiers.

'I wanted to talk and finished up wanting to scream. When I told Mama, all she said was I could have learned the game like other girls had. She said it just showed why I'm not married. Then we had the lecture about how she dislikes "an old bride".'

Harry's dark eyes were fixed on her face.

'How old are you, for heaven's sake? Twenty-two?'

'I call that brotherly love. I'm nearly twenty-four.'

'Ah. Of course. One foot in the grave. Now, Cath, listen to me. You're pretty and clever, and it's time you learned to ignore our mother's mania for child brides. One would think she was an Indian Maharanee.'

'Oh Harry, I do love you.'

'So you should.'

The garden party went on. The grass was flat and littered with dying rose-petals, children whirled round on the painted red-nostrilled horses or trotted by holding gas balloons of patriotic red, white and blue. It was after seven before the party began to end. Catherine was so tired. There had not been a single thing she had done the entire day without first having to consult her mother; that was more fatiguing than standing for twelve hours. Up the drive the villagers were trailing in a long procession; the Aston guests were leaving in their motors or had gone into the house. Servants were dismantling the stalls. Catherine was helping in the big marquee when Harry came looking for her.

'Come along. You're being kidnapped.'

'Harry, I can't. I promised to stack the cups.'

'Mother has thirty people running about after her and she can't have you any longer. Look slippy or we'll be nabbed.'

He took her across the gardens and through a gate into the meadows. They went along a path which skirted the hawthorn hedge, then climbed a steep rise of ground. On the crown of the hill stood a group of trees called the Astonwold Ring. It was the place where Harry used to take her when she was a small child. There was a pond among the trees: in winter it was black with rotting leaves and in summer it skidded with creatures called boatmen; Harry could never coax her to swim among those, but *he* did. Sometimes they both climbed the trees, sitting on the springy boughs. Catherine liked to pretend she was riding a fiery hunter and could jump high fences...

Now they sat down on the dry grass. She unpinned her hat which was heavy and dragged at her hair.

'Another Aston garden party over,' she said, yawning.

'Perhaps there won't be one next August.'

'Oh. I never thought of that.'

It was quiet after the noise of the afternoon. Gnats rose and fell in clouds over the water. Catherine was content. Harry had always been the brother she loved the best. The elusive one. The rebel against their mother, he still completely understood why *her* love and admiration for Millicent kept her meek. She looked at Harry smilingly, but his next words startled her.

'Did Father tell you he saw Stella in London recently?'

She stared. Then said slowly, 'Of course he didn't. We never speak of her.'

'That old feud.'

'It's scarcely a feud, Harry, it's too long ago. But Mama was right about her, it *was* dreadful the way she ran off and took Rupert's little boy. So cruel and vulgar.'

'You have the family strategy very pat.'

Catherine was hurt; she could not bear him not to be pleased with her.

'Don't you think she was cruel?'

He leaned against the tree trunk and said thoughtfully, 'No more than we were. Well, *you* may have been kind to her. The rest of us certainly weren't.'

Catherine said nothing. She knew she had behaved no differently from the others, but her conscience was clear about her sister-in-law. It was typical of Harry's contrary nature that he should feel, or pretend to feel, otherwise. How they had talked Stella over that spring when she left Aston! They had all agreed that her behaviour put her finally outside the pale. The problem of her taking the Flood heir with her would have to be solved eventually. But at present to do anything about Kit would mean a scandal. That had been her mother's ruling with which Catherine wholeheartedly agreed. From that time onwards nobody spoke about Stella at Aston, not even Harry. And their friends politely followed suit. Now that Stella was quite famous, thought Catherine, the drama was over. Not forgotten, but over.

'Surely Papa did not actually meet her?' she could not help asking.

'Oh, he didn't go as far as that,' Harry said, with an uncomfortable smile. 'He went to see her show, *The Daisy Chain*. Cosmo Derbyshire and his family persuaded him. I think it amused them that he had never seen her on the stage. He told me she sang like a bird and danced the tango.'

They looked solemnly at the incongruous image.

'But he didn't meet her?' persisted Catherine.

'Can you imagine Mother's face if he had?'

Harry did not know why, but his father's drawling description of Stella had told on his nerves. 'Damned handsome, my dear fellow, a figure like Venus. And that voice! Come on a trifle since she was at Aston, what?'

Harry had thought of Stella today. He remembered her at one of the garden parties, going to the shooting booth with Rupert and scandalising him by handling the rifle as expertly as a trooper. He remembered her in a white trailing dress and a huge ribboned hat, standing by the roundabout while Kit, no more than three years old, circled round astride a horse. He had seen in Stella's face a positive yearning to jump on the roundabout too.

He had been deeply shaken and bitterly guilty when Stella ran away. He had imagined horrors, until the letter arrived from a reputable solicitor saying she wished to sever all connection with the family 'until such time as her son comes into his inheritance'. It stated that she and the child were in good health, she was working for her living and had changed her name.

She had utterly disappeared from their lives, but not from his imagination.

Two or three years later, returning from a spell at sea, he had been in London and had walked past the Kean Theatre. He stopped very suddenly. Rogueishly smiling from under a lace parasol was a large picture of Stella. Stella Bredon, said the poster. He was surprised at how much her familiar face and great dark eyes upset him. He found it literally impossible to step into the theatre and buy a seat.

163

Other women had come into his life and left it. He was always in and out of some love affair or other. Why did he think of Stella? And why now?

Brother and sister were wrapped in their own thoughts. The country was full of little sounds. Birds chirped and gnats droned. The wind of evening faintly sighed and far away a village clock chimed. Down the hill, Aston's towers were full of shadows.

'Isn't it absurd, Cath,' he said at last. 'To think of Stella dancing away on the London stage, and all this time not one of us has seen her. Until the Derbyshires dragged my father to the theatre for fun.'

'You mean you would like to see her too.'

'Wouldn't you?'

Catherine thought about that. She remembered Stella as eager, spirited, and worrying. Most of all, she remembered the way she had sung.

'I might like to see her,' she said, with all Catherine's delicate caution. 'I would certainly like to see little Kit. Do you think it might be possible – with Mama, I mean? As it is all such ages ago?'

He laughed.

'Oh Cath.'

Chapter Eleven

After war broke out, Stella found miserably that she could not share the feelings of everybody else in London. She felt a resentful stranger. When Patrick assembled the company together that August morning, the news had been greeted, literally, with cheers and champagne in the Green Room. Stella had gone out into the street and people were rushing by with strange excited faces, shouting 'War! War!' Men and girls were marching down the road, their arms linked, chanting 'Down with Germany!'

It was September now, but the feeling of euphoria continued and everything in London had startlingly changed. The Kean and many other theatres were shut. Lights at night must be dimmed with only a few shaded street lamps allowed. Blinds had to be drawn in upper windows before rooms were lit. All this was 'to make the identification of places and buildings more difficult for enemy aircraft'. Many of the young actors from the Kean had enlisted and vanished into training, and everywhere in London there was khaki. As the troops marched by in their ill-fitting uniforms, people gaily waved. How warlike everybody had become. Stella could not bear it.

Teddy Collingwood came to Victoria Grove, very cast down because he had not been passed medically fit.

'How can I walk about in civilian clothes?' he demanded, adding in a martyred tone that she was unsympathetic.

'I don't share your Land of Hope and Glorification.'

'We've got to wipe Germany off the map.'

'Maybe they're stronger than we think.'

'*We* are stronger than *they* think. Your Dutch blood is showing.'

Stella sighed. After the unending summer, the lawn was

165

parched, its silvery dryness reminding her of another land. Not a walled-in London garden, but thousands upon thousands of miles baking in the January droughts . . .

It was a relief when Theo telephoned to say he was in London for a while and could he take her to luncheon if she was not too busy?

'Dear Theo, I long to see you and I am out of work.'

She walked through the park, inevitably seeing how much the familiar stretch of flowers and trees had changed in less than two months. No sparkling carriages. No elegant young men galloping in the Row. A few children with their nurses, and a group of khaki-clad soldiers marching towards Hyde Park Corner.

When she was shown into the drawing room of the Park Lane house, Theo was by the window, his heavy figure outlined against the autumn trees. He smiled when he saw her and came over to take both her hands: they never kissed when they met. His grasp was painful, and her rings bit into her fingers.

'Let me look at you. Very pretty. Sit down and amuse me, I've been in male company for too long. So you are out of work. That's a rare state for you, Stella.'

'Patrick closed the Kean when war was declared. Most of the shows closed except a revival of *Nobby, V.C.* and people are flocking to that. All I do is stupid charity concerts.'

'Are you not happy, then?' he asked.

Sitting straight-backed, small feet in bronze shoes crossed, she looked elegant and dispirited.

'Oh Theo, one is doing nothing useful. I know I'm wrong, but all this talk of honour and sacrifice makes me miserable. It does so remind me of the commandos. *They* sang hymns and in London it's recruiting songs but the result is just the same. Uncle Hendrik said they would drive the English into the sea. Over here they say we will eat our Christmas dinners in Berlin.'

'Ah, you've seen a war before.'

She gave her shoulders a little shake, and said he did not want to listen to her selfish anxieties.

'But they're feminine ones. I'm always glad to hear about those.'

They went to luncheon at the Ritz where she was given many interested glances. She was recognised wherever she went.

When Theo remarked on it, she shrugged.

'It's not having been at the Kean, Theo, as you very well know. It's those blooming postcards and I've you to thank for them!'

Two years ago Theo had met a young and ambitious photographer who was on the lookout, as he described it, for a new face to launch. Saying that he sounded like a man searching for Helen of Troy, Theo promptly sent him to meet Stella. Since then Stella's face was seen on postcards all over England. She smiled from photographers' windows, wrapped in furs against cottonwool snowstorms, leaning over country gates twined with calico honeysuckle. She stood on the summits of cardboard mountains, patted kittens, emerged from gigantic Easter eggs, wore meringues of tulle or ribboned bonnets or pearl chokers. People made Stella Bredon collections.

During luncheon Stella asked Theo about the journey from New York, wasn't it very dangerous now to cross the Atlantic? He shrugged the question away. He never wished to talk of himself. What he wanted was to be with this odd, beautiful woman, to listen to her with amusement, admire her and when she wished it, make love to her. She had a particular perfume which was nothing to do with his complexities of finance and the difficulty of getting to a Europe now at war. Studying her now, and seeing the dissatisfaction in her eyes, he suddenly said:

'If you dislike not being useful, as you call it, why don't you get some actors together and some pretty girls and go to France. To amuse the troops?'

She widened her large eyes.

'Ah, I see the idea appeals. It's better than brooding over the Transvaal. It might give you something more satisfying to think about.'

'But it's magnificent!' burst out Stella. 'Theo, surely it's

167

impossible? I can't just go to the War Office and ask them.'

'War is the business of the generals, Stella. Entertainment is yours. In this world, what is usually needed is an introduction.'

'Oh Theo.'

'What a glutton for work you are.'

Early the next morning a letter came from Theo by hand, saying that Sir Gerald Brooke-Gould would see her at midday. 'Look on it,' wrote Theo, 'as an audition.'

Dressed to kill in black and white velvet, and carrying a large ermine muff, Stella arrived at the War Office and was ushered into a lofty room commanded by a portrait of an elderly Queen Victoria.

Sir Gerald Brooke-Gould did not keep her waiting long. He greeted her courteously. A colourful figure, his scarlet tabs vivid, his gold buttons burnished to silver, thick-set and fiftyish, he reminded Stella of her father-in-law. It was something in the smile and the drawling accent.

It was obvious to her when she began to talk (Theo had said nothing in his letter about her plan, merely arranging the appointment), that the idea of entertaining the troops had never entered the General's head and that he rather wished it had not entered Stella's.

'But what kind of entertainment, Miss Bredon? How many actors would you take?'

'Six or seven. A show of music and dancing and jokes. Something to amuse the troops and bring them a message from home.'

'Who would finance such a project?'

'Mr Jensen says that he would be willing to do so.'

'Indeed. Most generous.'

There was a telling pause. He looked at her with an expression she had many times seen on the Marquess' face. It said, 'You are a mere woman, for all that you're a pretty one.'

'France now is scarcely the place for young ladies. There is great discomfort ... even hardship,' he muttered. His face cleared. He had the air of somebody who had found a way to refuse.

'I was in that other war, General.'

Seeing his surprise, she spoke about the Transvaal and Meidoorn. About food shortages. Dangers. They had been attacked. 'But we managed. We survived.' Tactfully she did not mention that the British had burned down the farm.

He looked at her now with a grudging respect.

'I see that I am faced with a warrior, although alas she was on the other side. Well. I did promise Mr Jensen I would give you a fair hearing, Miss Bredon, although he wisely did not tell me what I was to hear. Very well, I will put your proposition forward to Lord Kitchener. Does that satisfy you?'

'It would be wonderful!'

'I promise nothing. But if you were given permission, when would you wish to start?'

'On Christmas Eve.' It had been Theo's idea.

'My dear young lady, do you imagine the British Army is going to stop fighting at Christmas and sit down to a turkey dinner?'

'I just imagined,' she said engagingly, 'they would be pleased to see us.'

The General allowed himself a smile, and bade her goodbye. Stella walked thoughtfully down the staircase to the ground floor, bowed in reply to a smart salute from the Corporal at the door, and found herself face to face with someone entering the building.

It was Catherine Flood.

Both young women stopped dead, Stella surprised and smiling, Catherine blushing a painful crimson.

'Why, Cathy, what are *you* doing in the War Office?' exclaimed Stella.

'I am having luncheon with Papa,' was the embarrassed reply. 'He has a post here now.'

It was very obvious that despite the invisible bond of politeness which kept her, Catherine longed to escape. But Stella could not help lingering a little, thinking it extraordinary to see her again. She gave her a friendly look; she was composed and charming and startlingly elegant in her black and white. Catherine looked dowdy beside her.

'I have been trying to persuade a General to let me do some work in France,' she said. 'I am not sure yet if I shall be allowed.'

Catherine had stopped blushing. She now resumed, like a woman wrapping herself with a practised gesture in a cloak, her usual poise. With a faint gleam of interest she asked if Stella meant to take up nursing.

'Nothing so praiseworthy, I'm afraid. I want to take a concert party to France.'

The interest faded from Catherine's eyes as she nodded politely. Then said she must go, as her father was expecting her. They said goodbye and Catherine walked away.

Driving home, Stella thought about the brief meeting. She had forgotten how clearly one could sense disapprobation: of all the Floods, Catherine had always been the one who said the most by speaking the least. She has not forgiven me, thought Stella with indifferent wonder, so I suppose she is still reflecting her mother. Poor Cath, is she married yet? It would have been impossible to ask a Flood such a question.

A week after her visit to the War Office, Stella received a letter from the General saying that Lord Kitchener had approved. Enclosed was a copy of a telegram from Lord French, Commander-in-Chief in the Field.

'Deeply indebted to Miss Bredon for offering her services and those of other members of her profession. She will be allowed to give concerts in camps and hospitals at Le Havre, Rouen, Abbeville and Boulogne.'

When Theo came to Victoria Grove that day, Stella ran into the hall and threw her arms round his neck. Instinctively, he pressed her close. Then he said, 'And what is that for?'

'Oh Theo. Must it be for something?'
'Of course.'

Like every other actor, Stella disliked seeing a theatre dark.
The Kean had been shut since *Sweet Violets* ended on
August 4th. There were no bright posters outside, no
photographs of crowds of beautiful girls or better still, large
studies of Teddy and herself. Patrick was in his office on
the telephone. Waving her to a seat without smiling, he
continued to talk, his conversation consisting of little but
'Oh quite. Yes. Quite.'

He finally put down the telephone.

'That was a new composer I wanted for a show. He's just
joined up after five hours in a queue with hundreds of
others.'

He looked across at Stella with suspicion. She was
sniffing the bunch of Parma violets pinned to her fur
muff.

'Why are *you* here? Who's offered you a leading role
somewhere else?'

'As if I would leave you and the Kean.'

'You'd leave tomorrow if it suited you. There isn't a drop
of loyalty in an actor's veins.'

She giggled.

'As a matter of fact, I've come with a different kind of
offer,' she said, and took Lord French's telegram out of her
muff. 'I suppose you wouldn't consider managing the
concert party?'

He read the telegram.

Then he glanced up with bloodshot blue eyes.

'Of course I will. And you should have let me go to the
War Office. If I'd done so, we'd be in France by now.'

Patrick engaged eight players, including a pair of jugglers,
a Scots comedian and two pretty girls who called themselves
The Snowbells. He was tetchy when Stella had suggested
the girls.

171

'I've never been able to stick them. Powder puffs on legs. Squeaky voices.'

'They'll be just what the troops love.'

He shuddered.

'Dimples and ringlets. Very well. We will sign up the simpering Snowbells.'

Patrick's attitude not only to the two young girls, but to most women, interested Stella. He was deep as the ocean about his private life, and she sometimes wondered if he preferred men. But since he was at his theatre from breakfast until midnight, was there room for a private life at all? Theo once said that a man so absorbed in his work might find a celibate life suited him. Stella was not sure.

It was freezing cold when she left in a taxi for Victoria Station. A foggy December morning with moisture suspended in the smutty air. Nurse Digby had gone down to the Sussex cottage which Stella had bought some years before, 'to give Kit a little country air'. Kit and Nurse Digby would be spending their Christmas holidays there. Once again she, not Stella, would act as the boy's mother.

Stella, wrapped in a voluminous sable coat following Patrick's instructions to 'look beautiful and *keep warm*', stared from the taxi window. Flags everywhere. Drooping from windows and balconies, hanging above shops, stirring in the cold wind. They did not look festive, but simply echoed the posters which shouted '*England Needs You*'.

Last week a letter had come which had made Stella cry. It was on United Services Club writing paper.

'Dear Stella,

I wanted very much to meet you before I left but it was too late. By the time you get this I shall be "somewhere at sea". I want to tell you, Stella, that I've been wrong in not coming to see you, and not asking you to forgive me for anything I did to hurt you. It's a long time ago, but I've never forgotten it – or you. It is wonderful that you have made such a success, and I send my admiration

172

as well as my affection. God bless you. May I see you when – if! – I get leave?

Harry'

She could not reply for he gave no address. After that she found herself nervously looking each day in *The Times*, which had begun to publish casualty lists. There was no mention of Harry, thank God. She even went so far as to wonder if she could speak to Catherine and ask for some news. Telephone Aston? She must be mad.

She was glad to be leaving London. The city looked so dark now and more and more women were in mourning. The black-clad figures struck at the heart. There was a restless charged feeling in the very air. Excitement was gone.

Victoria Station seethed with soldiers weighed down with kit bags, their tin hats slung and jingling. There were such crowds, military police and nurses, men in the Red Cross, and all the countless families of mothers and children and old men and women. So many laughing and tear-stained faces, the air full of smoke and noise and emotion. Edging her way through the press of people, she at last made out a small stylish figure on the platform. It was Patrick dressed in a long dark coat with a fur collar, talking energetically to a group of journalists.

'There you are, darling, you are late and we need some pictures,' he said. 'Teddy,' impatiently to Teddy who was flirting with the Snowbells, 'bring the girls here. Stella, stand in the centre.'

The actors gathered, photographs were taken, and as Stella obediently smiled she saw that a little crowd had actually gathered to see *them* off. Mostly the admirers were elderly women. One of them shouted, 'God bless you all for going out to France!'

The crossing was choppy. Stella, a good sailor, preferred to be away from people who were not, and retired selfishly to her cabin. She tried to read, but lay instead listening to the throb of the engines and the roar of the sea. She thought of Theo kissing her, on a day like this one. Of Harry whose life was on the sea. She wondered if she would ever see him again, and memory which had been asleep for so long awoke and showed her Harry's face when it had been taut with love . . .

It was nearly dark when she peered through the porthole and made out a scatter of dim lights shining in the December evening.

'Stella? In the lounge in three minutes please, and try to look merry and bright,' called Patrick's voice, accompanied by a loud rap at her door.

A white-faced company mustered in the ship's lounge. The Snowbells had been very sick and huddled together on a sofa, looking like orphans.

'Our plans have been changed,' announced Patrick briskly. 'Our first concert was to be tomorrow afternoon in Boulogne, as you all know. But the officer in charge has particularly asked if we can fit one in tonight. At a hospital in Dèvres, and don't ask me where *that* is. I said yes. I hope you agree.'

There was a muttered, 'Of course' from everybody except the Snowbells. Patrick said sharply, 'Girls! pay attention!'

Trailing off the ship in the dusk, they arrived at a cobbled quayside smelling of fish. A knot of soldiers marching by recognised them as actors and there was a ragged cheer. Patrick marshalled his company into three waiting motor cars.

The country roads were rough and the journey slow. At last they drew up outside a building whose dim outline showed elaborate cupolas – it had been a casino.

Stella was nervous as she and the Snowbells changed into their costumes. The waiting audience consisted only of soldiers who had come back from Mons. Wounded men. Would the songs and jokes so cheerfully rehearsed in London sound empty and stupid? She found herself trembling slightly as she and the rest of the actors followed Patrick down a corridor towards two open doors. They heard a steady roar of whistling, clapping and laughter.

What had been a huge ballroom had been filled with row

upon row of beds. Nearly two thousand men lay there, and as the company came in there was a burst of welcome. The vast room, lit only with candles, glowed on the hundreds of pale faces. All the strain left Stella when the music started. The huge audience listened, shouted for more, responded to every laugh. She had seen men in a war once before but not like this. The battered riders coming to the farm, tough and weatherbeaten, had still been unhurt, still had the liberty of health. These men were struck down and had escaped slaughter. The candlelight glittered in their eyes as Stella leaned towards them and sang.

The concert party tour lasted for four weeks. They played in the Boulogne fish market which stank of fish, they performed in converted hotels, danced and joked and juggled in Red Cross huts, on makeshift stages of planks laid across barrels. They gave a show in the square at Amiens in the open, and afterwards stood with the soldiers in the bitter dusk, drinking coffee by a brazier. They played at Rouen after a twenty-three-hour train journey to troops just returned from the trenches, plastered with mud from head to foot and due to return next day. Wherever they went, whatever the obstacles, Patrick was cool, ingenious, curiously cheerful. Where was the irritable man who had sat in the Kean? He had scale maps of every journey they made, knew all that civilians were allowed to know of the war's progress and a good deal they were not. He managed the cinema projector at the show, and when the troops yelled for a film to be repeated, he re-wound it faster than was possible; when the projector broke, he found a Sapper to mend it. When the pianist ran a temperature, Patrick played the piano. When Stella's dance dress split, Patrick sewed it up, and when she caught a chill, he dosed her with real Napoleon brandy.

At last the tour was nearly over; they gave their last two shows at Le Havre to an audience of mixed French and English troops. They sailed home.

Victoria Grove was dusty and icily cold when Stella trailed into the house. Letters lay in the hall like autumn leaves, she simply walked over them. She went shivering upstairs to the deserted nursery, turned on the gas fire and crouched beside it. She was tired and strung up and sad. So many faces. Pale and drawn and wearing eager smiles. Jingling in her head was the song she and Teddy sang to them, 'Just a little love, a little kiss.'

There was a loud knock at the front door. The bell pealed. She sighed. It would be Teddy, already deciding he would enjoy coffee and a gossip about the tour, arriving to coax her out of her dark mood and drag her off to luncheon with his theatre friends. She would not be allowed the luxury of solitude.

Still wearing her furs, she went down the stairs again. Through the stained glass of the front door, lozenges of scarlet and blue, she saw a man's figure. It did not look like Teddy . . .

Standing on the step, holding an enormous bunch of yellow roses, was Harry Flood.

'*Harry*! But how did you—'

'Naval intelligence. Did they get it wrong? You look as if you've only just come back.'

'Yes . . . this minute . . .' She was bewildered and could scarcely grasp that she was talking to him.

'Naval not-so-intelligent. They swore the concert party was back yesterday. Am I allowed in?'

He dumped the roses into her arms.

'Oh, of course, how lovely to see you,' she faltered. 'I'm sorry to seem so stupid . . . but I only just came off the train . . . I feel as if I'm still travelling.'

As she closed the door she said hurriedly, 'It's so cold. Would you mind if we went up to the nursery? There's a fire.'

'Excellent idea.'

The fire burned noisily, the room was full of childish pictures and nursery books still kept by Nurse Digby, just as she kept the old rocking horse in the corner; it had recently been repaired and painted. Stella asked Harry rather shyly to sit down. She slowly took off her furs.

He put his hands to the fire and turned, his face half lit by its ruddy light.

176

'The bad penny. Did you think I'd turn up again?'

'I don't know. I had your letter. I'm sorry I couldn't answer but there was no address.'

She felt extraordinarily shy. The years between had done nothing to Harry Flood but make him more attractive. She recognised every detail of his olive-skinned face, the deep dimple in his chin, his expectant, mocking eyes. There was a barrier, though.

'Are you on leave? What a stupid question, Harry. Of course you must be. But for how long?'

'Sick leave,' he answered with satisfaction. 'I was wounded in a scrap off Scapa Flow. I was too near a piece of shrapnel. They fished it out and I've an interesting scar which made Cathy go green.'

'Why did you show it to the poor girl?' she asked, laughing.

'To get her reaction, of course. The drained face and the trembling lip.'

He paused and looked at her.

'Stella. I can't tell you how often I have wanted to see you. I've walked past your theatre. Looked at your pictures. But never even managed to get myself into the stalls; I wonder why. Of course like the rest of the world I never stop seeing postcards of you wearing ridiculous hats.'

'I wear delightful hats,' she corrected him.

'Not always. That was a monstrosity with the long ribbons and the strawberries. And the one of you on a donkey, with "Good Fortune Guard You" in rosebuds.'

'I looked rather sweet on the donkey, but he was a beast.'

'Are you going to have luncheon with me, Sister-in-law?'

'I don't expect so, Brother-in-law. I shall lunch with a friend.'

'A cruel cut. Am I an enemy, then?'

'It would be too easy to answer that.'

He looked at her reflectively. There was something both nervous and casual about her, and an awareness of her own

177

beauty, a desire for the world to share her pleasure in it. How large her eyes were.

'I still think you will have luncheon with me.'

'I'm sorry, Harry.'

'Ah, you will be if you refuse.'

During luncheon at the Ritz, a number of people, women, officers in uniform, came up to congratulate her on the French tour. She introduced them to Harry, thinking it odd to say 'Lord Harry Flood' again. And her friends looked too interested.

Eating little, she kept trying to make up her mind if she was going to allow Harry to make love to her again. There was never a reason for onetime lovers not to return to bed, if both were heartfree. Apparently he was, and she supposed that she was as well. Theo came into her thoughts just then. Their lovemaking had drawn them close but it always seemed as if they had both decided to keep their liberty. She could not imagine doing so with Harry Flood. The weeks she had just spent in France had been so hectic, so intense and sad that she felt marked by them. And Harry's presence had a stronger effect on her than she wanted. She felt nervous. Not he.

'Stella,' he remarked, during the coffee, 'I notice that you have not once enquired about my beloved family.'

'Why should I want to do that?'

'Come along, you can't still feel the way you used to.'

'Can't I, Harry?'

'Of course not. You're famous now. Singing away in the theatre and simpering on the backs of donkeys.'

'And you think that means I have taken a sponge and wiped out the past?' she asked with curiosity.

'Not exactly. Some of it was distinctly worth keeping.'

She pretended not to understand.

'Since you won't ask about my family,' he went on, 'then I shall demand news of yours. How is my nephew?'

'At school. Happy and getting rather elderly. He's twelve.'

'That's a curious thought. Twelve! Is he like you?'

'More like Rupert but sturdier. And has blond hair like me.'

'He sounds a handsome fellow. It's fun to think he'll be head of the family one day. Do I make you nervous, Stella? You practically jumped into the air. Don't worry, my father is in good fettle and should make old bones, as they say. There's no danger of waking up and finding your son a Marquess.'

'Poor Kit when that happens,' said Stella briefly. She was nervous, yes, and found it extraordinary that there was still resentment and even dislike in her attraction for this too-confident man.

'Now that is absurd,' he said, smiling. 'Aston's a great big prize. How pretty you look when you scowl, I shall go on talking about the family to annoy you. My mother has sold off all the hunters, the food is awful, there is bandage-rolling in the billiard room and parcels on every piece of furniture in my father's study. My mother believes to be patriotic means to be uncomfortable. All the young servants have gone to the wars, old Des is in Gallipoli, Elinor is expecting again (she has two little girls), and my father is at the War Office. He lives at his club and wisely avoids the Aston victuals.'

He watched the effect of his words.

'Let me see,' he went on, 'who's left? Ah yes, Cath. She continues to refuse every proposal of marriage and drives my mother to distraction. The trouble with my sister is that she behaves like a great beauty and a great heiress and is neither.' He spoke affectionately.

'She was always very pretty,' said Stella, who had decided not to tell him of her meeting with Catherine since it had scarcely been a success.

'Cath can't hold a candle to you.'

Compliments were part of Stella's life, like flowers and as necessary. She never replied to them. He wanted her very much just then, but made no move to go. The restaurant was emptying; he vaguely signalled for more coffee.

'Neither of us has touched on the most interesting topic of them all. Your disappearance,' he said.

179

She was silent for a moment, having the curious feeling of being on her guard.

'It was rather successful, wasn't it?' she finally replied. 'Like an act on the Music Halls. Find the Disappearing Lady.'

'Why didn't you tell me what you were going to do?' he said, ignoring the tone. 'Who helped you? We were fond of each other — you used to say you had no friends but myself.'

'It was true then. I found one or two more later.'

'So you intend to remain a sphinx. If you won't tell me, you won't. I shall get it out of you in the end.'

Stella looked at the tablecloth.

There was a pause, and he suddenly said roughly, 'You hurt me very much, running off like that. Until we heard from your lawyer, I thought I'd go mad.'

'Harry, don't exaggerate.'

'Strangely enough, it's true. Perhaps that was why when I *did* know where you were, I didn't want to see you.'

'Yes. I felt exactly the same about you.'

He looked at her strangely.

'We both had reasons for keeping away. They're gone now. Do you know what I think?' he went on, in a low voice. 'That we should take a cab back to Victoria Grove and make love for the rest of today. And tomorrow. And the next day.'

Chapter Twelve

Catherine was the only member of the family now remaining at Aston with Millicent. Both her brothers were away at the war and her father was in London at the War Office, only returning home occasionally for a day or two. Working beside her mother, Catherine had helped to put Aston on to a wartime basis. The changes had been extraordinary. All the gardens had been ploughed up and planted with vegetables. Troops of land girls now worked on the farms and in the fields. The house itself was given over to fund raising and work parties. Millicent's organising powers were as vigorous, her attention to detail as sharp as when she gave her famous pre-war garden parties. And as in those days, she allowed Catherine little responsibility but leaned heavily on her for energy and obedience.

Millicent herself was in good spirits. She enjoyed turning Aston upside down, and had not been so easy in her mind about her husband for years. The Marquess was satisfied with his work and his life at his club: visits to Paris for poodle-clipping were over. Millicent even managed to accustom herself to the dreadful breeches worn by the land girls. She had laid away her embroidered silks and velvets and now wore dark sensible suits which did not touch the ground, and showed a neat ankle. Catherine was expected to wear similar clothes. If it were not for her daughter's moods, thought Millicent, everything was going well.

One bright May morning she was in the breakfast room, reading a letter from Desmond. His regiment had returned from Gallipoli and, after the briefest leave, had been posted to France. Millicent's appreciation of Desmond, never her favourite, had grown steadily. She saw how deeply he felt about Aston. Even his letters from the Front were full of ideas for improving the estate: he might have been the heir. Rupert had never been like that. The memory of her eldest son no longer hurt as it used to do, piercing her heart with unbearable sharpness. But his face, sensitive, handsome, came often into her mind. Sometimes she went to the picture gallery to look at his portrait. He stared down, immortally young, looking just beyond her shoulder with his painted eyes. When she stood for a long time, she could almost believe that soon his glance would meet her own. In Rupert's invisible company, she always thought about his son.

Once, just before war began, Harry had had the temerity to suggest that she should see the boy and his mother.

'Don't you think, Mother, you are getting rather out of date? I could name you five actresses, three from the Gaiety chorus, who are now in Society. You can't even call Stella a nobody these days. She is quite a star.'

'Certainly Society is changing for the worse,' she replied freezingly. 'Foreigners, financiers, even men who own Canadian prairies are gaining entrée, simply because they have means. I shall never lower Aston's standards. Have the grace to remember that.'

He laughed and kissed her, although she tried to turn away her face.

Catherine, late for breakfast, muttered an apology as she took her place. Millicent passed her Desmond's letter. While the girl was reading it, her mother took the opportunity of studying her. She often did this, looking for evidence that her daughter might be losing her looks. Catherine would soon be twenty-five, an age which Millicent regarded as that of an old maid. Women of her class had a duty to marry young and well. Catherine had had brilliant offers, and by now could have been the mistress of a country mansion, with two or three children. Among all my crosses, thought Millicent, my sons fighting for their country, the burden of Aston entirely on my shoulders with William not giving me a shred of help, Catherine is the worst.

'Des sounds worried about the London air raids,'

remarked Catherine, giving back the letter. 'Did you write to tell him that Papa rather enjoys them?'

Her mother ignored that and said what was in her mind.

'You know Guy is invited for luncheon today.'

'Yes, Mama,' said Catherine in a changed voice.

'That will be all, Collins,' said Millicent to the elderly butler hovering with the coffee pot. He left the room, knowing why. Lady Catherine was going to turn down another one. She was set to be a spinster, just like her aunt Lady Beatrice, more was the pity.

When they were alone, Millicent said mildly:

'Guy has spoken to your father, and to me. He said how eagerly he is waiting for your answer. And you know quite well how soon his regiment will be sent to France. He's exactly the kind of young man your father and I wish for you, Catherine. I hope you are going to be sensible this time.'

'Papa said he looks like a ballet dancer.'

Millicent frowned. Guy Esterbrooke was small, fair and goodlooking. William was a fool to say such a thing.

'Catherine. There's something I wish to say.'

'But you already have.'

'Guy Esterbrooke,' continued Millicent with admirable self control, 'is a serious and affectionate young man, whose family have been friends of ours for many years. In my opinion, you must accept him.'

'Must?'

Millicent's hawklike face grew positively soft.

'My dear child, it is time to forget sentimental ideas about romance. You're no longer a girl, and you are our only daughter. It is only right, I might say it is your moral obligation to marry.'

'Mama, I have told you that I want to be a nurse.'

'And I have said it cannot be considered.'

The clash was a recent one, joining the wearisome argument which had grown in the last few years, over Catherine's obstinate maiden state. Society women were opening Red Cross hospitals and dressing stations in France

183

and taking their daughters with them. Some Amazons had a plan to ferry barges of clothes for Belgian refugees through the Flemish canals. Millicent listened to talk of these exploits by her friends and did not say a word. She was not affected by other people. When Catherine said she wished to nurse, she tactfully explained why the idea was impossible. A girl among soldiers, even among the wounded, could be exposed to untold sexual horrors. Catherine thought the excuse ridiculous.

'So it is still "No" to my being a nurse,' she said.

'Have a little talk with Guy, Catherine.'

The girl did not answer and ate nothing. Excusing herself very soon, she walked out of the dining-room and rapidly up the main staircase. Painted warriors and rearing horses, guarded by angels with swords of victory, fought and flew across the lofty walls, arrested in violent motion. Catherine went to her bedroom and shut the door. She was angry and resentful and the feelings were new. Until now she had literally seen with her mother's eyes. It had never been difficult to do what her mother wanted: she agreed with her.

But the war had brought its changes even to Catherine's heart, and she knew that Millicent was now wrong and that *she* was right. She had never thought such a thing before. Going restlessly over to the window she stood for a while looking at the rose gardens with their neat lines of cabbages, the parkland now given over to herds of sheep, the steely glint of the lake reflecting the sky. For no apparent reason, she suddenly thought of Stella. Not the actressy stranger who had spoken to her recently at the War Office, but Stella as she had been at Aston, with a certain expression in her dark eyes which for the first time Catherine understood. She must have felt as I do now, thought Catherine and sighed.

She went over to the dressing-table which her father had given to her for her last birthday. It was a pretty, elaborate little piece of satinwood, full of gilt-handled drawers and cubbyholes. By sheer chance she had discovered a secret drawer behind a drawer. And had begun, she was not sure

184

why, to hide money in it. She now had more than her mother would approve. Like Royalty, Millicent never handled money. Catherine unlocked the drawer and took out a purse already bulging. She was going to need it, she thought. For a moment she looked very like Millicent.

The spring was warm, the sunny parks crowded at weekends. Stella thought how cheerful people seemed. Yet that could not be true. The casualty lists in the newspapers grew; as the dreadful news touched every family, less and less mourning black was seen in the streets.

Mercifully, she had no reason to grieve but she was not happy. She even wished she had never returned to Harry's strong embrace, and hated the violence of her own feelings. On the first afternoon when they came back to Victoria Grove, she had really believed she could keep her head. Her body might not obey, but her mind still worked and her strong will too. It would never allow her to suffer a second time just because this man turned her bones to jelly.

Poor weak thing, had she actually believed that? Harry picked her up and put her on the bed in the empty house, and as he began to kiss her, she dazedly heard the grandfather clock downstairs strike four. It was her last consciousness of time until he left. They made love as men drink water after crossing the desert, lying flat, choking, near-drowning. For three days they scarcely left the house and once she fainted. He caught her just in time, and revived her by patting her face and hands. 'There's a compliment. You look dreadful.'

They loved like tigers, then talked for hours in bed or lying by the fire. They made jokes, invented poems, played games, and Harry constantly asked her to sing for him. Once she sang 'Do not go, my love', and remembered the long Aston drawing-room and Harry's still figure reflected in clouded mirrors.

Sometimes while they talked he asked her about Kit, he never tired of hearing about the boy. 'You didn't finish telling me how you chose his prep school.' 'Which was the race he won?' He demanded to see Kit's school reports, letters, photographs of him, and spread them on the floor, absorbed. 'You look sweet, but why is he pulling that face?' He read aloud a poem of Kit's, published in the school magazine. 'It's good.' She was touched by his affectionate interest, it was impossible not to be. But she recognised that Flood passion for anybody of the blood.

The three days which had begun as the clock chimed, seeming to Stella an endless prospect of joy, ended after a night of sharpest love. Harry in uniform was by her bed, while outside in the street the taxi hooted. He gave her a final kiss.

'I'll be back.'

'Swear.'

'Do you think I'll let anybody else have you?'

The slammed door reverberated through the empty house.

She looked round the bedroom. There were signs of him everywhere. Yesterday's newspaper in a chair, its cushion crushed by his figure. Two champagne glasses and the empty bottle. A game of chess, unfinished. A book of poetry, Browning, he had brought from the drawing-room and read aloud to her, 'Flower, you Spaniard . . .'

Since then, four months ago, she had received only one letter from him. It began 'My Dear One,' and said little except, 'You are not to worry if you see stories about the dangers we're in, you know how the newspapers exaggerate. By the way, do you realise you're an angel?'

She missed him at times so painfully that it was like being ill. It felt as if she were haunted. When Patrick told her he had 'At last!' found a new show, she welcomed the thought of hard work as the only replacement for love.

Patrick had been looking for a show and getting steadily more irritable as time went by. The only time he had been cheerful had been with the concert party in France. Now a new show metaphorically dropped out of the sky on to his desk. Its writer had composed the popular song 'You Haven't Kissed Me Yet' which was played by military bands and whistled by soldiers. Jack Lescher was commissioned into the Royal Naval Air Service, but proved as hopelessly incompetent at aviation as he was a born composer, crashed his plane twice and was dragged out of the wreckage. He spent his time in a convalescent home writing a show – *A Boy in Khaki*. Patrick read it – and sent for Stella and Teddy.

The show, starring them both – 'The Popular Pair' – opened in the early summer and was an immediate success.

Like every actor and actress Stella welcomed work, and like every woman without her lover she frantically filled up her days. She could not bear her lonely thoughts. She sang at charity matinées, visited hospitals, helped at auctions, played in *A Boy in Khaki* and often ended up at a party from midnight until two in the morning. Patrick said she was overdoing it and she told him to mind his own business.

'It is my business when you have to use too much rouge,' was the cutting reply.

She eased up slightly on the work and the rouge, but gave him no credit when she felt better.

One sunny morning she came downstairs at Victoria Grove, dressed *en grande tenue* in rose colour with an enchanting feathery hat, when the front door bell rang. Her elderly daily help – parlourmaids were of the past – asked if she should answer it.

'No, Mary, I'll go.'

A girl was standing in the porch.

'Catherine!'

'Oh – Stella – is it a bad time? Shall I come another day? You're just going out.'

'Not just yet. Do come in,' Stella replied, trying not to look amused. As at their brief meeting at the War Office, Catherine was blushing hotly.

'I've plenty of time,' added Stella. 'I'm due at Walsingham House but I always arrive everywhere too early. Come into the drawing-room. It's nice to see you.'

The sun was flooding through the garden windows at the far end of the room, lighting everything in its white simplicity – pale walls, pale furniture, bowls of pale flowers. Stella settled her guest on the sofa.

187

'I must apologise for turning up so unexpectedly.' Catherine was still nervous. 'But I – I came for advice.'

That, thought Stella, is obvious. She looked at Catherine and saw more than she had done at their previous brief meeting. Her sister-in-law was still as pretty as when they had been together at Aston, but she was no longer wandering out of childhood and the poise which had been touching in a girl of seventeen was now settled. She sat too straight, her manner was too stiff. Yet her face was mournful. Accustomed to stylish actresses, Stella thought her clothes wonderfully dull.

'Now what can I do for you?' she asked comfortably. 'I'm usually full of ideas, and I'll be glad to help if I can. After all, now I come to think of it, we are still related, aren't we?'

She couldn't help laughing.

But her visitor was absorbed in her own troubles and deaf to little jokes.

'I want to be a nurse and my mother won't hear of it. She simply isn't reasonable. If I even try to talk about it to her, she refuses to discuss it.'

Stella raised her eyebrows.

'But your mother has a strong sense of duty,' she said, trying to keep a dry note from her voice. 'She can't disapprove of anything so patriotic, Cath!'

Catherine looked embarrassed again.

'She says that it isn't proper. That – that men who haven't seen a woman for some time are "not themselves" as she puts it. It's all so *stupid*. I know at least six girls who have become nurses – but if you heard Mama talking about it!'

'Rape and pillage?'

The girl refused to smile.

'Two of my cousins are nursing in France at this minute, but she keeps on saying "No". And then – there's somebody who wants to marry me.'

'And you don't wish to marry him?' said Stella, who remembered what Harry had told her.

'No, I don't. There've been others and I refused them

too. My mother can't understand it. I'm not against being married,' she went on with a note of desperation in her voice, 'I would quite like it. But I don't manage to love anybody. I'm probably incapable of falling in love. Some people are, you know. It's like being born colour blind.'

There was a moment's silence, and Catherine did manage to give a tentative smile. Stella found that she was more affected by seeing her than she had at first imagined. She had forgotten the girl's extraordinary charm when she came out of her shell; there was something fascinating about her, though Stella had never discovered exactly what it was. She seemed to be both unassailable and vulnerable, and wasn't that impossible? And then, the past linked them for they had shared so much of it. The pale girl sitting here at Victoria Grove had wept over Rupert too. And had ridden out with her on cold Aston mornings, and come to sit in her bedroom while she was dressing. They had laughed sometimes over the silliest things. A thought struck Stella.

'The Marchioness doesn't know you're here, does she?'

'Oh no. And I'm not just in London for a visit. I left her a letter saying I was going to join the VAD. I said I'd write and give my address when I had one.'

Stella stared.

'Do you mean you've left Aston?'

'I suppose I have.'

They looked at each other. Stella had a sudden realisation of just what a huge step that was. All those years ago it had been so for her, and *she* was not a Flood. No wonder Catherine looked tense.

'Cathy, are you sure you mean it? If you go back home now, your mother will lecture you but she'll be far too afraid to nag in case you cut and run again. But if you're really serious about the VAD it isn't difficult to join. In fact it's easy, they're recruiting all the time. We could go to Devonshire House together. You'll have to take a course in nursing, naturally. I daresay there's lots to learn. And if you don't have to live in at the hospital to start with, you could stay here with me if you wish. The point is, Cathy – do you mean it?'

Catherine blushed for the second time.

'I want to nurse more than anything.'

'Oh. If you feel like that . . .'

Stella took her to Devonshire House where an interview was arranged with a certain Lady Handcross, a formidable matron whom Catherine already knew. After the interview Catherine returned in a cab to Victoria Grove, looking discouraged.

'It *would* be Lady Handcross in charge,' she said, pulling off her hat and collapsing into a chair. 'She's a gorgon. She says I must go through *three* interviews, *and* pass a first-aid test, *and* a home-nursing examination. She was deliberately making it sound difficult and making me feel pretty useless.' The afternoon had badly shaken her.

'You didn't imagine you'd be a nurse in twenty-four hours,' said Stella, laughing. 'It's always a smack in the face to find oneself a beginner.'

'I'm a beginner at everything,' muttered Catherine, accepting a cup of tea.

Stella raised her eyebrows.

She knew a score of things at which her sister-in-law was exquisitely trained. At wearing a tiara and entering a crowded drawing-room, curtseying to a king, finding the right light talk with a statesman; dancing with an Ambassador of sixty and making him feel twenty-five; doing the social things with a charm that never showed exhaustion or even emotion. A poised, cool lily.

'I must write to my mother,' Catherine finally said, after some minutes of thought.

'Yes, tell her they've accepted you. That will settle it.'

'Oh, Stella, of course it won't. She will pull strings with Lady Handcross and get me back.'

Stella burst into a loud laugh suited to backstage and not to the delicate ears of a Flood.

'My poor girl, don't you see that she can't! Everybody

is crying out for volunteers. Old Lady Handcross's guns are nine – ninety – times the size of your mother's. Telephone her and break the news. You may as well get it over.'

'I couldn't. I must write.'

'Perhaps a letter is kinder,' said Stella, struck now by Catherine's expression, and wondering how anybody who felt like that had screwed up the courage to come to London at all.

Stella left her to write the letter and later saw Catherine hurrying to the post box.

Two days went by. Although they did not mention it, because Catherine clearly did not wish to, they were both awaiting an angry telephone call. None came. Then Stella remembered that at Aston the telephone was rarely used for serious matters. The instrument was at the end of a corridor beyond the billiard room, with scarcely any light, and when a rash visitor wished to use it, he was provided with a lamp. The Marchioness never went down the corridor, but sent messages.

Catherine went to Devonshire House again, and after her various tests was finally told she had been accepted. Her training at St Saviour's would begin at once. She must attend lectures and spend part of each day on practical work. She would wear uniform. Looking brighter, she left the house early on a rainy day to collect her uniform at the Red Cross headquarters. She said goodbye to Stella who was still in bed, and Stella returned to sleep. She had come home at two in the morning after a supper party at Gatti's with Teddy, Patrick and a host of theatre friends, many of whom were in uniform and on leave.

The London morning went by and still Stella slept. She was dreaming of bells: church bells and dinner bells. Burrowing into her pillow, she began to realise that it must be a real bell pealing away downstairs. Her daily maid, she supposed, had come and gone. Nurse Digby was away at the Sussex cottage.

Half asleep, she myopically looked at the clock: it was after midday. She sighed and clambered out of bed, wandered over to look out of her window. A motor was drawn up at the kerb. Even after all the years that had passed Stella recognised it. She could see the crest on its door, and she knew the narrow-shouldered figure of the elderly chauffeur.

Throwing a robe round her shoulders, putting her bare feet into slippers, she went downstairs as the bell again rang as urgently as that of a fire-engine.

Millicent Flood, under a large black umbrella, faced her without a greeting.

'Fetch my daughter if you please.'

Darkly dressed, more weather-beaten than Stella remembered, her mother-in-law looked small and iron-faced.

'Won't you come in?'

Millicent merely repeated her request and said that she and Catherine would speak in the motor.

'I think you had best come in. Cathy is not here.'

'Then be good enough to give me her address.'

'Oh,' said Stella, faintly smiling, 'this is her address. At present she's somewhere between Devonshire House and St Saviour's, or she's at the Stores being fitted for her uniform. Moving about London, you know.'

It was the first time in her life that Stella had seen Millicent show a flicker of irresolution: she hesitated.

'I will come in.'

The rain beat against the windows, the chill drawing-room smelled pervasively of flowers. An enormous white vase of lilies stood in the empty fireplace, there were pink carnations on the piano and orchids in crystal on a side table. A silver bowl filled with gardenias was on the windowsill. Stella asked her visitor to sit down but Millicent, furling the wet umbrella, remained standing. Stella sat in an armchair and spread the robe of shot blue and green taffeta round her, pulling its frills to her chin.

Her appearance at midday was exactly what Millicent had expected and confirmed her conviction that Catherine had suffered a nervous collapse. How else could she choose such company? Everything about this one-time daughter-in-law was impossibly vulgar. The undress. The loose plait of hair. The bare slippered feet. The flowers unmistakeably sent to her by men.

'The Marquess and I require our daughter to return home at once. I shall wait until she returns.'

'Do wait,' was the polite reply, 'for as long as you wish.'

Millicent looked at her. She has changed, she thought; she's better looking and doubtless has money since she is a theatrical and a kept woman. She always had a hard centre, though. That was how she caught my son.

'I'm afraid I have to go out quite soon,' Stella said. 'There's a charity matinée at Lansdowne House. I'm auctioning some paintings. I doubt if Catherine will be back until this evening, but do make yourself at home.'

Millicent thinned her lips.

'What influence had you in this matter?'

Stella was surprised. 'I? What have I to do with it? Your daughter turned up out of the blue and told me she wanted to be a nurse, and that you disapproved. I've no idea why she came to me, I certainly never asked her. Perhaps she read about the concert party we took over to France and thought I might know something helpful. She is very welcome. But what Catherine decides to do is no concern of mine, Lady Tyrrell.'

Apparently the older woman believed her. She said almost to herself, 'She must see her father. Today. I shall expect her back at Aston tomorrow.'

Stella was silent.

'I brought this in case I failed to see her,' said Millicent, placing a letter on the table. Without another word she walked out of the house.

Stella shivered as she heard the motor driving away. She had forgotten the actual physical sensation of being disliked. It was like being forced to drink a kind of poison. Catherine was escaping in the nick of time. Better to nurse in the midst of this sad war than to rot like the Aston flags.

Catherine looked alarmed when Stella told her of the

visit. Her face drained of colour. She picked up her mother's letter but did not open it.

'Don't read it yet. It will only upset you,' Stella said.

'Of course I must read it now!'

'Why? You know perfectly well what's in it. So do I, I can see it in your face. All the old arguments. Look, let's put it here,' said Stella, propping the envelope against her white French clock, 'and when you come home tomorrow from St Saviour's, after an interesting day, you may feel strong enough. Did you get to the hospital? What was it like?'

'Huge and dark and smelling of carbolic.'

'Just what you dreamed of.'

'Oh yes. Beginners do trays,' said Catherine. She paused for a moment. 'Didn't you say Mama said I am to go and see my father?'

'That's right, and I've had an idea,' said Stella, who felt kindly towards her visitor and saw, in her position, a curious reflection of her own once upon a time. 'When you've braved the interview, come to our show. I'll leave a ticket at the box office. Afterwards we'll go to Rules to celebrate your new career.'

'With whom?' asked Catherine, polite but cautious.

'Are you expecting to fend off the Brigade of Guards? With nobody. We'll go together. They always keep me a table.'

'*By ourselves?*'

'Cath! A year more in Aston, and you *would* have been a fossil.'

For the first time in her life, Catherine resisted opening a letter. It stayed propped against the clock. As she was leaving for the theatre, Stella looked at it with a sardonic expression. She could just imagine the words folded inside it. Commands. Sentences using the words duty, honour, standards. Muffled in the envelope, they waited.

Stella was in her dressing-room, in her last Act costume of draped white chiffon sewn with stars and pearls when Catherine was ushered in by Bessy, Stella's dresser. Stella glanced at her quickly for signs that the meeting with her father had upset her. But apparently the Marquess had stayed true to form and uninvolved, for Catherine only looked shy. She had never been to the theatre alone before, and to be backstage was very extraordinary.

'It was lovely, Stella! The music is so sweet and the comic bits are so funny. You dance and sing beautifully.'

'Thank you, Cathy, I'm glad you enjoyed it.'

Catherine was given a chair and sat down, upright as young Royalty. Stella massaged cream into her face and neck and violet eyelids. Bessy was interested in the dully-dressed girl who was Lady Somebody. Doesn't look it in them togs, she thought.

'I like Jack Lescher's music,' ventured Catherine.

'Everybody does, bless you,' said Bessy.

Catherine was rather startled at being addressed by Bessy at all, let alone with a nudge of familiarity.

'You should see him play the pianner,' went on Bessy, brushing Stella's hair as if grooming a horse. 'He's got a diamond ring you could eat your dinner off-of. He puts it on the pianner lid. Careful, I told him, it'll fall in and then you'll never fish it out from all them strings.'

Stella groaned. 'Oh Bessy, not more stories about Jack!'

A knock at the door was followed by a curly head peering in.

'Like a swig of Black Velvet after our labours?' asked Teddy. 'It went well tonight, I thought. But one is exhausted. Drained. Hello, I'm Teddy Collingwood,' he added graciouslly, taking Catherine for an admirer. He waited for her to ask him to sign her programme.

'Catherine, this is Mr Collingwood,' said Stella through a mask of cold cream. 'Teddy, Lady Catherine Flood.'

The actor gave an enchanting bow.

'How do you do. I believe you and Stella are related, Lady Catherine?'

'Yes, we are,' was the reserved reply. Catherine looked at the ground.

But the actor with his alluring monkey face fascinated her. So did the room heavy from the scent of make-up and

195

an enormous basket of red roses. So did the lights glaring in an arch round the looking-glass. She stole a glance at Teddy Collingwood. He was real enough, but to her he still seemed to belong in the make-believe world she had just watched for two and a half hours, where he had danced and sung surrounded by beautiful and adoring girls. In a painted garden he had courted Stella. He had marched away to war and returned a hero. He was 'the boy in khaki'. The young man standing near her was a little paler and older than the god upon the stage. But he still had a kind of radiance.

'Shall we all have the Black Velvet?' he enquired.

'Thank you, Teddy, but Catherine and I are off to supper.'

'Accompanied, of course, by the *haut monde*?'

'No. As a matter of fact we are going alone.'

'Of course you are not,' he said promptly.

'Now, Teddy,' said Stella, passing the tortoiseshell pins to Bessy who began to coil her hair, 'Catherine has only just arrived in London and we are going to have a quiet evening.'

Teddy wasted no more time on Stella. He had taken a fancy to the dark girl sitting so stiffly and looking so shy. Like every successful actor he had met a good many Society people, but this girl was different from the usual drawling beauties. He used the full battery of his charm.

'Lady Catherine,' he said, falling on one knee as if about to sing a serenade, 'allow me, I beg, to take you to supper!'

'Mr Collingwood, do please get up,' said Catherine. She suddenly burst into a fit of giggles, the first Stella had heard from her since she had arrived.

Lady Tyrrell's letter must have been stronger than Stella feared for when she finally brought herself to read it, Catherine ran upstairs and locked herself in her room. She came down later, red-eyed. But a second letter came and although still angry her mother did not cast her off.

Unknown to her, Lady Handcross had known Millicent's reaction and had written to her in plain terms. Millicent found herself forced to write to her daughter that she 'respected her spirit of sacrifice'. But Catherine must come to Aston whenever possible. 'Naturally we cannot visit you where you are at present. Thank heaven you will soon be boarding at the hospital and supervised by responsible people. In the meantime I rely on your honour.'

Catherine said nothing about the letters but Stella saw that whatever Millicent felt she was not using money as a lever. Stella could not ask about that because her sister-in-law would be offended; the nobility were obsessed with money but it was vulgar for *you* to mention it to *them*. However, taking taxis, buying books and flowers and offering to pay generously for her keep (which Stella flatly refused) were indications that Catherine still had her allowance.

After the first supper at Rules, Teddy became Catherine's chosen companion. They met in the City for a sandwich at a shabby tea-shop whenever she could get away from the hospital. They met every Sunday. He wrote to her and sent her flowers, which she carried carefully up to her room.

Stella was curious about the friendship and watched the unlikely couple with amusement and a touch of alarm. If Catherine were at last falling in love, she could not have chosen a more unsuitable man. Teddy was a feckless creature who loved as easily as he danced; Stella marvelled why he of all men had found his way to Catherine's heart.

One evening she and Catherine happened to be alone at Victoria Grove, sitting together in the drawing-room. Catherine talked unselfconsciously about Teddy, who had taken her the previous day to a Kensington antique shop and bought her a Rossetti pencil drawing of a honeysuckle spray.

'He said it reminded him of me. He thinks of such silly things,' Catherine said, smiling to herself.

'Are you getting fond of him, Cath?'

The question was casual enough but Catherine's face

changed and the tenderness went out of it. The look she gave Stella was a fixed light behind barred windows.

'One must have someone to go about with. Teddy's not bad.'

'Oh, he'd be overwhelmed at that!' Stella took her cue.

So Cath isn't going to tell, she thought. Imagine my thinking that she would.

Certainly Catherine was touchingly happy, and amused Stella and Teddy with her stories of life at St Saviour's, of the floors she scrubbed, the eight pints of milk and seventeen cups of tea she only just missed from dropping, and of her cousin, wounded at Ypres, whom she had found in one of the wards.

'He shouted my name at the top of his voice and I started to laugh. How Sister glared!'

Teddy listened and teased, dragged her off to a concert or took her to St James's Park where they found the lake emptied and covered with ugly wartime huts built on the mud. Soon Catherine would be a 'real' VAD probationer, sleeping in at the hospital. But at present she was still free to spend time with a man who seemed to have changed her life.

'You're not going to break that girl's heart, are you?' Stella said to Teddy one evening after the show. Worn out after a day at the hospital Catherine was home at Victoria Grove, in bed asleep by half past ten. Teddy and Stella were having supper at Romano's where the place buzzed with the hectic gaiety of the 1915 summer.

Teddy poured more champagne.

'Has it occurred to you that it could be the other way round?'

'Cath break *yours*. When in the world, Teddy Collingwood, has your heart even suffered a bruise? You fall in and out of love like a tumbler. You even did with me.'

'Oh, you!' he said, packing the words with a good deal of meaning. 'Cathy's another story.'

'So she is. If you hurt her, she'll bleed.'

He studied the bubbles in the glass.

'You don't know how badly hit I am. I adore the guarded

little thing. I want to get into the castle, but suppose she locks me out?'

'Surely that could never happen. Aren't you irresist- ible?'

'Yes, thank goodness.'

Stella's life and Catherine's did not run in unison, they worked at different times. After a particularly wearing day of charity shows and an evening performance, Stella let herself quietly into the darkened house and went to her room. She found one shaded lamp had been lit, and there was a tray on her dressing table. It was laid with lace, and there was a plate of wafer-thin chicken sandwiches and a glass of milk. On the back of one of her visiting cards, Catherine had scribbled, 'I hope you are not too tired. C.F.'

Faintly smiling, Stella looked down at the tray. Every- thing about it, even to the shape of the sandwiches, was exactly like the little repasts left for Aston guests when they came home late from a Hunt Ball.

When the two girls happened to be at home at the same time, Catherine was always good company. But there was another jumpy conversation between them. Catherine said she would 'very much like to see Nursie. May I?'

'Of course. She's at the cottage and knows you are here. She keeps sending her love, as I told you. She'd be so pleased to see you.'

'I'll go down then.'

Silence.

'But you don't want me to see Kit, do you?'

'I'm sorry, Cath.'

Catherine's pale kittenish face looked fixed. She wore the smile again. It had stood her in good stead through many social crises at Aston.

'I quite see. Of course I won't ask. But—' looking towards the drawing of the child, 'he *is* like Rupert.'

With Kit at school and Nurse in Sussex, Stella had nobody with whom to share her life and she liked having Catherine to stay at Victoria Grove. But Catherine brought something to the house as well as her youthful presence.

Stella had not realised that she had invited in a living reminder of the past. Family resemblances were the devil. The girl's voice, light and at times rather meaningless, resembled Rupert's. How often she voiced opinions of her mother's as her own. Her bouncing walk was like her father's. Worst of all because it was very strong was a certain look, both mischievous and hard, which *was* Harry.

Stella had received another short letter from him which she had luckily intercepted before Catherine caught sight of it. Catherine herself had weekly letters from her mother, in one of which a letter from Harry was enclosed. She read it aloud to Stella, laughing. To Stella's sharpened ears the letter sounded more natural and affectionate than the one written to herself.

'Isn't it like him to ask for jam puddings from Fortnum's?' Catherine said with hilarity. 'He sends Mama lists of treats that she is to post him. She gets so cross. This time it is all the *Tatlers* she can find as well as puddings. In case there are any pictures of one's friends. Mama does dislike *having* to send things. Old Des is just grateful for anything she decides on. He never asks.'

Still looking through the letter with sisterly amusement, Catherine never saw the expression of suppressed pain on Stella's face when she heard Harry's name. She always longed for a mention of him, but could not bear to hear it. How unnatural it was to be in love with a man and never speak about him to a living soul. But when in her life had she confided in anybody? Catherine would be shocked and jealous and besides, Harry would forbid it. He had once shown only too plainly what his feelings were about Stella and himself, and his family. Yet listening to Catherine talking of him throbbed like an infected wound.

It was raining when the cab collected Stella to drive her to the theatre. Looking from the window, she thought how the sight of men in uniform was taken for granted now, it was a commonplace. So were the posters on every hoarding and bus and tramcar, 'Rally round the Flag!' Her taxi drove down Park Lane and she thought – how long it is since I have seen Theo. He had written that he would not be in England for a while. Financial matters, unspecified, weighty, kept him in New York.

At the theatre this evening the audience was crammed with officers in uniform and buzzing with expectant talk before the Overture. When the curtain rose and Stella and Teddy made their entrance and sang their opening number – 'There you are, my darling!' – she saw the sea of faces and felt the house's hungry demand. It was something she and Teddy had first been aware of in France, the avid desire for music, spectacle and talent as the audience waited to be made happy by the two hours' traffic of the stage.

The penetrating needle-thin rain had not stopped when Stella was driven home. London was very dark, and only a few nights ago there had been a bad Zeppelin raid. The great city lay each night in the ghostly radiance shed by a few masked street lamps, the tops of the glass painted blue. There were no lights along the river fronts or on the bridges, the windows of the buses were thickly curtained, the motors had no headlights. A dim world of apprehension. The music and the applause had evaporated, and Stella felt tired and low-spirited. She was vaguely surprised to notice a dim beam showing from a downstairs room as she walked up the path to the front door. Catherine was always in bed by the time Stella came home.

As she opened the door a voice called.

'Is that you?'

Something in the tone frightened her.

Catherine was crouched on the sofa. She said in a rasping, tearless voice, 'Harry is missing. His ship was hit in the North Sea.'

Chapter Thirteen

As 1915 dragged by, with its lengthening casualty lists of
the appalling losses at Ypres, Stella no longer believed that
Harry was alive. But in a city of grief to seem cheerful was
a necessity. The fierce excitement which had swept through
the country when war was declared had gone. Feelings were
sombre, recruiting desperate, everywhere the posters
shouted for men. 'Forward to Victory; enlist *now*.' When
Stella met women who had lost a husband or a son, she saw
none of that proclaimed pride written about in the
newspapers: 'Grieve not for your son killed, but glory in his
Fate.' Women's faces when they were bereaved were fixed
and bitter.

As if to force back the dark, London at night was infected
with a feverish gaiety created for – and by – the men on leave
from France. They wanted, needed, must have a few days
of solace. Theatres and restaurants were crowded, laughter
loud. And Stella who grieved for Harry every waking
minute was still willing to be caught in the hectic midnight
revels.

Not Catherine. She shunned company. Stella had lived
too long among the Floods not to know that *their* suffering
was private, other people were kept at arms' length. The
words carved in stone and running like a ribbon through
the Aston chapel, above the windows, round the tombs,
even the christening font, were 'never yield'. Catherine did
not wish to be comforted or to speak of her brother. Oh
most certainly she did not want Stella to indicate that in
being related to the family she shared the sorrow. Catherine
was now living in at St Saviour's and simply never came to
Victoria Grove for weeks at a time.

The person to whom Catherine turned but did not

confide in was Teddy. She was deeply in love, but it was a strange love which would not share its unhappiness. Whenever possible, she flew to him. She persuaded other nurses to exchange their time off so that she could see him on Sundays, the only evening he was not playing at the theatre. He waited for her at St Saviour's gates; the amount of time Catherine was allowed out was precisely two hours.

White-faced, heavy-eyed, rattling away cheerfully in her quick voice, Catherine walked beside him, making little jokes. Yes, hospital life was 'quite hard', and yes, she did sometimes stand for nine hours, 'Oh, Teddy, my feet swell up. Hideous!' They always went back to his lodgings to fall into each other's arms.

They were lovers now. Teddy did not know if grief had been the reason, or if she like the rest of the world was changed by the knowledge that life might be short. Teddy had hesitated, but the virginal girl who had refused a score of eligible men threw herself at him passionately. She made love blindly, hotly, never speaking of it afterwards.

Every Monday night Teddy came into Stella's dressing-room and leaned against the wall, shutting his eyes. His face was grey. Remembering the young man once so careless and heartfree, Stella's heart ached. He burst out that Cath was overworked and exhausted, and that he could see she felt ill with grieving. But she never, never talked about it, she refused. What could Stella say? That Catherine's desire for private sorrow was stronger than her love?

Stella herself could not get used to the idea that Harry was gone for ever. She wondered if all women felt like this when they received those dreadful War Office telegrams. In her thoughts Harry lived vividly. In dreams, he teasingly returned.

Walking through Kensington one icy winter morning, she saw that a War Shrine had been put up at the corner of Victoria Grove. The little shrines were seen all over London now. A wooden board was painted with the names of the men who had lived in the street and who were now serving abroad. And those who had been killed in action.

There was a cross, and on a ledge was a vase of frostbitten roses. She stood looking at the shrine. It was a way of sharing sorrow. *She* could be part of nothing so united, and it made her cry.

A Boy in Khaki ran through the winter months, and after nearly half a year of playing Stella managed to beg a few days off during the Christmas holidays; Patrick ungraciously agreed to allow her understudy to take over. Stella was busy packing when she heard a footstep, and looking up she saw Catherine standing in the doorway. Stella started.

'Oh Cathy, what ages since I've seen you! Shall we have some tea?'

She smiled with affection but Catherine only said without preliminary, 'Are you going away?' She looked pale and plain in her dark uniform, the nurse's cap pulled low on her forehead and hiding her hair.

'I'm off to the cottage to be with Kit for a little of the Christmas holidays. My understudy's playing.'

'Oh.'

Catherine remained in the doorway with the air of someone wishing to go. It was nearly three months since the night Stella had come home to find her crouched on the sofa, and after that night Harry had not once been mentioned between them. Stella knew that Catherine's changed attitude, her coldness and the removal of her friendship, were entirely due to Harry's loss. When her family was struck down, back in a rush came Catherine's passionate loyalty and her rejection of anybody who had dared to harm them in the past. Stella had left them and taken Kit. Stella had refused to be part of them. So in their time of grief she was nothing to do with them and must not dare to think she was. She became the enemy all over again just as Catherine, after her defiance, returned to being a Flood.

'I've come to collect my things. I am going to France,' was all Catherine said.

Stella sat back on her heels. A dozen questions came into

her mind. She looked up into a face that invited none of them. Expecting the snub, she still asked.

'Do you know where they are sending you?'

'To Étaples, I believe.'

'You *believe*?' echoed Stella, managing a smile despite the chill tone of Catherine's voice. 'Surely they've told you.'

'Matron would not say. I only know the rumours.'

Oh God, thought Stella, sitting on the ground and looking at the girl in her hideous uniform, why must you use your grief as a weapon against me? I can't admit to you that Harry was my lover but surely you must *feel* somehow that I'm unhappy too? But Catherine had lost her quickness, her lightness, her instincts for guessing at, even for caring about, anything but her own sorrow. Stella had a wave of strange jealousy.

'Do you mind if I go and look in the room for anything?' Catherine said. By leaving out the 'my' she made it sound as if Stella's house were a hostel or a barracks.

'Of course. There's nothing much except some shoes and a book or two. Go and look.'

When Catherine had gone out, Stella tried to concentrate on her packing, but found herself listening for movements in the bedroom next to her own. Not a sound.

Eventually Catherine came back, having apparently stowed her few possessions in the Gladstone bag she carried. She hovered in the doorway waiting – that cruel politeness – to take her leave.

From sheer bloody-mindedness Stella said, 'I should have thought you much too inexperienced to be sent out to France yet.'

'I'm as good a dogsbody as anyone else.'

Stella pressed her point home.

'But not a fully trained dogsbody, are you? Did you use influence to get to France? Of course you have a good deal if you want to use it.'

Catherine met her eyes and said nothing. The silence spoke. It told Stella to be quiet, not to dare any further. It was rather a terrible kind of reply. Even Stella, for all her strength, quailed.

'Good luck, Cathy.'

'Goodbye.'

The footsteps went down the stairs and the front door closed.

When Stella stepped from the train at Cuckstone, a sliver of moon hung in a clear sky, and the night smelled of winter. Getting away from London untied knots. The troops' trains at Victoria always rent her heart, the embracing couples hurt her and so did the procession of stretchers: the ache seemed to be in the very air. A dilapidated horse-drawn cab smelling of straw clip-clopped her to the cottage gate. As she walked through the garden, the door opened in a dull square of light.

'Stella? I thought I heard the cab.'

Nurse Digby had unwillingly learned over the years to call her by her name.

'Nursie.'

They briefly kissed; Nurse Digby never really kissed anybody but Kit.

'You look fagged, Stella. I'll get you a sherry and something to eat.'

'I'm afraid I'm not hungry.'

'You must eat all the same.'

Stella had bought the Garden Cottage on Theo's advice in 1912. It had been a tumbledown place, thatched, poky, beamed, flaking, with a tendency to eight-foot hollyhocks. It became a toy to her before the war. She altered it, improved it, made this room larger, opened up that window. She furnished it and furbished it. Theatre friends came down at weekends. George Christian played his music and Phyllis and Zena Dare sang. Nurse Digby and Kit took to the cottage and preferred it to Victoria Grove. There were long Sussex walks, a pony for Kit to ride over the Downs, country folk to talk to, the thyme-scented air . . . they persuaded Stella to let them spend much of Kit's school holidays there. Stella had been grudging about that, but had changed her mind since the war. She preferred them to be in Sussex.

Hazel Digby went out to the kitchen and Stella pulled off her hat and sat down by the fire. Places looked after by Nurse always had the same look, comfortable and burnished. There was a vase of winter leaves and berries, the fender shone like silver, Hazel's knitting lay on her chair. On a table nearby was a map of the Western Front, with a wavy line from north to south marked 'The British Line'. Stella knew Kit had been describing strategy and tactics to his nurse before going to bed.

It had been a gradual surprise to Stella to discover that her son and Rupert's was clever. She had never expected it and the realisation that he *was* clever gave her a curious sensation, as if she were faced with a being who was more than herself. He saw points too quickly, always went beyond them. There it was in front of her, that perceptive and reaching intelligence. Where did he get it from? *She* was not clever although she never denied that she was strong. As for Rupert, he would have been flummoxed by his son's keen and questioning mind. The person who was not surprised was his nurse: she never said why.

She came back with a tray, drew up a table, and sat down, waiting for Stella to eat as she had waited for forty years for children to do. In the way of children, Stella obeyed. Hazel then picked up her knitting, sitting close to the lamp which shone in a circle on her broad hands. She knitted in silence without looking at her work. The news of Harry's loss – Catherine had come down to break it to her – had marked her broad face. In repose, it was stony.

Stella broke the silence to say too brightly:

'How was the term? I don't expect Kit missed me: he never does.'

'Oh, he'll tell you all the news himself. You know he likes to do that.'

Stella drank her sherry.

'How were the end of term exams? Has he been in trouble with those midnight feasts he's so keen on?'

Hazel Digby looked at her, seeming embarrassed.

'I've been asking myself if I ought to warn you about something. Before he barges in tomorrow morning.'

Since Harry's death, everything made Stella nervous and the word 'warn' literally made her slightly frightened.

'His grandmother went to the school to see him.'

'*What?*'

'The Marchioness turned up. Two weeks ago last Sunday,' said Nurse Digby flatly. 'Apparently they telephoned from Aston and somebody, not the Marchioness, spoke to the Head. Then she came in the motor car and collected Kit.'

Looking at Stella's face, Hazel Digby felt a wave of compassion; she was as fond of her employer as of anybody except her children. Stella had always been generous to her and allowed her more sway over Kit than another mother would have done.

'Don't take it too hard. It was bound to happen sooner or later. In any case, Kit already knew who he is.'

'*You told him*!'

Hazel Digby put down her knitting and sighed. She said patiently, 'I did no such thing. You forbade it. I always told the child what we had agreed, that his father was killed, that you'd lived up in Northamptonshire, and so on. And that you'd met in South Africa during the war and were an orphan, all the true things as well. He found out three years ago. Imagine!' She smiled grimly. 'Saw it in the *Tatler*; they had your real name in brackets.'

'Why didn't you tell me?' wailed Stella, putting her hands to her face.

Hazel sighed again. Over the years Kit's mother had become more and more the actress. When they first left Aston the widow had been a reserved young thing, with a stubborn chin and a will of her own, but inclined to silence. Hazel liked that. But in that stagey atmosphere, surrounded by a pack of theatricals, what did one expect? Stella was taking this news with unnecessary melodrama.

'I didn't tell you, Stella, for the simple reason that the little monkey didn't tell me. Children can keep secrets too. He produced his bombshell last night when I went to the school. Got into the cab, gave me a kiss, and then came out with it cool as a cucumber. I nearly jumped out of my skin. He'll tell you all about it tomorrow so there's no need for me to say much now. What I will say is that he's been reading up about the family ever since he found out. Burke's Peerage. Debrett. Everything he could lay his hands on.'

'And all his friends know.'

'As a matter of fact they don't. He's been hugging it to himself.'

Stella was silent. In her mind she saw the old shiny Aston motor drawing up at the school. The woman and the young boy.

'Oh Nursie.'

'There, there, my lamb, it's not the end of the world.'

Stella slept badly and woke early. It was cold, but the sky was reddish and a winter sun was rising. When she pulled the curtains, she saw part of the frosty garden beginning to melt, the rest thickly white.

'I heard you pull your curtains,' said a voice, and Kit came in, ran across and gave her a hug.

'Get back into bed, Mama, and I'll sit the other end like I always do.'

Mother and son looked at each other with the length of the coverlet between them. Every time she saw him she noticed that he was slightly changed. Why don't I keep him close, she thought, instead of leading a stupid not-happy life of my own? But the boy at the other end of her bed seemed not to want that. He was handsome and clever, warmhearted and – with an absent mother and a long-dead father – independent. He liked to kiss and escape, like another member of the Flood family used to do.

Kit had a round face beginning to fine down, large speaking hazel eyes, and a thatch of hair slightly darker than her own. He was going to be tall.

He looked at her critically.

'I like it when your hair's down.'

Then, with a boy's desire to shock:

'Guess what. I met my grandmother.'

'Nursie told me.'

'What a spoilsport, it's my story! My grandmother arrived,' he went on, waving a hand, 'in the hugest old motor. And although it was quite a warm day she was wrapped up in a fur rug just as if she were on a steamer. She was in mourning for my Uncle Harry.'

Shock upon shock.

He looked at her with his beautiful eyes and said in a detached voice, 'You might have told me about the family. Well, of course, I knew. I've mugged it all up. Pages in Burke! But since *you* didn't say, Mama, I didn't either. My grandmother did. She told me about Aston and then she took me to Wragge's teashop and we had tea and she bought me the hugest box of chocs. I was sick later! During tea she talked and talked.'

'I see.'

'Then she drove me back in that spiflicating elderly car, isn't it funny? And the chauffeur called me "My Lord". That was even funnier. And when she left me she said she'd come to school again.'

'You were glad to meet her, I suppose,' said Stella, feeling she had to say that.

He made his eyes large, looking very like herself.

'Lord, no! It was embarrassing. I do wish you had warned me she might appear out of the blue like that. I nearly curled up under the table at Wragge's some of the time. So *embarrassing*. It was all right discovering who I was, I mean it was a mystery and I enjoyed that and I knew I'd find out why you and Nursie had been so owlish (I thought they'd disowned us!). But when this old lady appeared like a ghost – well. I didn't tell the boys at school who she was. I said she was an old relative with pots of money who might leave me some. I didn't like her very much. I bet she was as embarrassed as I was.'

'I am quite sure she was not.'

'Anyway,' he said broodingly, 'it isn't quite true, what I said, that I thought it funny knowing I was a lord. I don't much like that either. It makes me feel sick inside.'

'Then don't think about it.'

The large eyes again.

'But that's no good. I have to.'

'We left Aston when you were five years old,' said his mother miserably.

'I vaguely remember things. But when I used to tell Nursie I did she said it was all in Northamptonshire and we'd lost all our money after that.'

'I left because we were not happy,' she said, wondering if Aston had stamped some image in that youthful head which had always been with him. 'Why think about it now?'

He shook his head pityingly.

'Nursie says Aston will be mine one day. So did my grandmother – I suppose I must think of her as that. She says I ought to see it again.'

'I don't want you to.'

'Poor Mama,' he said incomprehensibly.

Nurse Digby called him just then, and Stella did not know whether to be glad or sorry.

To Nurse Digby, the appearance of the Marchioness at Kit's school was a huge relief. Like a parent who dreads her beloved child will eventually discover he is adopted and may turn on the one who loves him because she has lied, Hazel Digby had waited. She had never liked her old mistress, her love and loyalty were to the Floods, to the huge house and its curious history which was part of the village where she had been born. The Marchioness had behaved as if the glory were exclusively hers, and even made her husband 'look like nothing'. But Kit was Hazel's child, as his father had been. She had wanted him to know the truth. Now, when Stella was resting or out for a lonely walk, Hazel told the boy everything he wanted to know. She was a walking library of Flood stories. She had a few treasures hidden until now: a bible with the family crest. A photograph of a house party in 1905 when King Edward had stayed at Aston. There was Kit's father, thin-faced and boyish, standing beside a younger shyer Stella in white frills. In the centre of the picture, his hat at a rakish angle, was the King. Hazel Digby also had an ink-stand, a gift from the Marquess engraved with the Flood crest and the date, made from the hoof of a deer he had shot at Balmoral. Kit was fascinated.

He did not speak about the family to his mother again. Whether he did not want to upset her, or felt that she might upset him, Stella was not sure. She sensed his reserve. Only Hazel Digby knew his thoughts; in his last boyish years before adolescence he always turned to her. Stella had taken him out of the society life when he was a small child, yet he behaved exactly as if he had never left it. Boys of the nobility all belonged to their nurses until they grew up.

One winter evening Kit, after a long icy walk with a boy who lived at a nearby farm, went yawning to bed. Hazel Digby picked up the khaki shirt she was making, and said, after a pause:

'Stella – about what happened. Anybody can see it's upset you.'

'Of course it has,' was the sharp reply. 'And how did she find out where Kit was?'

'That's plain silly. You're a well-known actress, you can't hide your light under a bushel. She turned up at Victoria Grove, didn't she? I daresay she's always known where Kit was at school.'

'I asked Catherine not to say.'

'Then she wouldn't. She's very good like that. But the Marchioness, if you'll forgive me, is nosey. Can you imagine her *not* wanting to take a look at Rupert's boy? It would be just like her to have driven down before, got the chauffeur to bribe a porter, and sat outside in the motor waiting to get a glimpse of Kit. That would have satisfied her for a bit.'

Stella looked dark.

'She must have been pleased as punch to see what a corker he's turned out,' said Hazel, given to schoolboy slang. 'There's no cause for you to be hot and bothered. Get used to it. His Lordship won't last forever and then where will we be? At Aston again.'

'Never.'

'Oh, I daresay *you* won't, but Kit's a Flood in his bones.

I knew it the first time I set eyes on him when he was two hours old. Can't you see it?'

'I don't think I want to, and I don't think I want to talk about it either. I'm going to bed.'

Hazel Digby returned to the khaki shirt, pulling the thread through the cloth so hard that it made a noise like the string of an instrument. When she was alone, she took two letters from her sewing bag. One was from Desmond at the Front. 'You're not to worry, Nursie, things are going well. My motor bus brings parties of officers and men back from the forward villages, and we have first-rate practice at storming enemy lines, cutting wire, etc. What an excellent pair of socks you knitted me! Reminded me of the ones you made when I was running for the House.' The other, just as schoolboyish, was Harry's last letter to her. She had read both a hundred times.

A Boy in Khaki continued to run. There were raids on London, and bombs fell close to the Strand. The explosions made the theatre building shudder, and the word 'Zeppelins' ran through the audience like fire. But astonishingly, everybody remained in their seats. The actors went on with the show. The maroons sounded the 'All Clear' during Act Two, and there was a standing ovation at the end. Patrick in the wings said the audience was applauding itself.

Stella hated the raids, but Teddy was positively cheerful at any hint of danger: spirited, encouraging and brave. Stella and Patrick both felt a desire to protect Teddy now. All those hopes that the war would soon end were gone, the horrible casualty lists grew longer, and any man not in uniform was treated as a shirker. Twice in the street Teddy was publicly insulted by young girls and given a white feather. The second time it happened a thin tall girl pushed the feather into his buttonhole and said savagely, '*That's* what you are.' He walked straight to a recruiting centre and, ashen-faced, went through the whole rigmarole again, finishing up with a medical certificate which told him something he had suspected, that the patch on his lung had flared. He had to leave the show and was sent to a sanatorium in the country. He was shocked and upset, and only mildly comforted when Stella visited him and told him the actor who had taken his place was florid and unfunny and fattish. But when the show closed in February 1916, Stella declared it was entirely because of Teddy's absence. That did please him and it was true.

She was restless and irritable in this new year. There was a strange thing about sorrow. You were strong to start with and steadily grew weaker. As time went by she missed Harry more.

With no theatre to hurry to, she dreaded the evenings and sadly missed Teddy's company. She disliked the shows given to raise funds for 'Comforts for the Troops' at which she was continually being asked to sing. They were held in the great mansions of Mayfair and Belgravia, now given over to war work organised by their Society owners. Stella thought the ladies in question officious and smug. One afternoon when she was singing in what had been the ballroom of Fitton House, Stella looked straight across the room – and saw Elinor Flood. Elinor wore deep mourning for Harry. The moment she saw that Stella was looking in her direction, Elinor gazed at the floor. She left the concert without speaking to Stella.

Patrick wanted to take another show to France, and now his theatre was dark he went to the War Office to see what could be arranged. Since that first 1914 venture, the organising of concerts had grown enormously. He was amused to be told a Colonel Frampton would see him, remembering that Stella had been received by a General.

Colonel Frampton was long-nosed and grey-haired, and informed Patrick that yes, a party could be sent out to France soon. Soldiers, he said, must have time to relax and rest when out of the line. They should not have too much time to think as individuals. That would undermine Army discipline.

'The Army encourages games, you know. Football for the men, Rugby and cricket for the officers.'

'I see,' said Patrick, seeing a good deal.

'Hard training in the mornings, games or entertainments in the afternoons or evenings,' said Colonel Frampton. 'And no lounging about. Let me see. This month we have the Whizz Bangs and the Brass Hats giving shows. We can fit you in at the beginning of March.'

Patrick collected some of the previous members of his concert party, and sent a message asking Stella to come to the Kean. When she walked into his office, he thought she looked strained. Too much rouge again.

'Teddy's back from the sanatorium,' she said brightly.

'Yes, but not allowed to dance yet. However, he's coming with us and can sing. Can you manage the dances alone?'

'I suppose so.'

He was silent for a moment and then said that the two jugglers who had come with them in 1914 were both dead.

'Oh Patrick.'

'So many friends,' he said and shut his eyes. His turnip-shaped face was like a mask of grief – for whom? It was not only the Floods who kept people at arm's length.

'Do you believe the dead are still with us?' he suddenly asked, opening his eyes.

'I don't know what I believe.' She was struck and chilled.

'The troops do. They say the dead come back and fight beside them. You said once you used to have strong ideas about religion, Stella.'

'Oh yes. Brought up in the Dutch Reformed Church. We didn't just hope, we were rock positive.'

'What luck. How could you throw it away?'

Teddy was on his feet again; he looked frailer but the doctors allowed him to work. He carried his medical exemption certificate with him permanently, for red-capped military police had begun stopping men of military age in the street now that conscription had come in. The police demanded to see proof of why a man was not in

215

uniform. At the exits of the Kean and other theatres and music halls after the show finished were groups of police who spoke to all the men wearing civilian clothes and asked to see their badges proving that they worked on farms or in munition factories. Teddy had come to terms with such encounters and confided in Stella that he was developing 'a little shell of toughness'.

'Not too thick a shell,' she said, pressing his hand. 'I couldn't bear you to change.'

'Darling, as if I would.'

He was comforted by letters from Catherine who was nursing in a converted château in Normandy. There was a faint chance that Patrick might be able to give one of their shows there during the tour.

The Channel crossing was tense with fear of submarines, and mute relief when the ship safely berthed at Calais. Met by a young Duty Officer, Patrick and his actors were driven to a battered building which had been a school. They were to be billeted there, give three performances and then move on. Patrick gathered his troupe together in the assembly hall.

'We'll rehearse the opening number. There's a good half hour before the show.'

The elderly pianist struck up, muttered, 'Out of tune' and began to thump the opening chorus. The actors began to sing. Then high above them the maroons began to wail, followed by gunfire so earsplitting that it felt as if hell itself was the gunsite. In between the shattering fire there was a drone of planes and one – two – three explosions. Everybody threw themselves to the ground; the building shuddered. The hall door burst open and the Duty Officer shouted, 'Chapel's got a thicker roof, shall we skedaddle?'

The whitewashed chapel was piled with Army crates and blankets, but the altar was still there, and framed Stations of the Cross and a dusty confessional box. Huddled in this place of prayer and war, the actors waited. There it came again, a deafening explosion closer than the rest. Down they fell on their faces. The Duty Officer was the first to put up his head. Guns roared. Then, in a pause of blessed silence, he remained listening intently. As he stood up, the 'All Clear' wailed its cheerful message.

'Good job we moved you, Mr Bird. Sounds to me as if the assembly hall's been hit.'

He and Patrick went out of the chapel.

Teddy pulled Stella to her feet. As usual in an air raid, he was grinning; he dusted her skirts. The Snowbells patted their blonde curls.

'We bin in Zep raids,' said Edie, the married Snowbell. 'Nine people killed on a bus just near our street. People don't talk of nothing but Zeps, fair made us sick.'

'You'd have thought,' piped up Elsie, the young plumper Snowbell, '*their* war was worse than this one.'

The Duty Officer was right, for the hall where the show was to have been given was a sea of broken glass. After hurried consultations, the actors were bustled out into the street to a large YMCA hall nearby. To Stella it was extraordinary that after the raid people were now coming out of houses and shops, looking more annoyed than frightened. Soldiers on horseback trotted by. Vans hooted.

At the YMCA Stella and the two girls were apologetically given a stone-floored lavatory for a dressing-room. Pulling on her pierrot dress, painting her eyes, Stella envied the calm Snowbells. Like Teddy, they were now at their best. Stella was terrified by air raids. She could bear danger if she were not its helpless victim, but she needed action. In that distant Transvaal war, you had time to seize a rifle and face the enemy. Here you waited to be blown to bits.

The hall was filling up with so many troops that those at the back stood on chairs or packing cases, others overflowed into the street. There was a trap door in the roof and four enterprising Tommies shinned up, opened the trap, and hung expectantly round its opening. They looked like haggard angels on a church ceiling. The audience had just returned from the front to a rest camp in the second zone, described as 'semi-immune from shellfire'. They were solid Yorkshire.

A line of candles for footlights burned in a hot flickering glow lighting the white-daubed faces of the actors, their black and white costumes, ruffs and pointed hats. In serried rows, tin helmets pushed back to make haloes round their tired faces, were the soldiers. They roared applause.

The actors gave three performances in Calais next day, and four the day afterwards. They thought they had not a spark of energy left, but when 2,000 more troops poured into the hall, the company played, hoarse voices recovered, old jokes were mint new. Finally, on a morning of cold rain, Patrick gathered his people and they climbed into an old London bus, today's transport. The rain beat down as they trundled over the cobbles and left Calais. Tired out, the actors dozed.

Teddy sat next to Stella.

'Do you know where we're going?' he said. 'To Bézaincourt where Cath's nursing. Patrick has actually managed it. He told me last night.'

'Oh Teddy, how wonderful for you!'

He squeezed her hand.

Although she *was* unselfishly glad for Teddy, the thought of seeing Catherine was depressing. Catherine's grief and unkindness were going to hurt her all over again. I shall just have to try and avoid her, Stella thought. Sitting beside her, Teddy was unusually silent and Stella, too, was quiet. The bus drove past a big hospital set back from the road. An ambulance was drawn up outside and orderlies were carrying out the stretchers: there must have been at least ten stretchers, each with its blanket-wrapped figure.

'Christ, I feel a fraud,' Teddy suddenly muttered to her. 'Every other man in the world is fighting or wounded and I should be with them. Not wearing a frill round my neck like a circus dog.'

Astonished, she felt a wave of anger at his self-indulgence. She whispered fiercely, 'We all feel guilty but they *want* us, don't they? They can't show us more strongly how they want us *so shut up.*'

The bus was making its way now down long roads across open hedgeless country. Wagons trundled by laden with great logs of poplar destined to line the trenches. Troops passed on horseback, then a huge howitzer mounted on a truck and pointing skywards. Ahead were two sentries posted in the centre of the road. They stopped the bus.

Sighing, Patrick climbed out.

The actors waited.

'Sorry, everybody,' called Patrick, getting in again, 'the road's being shelled further on. The sentries say the Boche can make out every vehicle, and this bus is a beautiful target. We have to walk the rest of the way, it's about a mile and a half to the village. We must keep a hundred yards apart, and only two people may walk together.'

Teddy and Stella set off first in the rain. Bare fields stretched away towards woods on the misty horizon. Somewhere in the mist Stella made out a dim line of tents, but apart from that sign of life, she and Teddy seemed to be the only people left in the world. They passed a roofless farm, its gate hanging, a dead horse in the yard. In the orchards, the apple trees sprouted with mistletoe. Far off, now and then, was the shriek and shuddering explosion of shells.

Uselessly bent against the rain, they walked on, reaching the straggling edges of a village at long last. Brick houses of dark blood red, with stone facings and yellow shutters, some of the houses decorated with squares of blue tiles. An iron crucifix in the street, with a bunch of chrysanthemums at its foot. Soldiers slouched by, whistling.

'Miss Bredon, Mr Collingwood?'

A young officer on the lookout saluted them smartly.

'Name's Trotter. Sorry about the bus, but the Captain thought it a pity to lose you all, just when we're getting keen to see the show!'

He laughed and accompanied them up the street. On the left was a pair of tall iron gates held open with chains. Thick trees, a straight drive and a lake reflecting the great oblong shape of a château, its symmetrical windows shining through the rain.

'Bézaincourt,' announced Lieutenant Trotter. 'Convalescent home for men before they're sent home.

Requisitioned for us by the French Government. I'd best collect the rest of your party, can you make your own way? Ask for something hot to drink. I must say I'm looking forward to hearing you sing, Miss Bredon. One of your devoted admirers.'

With another smart salute, he strode away.

Teddy and Stella walked under the dripping trees to the château. Rows of motor ambulances were drawn up in the courtyard, the main doors of the château were ajar. As they went into the house they were hit by a wave of warmth and the smell of disinfectant. The place sounded as well as smelled like a hospital, it echoed with voices and footsteps. Nurses in starched white veils and spotless aprons to their ankles went by without glancing at them. Teddy stared at each young woman in turn, with hope and disappointment.

Stella looked round curiously at the marble-floored hall, the huge curved staircase with gilded banisters, the silk-covered walls on which were the faded squares of missing pictures.

'I suppose we must find somebody,' she said, 'I long for that hot drink, even watery cocoa.'

'Where do you think Cath is? You do believe she's *here*, don't you? Should I find the Matron?' He looked at her helplessly and Stella was ashamed of her own selfishness. But she was still cold and wet and thinking of the hot cocoa. As they stood in the hall, looking about and irresolute, a voice suddenly called '*Hello!*'

Down the stairs came a bouncing figure in starched white and floating veil. Catherine jumped the last three steps.

'I knew you'd come! Sister said nothing was definite, but I knew Patrick would manage it!'

Her face beamed with smiles as she kissed them impartially. There was a good deal of laughter over some of Catherine's weak jokes. She looked wonderfully pretty in the severe uniform, her heart-shaped face smiling, curls spiralling from under the nunlike veil. Teddy said, 'Oh, my dear girl.' Her answer was to laugh.

'I've been at the château for over a month,' she said.

'We've only just moved in, you know, and the men love it. Thirty-seven beds in the ballroom and forty-two in the state dining-room. We've used up all the conservatory furniture, wicker chairs instead of hospital ones. Most of my patients aren't badly wounded, but I do have one sweet man who was wounded fourteen times. Little wounds, but imagine! Whenever I change his dressings he says '*Doucement, Chère Mademoiselle*, so that's what we call him. Doucement.'

She chattered on about the life at Bézaincourt. Already some of her patients had gone home and she had received postcards signed 'Bed 32' and 'Frozen Feet'. The person running the château was Mrs Roper de Courcy, 'A distant cousin and a Tartar', who had managed to get some money from Winston Churchill, and was now in Paris, digging more out of the French.

Listening, Stella marvelled at the change in her. Was it work, satisfying, even heroic? Or the joy of seeing Teddy? Stella envied her spirit of recovery. *She* felt Harry's loss was a wound which would never heal.

Catherine, who had been talking to Teddy, turned her brightness on Stella.

'I can't tell you how my patients are looking forward to this evening. Doucement knows all about you, he has one of your postcards from an English cigarette packet. Of course the English patients talk about you all the time. Everybody is simply longing for the show. Oh bother, I must go or Matron will be after me. I pretend to be frightened of her. I'll see you later.'

Teddy took her hands and would have kissed them. But Catherine took them away, looking at him mockingly. She blinked her eyes. As she turned to go she said, 'You saw it in *The Times*, of course? Harry in Holland, I mean. Isn't it just like him to get himself interned? Mama says his letter was absolutely furious!'

Chapter Fourteen

On a clouded day in May 1916, the house in Park Lane had two blinds raised, enough to show that life was back in the long-deserted place. Timing his return as if in the knowledge that he would find Stella happy, Theo had once more braved the U-boats and turned up in London. It was over a year since she had seen him.

She had been singing at a soldiers' canteen in Grosvenor Square, and arrived for luncheon rather early. A strange man with an American accent and the face of a boxer opened the door, knew who she was and asked her 'to be good enough to wait in the lobby'. He disappeared. Stella presumed this was a new name for the hall, now a dreary place which looked as if it had not seen a visitor since the outbreak of war. She walked up the staircase.

The light from tall windows shone down on acres of sheeted furniture. A roomful of ghosts. Stella carelessly pushed back a dust sheet and perched on a sofa, content to wait. She had received a letter from Holland yesterday in answer to her own. 'Dear One,' Harry wrote, 'How wonderful to see your handwriting. Do you know what I want most of all? A photograph of you.' He knew it sounded absurd, for even interned sailors had postcards of her, but somehow those would not do. He wanted a photograph taken specially for him.

She smiled dreamily to herself. Good news seemed impossible to grasp when every telegram or newspaper made the heart turn cold. Stella remembered how Hazel Digby had looked after receiving the letter from Catherine. As if a dark curtain was lifted. Like Stella she seemed scarcely able to believe it. Oh, you're loved and yearned over, Harry Flood, Stella thought.

222

Knowing that Harry was alive made her pleasure at seeing Theo even greater, as if one love enriched the other. She had thought about Theo so often – and his letters were so unsatisfactory. Theo at his most Dutch. Only his presence could make their long loving-friendship real again. She sat in the shrouded room, waiting to hear his footstep. Yet she was taken by surprise when a broad-shouldered figure suddenly stood in the doorway.

'My dear girl, what on earth are you doing up here!'

'*Oh Theo!*'

She sprang up and ran towards him with her hands outstretched. He took them and gripped them hard.

'Oh, Theo,' she said again, 'I have absolutely missed you.'

'Have you indeed? That must be why you are looking so beautiful. You have been pining.'

He took her in with his familiar expression of sardonic good humour. As they stood together in the doorway of the sheeted dusty room, a light from the high skylight fell on his strong heavy figure and saturnine face.

'You're the first pretty woman I've seen in London. Where have they all disappeared to? The drabness of civilians now. It seems to be the fashion to look shabby deliberately, as if that will prove you are doing your bit, as they call it. And girls driving motor drays and working the elevators. With not a lace frill or a small waist among them.'

She giggled unpatriotically, saying that women were doing wonderful work.

'Oh, I don't question their wonderfulness, I merely complain of their looks. Come along, pretty actress, I am taking you to luncheon. This morgue is no place for you.'

A large motor was waiting outside the house, the chauffeur at the wheel. Theo, it seemed, had no misgivings about still looking rich and the 'Spend Less: Save More' posters left him unmoved. During the drive he was silent. A younger and less consequential man after so long an absence from her would have been incapable of leaving her

223

in a corner and thinking about other things. Stella did not mind.

The car drew up in a small Mayfair street.

'This looks like a private house,' she remarked, as they were ushered up a pretty staircase and settled in a well-arranged dining room crowded with officers. There were few ladies.

'It was. It belonged to Marcia Fane, did you know her? Perhaps not, she was after your time in Society. She sold this house lock stock and barrel when her husband was killed. They tell me it's the only place in London where the wine is still drinkable,' grunted Theo. The head waiter stood at his elbow without being signalled and Theo gave his order. Then turned to look at her appraisingly.

'In full bloom, I see. I must come to your show tonight. How is it going?'

'Very well, thank goodness. The score's lovely and they go out humming bits.'

'I daresay Stella Bredon is lovely too.'

'They seem to think so,' she said airily. 'It's all pierrots now, you know, jokes and white faces and frills round our necks.'

He smiled. He was, more than anything, the easiest man she knew. You can only be like this, she thought, if you are very strong.

'Do the raids still frighten you, Stella?'

'More than ever, isn't it stupid? Specially as Teddy is so brave, he actually laughs when we hear horrible great explosions and the theatre shudders. There's a machine gun on the roof of the building opposite and during the raids the shrapnel rattles down on *our* roof and that's quite frightening too. I'm all right when I'm on stage. It's when I come off I shake in my shoes.'

'Don't they say that nerves are a sign of talent?' he said, teasing her.

During the meal it was Stella who talked and Theo who listened or asked questions or gave his deep sudden laugh. Stella had stopped trying to persuade *him* to talk a long time ago. If he wanted to tell her something, about his life away from her or about his thoughts, he did so and she was pleased and interested, always wanting more. But the feminine gospel that 'If you are talking he is not enjoying himself' could not have been further from what Theo liked from her. She supposed he always made crystal clear what he wanted from everybody. Talking of his own affairs, except rarely, would deeply bore him. All he required from Stella was that she should look beautiful and be happy.

The fact that she had had a violent love affair, had grieved for months as deeply stricken as a war widow, had now recovered and was in 'full bloom' had nothing to do with her feeling for him. She was at home with him and spoiled by him and she became more than herself in his company; she flowered in his steady sceptical admiration, conscious that her power over him was limited but strong.

'The Park Lane house is uninhabitable. I'm closing it and moving into a furnished flat in South Audley Street,' he said as they finished the meal. 'Come and see if you approve.'

They walked down Curzon Street in the sunshine. And all the way to South Audley Street, Stella wondered . . .

The flats had been built twenty years ago, they were handsome and solid. Glass-fronted doors opened on to a Turkey-carpeted hallway. The glass, the brass and the mahogany shone which was pleasant after so many dirty shabby houses now. A porter of about seventy years old sat in an old-fashioned hooded chair of the kind she remembered at Aston. He took them in the lift to the second floor.

Stella looked round the flat with interest. It was spacious and high-ceilinged, darker than the blazing rooms of the Park Lane house with their expanses of sky, and furnished by somebody with a taste for bric-à-brac. Small bronzes and wall chandeliers and glass candelabra. Stella walked from room to room, ending up in a big double bedroom overlooking the well of the building. Theo's silver hairbrushes were on the dressing-table.

'I moved in yesterday,' he said. 'You think it dull and rather pompous, I daresay. Not your style, mm?'

'I'm sure you'll be comfortable here, Theo.'

He roamed about, picking up a leather box, a porcelain dish. He sat down on the bed.

'I've a good deal to do in London. Some of my Yankee friends and I must see the Treasury. We neutrals are not so very neutral, you know. I also have to entertain a pack of people tomorrow night, to get one of my schemes going. Would you be my hostess? After the show, naturally.'

'Of course. I'd like to, Theo.'

He sat looking at her without stirring. Since their beginning together, it had been like that. He never touched her or pulled her towards him or kissed her. Simply gave her a heavy-lidded look, and she could take it or leave it. If she refused the unspoken question he never did anything but give a grim smile. As he did now.

The following evening, during the third interval, the wail of the maroons sounded. Stella, changed into her third-act costume, a pierrot-in-reverse, black skirts and white pompoms, was lying on the sofa in her dressing-room.

'*Damn.*'

Teddy's rap at the door. He darted in, merry as a cricket. 'You must come out and look, darling. All the audience are in the street gawping!'

'I don't want to go out in the street, Teddy Collingwood, I feel safer indoors.'

'Come along, darling, don't be feeble, we must have a dekko!'

They were both in costume, but he took her elbow and pushed her down the corridor and out of the stage door. They joined a crowd of chorus girls in white frills, and a bigger crowd of the audience, soldiers and civilians. Everybody was staring at the sky.

'Look!' shouted somebody. 'Up by the church spire.'

'It's nothing.'

'Yes, it is – no, it isn't!'

'*Ah!*'

The crowd gave a groan of satisfaction. The pencil beams of the searchlights crossing and recrossing the sky had found what they were looking for. The thing hung motionless, a silver cloud.

'*The Zep!*'

There was a moment's pause as hundreds of eyes stared, then a man shouted venomously.

'Why don't they shoot the bloody thing down in flames like we saw last week?'

Theo had suggested that Stella might like to bring some friends to his party, but she decided against it. Actors always sang for their supper, but what had they in common with rich business men? What actors liked after a performance was simply shop talk at the Savoy. She did ask Teddy, but he refused.

Teddy's mood alternated between gaiety and deep depression since the concert party came home from France. The new show at the Kean was packed, as all the theatres were, and Teddy had never been more popular; he was becoming a celebrity, interviewed by magazines, as much in demand as Stella. Perhaps seeing Catherine at Bézaincourt in the real war brought home to him, with a worse pain, his own position. When he received news of friends killed in action, Stella had seen him weep. He was still stopped by the military police on occasions, and once when he and Stella were walking to the Kean and passed a group of soldiers one of them shouted: 'Why aren't you in uniform? And what's the lady doing out with the likes of you?'

Stella yelled back furiously, 'He's an invalid and *don't you dare judge him!*'

Her rage delighted the soldier who shouted, 'Sorry, Miss!'

When she took Teddy's arm, he was trembling.

He behaved absurdly when he did not hear from Catherine, always declaring that he knew the château had been hit. To which Stella always gave the same patient reply – had he asked at Devonshire House? Yes, he had, and there was no bad news.

'But hospitals do get hit,' he had taken to repeating

lately. 'The French use hospitals to protect their railway lines and the German raiders know it.'

'Teddy, you can't suffer agonies over the whole war. She must be all right if the authorities say that she is.'

'She hasn't written. If you love somebody, you write.'

His misery at being a civilian, his dread of being accused in the street – where, oh where was the little shell of toughness? – had become concentrated in his miserable worry over Catherine. The reunion at Bézaincourt had been a passionate affair. Released from the ice of grief Catherine had rushed into his arms. Teddy was used to lighthearted affairs with chorus girls and he was knocked sideways by Catherine. He saw her as a goddess from a world he knew nothing about.

Stella was sorry not to have his company when she went down South Audley Street made spectral by the blue-painted lamps. The old porter had gone home for the night, the entrance hall was empty and dimly lit. But as she went up the stairs she heard the buzz of voices. Theo's front door stood open and the man with the boxer's face took her cloak and said something which to her amusement sounded like 'You're sure welcome.'

After the darkness of the streets she was dazzled as she went into the crowded drawing room. To do Theo honour she was wearing a new dress from Worth of yellow chiffon with sprigs of mimosa sewn to the floating skirts. Several men turned their heads to look at her.

'Very pretty indeed,' said Theo, taking her in. 'But I'm afraid I have a shock for you. The villainess from your past is here.'

'Oh Theo, no!'

'Oh Stella, yes. I could not avoid asking her, I will explain why later. I'm also very sorry to tell you that Desmond Flood was killed last week. He was leading a raiding party, with great gallantry I heard.'

She looked at him in a moment of disbelief. It never grew less, the sickening shock of hearing that somebody you knew had been cut down like scythed grass. She had never even liked Des, nor he her. But all she saw just then was his tall thick-set figure and a specially kind and friendly smile as he stood at the door of her room the morning after Kit was born.

'I must tell Lady Tyrrell how sorry I am.'

'So you must. Now come and meet the General.'

Surrounded by Theo's acquaintances, all of whom were middle-aged men with the curious authority of money, Stella did not catch sight of her mother-in-law for a while. She was introduced to a great many people and was, so to speak, on show. She reacted with smiles and charm and a warmth she was far from feeling. Theo's influential neutrals were impressed, and showed it.

After more than half an hour, a young Guards officer came up to her, apologised for interrupting and said that the Marchioness would like a word.

Stella nodded and he took her to the other side of the room where, sitting by the fireplace, Millicent was waiting. She was in deep mourning, the Flood mourning ring, a great black stone in diamonds, on her hand.

'Thank you, Edwin,' she said, dismissing the Lieutenant. 'Good evening, Stella.'

Millicent scarcely knew why she used the name she had never uttered until now. Perhaps because the actress was her hostess. 'Would you sit, please. It hurts my neck to look up.'

Stella sat down. It was scarcely a year since Millicent had appeared like destiny at Victoria Grove, but she looked frail. There were fresh lines round her fine unforgiving eyes.

'Would you tell Nurse Digby that Desmond has been killed,' she said abruptly.

'Theo Jensen just told me. I am so very very sorry.'

'There is no need for condolences. He was not a friend of yours.'

'But I may surely say that I grieve for the family?'

'No,' said Millicent, 'you may not. Just tell Nurse Digby. I asked General Sutton to bring me here this evening as I wish to speak to you. If I asked you to visit me, I have no doubt you would refuse.'

229

Stella said nothing. She was free of this woman's power and she pitied her. But why did everything about her still set her teeth on edge? The immovable face. The condescending voice. The manner, oh most of all, the manner.

'I will tell you what I wish to say,' continued Millicent. 'The family is diminished. Rupert and Desmond gone. My son Harry interned. The Marquess is far from well. It is time Kit came to Aston.'

'I would prefer not.'

The flat reply had no effect on Millicent, who merely shifted impatiently, clasping and unclasping her dry hands.

'Yes, yes, we know all about that. Naturally the boy told you I have visited him at school. I am pleased with him. There is room for improvement, but he is very much Rupert's son. He must come to Aston.'

'No, Lady Tyrrell.'

The old woman gave a slight laugh.

'Ask *him* if he wishes to do so,' she said, and beckoned the Lieutenant, respectfully hovering.

'Edwin, take me home. Goodbye, Stella. I shall write to the boy.'

Theo's habit of refusing to take her side when she was angry – Teddy always sided with her – was particularly annoying the following day. Stella was still seething and when Theo took her to the Savoy Grill, he enquired about the meeting with Lady Tyrrell.

'What did your old enemy want?'

'To take Kit to Aston. I said no.'

'You sound a trifle hard,' he observed. 'Kit is her grandson after all. Surely an ageing woman may take a peek at him now and then? And let him take a peek at Aston. Particularly as her son has just been killed. Awarded a posthumous bar to his MC, I'm told.'

'They'll put it in the Great Hall to rot with the rest of those horrible flags.'

He raised his thick eyebrows.

'Not one of your best roles, Stella. Your boy will inherit Aston. There's not as much Flood money as there used to be, but enough. How much longer can you stop him from seeing that very extraordinary place?'

'I didn't know you'd been there.'

'Once,' he said blandly, 'for a weekend party, long after *you* escaped from its marble halls. I did not tell you at the time because I knew you'd look exactly as you do now. I enjoyed myself.'

He annoyed her. She returned to the subject of Kit, saying defensively that he was only fourteen.

'Only? In three years he will be a man and that's a fight you can't win.'

She recovered her temper eventually and for once it was Theo who talked – about the strong feeling among many Americans that they should join the battle going on in France.

'Is that why you are in London?' she asked.

He gave a grimace.

'You've sometimes said you don't feel it's right to be an actress in times like these. You see women doing men's jobs and you want to be a heroine too. Well, I've told you that what you do gives pleasure and lifts the spirits. I doubt if anybody would hire you, Stella, to dig turnips. So. That's what I tell myself. That my work, too, has its uses.'

With few petrol-driven vehicles left in London, Theo still travelled in the large motor which waited for him wherever he went. When Stella teased him about it, he mildly asked, 'Would you prefer me in one of those Victorian four-wheelers they seem to have dragged out of the stables recently?'

'Oh, I wouldn't have you any different.'

As they were being driven back to Victoria Grove, he said casually, 'By the way, the old Marchioness wanted something from me as well. Her youngest son, Harry Flood. She told me his ship went down. He's interned in Holland.'

'Yes, Catherine told me,' said Stella with commendable coolness.

231

'His mother asked me to help get him back on compassionate parole. His father is ill.'

Her heart began to thud.

'Surely the Dutch don't allow men back?'

'Sometimes. If an interned man falls ill. Or on compassionate grounds as this apparently is. Of course the Marquess may not be as ill as all that.'

'The Floods never lie. They don't know how.'

Her certainty amused him.

'You're right. Odd, isn't it? These old families with their high and mighty principles. And all of them descended from pirates like you and me. However. I promised to do my best. It's not impossible we could get him back on a three month parole.'

'Why should you?' she asked, with wonderful indifference. 'The Floods are no friends of yours.'

That did make him laugh.

'That's true. But there's a cousin – how many cousins these people have – whom I want on my Finance Committee.'

'Why didn't I guess?'

'I think, Stella, I prefer it when you don't. It's very touching when you believe I do things from selfless motives.'

He pressed her hand when they parted. They had not made love but her refusal, if so delicate a hint could be called that, seemed not to affect him – he invited her out the following day. Is he a cold fish or just a clever one? she thought, waving a gloved hand as he was driven away.

Alone in the house, she had a violent fit of trembling.

When she received a letter from Harry it was mostly about his father, although now and then a loving tone broke through. It seemed that his father had been taken ill immediately after the telegram came announcing Desmond's death. The Marquess had become to Charing Cross hospital where, Harry wrote in a moment rare with the reserved Floods, so many of the wounded from France 'must have upset him badly'. He was now being nursed at Aston but was still very ill.

Harry did not know if he would be given parole, he thought it possible. He did not know when, it could be soon. 'It seems,' he ended, 'a sad reason for being allowed to see you again.'

Knowing Harry was alive had at first filled Stella with passionate relief, the joy swamped her, after believing she would never be happy again. But then she grew restless. It was so strange knowing he was *there* across the sea a few hundred miles away. He woke and slept without her. Did he know how she longed for him and how tormentingly he stayed in her thoughts? Sometimes walking in London she thought she saw him and suffered moments as sharp as knives. A figure in uniform in the distance coming towards her, a man's back, a profile glimpsed in a taxi – Harry, always Harry. She felt as if she were haunted.

Emotion was everywhere in wartime London. It was in the long columns of fresh troops marching so cheerfully, in stations reeking of goodbyes, in the ambulances, and the newspapers which people could scarcely bear to open. It was in their eyes. Few women wore black now, only their faces mourned. The very wind in the streets smelled of passion, love and death and Stella breathed it in. She could think of nothing but making love to Harry again, and inextricably mixed with her longing was guilt because she lived in a city of sorrow. News came every week of friends who had been killed. There was not a home in England that did not grieve.

The days went by and Stella was hopeful and hopeless. But while she never stopped thinking of Harry and inventing fantasies of their reunion – she would meet him at the station and throw herself into his arms – she would wait at Victoria Grove and hear his step and rush down to be kissed until she could not breathe – she had the grace to remember her old enemy. Yes, she did pity her now. Millicent had always been proud and brave and she needed to be. She had cruelly lost her favourite son, the apple of her eye, years ago. Desmond whose tough centre and pride matched her own was dead in France. And now the vain and enigmatic old man who had given Millicent her glory was dying. The family seemed in an uncanny way to reflect the times. Perhaps they always had.

Close on the news that Harry might come back, Catherine returned from France. Teddy went to the station to meet her and took her back to his lodgings. After a single night together they parted. She took the train for Aston.

Teddy came into Stella's dressing-room the night after Catherine was gone and stood in that way of his, and talked about her. She had been so tired, he said, her face had looked as if it had been smudged with dust. She had travelled for two days and before that had been nursing at Bézaincourt with scarcely any sleep. It was no longer the easy convalescent home that it had been; the seriously wounded were being sent there and many died in great pain. Now Catherine had been dragged unwillingly from the place where she had worked and suffered, from her patients and the château which were still her only realities.

'She couldn't stop talking,' he said. 'Cath! Always so glad to be quiet.'

Her stories had all been soldiers' stories. Of dead companions who joined their friends when they went over the top. Of apple orchards filled with German snipers waiting for the French troops to come and pick the apples – and then they slaughtered them. She spoke of the colossal gilded statue of the Virgin and child at the top of the tower of Notre Dame des Brebières. The basilica was continually being bombed and shelled. The huge statue had been hit but not destroyed and now it was still on the tower but lying horizontally, as if the Virgin were reaching out to save her baby who, like a soldier, was about to fall. 'The war will end when she comes down,' Catherine had said.

She had been forced to break her nursing contract to come back to England. Nursing discipline was rigid and no matter how much the nurses were needed in France, 'if you once break the rules they will never never allow you to come back' she had told Teddy in a trembling voice.

'But perhaps that is best for her,' said Stella, struck and sad.

He did not think so. He loved and understood her and knew where she wanted to be; yet she could not bear, he said, for her father to die without her.

It was a strange waiting time for Stella. Theo was still in London, then he travelled to Paris for a while to arrange loans to one of the French armament manufacturers. He brought Stella back a flame-coloured dress sewn with glass beads. He grimaced when he described the city to her. The French troops, he said, were so bitter against the civilians. From Verdun the men had come back to Paris chasing after pleasure, to boulevards and restaurants thronged with people apparently indifferent to the war. Stella did not believe that. She had been to too many hectic parties on nights before leave was over. Wasn't that a way to bear what was unbearable?

She had heard nothing more of Harry's return and could not ask Theo. She knew his shrewd eyes might see too much in the question. He seemed very taken up with financial affairs and he did not see as much of her as usual. He did not make love to her. She knew he wanted her, she felt it in the air rather than seeing it in his eyes but he never made a single move towards her. He left for New York sooner than she had expected; she was too wrapped up in her own anxiety to notice, until later, that he did not drive round to Victoria Grove but telephoned to say goodbye.

All the London shows were full that winter. Indignant people wrote to the newspapers demanding that theatres and music halls should be shut altogether, 'Until we vanquish the Foe'. The public disagreed. It wanted spectacle, music and romance.

One frosty evening Stella arrived at the theatre and was told Patrick wanted to see her. When she went into his office she stopped dead: the desk usually littered with scripts was shut. The bookshelves were bare. Patrick, arms folded, waited for the effect.

'Yes, darling. The Rifle Brigade and black buttons. Do you think the uniform will suit me?'

'But you're—'

'Too old? Not any more, and I changed my birth-date a

235

fraction to please them. Don't look aghast, I'm not Methuselah. Men older than I am are riding around at the head of their regiments. Besides, darling, you know how I like to be in fashion. And Civvies aren't in style any more.'

He looked at her mockingly, wearing his mystery.

'I hope you're not going to cry, or I shall howl like a banshee,' he added.

'I never cry,' she said, bright and untruthful.

'I've noticed. Truly, Stella, it's time I was with the others. Don't think I want to go, I dread it. But I can't be happy any more and not be part of what's happening.'

Like everything he did, Patrick's departure was perfectly organised. He handed over his theatre to a tall elderly man, Julian Crabbe, who had worked in the provinces 'for eternity', said Patrick briskly. 'He has always thirsted for London and will give you both no trouble whatsoever.'

'Perhaps we like trouble,' said Teddy gloomily.

Stella gave Patrick a farewell party at Victoria Grove. It was crowded with celebrities and echoing with music. Patrick was the last to leave at nearly five in the morning. He wandered out of the drawing-room, where the out of season lilac drooped in the smoky air. Stella, in her yellow mimosa dress, leaned against the door.

'Well, darling,' he said, looking at her with a strange smile.

'Oh Patrick. How can I work without you?'

'Now, there's a question,' he said and laughed.

He disappeared from her life and from the Kean with its tunes and thump of dancing feet, to reappear later in Rifle Brigade uniform. It fitted his slender middle age to perfection. He looked almost handsome.

'We sleep in a positive prison,' he said. 'Why must barracks look like barracks?'

One day at the theatre, Stella and Teddy both received identical cards from France. The messages on them were printed – soldiers were expected to scratch out what did not apply. 'I am well,' said the card. Patrick had added three large exclamation marks.

236

Aching for news of Harry and scarcely able to think of anything else, Stella often reflected how absurd it was that she and Teddy could not share their anxious feelings. They both loved members of the same family. Their thoughts were linked. And Teddy had been her friend for so long. But when it came to the point, Stella could never bring herself to tell him about Harry. Harry's love was still his secret. Even in her mind, she knew that he forbade her to speak.

Teddy missed Catherine painfully. Once he even took a train all the way to the little station of Aston Magna, and telephoned Catherine when he arrived. She came to see him in a pony cart, but could only stay twenty minutes. She was nursing her father, she said, and was needed all the time. She was very nervous and pathetic, and Teddy returned feeling more miserable than before. Without her he was not himself. His good spirits deserted him and he was too much alone, and never went out at night after the show. Only audiences or danger stirred him. There were more Zeppelin raids on London, two were brought down in Essex and one came down in terrible flames, like a burning star. It seemed the beginning of Armageddon.

In late November there was a string of beautiful clear moonlit nights, welcomed by Londoners, for the Zeppelins, too easily spotted, stayed away in moonlight. Theatres advertised, 'It's a moony night, come to the show!'

Returning home at midnight, Stella thought how magical and quiet it was. She asked the driver who brought her home each evening from the Kean to drop her at the corner of Victoria Grove. She wanted to walk the rest of the way. She wandered slowly home, looking up at the sky full of stars. It was like a night in Africa, mysterious, diamondlike and hushed. Impossible to believe what was happening now, this minute, on the other side of the narrow sea. She opened the gate and walked through the garden. Suddenly she felt a pang of fear. A figure came out of the shadows.

'Stella?'

'Oh Harry, Harry!'

She stumbled towards the dark figure. He caught her in his arms and lifted her off her feet.

'You weigh nothing. How dare you get so thin! Is it possible you've missed me, my love?'

The next morning, exactly as his sister had done, Harry left for Aston. Stella did not ask when she was going to see him again, and he rewarded the impossible silence by holding her very close and saying, 'Leave it to me. I'll get to see you somehow.'

She lived from day to day, from one meeting and parting to the next. Sometimes he telephoned her in the middle of the night. When they talked, she imagined him in that dark corridor, while the great ancient house kept vigil over its dying master. He would appear at Victoria Grove for a night, for an afternoon. When they were together, he made love with a violent passion but rarely laughed or teased. She tried to ask him about his father, but he fended her off, always saying, 'Oh, you know, not too good.' He did once speak briefly about Desmond. 'It upsets me a lot. Elinor is so brave. And those poor children...' Yet when Stella spoke about Elinor, he said decisively, 'I don't want to talk about the family, my love.'

He was full of checks.

He did, at least, talk of his own life in Holland. His ship had been hit by a lone-wolf submarine raiding along the East Coast; the torpedo had blown a hole in the ship and most of the crew had been killed. Harry was in the sea for many hours before a Dutch fishing-boat picked him up. He detested being interned, and loathed the idleness and safety.

'What we do doesn't make a pin of difference to anybody on earth. We can't help. We can't fight. We're not even allowed to die.'

'Thank God for that.'

He did not respond.

'We're out of the real world,' he went on, 'exactly as if we _were_ dead, but dead to no purpose. In limbo. I know we

238

should be grateful. Until recently the Dutch kept interned men in civil prisons under lock and key. Now they've given us permanent parole and we're allowed to move around. I'm living at Rynwyr with Harvester, our cousin from Norfolk, remember him? Big chap with fair hair. We're in a crumbling old place which has seen better days, with a Dutch baron and his family. They're good to us. Once a week we have to report at the office of the District Commandant. And that, God help us, is all we do towards winning the war. If only I could get back into the Navy.'

Stella listened in miserable silence.

'One of my friends came home on compassionate parole,' Harry went on restlessly. 'When he was back, it was easy enough to get the parole extended. Then he simply disappeared off the records. Of course he went back to his regiment. The Dutch don't ask, they don't want to be embarrassed. And they very much don't want to be caught up in the war, with nothing to gain and everything to lose. They're keen that the Germans see how well they're observing their neutrality. The truth is they don't much care for the responsibility of allied troops shut up in their country.'

He put his arms behind his head. The light from the bedside table lit his olive-skinned face and the dark halfcircle of hair on his forehead. The Stella of a few years ago, unthinking and uncomplicated, passionate and set on getting what she wanted, would have burst out with questions. Why not do the same? If he was unhappy, why not break *his* parole? Return to the 'real world' and its real dangers. But she held her tongue. She understood the set of laws obeyed by people like Harry. Whatever other men did, Harry would not break parole. He had signed a promise on his word as an officer not to escape. He would go back to Holland.

For three icy months of winter, until the first mauve and yellow crocuses flowered in the unkempt garden, Harry appeared and vanished from her life like the god who only made love in the dark. The Marquess died in March. Harry telephoned from Aston very late at night to tell her. He said he could not see her for some time.

Sore at heart, Stella went to Sussex on Sunday. It was colder and frostier than London, the fields were white and the hawthorn hedges glittered. As Stella came into the cottage, Hazel Digby greeted her without surprise.

'I thought you'd come. You heard the news?'

The old nurse wore a black armband; she had worn it since Desmond died, and had put away any clothes which were not black or dark-coloured. Stella said yes, she had heard that the Marquess was dead. She followed Hazel Digby into the sitting-room where a fire crackled and the countrified room spread its simple welcome. The nurse went out to make tea, and Stella crouched by the fire. I suppose I came here because she is part of it, she thought. Hazel Digby came back with the tray, and sat down. Her hands for once were empty of work. She looked worn and sad. But she had bad news to break and it must be done.

'Kit is at Aston, Stella. Harry went to the school three days ago and fetched him back. Before his grandfather died. Did they tell you?'

She knew that they had not.

Stella froze.

'Can't blame them for wanting Kit there,' added Hazel Digby, watching her employer's stony face.

'They should have asked me,' Stella said at last in a voice which did not quite conceal her hidden fury.

'Didn't want an argument at a time like that.'

Silence.

'Kit's still there,' added Hazel Digby. 'He'll stay for the funeral. Harry telephoned and asked me if I'd like to go. Just like Harry. If you don't mind my leaving the cottage for a couple of days, I think I'll attend. His Lordship was kind to me in his way and I'd like to pay my respects. And with Des gone . . .'

Stella was scarcely listening. She was imagining her son walking through that vast, forgotten house which she had first seen floating at the end of its two-mile drive like a vision. The boy conceived in the African bush, the bastard

240

for whom she had forced Rupert to marry her. She knew how brilliant Kit's eyes would be when he saw his extraordinary inheritance. Looking up, she caught Hazel Digby's look.

'You're pleased he's there!'

'It isn't my place to be pleased or displeased.'

'You could be honest with me for once.'

Hazel Digby rubbed her chin in a gesture like a man's.

'Well. Since you ask, I'll tell you. It seems to me Kit would be an odd kind of boy if he didn't want to take his place in the world. Oh, I know you weren't happy, we all knew that. The Marchioness was hard on you. She'd set such store by Rupert, you can't think what a fuss she made of him when he was a boy and pardon me, but you were a disappointment. All that's over and done with, though, isn't it? What comes next is what matters. You can't expect Kit to give up Aston, his name and position, his grandmother's fortune and everything else because of some old troubles in the past. It wouldn't be human nature. *They* know he never will, that's why they fetched him back. Shall you go to the funeral?'

'They haven't asked me.'

Kit's hoarse voice telephoned his mother at Victoria Grove one morning the following week. He was back at school and hoped she was well and would 'tell her all about everything' during the Easter holidays.

'I can't talk now, you understand, Mama, don't you?'

She knew it was cowardly not to go and see him at school. She promised to write. They both promised.

Harry sent one of his telegrams at the end of the month, after a long silence since his father's death. The telegram said he would be in London that night and would come to Victoria Grove. Waiting for him at home, she thought her heart would burst. But when he arrived and kissed her, she saw exactly what she had been afraid of. He looked drained. He scarcely seemed with her at all. He said nothing of his father's death, and so she could not ask him. Like Catherine another time, he kept her at arm's length. He gave her nothing except his prolonged lovemaking, to which she responded with desperation, and after which she felt sadder than before.

He left for Holland next day.

Stella knew she must go on being grateful that he was alive. It was a sin not to be, in this world of grief. Chorus girls, dressing to dance on to the stage with happy smiles, cried in each other's arms. Boys of twenty were carried off the trains at Charing Cross on stretchers. England was turning into a land of women, old men and children. How dared she be sad with only separation to bear? But after Harry was gone she felt tired and rather ill. She went to see her doctor one afternoon and he confirmed her fears. She was pregnant.

Chapter Fifteen

The news that the popular musical comedy actress Miss Stella Bredon had married a captain of French Artillery and gone to live in France did not appear in the newspapers until the actress to replace her in *Pins and Needles*, the show at the Kean, had been announced. Theatre friends all exclaimed that Stella was a sly one and sent her long telegrams to Victoria Grove. They lay unopened in the empty house. Theo sent a huge cheque, no letter and a visiting card with a question mark on it, but Stella did not receive that either. Teddy, bitterly hurt by a brief enigmatic letter from Stella, told everybody in the theatre that he had known about the romance months ago.

The only two people whom Stella actually saw before sailing from Dover were Nurse Digby and Kit – she had telephoned a horrified Julian Crabbe. Stella drove down to collect Kit from school and took him to spend the day at the cottage. He looked well and handsome, laughed a good deal and talked about Aston with a tact older than his fifteen years. Stella and he went for a walk that afternoon. Sitting on the springy downland turf in the sun, she broke the news. She had rehearsed it fifty times but it still sounded appalling. She was to be married and was leaving for France. The boy's face, bright as the Sussex day, dreadfully changed. He looked as if he were going to cry.

'*But I've never met him!*'

'Darling, how could you? He and I only met in Normandy when I was there . . . and we've written . . . and he's with his regiment.'

She hated the lies.

'You should have let us meet.'

'I only wish I could have done. Oh Kit! I can't bear it

243

when you look like that!' She was as upset as he. 'René is a dear man. You'll like him. He's so interested in you.'

Lie upon lie.

On the way back to school, he scarcely spoke a word.

Stella returned miserably to the cottage. Nurse Digby was quiet and unusually kind, helping Stella to pack. She went with her next morning in the old horse-drawn cab to the station. Birds were singing in the lilac trees in the station yard. The train drew in and Hazel Digby heaved Stella's suitcases on the rack.

'You look after yourself, and I'll look after Kit.'

A whistle blew. She gave Stella an unexpected kiss.

'Try and be like the song. What's the use of worrying, it never was worthwhile.'

Stella travelled to Paris and stayed in a quiet hotel near the Madeleine. She remembered what Theo had said about the city and it was true. It had a curious gaiety still, in contrast to London's drab streets. It was strange to see the soldiers in the boulevards eyeing the bright painted women. The restaurants looked positively festive. The next day she left the capital in a slow grimy train eventually bound for Provence.

Patrick had once said to her that every act reacts and Stella remembered this as the antiquated train crawled down the map of France. She had made another such journey when she had been sixteen years old. Pregnant and unhappy, she had travelled across Africa, knowing exactly what she was going to do. The man who had seduced her must make her his wife. There was no simple answer now. If her pregnancy were known, there would be a searing scandal and her career would be finished. Would Harry make her his wife, supposing *he* knew and she could get to him? She had American blood and Dutch origins, it was not out of the question that she might have crossed to Holland. She had known two women in London Society who had managed it. But she would no more beg Harry Flood to marry her than she would search out a doctor to give her an abortion. Both ideas made her sick. She was going to

244

have this baby, and she must keep her head. I did it last time, she thought. I'll do it again.

How tired she was. Hour upon hour in the corner of the stuffy compartment she dozed or stared from the window at the great changing country outside. Nobody recognised her: she was free, lonely and free. Officers and ladies entering or leaving the compartment glanced sometimes at the pale woman.

Of all the distant places where, protected by Rupert's thick wedding ring, she could go to hide she had chosen a village in the Var. Years ago she and Rupert had once spent a winter holiday in Cannes – a happy time. On the train journey, looking from the window she had idly mentioned the village they were passing through. Ardisson. Rupert prided himself on his French and said that it meant 'the tongue of a buckle', and he supposed the local people made buckles of wood or metal. But when Stella looked up the word, he had wrongly remembered for that was 'ardillon'. In the unaccountable way of memory, Ardisson had stuck in her mind.

At last the tiny local train from Aix-en-Provence toiled into the station and halted. She was the only traveller to descend. The compartment had green blinds and when she stepped on to the platform, the sun hit her like a blow. There was no one to take her ticket, she picked up her suitcases and went out into the road. Stone houses faced a little tree-shaded square, water ran into a carved marble basin which looked as if it had been there since the Romans came. A soft white dust lay on the ground. Beyond the square at the turn of the street were vineyards stretching as far as she could see, some tended, some on the terraced hills grown wild.

She lifted her face to the fierce sun as to an old friend. This dry dazzling landscape, the mountains wavering in the haze, the relentless sky and the insects thrumming like machines were like Africa. She walked slowly into the square and turned into a bar. It buzzed with flies. Two old men in a corner turned to look at her with expressionless sunburned faces. Stella put down her suitcases and said in passable French: 'Goodday, messieurs. I seek a house to rent.'

And waited with a polite, questioning expression.

Les Platanes was big and ancient and square as a box, with broken shutters and floors of octagonal red tiles. The house was at the end of a drive overgrown with weeds, and surrounded by plane trees. The owner of the hillside vineyards had lived there, he and his two sons were killed at Verdun, his wife was dead. An ancient godmother had moved in, but she too had died. Nobody knew who owned the house. A cousin in Paris, perhaps? An elderly lawyer travelled from Aix to make painstaking arrangements for the safe banking of Stella's small rent.

She called on the Curé. He lived in a large shabby house by a large mouldering church of exquisite golden stone. She introduced herself as 'the widow of le Capitaine René Laccombe.' It was a name she had seen chalked on a cross by a roadside in Normandy.

'This is a land of widows, Madame,' said the Curé, who was old and thin, wore a dusty cassock, and had a manner as dry as the landscape. Ardisson would be glad to welcome her, he said. Only the old remained here, and they had begun to disown the war, he had heard them speak of 'your war' to poor northern refugees.

'There is much to forgive in the human heart,' he said. 'But they are old and you are the future.' With one hand, he indicated Stella's slightly swelling shape. Now I know I am in France, she thought. An Englishman would not have seen. Or pretended not to.

'I came to Ardisson because René and I saw your village from the windows of a train, Monsieur le Curé, and spoke of it together. I do not feel I can at present return to England.'

'You wish your son born in his father's land. That is good.'

Through the Curé's help, Stella found Madame Torelli who took on the task of housekeeping at *Les Platanes*. Madame Torelli was half Italian, her hair as dark and springy as Catherine's, her lined face vivacious. She was given to jokes and dramas and reminded Stella of an actress; like theatre friends in distant London, Madame Torelli told long anecdotes and played, so to speak, to the gallery. She was widowed, 'Ah! the poor Hubert. A pearl among men.' She was childless. 'A blessing. Forgive me, Madame, but during these times who can deny it?' She taught Stella to make good food from poor ingredients, a few olives, rationed oil, and the spiny Mediterranean fish with pink skin and silver scales. Both women sewed baby clothes, and Madame insisted on Stella going to put up a weekly candle to the local saint in the great stone-smelling church. 'Sainte Réparate. Scarce fifteen when the Romans cut off her head. Such a *sympathique* little saint.'

It was lucky for Stella that she had so spirited a companion, for letters from England, forwarded through Poste Restante and taking weeks to come, were dreaded. After receiving her letter, Teddy wrote faithfully. He forgave her for not telling him she was married, he said, adding that he had informed the whole London theatre that he had been in on the secret and had attended the wedding in Normandy. 'How is your French capitaine, darling? I pray he is safe.' He saw Catherine now and then, he wrote; she managed to get to London and wanted to nurse again.

Stella did not tell Harry of her invented marriage, but he must have heard through his sister, for she never received a letter from him, or from Theo either. Kit wrote schoolboyish missives, but they had changed. The old natural facetious letters were no more. Other letters told only of sadness and the death of friends. So many young men from the different chapters of her life. Names scrawled in the Flood visitors' book, boys who had courted Cathy, boys who had sung with Stella onstage at the Kean. A roll call of the young dead. The worst news came when Teddy wrote to say Patrick had died. He was killed on the Western Front, when the Third Army broke through the Hindenburg Line near Cambrai. Stella cried for a day. The tears kept running down her cheeks and she could not stop them. She had no Teddy to run to. Nobody but Madame Torelli who kissed her and was kindly silent. Stella went walking along the hot dusty road by the vineyards, thinking about Patrick. 'Do you think this uniform will suit me?'

Saddened, mourning, the cloak of pregnancy still protected her and she lived from day to day. The weather reminded her of the climate of her childhood; great purple clouds massed, days of exquisite sunshine were followed by a wild mistral against which she could scarcely stand upright. There were heavy tropical rains. When she told the Curé how much the country had captured her, he was unsurprised. Provence had never been fertile, he said. 'We never produce abundant harvests, we never achieved great feats of arms. But we have one power. We turn strangers into our sons and daughters.'

Alone a good deal, Stella was not lonely. And when she lay in the old-fashioned Provençal carved bed at night, in the big room overlooking vineyards run wild, the child in her womb kicked violently.

January came, the reddish earth was drenched with rain and on a day wilder and wetter than the rest, Harry's son was born. The midwife from a large village some miles away arrived just as Stella and Madame Torelli had begun to think they must manage on their own.

'You're strong, Madame,' observed the midwife, a brown-faced woman with great broad arms. 'And not nervous. It is your English phlegm.'

'I was born an American.'

'*Tiens*,' said the midwife, expertly rolling the baby in flannel bands. 'Our new ally. But your son is a Frenchman.'

Stella took her baby to the church one sunny late January morning to have him christened. Madame Torelli stood in as godmother, the baby was wrapped in a lace shawl in which she herself had been married. He was christened 'Patrick Vredenberg Laccombe', and slept disinterestedly through the service.

A small feast had been prepared at *Les Platanes* by the surrogate godmother. A cake decorated with blue and white sugared almonds. Good white wine. And most important, the Provençal tradition for the new born: on a plate edged with a few January roses were arranged an egg, a loaf, a dish of salt and a lighted candle. Madame Torelli waved expansively.

'The egg is for integrity. Salt for wisdom, of course. The candle will light the flame of honesty in your son. Bread is for bounty.'

'Big virtues for a small creature,' remarked the Curé, opening the wine.

With Patrick Vredenberg Laccombe safely arrived and now a Christian soul, Stella settled back into the old house. What the Curé had said was true, the country calmed her, balanced her. She waited without impatience for the spring to begin.

She wrote to Nurse Digby and Kit, to Teddy and Julian Crabbe at the theatre, to say her husband had been killed, and her son born. The lies no longer worried her, they were simply a means to protect the strong little boy thriving in the cool sunshine. When she was at last convinced that it was safe to travel with him, she was tearfully kissed by Madame Torelli, blessed by the Curé and – she hoped – by the youthful Sainte Réparate. She set off for home.

To eyes accustomed to the huge skies and opalescent colours of the South, London in March 1918 looked horrible; Stella literally shuddered. The city was shabby, worn out, dirty and sad. There were still soldiers everywhere, as there had been for nearly four years, but now there were many many more figures in the blue suits and scarlet ties of the wounded. Men on crutches, men with only one leg. And women in all kinds of uniforms, from women porters at the station to window cleaners. Thinking of Ardisson with a wave of longing, Stella put up at a Kensington hotel: she did not yet feel brave enough to face the dust of Victoria Grove. The baby, an undemanding person, slept in his basket.

She telephoned the cottage.

'Welcome home. It's nice to hear your voice,' said Nurse Digby matter-of-factly. 'Kit is at Aston for the Easter holidays. He asked me to go, but I said you'd prefer me to look after the cottage.'

'Thank you, Nursie. I long to see him.'

'And he to see you. I was sorry to hear about your sad loss,' said Hazel Digby. 'A dreadful shock, and just after the baby too.'

Did Stella detect a flavour of irony?

'Kit finds it strange, you know. A brother he's never seen. How is Baby?'

'Very fat and good. He's dark.'

'I expect his Daddy was.'

'Oh yes,' said Stella lamely.

There was one of the pauses she dreaded.

'There's something I'd like to ask,' Hazel Digby said.

She wants to go to Aston, of course, thought Stella.

'Would it be any help if I came to London to look after Baby?'

Stella gasped her thanks. When Hazel asked more questions about the child, the irony in the voice was gone.

Bringing cases full of starched aprons and an air of authority, Nurse Digby arrived at Victoria Grove, took one look at Patrick Vredenberg Laccombe and annexed him. The house was cleaned and polished, the nursery repainted. A routine was established, orderly and calm and entirely for the baby's benefit. It occurred to Stella that the only completely happy person in London was Patrick's elderly nurse.

Free of the monotonies and rewards of her baby's company, of the knowing looks and toothless grins, Stella had no excuse not to pick up her life again and to face everything she had left behind when she climbed on the train to Provence. Escaping had been lonely, but it had had a wonderful simplicity. Nothing was simple now. She must see Kit and get him to accept a new brother and his mother's official widowhood. She must work, always provided, she thought with an actor's self-doubt, she was still wanted. London affected her, its atmosphere was grim, the dark-clad people looked weary. The coming weeks stretched ahead like a series of dauntingly high hedges over which she must ride and fly, or fall.

She telephoned Aston and asked for Kit. The title slightly choked her. When he answered she scarcely recognised his new, deep voice.

'I kept hoping you'd be in England soon, Mama. Shall I come to London today? Tomorrow?'

'As soon as you like, my darling. You must meet your brother Patrick, you know.'

'Is that his name? You forgot to say in your letter. It was my great great grandfather's name.'

'I remember, darling,' lied Stella.

He arrived at Victoria Grove the next day, and when he came into the house Stella could scarcely take in this tall stranger. He had grown two inches, was handsome and strong-looking, the faint trace of a moustache shadowing his upper lip. His manner was awkward. But he hugged Nursie and was insulting about his brother. 'No teeth, no hair and can't talk. How can you expect me to take him seriously?'

He disappeared into the nursery for a private talk with Hazel Digby, then spent the rest of the day with his mother. She was watchful, and tried to disguise it with her prettiest manners. But she could scarcely miss the embarrassed voice when he spoke of his 'Stepfather', whom apparently he wished to forget. Her imaginary marriage seemed to have damaged part of his love for her. But he was unembarrassed when talking about Aston. Kit might be almost a man, but he still had the child's gift of accepting very extraordinary things. Nothing interested him so much as the house and its history. Fascinated by the past, his memory like unmarked wax, he told her Flood stories she had never heard in her life. He knew the name of every battle which had won them the flags in the Great Hall. He laughed over scandalous history the family preferred to forget – the traitor beheaded by James I, that pirate friend of Raleigh's who had reminded Stella of Harry, the embezzler sent to gaol in Walpole's day. There were tales of a drunkard who fell from a window in St James's, and a duel in which the

251

Flood opponent had hidden in the privy. He knew the ghosts of Aston and swore he had seen one. The wild daffodils were out in Middle Hollow, he said, and Boy Scouts were working on the farm. 'Do you know, Mama, I *faintly* remember the house. I mean carpets. And a staircase. And the stable arch.'

But he spoke too little about his relatives for it to be natural.

As he talked, he lifted his chin in the way she did. Facing a different destiny from her own.

Kit returned to Aston which with a slip of the tongue he called 'home'. After he had gone an ancient four-wheeler made its way up Victoria Grove, there was a double ring at the bell and the caller, not waiting for a reply, walked into the house. Hearing the ring, Stella came running and threw herself into Teddy's arms.

'Oh! I needed you when Patrick died.'

'And I you.'

They stood embraced and silent. Such an incongruous figure to turn into a hero. They were thinking of Patrick's immaculate figure and ugly red-veined face, his merciless eye, his impatience and severity. Patrick in a long fur-collared coat bustling them into a hall filled with muddy soldiers. Patrick onstage, surrounded by flurried chorus girls. Patrick lingering in this room, wearing a strange smile . . .

They sat down. He said briefly how grieved he was for her loss. 'I never met your husband, darling, and I wish I had.' But Teddy had already written to her in France in answer to the news, and she was spared too much sympathy now. Every time people spoke of her widowhood, she felt she betrayed again the poor name on the roadside cross.

Teddy looked handsome but very thin. Although in good spirits, she thought he seemed reserved. He told her that Catherine had finally left Aston, 'that place your son apparently *reigns* over!' and was back at St Saviour's. They saw each other all the time.

'And you,' he said with a note of smiling criticism, 'must work again. You're getting a little fat.'

'I am nursing the baby.'

'Can't it be weaned or whatever one does?'

She replied coldly that that was what she was doing.

'I don't expect it interests you that Julian has a new show,' Teddy said. '*Night Lights.* I suppose hundreds of offers are dropping through your letterbox.' He sounded as jealous as Patrick used to do. It was true that offers were coming in now it was known that she was back. The management at Daly's wanted her and so did the Princes. But she was happy to return to the Kean, with Teddy again as her partner. Patrick's successor, Julian Crabbe, eagerly welcomed her and the show opened in May. Pictures of Stella in pierrot frills and pom-poms appeared in the *Tatler*: 'The beautiful war widow now bravely returned to the Stage.'

At first her theatre friends looked embarrassed when they met her again. But when they saw Stella and not a figure of grief they were relieved and impressed and she felt she cheated them.

Soon she was part of London and its spirit of grim resolve. The shabby streets and shabby crowds no longer gave her a feeling of revulsion; the golden vision of Provence faded. But although the days fell into the old pattern of troop concerts and charity work as well as playing every night, there was one marked and painful difference. It was in Teddy. When she had come home he was as warm and welcoming as she was. She had been full of joy at finding him again. It had never occurred to her that in all the world her dear companion could change. But he had. He began to avoid her.

Every night they were together on the stage, twin pierrots dancing and singing and gazing into each other's eyes.

> You're the one I need, little girl,
> You're the one I love, little girl.

sang Teddy fondly as he swung her hands to and fro. But when the curtain fell he never came to her dressing-room, never asked her out to supper. He never again called at Victoria Grove.

She simply could not understand it, and was far too

proud and spoiled to ask him why. But she was chilled, and found herself constantly wondering what had happened to explain anything so upsetting and so strange.

One night when she was leaving the theatre she almost bumped into him at the Stage Door. She heard his attractive, slightly nasal voice exclaim, 'Ah, my darling!' and for a moment, in a rush of happiness, thought he spoke to her. But then she saw that he was looking beyond her, at a figure in a green velvet cloak. It was Catherine.

'Why, Cathy!' exclaimed Stella, forgetting everything but pleasure and surprise and giving a radiant smile. She swept forward with her hands outstretched. For that split second when truth shows, Catherine looked actually alarmed. Then, without taking Stella's hand, she managed a nervous smile. But Stella's natural warmth still carried her along and she said impulsively:

'What an eternity since I've seen you, Cath! Why has Teddy been hiding you?'

Behind her Teddy murmured something Stella did not catch. Catherine, ignoring the question as she had the outstretched hand, spoke as if to an acquaintance:

'How are you, Stella?'

The words were a shock. Spoken in the Flood manner, they were woundingly, ludicrously inadequate. Undeserving of sympathy for the poor dead man she had invented, Stella was outraged that he had been ignored.

She stood in the narrow passageway so that Teddy could not get by, and said sweetly, 'Aren't you going to ask about my new baby?'

'Of course.' Catherine's eyes were on Teddy, but they returned to Stella. 'He's well?'

'Wonderful. Kit is not sure if he likes having a younger brother, though,' Stella answered and laughed.

'What a pity,' said Catherine brightly.

My God, thought Stella, still with her smile, you could be your mother speaking. She saw the same coldness looking out of Catherine's pretty eyes, the same stiffness in her rounded, graceful figure. Stella had half a mind to say something cutting as a revenge – but suddenly she was aware of just how still Teddy was.

'I'll leave you two and get back to my little Patrick, then,' she said, and with a nod as gracious as that of retreating Royalty, she left them.

But on her journey home her thoughts were still bitterly offended. What *was* it? Why should Catherine again dislike her so thoroughly? When Harry had been missing, Stella had guessed the reason for Catherine's unkindness. There had even been a mad sort of sense in the fact that when the Floods were grief-stricken, old enemies must be kept away. But all that was over. What had she *now* done which could account for such treatment? She wondered if she would force Teddy to give her an explanation. However much he avoided her, Stella knew she could always succeed in making Teddy do what she wanted. She always had. But what was the use? With a violent swing of feeling, Catherine had once more turned against her. I can do without the Floods, thought Stella grimly. And without Teddy too if he wants to be part of them.

There were other anxieties to chill the spirit: news of the great German offensive. Reading of it, Stella and Hazel Digby had looked at each other in horrified silence. But the German victory did not come, and the Americans did. They poured into London on their way to France, fresh and strong and filled with hope, to join the exhausted men who still survived and hung on in the trenches.

London's wartime look had become permanent. The great Mayfair houses which Stella had known as a girl were entirely given over to United States and Dominion troops. Stella sang in ballrooms which had been turned into canteens. She seldom went out at night now, after playing at the theatre, although there were many invitations. When she remembered the hectic nights of 1916 and 1917 they seemed a kind of champagne nightmare. She had the war weariness too.

There were paradoxes in the grim old city. People had money and the theatres had never been so full – it was difficult to get a seat for even the most mediocre show. *Night Lights* went on being packed.

When summer came it was suffocatingly hot and Stella insisted that Hazel Digby should take the baby down to the cottage – it would be better for both of them. The old nurse grumbled and seemed oddly unwilling to go. When Stella saw them off at Victoria Station, Hazel Digby suddenly said,

'Don't like leaving you. You need company.'

Good grief, thought Stella, waving as the train drew out, she's sorry for me.

But Hazel Digby was right, for she missed her, and missed the little child even more. He had taken recently to waving a fist which he held speculatively aloft, marvelling at the wonder of the world.

She was in bed on a hot June Sunday morning, trying to make up her mind whether to take the train to Sussex, when she read in the newspaper that 'Mr Theodore Jensen, distinguished financier and friend of His Late Majesty King Edward, was in London after a long absence.' The news depressed her. She had lost Theo as she had lost Harry, exchanging both friendship and passion for the ghostly embrace of poor Capitaine Laccombe. But she was vain enough to resent both men rejecting her. As she lay looking irritably at Theo's printed name the front door bell rang. She sighed aloud, remembering the pre-war maids who had answered that peremptory sound. Climbing out of bed she looked cautiously through the window.

A grey Rolls Royce was drawn up at her gate.

Rushing down the stairs she wrenched open the door.

'Theo!'

Her trailing white satin had fallen off one shoulder, her fair hair streamed and her feet were bare. He grinned at her disarray. With the front door shut behind them, he permitted himself the rare gesture of a kiss in greeting.

'Why didn't you telephone? How dare you appear like this when I look so dreadful!' she wailed. *He* looked perfection, with a gardenia of exquisite whiteness flowering in his buttonhole.

'My dear Stella, I only called to ask if you might perhaps dine tonight? I am staying at the Hyde Park. Could you possibly manage to come?'

'With all my heart.'

'I'll send the motor for you.'

Without a word about their separation, he left.

Theo had a suite with a private sitting-room overlooking the summer trees and when Stella was shown in she saw him framed against a green background, as she used to do at the Park Lane house. He turned and looked at her thoughtfully. She wore thin glittering grey silk shot with peacock blue.

'That colour suits you. But what doesn't?'

'Missing you didn't suit me at all.'

He poured her a glass of champagne.

'I read in the *Tatler* that you're a widow for the second time. You seem to go in for losing husbands.'

Before she decided to do so, she blurted out:

'I didn't marry poor Captain Laccombe. I invented him.'

He scratched his nose.

'You might have the grace to look astounded!' exclaimed Stella indignantly. 'I wish for once in my life I could see you overcome with stupefaction. Even *surprised!*'

'You surprise me all the time, but not in the way you imagine. I never thought you were married, my dear girl. It was too neat. You bore another son, I'm told. And how is he?'

'Beautiful and fat and you don't care a straw for children.'

'I never objected to Kit, now apparently the Marquess. There's something that can't please you.'

'I try to get used to it. *He* likes it but won't say so,' she said impatiently, then leaned forward. Her face, with its planes and angles, was as eager as a girl's.

'I don't want to talk about the *Floods*. I want to talk about you and me. Why did you throw me over?'

'*Enceinte* ladies have never been my speciality. You

257

managed it very tidily, though. I admired from a distance. Might one ask who is the father?'

She was ready for the question.

'It wasn't you, Theo. If it had been I would have told you.'

'I knew that.'

Dusk was falling. He had not rung for dinner and Stella walked to the open window; through it came a scent of grass, a good smell in the sad old city. She turned away from him.

'I can't tell you who it was. Would you rather not see me any more?'

Her back was still to him, and Theo studied it, noticing for the hundredth time the shape of her long neck and the way the hair grew in fine tendrils, however much she pinned it away.

'Does that mean the man is still your lover?'

She spun round.

'He isn't in England, but he is still alive. That's all I can say.'

He said nothing, reflectively sipping his champagne. It would have been extraordinary in any other man in the world, she thought, to sit there so coolly, still with his friendship and affection although he knew everything about her. His very composure was attractive. When he looked up, she smiled with a certain deliberate allure. Oh, she had missed him. Missed the tough sturdy figure and the mind to match. They were alike, Theo and she. They shared the same Dutch stubbornness, the same blood. To lean on him was leaning against a rock. When had she felt that for a single moment with Harry?

She did not want to lose Theo. She had Harry's son but he was gone and who could say if he would come back or whether she could bear it if he did? What she wanted now was her own way – to keep Theo.

'Perhaps I won't give up the contest just yet,' he finally said.

'You don't treat me very seriously,' she said now,

undecided whether to be pleased or offended. 'Sometimes I wonder why you bother with me.'

'Don't fish.'

'Why not? I like to fish.'

The ground was dangerous. She rather enjoyed that. Whether her confession had cleared the air or clouded it, she was in a mood to tease the big watching man.

'What exactly is it that you want?' he enquired, bringing back to Stella for a moment the first time they had met, when his whole attitude to her had changed the moment she asked for help.

'Not much,' she said airily, 'except to ask the unaskable question, about your feelings for me.'

'Since when in the years I have known you, Stella, have we dealt with those? It is you we deal with. And up to the present very successfully.'

Simply because he did not want to answer, she said with a teasing break in her voice, 'I just wondered if you might perhaps love me?'

'Oh, I might. You're very engaging. And very handsome, for a widow. Which reminds me to tell you that I am also in mourning. Mrs Jensen died six months ago.'

'I never thought of you as married,' was the unsympathetic reply.

'Nor did I. Nor did she. However,' he rang the bell for dinner to be served, 'it has occurred to me that you might consider me as a husband, one of these fine days.'

Her face made him laugh outright.

'That's taken the wind out of your sails. I can see that it has never struck you, Stella, how well it would suit you to be rich.'

She did not answer the curious proposal then or later. She left it between them, hovering pleasantly in the air. She indicated that she would like to talk to him about it again. Theo had never seemed so attractive a companion, he was so easy to be with, so amused and amusing, and he spoiled her – up to a point. He was her friend. They did not make love, but the proposal of marriage made this acceptable between them.

Stella was relieved and relaxed. Love of any kind but friendship was an age away; it had utterly stopped on the unhappy morning when Harry had left for Holland. The desire for it, in just the way that had happened to her when she was expecting Kit, had disappeared when she found she was pregnant. Perhaps it was something to do with Harry which caused it to stay away now. What Theo gave her was a feeling of security which, like a suitor carrying a ring in his pocket, he would slip on her finger simply if she wished to hold out her hand. She could decide to wear it or he would take it back. She was safe yet free. He wanted nothing but her company, her trick of being able to make him laugh. And that she should in a world of drab women look beautiful.

One summer weekend Julian Crabbe suggested that she ought to have two or three days off. He was very unlike Patrick in his nervous care of his actors: he said that he thought she needed some country air. Stella thanked him and accepted, noticing that her young understudy found it difficult not to look pleased.

The following day Stella travelled down to Sussex to Hazel Digby and a sunburned little boy.

'This came for you,' said Hazel Digby when they had greeted each other, and Stella had hugged the child.

It was a letter with a Dutch stamp.

'Daresay he's heard about your poor husband being dead. He was always punctilious, was Harry,' said Hazel Digby, and walked out into the garden.

Stella felt slightly faint as she opened the letter. It was very short.

'I heard from Catherine that your husband had been killed in France, Stella. I am so very sorry and I send you all my condolences and my thoughts.

Brave men die every hour of every day, and I know you have a courageous heart to bear your loss. Catherine also writes that you have a son, half-brother to my nephew.

I hope your children will help your recovery, and will
bring you much joy.

My life at Rynwyr goes on in the same dull way. My
cousin Harvester was ill, and they shipped him home
where I hear he is slowly recovering. Without him things
seem rather worse. I now have a smattering of Dutch,
which I learn to keep my brain from rusting.

Please give my affectionate greetings to Nursie.

H.F.'

Up in the cottage bathroom, Nurse Digby was getting the
baby ready for his bath. He lay on a towel on her knee,
kicking his legs and stretching his arms, concentrating on
every movement, his dark eyes fixed on his nurse. Stella
came into the bathroom and gave her the letter. The elderly
woman read it, and returned it. She sniffed.

'Isn't that Harry all over. "Half-brother" indeed. *We*
know you aren't half of anything, are you, my Lamb?
You're a whole great beautiful treasure, that's what *you*
are.'

Stella had a rush of gratitude so sharp that tears almost
came to her eyes. She had never known how much she had
wanted to hear just that: Nurse's allegiance was not to Kit
and his magnificence. It was all for the fatherless infant on
her lap, who gave her in return a sudden, knowing grin.

Before the summer holidays, Kit wrote from school to
ask his mother if she would allow him to spend them at
Aston, 'if you don't mind too much?' She found that she
did, and felt strong enough to ask Hazel Digby's advice.
The answer was prompt. 'Of course he must come home.
Tell him so.'

She replied firmly, and Kit duly arrived at the cottage,
spirited and affectionate. Nothing was said about Aston,
but coroneted envelopes flopped through the letterbox
weekly. Kit spent his time on the Downs or in the woods
with his friend Clive, son of a local farmer. They returned

261

grass-smeared, with tales of moles and ferrets and badgers and blackbirds.

Night Lights played on into the autumn. There had been no raids since May, but a new danger came suddenly, not from the enemy yet out of the air. It was an epidemic of Spanish influenza. It began in Lancashire and Yorkshire during the summer, and spread with frightening swiftness, filling the hospitals, disrupting life in London, putting its dark hand across the obituary columns. Deaths were not only 'In Action', but 'by pneumonia following influenza'. The disease struck people down in the street, pavements were sprinkled with disinfectant, outside chemists' shops were long anxious queues. As in a time of plague, people began to shun each other's company. Schools and cinemas were closed down, and Julian Crabbe, calling the actors together one cold October morning, said that the show must end.

When the company trooped offstage, depressed and whispering, Teddy followed Stella into her dressing-room. She began to clear her table in silence and to unpin the telegrams from round her looking-glass. What was he here for? When she turned round and faced him, he looked painfully self-conscious.

'Well?' was all she said.

'Stella – I – there's something I must tell you. Cath and I are married.'

She simply stared.

'Yes, months ago, in Hanover Square by special licence,' he went on hurriedly. 'Witnessed by the church house-keeper and the curate, pathetic, wasn't it? Cath made me swear to keep it a secret. She didn't want her mother to know yet. She said it would be such a shock – well, of course. They've lost so many. Her brother Desmond, two uncles, and cousins – God knows how many. They all seem to be related, don't they?' he added incongruously.

She felt extraordinarily forlorn.

'It's much too late, Teddy, but I do wish you joy.'

'Thank you, darling.'

There was a miserable pause. He had been her closest

262

companion, her dear friend, for years. They had begun their working life, shared its music and its excitements, together. They had risen to fame, bathed in applause, and sometimes danced without touching the ground. His unkindness lay like a dagger between them.

He leaned against the wall as he used to do.

'Another thing. You know they're taking a tour of *Night Lights* to Melbourne? I've signed to go. We sail on the *Ormus* from Tilbury in a fortnight.'

He laughed shakily.

'I always said I'd never tour abroad. It's Cath. She suddenly made up her mind Australian sunshine would be good for my stupid health. So she screwed up her courage at last, and told her mother we are married.'

'Oh darling!' Stella burst out, 'she must love you!'

Then he did, for a moment, look his old self.

'I suppose that amazes you.'

They wondered if they should kiss.

'I haven't been very nice lately – oh, don't look like that, Stella, you'll break my bloody heart! It's just that ... that it's been hellish difficult with Cath and her family and everything. I can't explain now, but I will someday. Darling, darling Stella.'

He took her hands and kissed them, and rushed from the room.

Stella sat staring at the door and thinking of Catherine. She remembered her in a white dress walking down the staircase at Aston, with those painted battle scenes making a great violent panorama behind her. Catherine had been the princess courted by a string of suitors; she had refused every one of them, only to read their names in the long death-columns of *The Times*. She thought of Catherine's laughing face when she had first lived at Victoria Grove, and how her eyes had swum when she began to fall in love. And the coldness of those same eyes the other night. Would Millicent forgive her daughter for marrying an actor, and was that the complicated reason for that disliking look? Stella did not know. She had loved Catherine in a way. It was sad.

Teddy did not come to see her at Victoria Grove, but telephoned to say goodbye. He sounded as if he were crying.

Theo was still in London, and he was particularly kind when she told him about Teddy. He remarked that families could be the devil, and talked for a while about his own stiffnecked New England family. It was an uneasy nervous time, made more painful by recurring talk of peace. In the newspapers and politicians' speeches the words 'the great drama is ending' sounded like a roll of drums. Then one night it was announced that the enemy had begun to retreat – they had turned their faces towards Germany.

Stella was alone in Victoria Grove on a cold grey November morning which threatened rain when she heard the deafening sound of maroons. They were fired from the police station and the fire station, and echoed and re-echoed as other maroons took up the warning across London. An air raid? It was six months since enemy planes had come, and now with talk of a retreat surely it was impossible. Pulling on a coat, Stella hurried out of the house. A crowd had gathered at the end of Victoria Grove and as she ran towards it she heard a man shout, 'The Armistice! It's the Armistice!' And other voices began to call, 'The war is over.'

She could not believe it. She rushed back to the house, thinking she must telephone Hazel Digby or Theo, she must share what was happening – but before she came to her gate a taxi slowed up, crammed with laughing people. The door of the taxi flew open and a soldier shouted, 'Come and join us, lady!'

For the next few hours she was caught in the strangest rejoicing of her life. The taxi was full of girls and soldiers, Stella sat on the knee of a Sergeant whose huge hands held her close as the cab jolted to a halt in the crush. There were crowds in the road, crowds wandering through a growing press of motors, taxis and buses. Everywhere the people surged and ebbed like the sea, singing and dancing and kissing and laughing. In Kensington their taxi passed a flower shop and a girl came running out to pelt the inside of the cab with orchids. In Hyde Park people were marching by, blowing whistles and banging tin trays. At Knightsbridge Stella managed to extricate herself from the strong arms of the Sergeant who kissed her, saying, 'What a beauty. Just like Stella Bredon, you are.'

Laughing and gasping, she stumbled through the crowds, up the steps of the Hyde Park hotel in search of Theo. The place rang with music, but he was not there. She was shown into his empty suite. Outside the noise roared and reverberated, the bells rang, the motors hooted and there was the sound of voices singing.

She burst into tears.

Chapter Sixteen

Fog invaded London like the desolation in so many hearts. It shrouded the street lights bravely shining and crept like a spectre into the ballrooms during Victory celebrations, clasping the chandeliers with grey fingers. When Stella saw a regiment marching through Kensington Gardens, they seemed like ghosts. The ghost soldiers whom Catherine had said her patients swore had kept them company in the trenches, the shadowy figures beside them going over the top. It was a haunted time.

Hazel Digby had braved the fog and gone to meet some friends, and Stella was looking after the baby. She had never taken care of Kit when he was very young, and she enjoyed the little child who was easy and good-natured. There was talk of giving a Victory show at the Kean, and she sat down at the piano, holding the baby on her knee, and strumming the melody of a new song with one hand. The front door bell rang, and her old daily maid answered it. There was a murmur of voices.

The drawing-room door opened.

Harry Flood walked into the room.

They stood frozen for a moment. Then moved simultaneously. But before they could touch, the child began to cry. He continued to shout until Stella sat down again and bounced him on her knee. Still occupied with him, she managed to say with a smile, 'I didn't know you would be home so soon.'

And pressed her lips to the baby's soft little head.

'I didn't know either. The Dutch wanted to get rid of us,' Harry said. 'I've been at Aston, but only for two days. I telephoned you, but the number was engaged time and again. You're difficult to catch.'

He sat down, ignoring the child dangling in her arms, and said oddly, 'It's extraordinary to see you again.'

They both saw changes. To Harry she seemed older, more enigmatic and more seductive. Jealousy stabbed him. But the changes in him frightened Stella. He looked drawn and rather ill, worse than when he had been on parole. He did not smile at all, and his eyes were strange. He does not love me, she thought. That's what happens when you're dragged apart. How could I possibly tell this man about his son?

She talked brightly about peace, London, the Armistice. The child gave a small yawn.

'He's tired, poor man,' she said, smiling. 'I'll take him up to the nursery. I won't be long.'

But Harry followed her up the stairs. She put the baby in his cot, covered him and watched him for a moment; he was already half asleep. Then turned to indicate to Harry that they should leave the room quietly. He was staring at the child as intently as, five minutes ago, he had looked at her. She thought – will he see? Can he? The likeness to *her* eyes was startling; it was in the bumpy forehead, the silky dark hair, the long upper lip, the dimple pressed into the centre of the chin. She knew very well that Hazel Digby had seen it though she had said nothing.

When they were back in the drawing-room, Stella asked him pleasantly if he would stay to luncheon. He did not hear a word she said.

'You're a bitch,' he said savagely.

'*What*?'

'A bitch,' he repeated, looking as if only a fierce effort prevented him from slapping her face. 'How dared you keep it from me that you had had my child? How dared you?'

'You don't know that he is,' she said stupidly.

'Don't know! Any fool can see it, let alone his own father. There isn't a trait that isn't family – nose – forehead – chin. You might as well announce it in *The Times*. Christ!'

He flung off to the other end of the room and catching

his anger she ran after him and hit his shoulder with her clenched fist.

'*Yes*, he's yours, and why didn't I tell you? Because you said we'd never marry. Because I was pregnant and alone, as I was when I carried Rupert's child, as I always will be!'

'How do you know what I would or wouldn't have done? Slinking off to God knows where to have my son. Calling him some claptrap foreign name. Pretending to be a widow.'

'Oh, I don't *pretend* to be a woman without a man, I don't *pretend* my loss!' she cried violently. 'I hate you, Harry Flood, go away and leave me alone, I never want to see you again.'

'Don't you? Don't you?'

He threw his arms round her waist and kissed her, forcing open her mouth.

Passion made no sense. He broke into her life as destructively as he had done in the past, invading her mind as well as her body, setting light to a fuse which ran through her in a line of flame. She could not bear him out of her sight. They never parted until after midnight, when he left the house and walked back through the bright streets to his club.

Greeting his old nurse again, he hugged her as tenderly as he did Stella. Hazel Digby asked no questions and took his presence without apparent surprise. Perhaps she did not care. Her nursery was filled again, and with a baby of less than a year old life stretched into infinity.

Harry stayed in London for four days and spent them entirely at Victoria Grove. He arrived early, lunched with Stella, walked beside her in the park, or sat in the nursery with Hazel Digby and his little son. He and Stella dined, and she played and sang to him. He was altered from the man who had come from Holland almost two years ago. She had been uneasy then, but now she was distressed. It was something to do with Desmond's death which had told on

him more cruelly because of his own impotent imprison-
ment. It was the reaction everybody felt now after an
intensity of feeling. It was more than both these things. He
scarcely spoke of his family except, perhaps, to his old
nurse when Stella was not there. And the matter of Kit
hung between them, an unresolved question. Stella felt that
Kit was part of Harry's malaise.

She could not have said she was happy when they walked
in the foggy park together, only that there was nowhere else
in the world she wanted to be. Sometimes they exchanged
silence rather than speech. Rarely did she manage to make
him laugh, but then his face wore its familiar expression of
love and scepticism. There were constraints, except when
they made love – and even then, when it was over.

Finally he said he must go home.

'Perhaps,' he said, and kissed her, 'I should take you with
me.'

She had no idea what that could mean.

When it was time to leave, he lifted her chin, looked at
her searchingly, said 'My dear one,' and left the house. She
did not watch him walking down Victoria Grove. Since the
beginning of the war, she had never watched anyone going
away.

With Harry vanished into the foggy week, everything
had to start again. The very clocks in the house seemed to
Stella to have stopped. She had not telephoned Theo,
spoken to Julian Crabbe or Jack Lescher, both of them
worried about a show without Teddy. She had not even
read her letters.

After a restless night, she came downstairs early. The fog
outside pressed against the window panes, the drawing
room was bitterly cold. A huge bunch of clove carnations
which Harry had given her were still fresh, filling the room
with scent. She put her face into them. Then picked up the
heap of letters which had steadily grown through the week.
Letters from friends and from managements, from charities
and strangers, invitations, bills. She went through them,
putting them in careless heaps. To answer. To pay. To
forget. One letter on thick old-fashioned paper was

probably from somebody in society asking for money, or for Stella to sing for charity. It always was.

She opened it. It was headed 'Elliott and Hawkes, Temple Yard.

Dear Madam,

Our client the Dowager Marchioness of Tyrrell informs us that it is your intention for the Marquess to spend the Christmas vacation with you, either in your London or Sussex home. The Marchioness has instructed us to say that she cannot give permission for this.

She considers that the Marquess' rightful place must be at the family home at Aston. He is still under age, and there is therefore the matter of the Marquess' custody. Which matter we will be willing to discuss, if you will be good enough to call at the above chambers.

We are, Madam, your obedient servants.'

A moment of pure rage swept through Stella. How Millicent still hated her. But then looking at the letter she saw other things. Harry could not have known of this; his mother must have kept it from him, realising he would try to stop her. But another member of the family had known. With the click of a freshly-oiled lock Stella knew that it was Catherine. *She* had known all the time that her mother was determined to get legal possession of Kit. Stella could imagine the consultations with lawyers, the talk between mother and daughter. Catherine had sat at her mother's side, tactful and affectionate, deferring and agreeing. All the while she played a double part, a Flood loyal to the clan, yet married out of her own class and kind. Now Stella understood why Teddy had turned into an agonised stranger, and what she had seen in Catherine's eyes. You always dislike people, thought Stella, when you intend to wrong them.

The taxi crawled down Fleet Street at a snail's pace as the driver leaned out to watch the kerb. The fog had thickened and daylight turned into yellowish night. Occasional flares made the scene hellish, lighting faces with a sudden fierce red glare, then dying away into the murk. Stella saw nothing; she simply sat with the letter folded inside her muff.

'Sorry we took so long, Miss, shocking, isn't it? Can't see yer hand in front of yer face,' said the driver. He opened the taxi door into the swirling obscurity of the Temple.

The taxi drove away and Stella stood facing a long frontage of ancient dim-lit houses. She went up a flight of hollowed steps. A clerk took her card, and she was shown into a waiting room. A few moments later a small man, dark and thin with a face smudged with fog, came in.

'Lady Coryot? I beg your pardon, Madame Laccombe. Mr Elliott will see you now.'

The low-ceilinged room was littered with papers and briefs which were piled on shelves and tables, even on the chairs. A banked fire glowed but wisps of fog hung at the top of the dusty curtains. A man who could have been a Master of Foxhounds stood up as Stella came into the room: he had thick white hair and red cheeks. There was a woman seated by the fire: it was Millicent.

'Madame Laccombe? I am Fabian Elliott, how do you do. Pray be seated,' he said, drawing up a chair. 'It is very à propos that you managed to call this morning. As you see, my client is here.'

He bowed towards Millicent who made no sign of acknowledgement to him or to Stella.

Stella arranged her black velvet skirts. Then she put the letter on the desk in front of him and said freezingly:

'Explain this, if you please. The Marquess is my son. Custody is therefore mine until he comes of age.'

Fabian Elliott gravely shook his head. His visitor impressed him. He considered her very beautiful and it shocked him to remember that she was loose. His deep service was to the Floods, the ancient family that his own family had served for nearly a hundred years. But he was a man. And there was something alluring and fragile about the fair woman sitting opposite him.

'I am sorry, Madame. But the law states that a child may

271

be removed from its mother, and indeed should be so removed, if it can be proved that she is – ah – not of sound moral character.'

There was a silence.

Millicent leaned back against the chair. She wore a veil and when she spoke it moved with her mouth as if her veiled face were a talking mask.

'We have undeniable evidence of your immorality,' she said. 'That child you are supposed to have borne to some dead French captain – the child is illegitimate. You never remarried.'

How much trouble and money, thought Stella, you took to discover *that*. No wonder Millicent's eyes shone through the veil.

'Yes. It is true. I never remarried.'

Fabian Elliott looked horrified.

'You admit it!'

'Oh yes, I invented the marriage. To avert scandal,' said Stella with irony.

'And do you suppose,' Millicent took it up, 'we will permit a woman of your confessed repute to continue as mother to the Marquess. Rupert's son must be protected. It is already very clear that he wishes to take his rightful place. He shall. When you left Aston you wrote to me that you wished to get out of our lives. That is what you will do in the future. Relinquish your rights, and sign the necessary documents.'

A piece of coal in the grate fell in a shower of sparks. Fabian Elliott, troubled by his visitor's composure, wondered if she grasped exactly what she was being forced to do.

'If you will sign here,' he began with unconscious sympathy.

Stella shook her head. She was thinking about Harry. She had always done as he wished, and held her tongue. But now it was too late. Must she choose between losing Kit and keeping Harry's love? There was no choice in that.

'Do you know who is the father of my younger boy? I think it might interest you, indeed perhaps concern you.'

Millicent stiffened and Fabian Elliott said with distaste, 'The Marchioness scarcely wishes to discuss that.'

Stella ignored him.

'He is Harry's boy, Lady Tyrrell. Your second grandson and Kit's brother.'

Fabian Elliott looked appalled. Millicent was very still. Then turned and said, 'Leave us, please, Mr Elliott.'

He went out of the room.

In the silence which followed Stella looked at her old enemy. Millicent had taken a small lace handkerchief from her handbag and spread it on her knee. She straightened it, folded it, straightened it again.

'I'm sorry if I gave you a shock,' said Stella in spite of herself. 'But I can't let you steal Kit. You always hated me. I did you no harm.'

Millicent looked up.

When she spoke, her voice sounded quite strong.

'Yes, I hated you,' she said. 'Did you think that we would accept you? Everything we hoped for Rupert was gone the day he brought *you* to Aston. You forced him to marry you and you ruined his life. Now you say you have borne Harry's child. I daresay it is true. Do you imagine that will make any difference? That I would receive a whore at Aston?'

The words, unspoken and hovering between them since the first day they had met, passed Stella by scarcely stirring the air.

'And Catherine married to some lowborn actor,' added Millicent, standing up painfully. 'Your doing. My God. It was an evil day for Aston when you came into our lives.'

She went slowly out of the room, a little black-clad figure leaning on a stick.

Stella managed somehow to make her way out of the fog-muffled courtyards of the Temple into the Strand. Jostled by the crowds, the sour air stifling her, she saw a glow of windows, and went into a large shop to find a telephone box. She asked for the Aston number. It rang and rang. At last a servant answered. Another wait. Then Harry's voice.

'Stella?'

'Harry, I must see you!'

'My dear girl, I can't manage to get back to London just yet,' he sounded surprised. 'My mother's away but she will be home this evening. She is very tired and sad, and I promised to stay for a while. I'm sorry, dear one,': his voice was so tender that it made her cry.

'Oh Harry, don't you know what she tried to do?'

Sobbing with reaction, she blurted out the story. 'You didn't know, did you? Forgive me for telling her, Harry, but what could I do? She tried to take Kit from me. Do come to me, I need you so.'

There was a complete silence.

'Harry?'

'Do you mean to say you told my mother about our son?'

'She wanted to take Kit – she called me a whore!'

The tears were streaming down her face.

'You *told* her,' he repeated, not listening. 'How could you do such a thing! She doesn't understand a life like yours, it's incomprehensible to her. Don't you realise you will make her ill? You haven't changed,' he finished savagely. 'You're the same barbarian I begged Rupert not to marry.'

He slammed down the receiver.

She did not go home. She walked slowly through the fog to the theatre. The Stage Doorkeeper greeted her, saying Mr Crabbe was in his office with Mr Lescher.

Stella went down the corridor, and up the stairs to her dressing-room, put on the light and lay down.

She thought of the empty auditorium which all through the war had filled and emptied with people and applause for three brief hours. She remembered another kind of river, which filled and filled, pouring into the rock basin beside which Rupert had made love to her. She saw him lying in the bush, bleeding and near death, and remembered the porch under which he and Harry had stood, waiting as she crossed the churchyard. Aston floated again like a vision in the September sunshine, with its towers and terraces, the